"You will not leave me again."

Morgan looked fierce as he said it.

Kathleen stared directly into his dark eyes. "Morgan, I can't change the past, and you don't want to forgive me for it, so where does that leave us?"

Tears spilled without warning onto her flushed face. Morgan groaned, then lowered his head until their foreheads were touching. "I didn't mean to make you cry."

"Don't hate me. I accept your resentment, but I couldn't bear it if—"

His kiss surprised her, but the flash fire of longing that came afterward did not. Kathleen slid her arms around his neck and leaned into the embrace. His anger softened, turning to a wild hunger. The kiss ripped through the years of lonely days and empty nights, filling her with an intense desire to belong . . .

By Sharon Sala

SHARON SALA
writing as
DINAH McCALL

TALLCHIEF

HarperTorch
An Imprint of HarperCollinsPublishers

This is a work of fiction. Names, characters, places, and incidents are products of the author's imagination or are used fictitiously and are not to be construed as real. Any resemblance to actual events, locales, organizations, or persons, living or dead, is entirely coincidental.

❦ HARPERTORCH
An Imprint of HarperCollins*Publishers*
10 East 53rd Street
New York, New York 10022-5299

First HarperTorch paperback printing: December 2004
First HarperCollins paperback printing: April 1997

HarperCollins ®, HarperTorch™, and ❦ ™ are trademarks of HarperCollins Publishers Inc.

Printed in the United States of America

Visit HarperTorch on the World Wide Web at www.harpercollins.com

10 9 8

As we are born, we come into this world with some things predestined, such as our appearance and our capacity for learning. And even though we are varied in color, shape, and sex, to a person, we have one thing in common. We are all born with a God-given gift. Whether it's put to use or not is often left entirely up to us.

My gift was being able to tell a story. I thank God every day for the joy it has brought me, and I dedicate this book to each of those who choose not to let their gift go to waste.

One

A small dust devil was beginning to form at the end of the track field as competitors made their way to the starting line for the finals of the hundred-yard dash. For these young high school athletes, the annual state track meet was their last chance of the year to compete for college scholarships. The chance to leave their mark, however small and insignificant, on the roster of yearly winners.

Parents from all over the state lined the bleachers, oblivious to the burning heat and hot wind, staring fixedly down the track, waiting for their son or daughter to get a chance to shine. Students ran up and down the aisles, cheering on fellow classmates and exclaiming loud and long when a rival school won an event. College scouts interspersed themselves throughout the crowd, always on the lookout for the gifted, the strongest, the best.

More than one scout had his eye on the tall, lithe Indian boy who was lining up with the other runners down on the track. They didn't care that Morgan Tallchief's thick black hair was hanging far below his shoulders or that he rarely smiled. They saw speed in his long, powerful legs, strength in the breadth of his chest, and spirit in his eyes.

In their eyes, he was an athletic prodigy, a once-in-a-lifetime find. But he knew he ran for the love of it, for the joy of feeling the wind in his hair and the ground beneath his feet. He knew there were few things better in life than the feel of perfect synchronization between himself and Mother Earth. He believed that he could run forever.

"On your mark!"

Six athletes suddenly dipped into starting positions as the noise of the crowd began to subside.

"Set!"

The announcer's voice echoed across the stadium, dissipating with the hot wind that blew about the track.

The sound of gunfire reverberated from one side of the bleachers to the other, and then they were off. Like a pack of young wolves, the runners bolted forward with muscles bunched and legs churning, focusing intently toward the finish line only a hundred yards ahead.

All, that is, except Tallchief, who came out of his set like a slim brown arrow, black hair flying out behind him as he leaped into his lane and kicked into stride.

For Morgan Tallchief, there was no awareness of

the athletes on either side of him or of the goal that he must cross. There was nothing in his mind except the light, almost nonexistent impact of his feet against the earth and the rhythm of his heartbeat as it pounded in his ears. He didn't hear the sudden roar of the crowd or see everyone jumping to their feet. He was lost in the run.

There wasn't a single person watching who didn't understand what they were seeing. Morgan Tallchief was muscle in perfect motion, and he was running with a joy on his face that no one could miss.

When Tallchief flew across the finish line, the announcer's voice was a shriek lost in the crowd's resounding ovation. Still caught up in the race, Morgan was only vaguely aware of his coach's voice yelling for him to stop as he ran out from the sidelines and onto the track.

Morgan's mind shifted gears as he automatically shortened his stride, mentally pulling himself back into reality.

"You won, boy! You won!" Coach Teters shouted.

Morgan let himself be manhandled as his teammates surrounded him. He wouldn't tell them that the coveted medals awarded to the winners were secondary to him. They wouldn't understand that long before the race began, in his heart, he'd already won just by being a participant.

In the midst of rowdy laughter, someone on the sideline screamed with excitement. A resounding cheer went up from the crowd in the bleachers and then they began to chant.

"Tallchief! Tallchief! Tallchief!"

The sound of his name echoing out across the field

stopped him in his tracks. The skin crawled at the back of his neck, and he shivered as the sound of his own name engulfed him. Confused as to the reason, he turned and looked up, staring out across the heads of his teammates to the bleachers beyond, searching for an answer to the sudden and unexpected accolade.

The coach's face was ecstatic as he pushed his way through the crowd around Morgan and nearly lifted him off his feet in a wild, boisterous hug.

"What happened?" Morgan asked.

"You set a record, boy! A national, by God, record!"

Morgan grinned. Even for a boy who loved the run better than the prize, that was quite a concept. Before he could comment, his teammates suddenly lifted him into the air and started around the track with him on their shoulders, as if they were bearing the trophy of the day.

In spite of his normal reticence, Morgan couldn't help but respond. He lifted an arm to the crowd. Smiling a slow, easy grin, he began to wave.

As they circled the track, Morgan searched the crowd for one certain girl with long brown hair, clear blue eyes, and the face of an angel. He loved to run—but he loved Kathleen Ryder, his algebra teacher's daughter, as well. Yet no matter how hard he looked, the faces all seemed to be one big blur. And then for no reason other than instinct, he suddenly looked up and she was there, standing on the highest bleacher, her arms above her head, waving in wild delight.

His pulse skipped, and that slow, easy smile stilled. He lifted his arm to wave back, and in that instant it was as if the hundreds of people had suddenly disappeared and they were alone.

He felt her gaze only, believed that he heard her laughter above the noise of the crowd, and his heart soared.

Kathleen!

The steady roar of a motor had all but lulled them into an easy, sleepy silence. Nightfall had come and gone as the success of the day settled wearily on the shoulders of the young athletes who were on their way home. Many dozed as the Comanche Public School bus made its way south. A few, like Morgan and Kathleen, sat arm in arm in the back of the bus, stealing kisses when no one was looking and aching for more as only young lovers can.

Kathleen's gaze raked the stern profile of the young man she loved without caution, seeing past the solemnity of his expression to the gentleness she knew was within. She slid her hand across his thigh and felt the muscles contract beneath the fabric of his jeans as he acknowledged her and her right to touch. She held her breath, waiting for him to turn, for those dark, fathomless eyes to pierce her soul. When he did, the slow smile on his face stilled her heart.

"You were wonderful today," she said softly. "I was so excited I thought my heart would burst when you crossed the finish line. Oh, Morgan, if you could only see yourself run!"

He smiled in the darkness, then slipped his arm across her shoulders and hugged her close. There was no way he could make her understand, but he *did* see himself when he ran.

But the run was in the past, and right now, there was nothing on Morgan's mind but this woman/child who'd stolen his heart. Slowly, he threaded his fingers in her hair and then began combing through it in a sensuous, repetitive stroke.

"Your hair feels like silk on my hands," he whispered, and feathered a kiss near the lobe of her ear.

Kathleen shivered, wishing they were alone, wanting those hands to touch her in other places, aching for that beautiful mouth to take her breath away. Instead, she sat motionless, letting him do what he chose. She loved him too deeply to deny herself—or him.

In the dim light, she could almost see the expressions changing on his face as he touched her hair, touched her cheek, traced the shape of her mouth with his hand. Eyes so dark they seemed bottomless suddenly blazed with a longing she recognized—and feared. Loving this boy was the center of her world. She dreamed of making love to him, of lying naked against his strong, brown body and feeling his long, dark hair cloak her face as they kissed; wondering what it would feel like when he was inside of her. Heat surged low in her belly. Her breath slipped out in a near-silent moan.

She shivered, and Morgan's hand stilled. When he heard the catch in her breath and felt her shift uneasily in the seat beside him, he knew what she was thinking. In that instant, his own body betrayed him. Blood surged through his veins as his nostrils flared. He sensed her longing as intently as he felt his own. Swiftly, he traced the fragile curve of her neck, feeling his way through the darkness to the place where her lifeblood flowed. Unable to deny himself or her, he lowered his head.

When Morgan's mouth slid across the pounding

pulse threading down her neck, Kathleen closed her eyes. She gave herself up to the longing, leaning into his caress because she had to, and it was not enough.

Her pulse hammered beneath his mouth. Transfixed by the sensuousness of knowing her in this way, he traced her neck with the tip of his tongue and pictured them somewhere else, doing more—much more.

At the point of foolishness, he stopped. There was an ache in him that had no end, but he had to stop what he was doing before he got them both in trouble. Coach Teters let some things pass, but not out-and-out necking. The last thing he wanted was for the other guys to watch what he and Kathleen might do, even if it was nothing more than a kiss. What he felt for her was too special to share.

When he broke the contact, she looked up and then sighed. "We're almost home."

If she could have her wish, they would ride in the dark forever on a bus bound for nowhere.

He looked up, and even in the dark, recognized familiar landmarks. "Yeah, almost," he muttered with reluctance.

"Are you going to catch a ride home when we get to the gym?" she asked.

He smiled and then bent down and whispered in her ear. "No, I'm going to walk you home."

It was what she wanted to hear, but she knew what it would cost him to do it.

"Then that means you'll have to walk home, too," she reminded him.

He shrugged. "It's only two miles."

"But it's dark."

He tweaked her nose and laughed beneath his

breath. "Two miles is no longer at night than it is in the day, only cooler."

But her guilt overrode her joy. "Your grandmother might worry."

Ever since his parents' death years earlier, Morgan had lived with his grandmother. His older brothers and sisters had left home long ago. Most had already started families of their own, and raising a half-wild teenager who lived on an edge few of them understood was a challenge none but the grandmother had wanted to accept.

"Grandmother will not worry. In a couple of weeks I graduate. In her eyes, I am already a man."

The word "graduate" made Kathleen ill. With all his opportunities for athletic scholarships, Morgan was going away to college, though he hadn't yet decided which one. Chances were he could even become famous. With all the wisdom of a young and untried woman, she feared if that happened, he would forget her.

Morgan sensed her concern. "I haven't signed anything yet. I am waiting for your father to decide where he can send you."

As a schoolteacher, Kathleen's father's resources were limited. Kathleen had told Morgan he was still trying to get some financial aid for her, or else she might end up at a community college.

She caught his hand and held it to her heart. "No, Morgan. You're the one with the opportunities. You pick the best school for you. I will try to follow."

Her promise cut right through his heart. He had never felt so sure about being loved.

Then the dome light came on inside the bus as the

coach began waking students up. In the distance, streetlights from the small town of Comanche could be seen.

"We'll be at the gym in five minutes," Teters shouted. "Don't leave any bags on the bus, and managers, make sure you store the equipment in the gym before you go home. Also, my office will be open in case anyone needs to call their parents for a ride."

Students began to stir, gathering their wits and their belongings. No one paid much attention to the coach's speech because they'd heard it all before. It was the same one he made after every meet.

Morgan looked up just as Coach Teters looked down the aisle, making a mental head count of the students just as he'd done when they'd started home. He knew that, like the coach's speech, the head count was out of habit.

He waited for Coach Teters's gaze to fall on the place where they were sitting, well aware that the arm he had around Kathleen Ryder's shoulder was going to cause a frown. When it happened, Morgan met his gaze with gentle defiance. To his relief, Teters cocked an eyebrow and then turned away.

The bus rocked to a halt. When the door opened, the students began to file down the steps. One after the other, Teters bid them good night, reminding some to call a parent, reminding others to go straight home.

When Kathleen Ryder started down the steps, Teters reached out to steady her. She was a fellow teacher's child, and as such, warranted an extra caution.

"Kathleen, do you have a way home?"

She smiled, then looked back at Morgan who was getting off the bus behind her.

"Yes, sir. Morgan is going to walk me home."

Morgan slid his arm around Kathleen's shoulder, nodded at the coach, and started across the parking lot. They were several yards ahead of the bus when Teters's voice boomed out across the near-empty lot.

"Tallchief!"

Morgan paused, then turned, unaware of the elegance in his movement or the patience on his face.

"Sir?"

"You did a fine job today. A real fine job."

Morgan nodded again, then looked down at Kathleen and smiled. "Yes, sir . . . thanks." They walked into the shadows on the other side of the gym, and then were gone.

Traffic in Comanche was usually sparse. At this time of night it was nearly nonexistent. Most of it was nothing more than the coming and going of parents from the gym and a few early customers heading for a bar outside of town. The night sky was slightly overcast, and the quarter moon played hide-and-seek through clouds scudding across the sky. A soft breeze was playing with the ends of Kathleen's hair and mating her T-shirt to the thrust of her breasts. It was enough to drive a strong man wild. For Morgan, who was just shy of being a man, it was all he could do to keep walking.

Kathleen could feel his eyes upon her face, upon her body. In the shadow of an alley, she paused, then looked up at him. His face was in profile, and yet she knew each feature as well as she knew her own.

The strong, almost hawklike nose and high, proud cheekbones were chiseled out of a face of dark beauty. A full, sensuous mouth that could curve in a smile or a twist of disdain did things to her senses she knew she should ignore. But it was his eyes, those black, fathomless eyes that glittered constantly, alive with emotions he tried not to show, that were the soul of the boy that she loved.

"Morgan."

Her voice was soft, almost a whisper. But Morgan heard more than the call of his name. He heard longing. And when he looked into her eyes, he saw need. His mouth firmed, and his eyes flashed as he grabbed her by the hand and started dragging her faster down the street, trying to ignore the sudden rush of blood thundering through his veins.

"What's wrong? What did I do? What did I say?" she gasped, trying and failing miserably to keep up with his long-legged stride.

And then as suddenly as he'd started, he stopped and pulled her into the shadows of the heavy shrubbery surrounding an abandoned house. It had been empty so long no one could even remember who had lived there last. The only thing that still flourished was the rose of Sharon border that grew on both sides of the street, sheltering the house and its imminent decay from sight of any passersby.

Morgan dropped his bag on the grass and wrapped Kathleen in his arms, rocking her back and forth against his body in a slow, even motion.

"I'm sorry, so sorry," he said softly. "I took something out on you that was not your fault."

Near tears, Kathleen could do little more than whisper. "What's wrong?" she asked.

Morgan took one look at the pain on her face and knew he shouldn't have stopped running. With a groan, he lowered his head. His mouth centered upon hers, and then he shuddered as wait gave way to want. Weaving a wild, erratic pattern of kisses across her face, on her lips, and in her hair, he traced her body with his hands, memorizing the gentle flare of her hips, the swell of her breasts, the narrow indentation of her waist. She might be a girl in the eyes of the world, but in body and in spirit, she was woman to his man.

She shuddered, then wrapped her arms around his neck, moving against the ache in his body, wanting all there was of this boy who'd stolen her heart.

"I love you, love you, love you," Morgan whispered, and then tasted tears on her face. "God, Kathleen, don't cry."

He stopped instantly, hating himself for manhandling her in such a way. Cupping her face with his hands, he bent until their foreheads were touching. Slowly, he began tracing the source of her tears with his thumbs.

"I didn't mean to scare you. Please forgive me."

Kathleen shuddered and then lifted her head until their gazes locked. Even in the darkness it was impossible to miss the fire blazing from within him. Morgan's eyes traced her beauty, memorizing the heart-shaped face, the fine, straight nose with just a tiny tilt at the tip, eyebrows that rose and fell with more expression than some could voice, and eyes as blue as a hot summer sky. Her mouth quivered, and he knew all too well how sweet, how soft, how giving it would feel beneath his own.

And then she took his hand and pulled him deeper into the shadows, farther back from the street until they were lost in the night.

"Kathleen . . . this isn't a—"

She pressed her fingers across his lips, silencing what she knew he was about to say, and then took his hands and laid them gently but purposefully upon her breasts.

"Make love to me."

She filled his palms and he shuddered as her words rolled through his mind. Even when he knew he should be pulling back, he found himself pulling her T-shirt over her head instead.

Clothes fell away as urgently and as quietly as the breeze that moved across their bodies. And when he laid her in the cool grass and slipped between her knees, Kathleen thought she might die from the joy. Every rule her parents had ever taught her was forgotten in Morgan Tallchief's arms. There was nothing that mattered but him and the love.

Morgan was shaking, both from want and from fear. He was deep inside her when he felt the resistance to his intrusion. His mind was reeling with the knowledge that he would be the first and that he wouldn't be able to stop the hurt. His whisper was soft against her cheek when he paused.

"Forgive me," he groaned, and then thrust, holding her close when she arched up in pain, covering her lips with his mouth and swallowing her gasp of surprise as her body began to accommodate him. He held himself motionless, shaking, waiting for the shock to her system to pass.

Tears were on her face as she wrapped her arms around his neck.

"I waited all of my life for this moment," she whispered. "Thank God it was you."

Her revelation made him weak in ways a man should not admit. For Morgan, there was only one way to respond. Slowly, he began to move, pacing himself as he did in a race, feeling one with Kathleen as he did with the elements through which he ran, sharing heartbeats that raced to a finish line so far ahead.

Tears ran in a steady stream down Kathleen's face as Morgan took her by storm, and although she'd dreamed of this moment for months, she was still not prepared for the onslaught of her own emotions.

She'd known that the first time would hurt, but she hadn't been prepared for the feel of his power as he moved within her, or the hot, silken thrust of young manhood awakening fires in her she hadn't known could burn.

When it started low in her belly, tingling in an urgent, achy way, she clutched Morgan's shoulders in a sudden frantic grasp, as if she'd been teetering on the edge of something and was about to fall.

Morgan looked down at the girl beneath him and saw unexpected passion flare high on her face. Knowing that he was giving her pleasure gave him joy. With a groan, he deepened his thrusts.

Kathleen gasped as the tingle gave way to a hard need to move, but to where—and against what?

"Morgan?"

Her voice was shaking as her fingers suddenly dug into his arms.

"Don't fight it, Kathleen. Come with me. Let it go."

With his words, the rush came upon her, all in one place, all at one time, hitting center and then flying in a thousand pieces throughout her body, leaving her blind to anything but the touch of his mouth and the sweep of his hands. And when he suddenly groaned, arching his body deep, then deeper, she shuddered with new joy, and held him when he fell.

"Oh, God. Oh, God."

It was all he could say. His body was weak, but his heart was full. This moment had been a long time coming, and although he knew the risk that they'd taken, he didn't regret it.

"I love you, Morgan, so much."

"Thank God," he whispered, raining down kisses on her soft, tearstained face. "I love you, too."

Long minutes later, they began to dress. The embarrassment Kathleen thought she might feel was not there. She was still caught up in the love that had come with the act. Clothes went on much slower than when they'd come off, and finally, it was Morgan who picked up his bag, took her by the hand, and led her back onto the sidewalk.

Reluctance measured their steps as they neared the street on which Kathleen lived. An odd panic began to set in as she saw the streetlight shining down on her front gate. For an instant, she had the strangest urge to turn and run. Instead, she tightened her hold on Morgan's hand and slowed her steps even more as she finally admitted. "I don't want to go inside."

He slid an arm around her shoulders, pulling her closer to him as they continued to walk.

"I don't want to let you go, either, but we have to," he said. "Your father would skin me alive if you didn't come home, and Grandmother would worry if I did not."

Kathleen smiled through tears, remembering his

earlier claim that his grandmother already considered him a man. "Even a man has rules, right?"

He grinned. "Right."

The gate swung open, creaking loudly on hinges in great need of oil and disturbing the quiet of the night. A few doors down, someone's dog barked twice in the backyard, and the squall of car tires on pavement could be heard in the distance as some driver took off in a rush.

The urgency of the sounds echoed in Morgan's heart. He knew what Kathleen was feeling. He didn't want this night to end, either.

The wooden boards on the porch gave way to their weight, squeaking gently as they walked to the door. Kathleen's hand was on the knob when Morgan pulled her back into his arms and stole what was left of her heart.

His mouth was cool and firm when he kissed her lips, but his hands were shaking as he wrapped them fast in her hair. Even though they'd made love only minutes ago, his body was aching for her again.

Kathleen sighed, feeling the surge of his body against her belly, and gave herself up to his touch. Long moments later, he tore himself away.

"Can I call you tomorrow?" he whispered.

She nodded, and then stood on the porch with her hand on the knob, watching as he jumped from the steps and back onto the street. Within seconds, he broke into a jog, and as Kathleen watched, his long legs began to stretch, and his body began to move with the motion, and by the time he was halfway down the block, he was running.

Morgan was all the way to the corner and about to

turn left when he heard her first scream. And he had no doubt that it was Kathleen that he heard. Shocked by the sound, he froze in midstride, and then spun, staring back up the street toward her house. By the time the second scream came, he was already running.

He ran with his heart in his mouth. Pushing himself beyond any limit he believed he possessed, he was passing through the gate when the first blast came. The impact knocked him off of his feet and onto his back. Long seconds passed while he stared up at a sprinkling of stars and wondered how he'd come to be there. But sanity returned with a flash, and he was struggling to his feet when the second blast came, blowing what was left of the glass out onto the front lawn and sending snakelike fingers of fire licking up the inner and outer walls at once.

"No, God, no!"

His cry was a rage against the impossible, and had he not been restrained by a neighbor who suddenly arrived on the scene, he would have run into the fire. Instead, he was dragged, screaming and fighting, back out into the street, away from the flames—away from the girl that he loved.

Flames boiled out of every crevice of the Ryder home, eating at the wood like a voracious dragon and lighting up the night sky. People began to gather, pulled to the scene by curiosity, then crying aloud at the horror of an entire family's demise.

Morgan stood alone in the street, oblivious to the fire truck that pulled up, unaware of being jostled and moved aside as volunteer firemen ran frantically toward the house in a futile effort to put out a fire that had already done its worst damage.

Inside, he was dying. The joy that had carried him through life was over. The thing he did best had not been enough to save the girl that he loved. Today, he'd set a national record on a track field, and yet when it had mattered most, he had not been fast enough to rescue Kathleen. Something curled up inside of him, leaving a dark, vacant hole where his heart had just been. His mind went blank as the heat from the fire scorched his face. And then someone took him by the arm and moved him from where he stood.

"Morgan . . . son?"

Morgan blinked, then shuddered as Coach Teters took him in his arms.

"What happened, boy?"

Morgan couldn't answer, because he couldn't talk.

"Are they all . . . uh, did the fire start after Kathleen went inside the . . . ?"

Teters's question ended as Morgan suddenly dropped to his knees and covered his face with his hands. The coach followed, intent on giving comfort, when he heard the boy moan. It was a high-pitched keening sound unlike anything he'd ever heard—a wail from a man with a broken heart.

"Come on, boy, I'm going to take you home," he muttered.

With help from a neighbor, they got Morgan on his feet and into the coach's car. Teters drove out of town with a nervous eye on the road and another on Morgan.

He was so silent and so still that time and time again, Teters caught himself listening for the simple sound of a breath being drawn. But it was the constant flow of silver tears running down Morgan's face that proved a heart still beat, even if it was only his body in motion. The boy Morgan had been was dead, along with the girl that he loved more than life.

When Monday came and the school day arrived, Morgan did not. Teters was in a panic. There were messages all over his desk from scouts across the nation, wanting their chance to recruit the boy who'd set a national record. That evening, he drove out to Morgan's house and came face-to-face with a small, brown-eyed woman who refused to let him inside.

With a heartfelt plea, he began begging the grandmother just to let him see Morgan. To his dismay, she refused. She was a small but valiant wall between her boy and the hurt life had dealt him.

"Morgan wasn't in school today."

She nodded.

Teters shoved his hands in his pockets and tried not to yell. Fear mingled with frustration as he stared in that bland, implacable face.

"You've got to make him come back," he said.

"He will do what he must," was all she would say.

Teters tried not to shout. "What he must do, Mrs. Tallchief, is finish high school. He graduates in two weeks. Surely you don't want him to go through life without so much as a high school diploma! And what am I going to tell all those scouts?"

And then, to Teters's relief, Morgan came out of the house and stood directly behind his grandmother. His face was drawn, his eyes a flat, expressionless black as he answered his coach's question.

"You will tell them I do not want to run anymore."

Teters was dumbstruck. "You don't what?"

"Today I joined the navy. Three days after graduation, I report for duty in San Diego."

Teters wanted to cry. "You can't mean that."

"It is already done," Morgan replied, and walked back inside the house.

Teters stared at the doorway through which Morgan had disappeared, and then down at the old woman who stood between him and the greatest athlete he'd ever known.

"Can't you make him see sense?" he begged.

She shook her head. She hadn't lived all these years without seeing most of the sadness that life had to offer. Regret was there in her voice, but her words were strong and sure.

"My Morgan is a man. He has to find his own way out of this pain." With a nod of her head, she started indoors.

"But he's giving up everything," Teters begged.

She paused and then turned.

"Don't you understand?" she said quietly. "In his mind, it is already gone."

Two

Santa Fe, New Mexico
Sixteen years later

Wind blasted across the desert, carrying a wall of dust with it as it blew. Morgan stood in his studio, staring out at the storm and thinking that if he would just take one step outside, he could run with the tumbleweeds that flew through the air and lose himself forever within the blowing sand. Then he focused on his reflection instead of the storm and turned away from the windows, muttering in disgust.

"Indian, you've been alone too long."

He'd come close to getting himself killed more than once during his years with the navy due to this kind of thinking. His stomach growled in defense as a wry grin split the somberness of his face. He tossed a paint cloth onto the table beside his easel and poked the fan brush he was holding into the quart jar beside a near-empty palette.

"So, belly, are you saying I should feed you and not my spirit?"

His own voice echoed as the wind continued to howl outside the studio, reminding him of his solitary state. The scent of oil paint filled the room, mixing with the faint but unmistakable smell of dust as he went about the task of covering the painting in progress. Yet even as he shut down his work, his fingers began to twitch, and the muscles in his legs tensed and jerked, as if straining against the unwelcome inactivity.

But it wasn't the storm that made Morgan nervous, it was what happened to him when his mind stilled. After all these years, the thought of Kathleen Ryder's scream, the memory of the heat of the blast as it knocked him flat on his back, as well as the knowledge that he had witnessed her death still had the power to stun him into momentary immobility.

Afterward, he would always be angry with himself for showing weakness, but it was a wasted emotion. He'd long since faced the fact that he was a one-woman man. There'd been other women in his life, but none that had mattered. None who'd been more than a means to an end. For all intents and purposes, Morgan Tallchief's plans for a future had ended on the same night as Kathleen Ryder's life.

Morgan paused on his way out of the studio to look back at the standing easel on the other side of the room. The blank white cloth he'd dropped over the unfinished painting taunted him, reminding him that his heart and his life were just as empty as its surface.

His dark eyes narrowed, and the cut of his mouth thinned as he rejected the image. His chin tilted as he stalked back to the easel.

With a flourish, he yanked the cover from the half-finished painting, picked up a clean brush, and swiped it across a palette, dipping deep into burnt umber, then swirling through alizarin crimson before finally tipping it with a soft, glossy black.

Minutes later, he was lost in a world where warriors on ponies chased through his mind. He forgot the storm raging outside his home. He forgot everything but the story coming to life on the canvas before him. Brushstroke after brushstroke, the painting was slowly being born while his mind continued to wander in and out of the past. To the time long after Kathleen—when he'd taken one too many chances with his life. To the day that Polchik, a short and stocky, by-the-book naval officer who was Morgan's commander, had refused to ignore his latest stunt.

Goddamn it, Tallchief! When I give an order, I expect it to be obeyed! Is that understood?

Morgan pulled a palette knife loaded with a mixture of blue and gray paint across the canvas, nodding in satisfaction as a distant mountain began to take shape. The color of the mountain was the same shade as the veins that had been bulging in Polchik's neck that day.

What the hell were you trying to do out there, kill yourself?

The knife hung loosely between Morgan's fingers as he stepped back to study the scene. The Indian woman kneeling by the mountain lake was in mourning. Her beaded tunic was streaked with blood from self-inflicted gashes and wounds. An empty cradleboard lay in the grasses nearby, while the woman seemed mesmerized by the bottomless depths of the lake by which she knelt.

You're not a goddamned fish, Tallchief! At those depths, when your tank runs empty, you can't breathe! Did you fucking know that?

Morgan's eyes narrowed. Without hesitation, he dropped the knife onto the table and squeezed a small portion of white paint onto the palette, then delicately feathered the tip of a brush through the color.

The strokes, almost indefinable, gave birth to the ghostly image of a toddler suddenly walking just above the surface of the water. Its presence was made all the more gripping by the transparency of its tiny form as it moved into a dimension the mother could not follow.

It didn't take a genius to follow the grieving mother's train of thought as she gazed with longing out across the lake to the child only she could see.

This isn't the first time you've pushed my buttons, but this time I want the truth! If Lieutenant Anson hadn't pulled your sorry ass out of the water, would you have come on your own?

Morgan dropped the brush into a jar of cleaning solution before picking up the palette knife again. With a sharp twist of his wrist, he thrust it into the dollop of white. In a confident motion, he cut through the color, leaving nothing but a thin roll of paint along the edge. With a quick sweep of knife to canvas, snowcaps suddenly appeared on the distant mountains.

Damn your sorry ass to hell, Tallchief! I'm ordering you to report to the infirmary on the double. Not only are you going to get a thorough physical, but you're about to get your stupid head examined as well. I don't care whether or not you cooperate with the shrink, but I want it on record that, in my opinion, you fucking well need one.

Dismissed!

Morgan squinted, then nodded in satisfaction as he stepped back to view the painting. He winced as a blast of wind whistled through a crack in the windowsill. The wail reminded him of the day of Grandmother's funeral. His sisters had cried for hours, but he'd been unable to shed any tears. Grandmother had lived a good long life. She hadn't been sorry to go. He knew because she'd told him so in a dream he'd had the night before the funeral.

But that was ten years ago. Today, Grandmother was safe in the arms of her Maker, while Morgan was still wrestling with the devil, as he had on the day he'd once again become a civilian.

James, this is Morgan. I'm coming home . . . this time for good.

Little brother! It's about time you gave up living on water and came back to the good red earth of Oklahoma.

I'm driving, so it will take a while. Look for me when you see me coming, okay?

The windows in his studio rattled and Morgan glanced up and then out, startled by the force of the wind and the blast of sand against them.

Santa Fe.

It was to have been an overnight stop. But he'd looked out of his hotel window and into the desert, seen the mountains far into the distance and felt them calling to him in a way the sea had not. It wasn't home, but there hadn't been a home in his heart for such a long, long time.

So, little brother . . . you're not coming home?

I'm not sure, but I think maybe I might already be there.

What will you do out there all by yourself?

I don't know. Maybe Grandmother will tell me. She always did, you know.

Morgan . . . Morgan . . . you're starting to worry me. Grandmother has been dead for years.

Since when would that stop her?

A shutter came undone in the storm and slammed abruptly against the frame, just as suddenly as James had laughed that day. He spun toward the door and would not have been surprised if James had suddenly entered the room. His thoughts were so deep in the past, it seemed a day for reunions, both with the living and the dead.

Morgan frowned. He might be thinking of the past, but he didn't like to. What he needed was a good run. Then this antsy feeling would go away. But there was the storm, plus the fact that tonight there would be no moon. It wasn't for company, it was merely for light to see by. And he ran not for the love of it, but to wear himself out enough to be able to sleep. His stomach growled again, reminding him that he'd put off the food that his body needed.

He took a clean rag from a shelf above the sink and began cleaning the paint and paint thinner from his hands, remembering another day only months after he'd settled in Santa Fe, and the boredom that had almost overwhelmed him.Only a couple of months into his self-imposed isolation, Morgan had found himself without food in the house. He'd needed to make a grocery list, and the flat, empty surface of a brown paper bag was nearest at hand. He remembered picking up a pen, shifting the sack to a better angle on which to write, and while he was thinking of cereal and milk, Grandmother's voice came to him as clearly as if she was standing at his side.

Spotted Pony! Remember Spotted Pony?

Hours later, Morgan had looked up to see a setting sun and realized that the day was almost gone and he had yet to go to the store. He remembered feeling stunned as he'd looked down. There was no grocery list, only a collage of faces and places he'd put on the paper.

Grandmother smiled back at him from the corner of the sack while the pony he'd had as a child grazed on sweet spring grass from the center of the surface. A hawk hovered on the lower edge of the bag right near a fold, making it seem as if it were about to fly off the edge.

The pen fell from his fingers and clattered to the floor. Only then did he realize how much his hand ached and that the muscles in his arm were jerking from the stress. He remembered staggering backward until connecting with a barstool, then sitting in total silence while he absorbed the power of what was on the paper.

Now, Grandson, you will be all right.

And he had been. Grandmother had told him what to do. She'd reminded him of a skill he'd never realized he had. One that would give him a purpose.

The wind was down to a low whine as Morgan hung up the towel, giving his finished painting a satisfied glance. Only after he caught himself squinting did he realize daylight was fading. It was the first week of May, and it would be a couple of months before light would linger into the nighttime hours. The sun was minutes from setting, and while a thin veil of dust still hung in the air, it looked as if the storm had passed.

Rubbing wearily at the back of his neck, he groaned, then stretched before covering the painting with a clean, damp cloth. This time when his stomach grumbled, he obeyed the call.

As he stepped out onto the patio, he paused, stretching again and wrinkling his nose at the scent of dust. Even now, the air was cooling. Before long it would be chilly where it once had been hot, although the thick adobe walls of the sprawling house that was his home were fine shelter from both extremes.

Halfway across the breezeway, the skin suddenly prickled on the back of his neck. It was something like the feeling he used to get in the navy just before he went on a mission. Instinct told him he was no longer alone. He turned, his senses on alert as he stared intently into the dusk, barely able to make out the shadowy images down the road of two people on foot. It was too late to disappear into the house without acknowledging their presence. And the porch light he'd unthinkingly left on all day was now a beacon in the oncoming nightfall.

"Damn it. I'm not in the mood for this," he muttered.

The loner that he'd become didn't welcome visitors, yet his conscience prevented him from ignoring them. From past experience, he knew they were probably stranded travelers searching for help. And while there were two of them and only one of him, he felt no sense of concern at the isolation in which he lived. He'd had worse odds. Death obviously didn't want him, at least not yet. He shifted position and leaned against a porch post, watching their approach.

A faint, cooling breeze sifted through his short, thick hair. Wide shoulders pushed at the boundaries of his blue denim shirt, while his dark eyes glittered from a face filled with secrets. The boy that he'd been and the man he was now were as different as daylight and dark. The lithe, slender body of his youth had given way to the strong, hard body of a mature adult. His years with the SEALs had bulked muscles that had broken men's necks with little effort. It wasn't something he dwelled upon, but it was a part of who he'd become.

He glanced west toward the fading sunset. If they didn't hurry, they'd be caught by the dark. And as he watched their approach, something about the way one of them walked seemed slightly familiar—an easy sway of hip with a long-legged stride. For some odd reason, the notion made his heart skip a beat.

A swift gust of wind came whipping around the corner of his house then danced down the road, buffeting the people on foot and swirling the long hair around their faces before settling it back down on their shoulders. It was then he knew they were women.

Julie Walkman shifted the bag she was carrying to her other shoulder and then glanced at her daughter, assuring herself that Patricia was managing her own bag just fine.

"We're almost there," she said, pointing to the house in the distance.

Fear of the unknown put a tremor in Trish Walkman's voice.

"Mom, are you sure it's the right one?" As soon as she spoke, she wished she had not. If her mother knew she was still afraid, she would start blaming herself all over again, just as she'd done most of Trish's life.

Julie Walkman never missed a step. Her voice was just as firm as the steps she was taking.

"It's the right house."

Trish nodded, then sighed. She had lived her whole life on trust. Now was not the time to question it. Taking a cue from her mother, she swung her duffel bag to her other shoulder, wincing when her long black hair got caught in the strap.

"Ouch," she muttered, and yanked at the bag, frowning as strands of hair were pulled out of her scalp.

Julie heard more than pain in her daughter's voice. She heard frustration, with tears not far behind, yet sympathizing with Trish would only make things worse. For a child born into a life on the run, she'd grown up with more sense than one might have expected. And if Julie's instincts were correct, they weren't through running.

Five days ago Julie had buried her father. The day before yesterday on her way home from work, she'd picked Trish up from her last day of school. Her hopes had been high. Officially, they were no longer under the care of the program. All the people involved in the original situation were dead.

It was over!

Julie had three weeks of vacation coming and big plans. In her heart, she believed there would be a way to explain everything that had gone before. In her mind, she wasn't so sure, but she'd waited all these years for the chance, and now that the time had come, she wasn't going to waste time second-guessing.

But that was before she and Trish had found their home in a state of disaster. Everything they owned was out of drawers, off of shelves, on the floor, turned upside down. And the phone had been ringing and ringing and ringing.

A shiver slid up her spine as she remembered picking up the receiver. Later she would think it had been a stupid thing to do. But she'd been in shock, and the ring had been so persistent. To her dying day, she would never forget the raspy voice on the other end of the line.

I want what's mine or I'll take it out of your hide.

At that point, fear had taken on a new meaning. She'd dropped the phone, taken one look at the house and then her daughter, and wanted to scream. It was happening all over again, and this time they were alone—except for Morgan.

After that, the hours became a blur. They dug through the jumble of clothing dumped everywhere upon the floors, packing only what they could carry. With cash in her pocket and gas in her car, Julie Walkman drove south out of Seattle on Interstate 5, stopping only for gas or rest when absolutely necessary.

She drove with fear in her heart and panic on her face, and she never quit looking behind. At Bakersfield, California, she headed east and began breathing easier. At Albuquerque she turned north, convinced that their troubles were behind them. Then the car stalled in the middle of the sandstorm. When it passed, they got out and started walking. To Patricia's credit, she never once complained.

Julie heard her daughter's long-suffering sigh now as she shifted her bag once more. She glanced at her and winked. Trish managed to return the favor.

In a few months Patricia Lynn Walkman would be sixteen years old. Julie was proud of the fact that she was growing into a beautiful young woman. Her skin was a warm coffee color. Her long black hair framed a face of exotic beauty that had yet to mature. Her legs were slim and firm, the muscles in her body taut and shapely.

Unconscious of the way her young breasts moved with her stride, Trish quickened her pace to keep up with her mother and wondered what they'd find at the end of this road. Technically, she knew *who* they would find, but mentally, she couldn't put a face to the man. Morgan Tallchief was his name, and said aloud, it never failed to make her mother cry.

Trish saw her mother stumble now, then come to a sudden stop. She grabbed her by the arm, afraid she was about to fall.

"Mom! Are you all right?"

For the first time since the day of Trish's birth, Julie tuned out the sound of her daughter's voice. The bag she was carrying slid off her shoulder and to the dirt.

There! Standing on the porch, then stepping out on the grass!

Oh, God! She knew him by the way that he stood, and then the way that he moved, but he was bigger now, much bigger than she remembered. The setting sun caught his face. Even at this distance she would have known that seal black hair anywhere.

Julie caught back a sob.

"He cut it," she whispered, and then almost laughed.

Of course he'd cut his hair. He'd been in the military forever.

"Mom?"

The panic in Trish's voice sank in.

"It's him, honey. Dear God, it's Morgan."

Julie started to move, one step at a time, then faster and faster until she was in an all-out dash. Forgetting the bag that she'd dropped, forgetting the child she loved, Julie ran as she had tried to run so many years ago—back to Morgan's arms.

When the woman suddenly stumbled, then stopped, Morgan's heart sank. He watched the other woman reach out to steady her, and frowned. Damn, what if she was sick or hurt?

But manners overcame his reticence, and he started across the yard. A flash of pure gold, and then another of hot pink caught the corner of his eye, and he knew that the sun had just set. Within minutes, total darkness would engulf them. That knowledge caused him to increase his stride, aware that carrying an injured woman to his house in the dark wouldn't be easy.

But when the woman went from walk to run, Morgan paused and then stopped, squinting in the half-light and wondering about her behavior. And then he focused on her face.

Dear Lord!

It was instinct that made him take a step back— away from the ghosts—away from the pain. He groaned and covered his face with his hands, telling himself it was nothing but a hateful trick of the light.

But then she called his name and the skin crawled

on the back of his neck. The last time he'd heard that voice it had been in a scream.

Afraid to look and afraid not to, Morgan dropped his hands and then opened his eyes. She was standing before him, her breasts heaving slightly from the run, her eyes wide and slightly frightened, as if preparing herself for something she didn't want to face.

"Kathleen?"

His hand was shaking as he reached out, needing to touch her, yet afraid that when he tried, she would disappear before his eyes. She seemed the same—and yet different. It was then he remembered the passage of time. He thought it odd that her ghost had aged when his memory of her had not.

Like him, she'd matured in body, and from the fire he could see in her eyes, in spirit as well. The lithe-bodied teenager had become a woman—but was she real? When his hand connected with warm, solid flesh, his fingers instinctively tightened around her wrist. Once, a long time ago, he'd turned her loose and lost her.

And then she whispered his name on a sob. The sound racked his body as painfully as on the night of the explosion when he'd stood in the street in front of her house and watched it burn.

"Kathleen? My God . . . it can't be you! I saw you die!"

All the pain of the past was in his voice and on his face. She swayed on her feet, praying that she would be able to find the words to make this right. Her hands cupped his face, touching, feeling, absorbing the flesh and blood image of the man she'd carried all these years within her heart.

"Morgan . . . Morgan . . . it's me, Kathleen."

The sound of her voice stunned him. In a sudden rage, he closed his eyes and lifted his face to the heavens.

"Ah, God . . . don't do this to me . . . not again!"

And then she took his hand and lifted it to her face, urging him to touch, to test, to take whatever it was from her that he needed to assure himself that he wasn't finally losing his mind. When she did, Morgan blinked and looked down, straight into the clear, true blue of Kathleen Ryder's eyes.

"Sweet Jesus! It's you!"

His hands were shaking as he threaded his fingers through the rich, silky texture of her hair, remembering the way it felt on his hands, on his face, on his body.

Kathleen stood without moving, barely breathing, praying more in these last few seconds than she had in her entire life. Praying that she would be able to find the words to make him understand, to make him forgive the deceit she'd been forced to practice. Praying that he still loved her as deeply as she did him.

Unable to bear the small distance between them any longer, she threw her arms around his waist, laid her cheek against his chest, and began whispering his name as she tightened her hold.

Morgan choked, then slid his arms around her shoulders as her entire body trembled against him. With resigned acceptance, he held her, facing the fact that either she'd just come back from the dead or, somewhere between dawn this morning and the sunset that had just occurred, he'd died and gone to heaven. Right now he didn't give a damn which was right. The only thing he knew was, Kathleen Ryder was back where she belonged.

Overcome with more than emotion, she swayed. As he felt her strength ebb, he stepped back and looked down, mesmerized by her presence as well as the look on her face. His eyes were glittering darkly in the half-light as he lifted her off of her feet, holding her suspended against his strength.

Dusk encompassed them as he spun them both in a slow, sweet circle, realigning their bodies to fit the changes that time had made. They were different—and yet so much the same.

Just when he thought he would die from the joy, the silhouette of another woman caught his attention. It was then he remembered Kathleen was not alone. When he looked, he saw, with some surprise, that the other person was just a young girl.

And that girl seemed speechless, apparently spellbound by the sight of them in each other's arms. When Morgan might have smiled at her, their gazes locked and Morgan was stunned by the color of the young girl's eyes.

They were so blue. Just like Kathleen's. Dear God, could this be her child?

Staggered by the thought, he had to accept the fact that she would have had other men besides him. He stared at her, separating the traits he recognized as Kathleen's from the others. What could the man have been like who'd taken Kathleen—a man who'd been with her just as he had—once in another lifetime.

The girl seemed to tremble beneath his scrutiny. He could see he was making her nervous, but it was impossible for him to stop. Anything that pertained to Kathleen Ryder, pertained to him.

His gaze went from feature to feature, trying to pick out the familiar, wanting to ignore what was not.

Her hair was straight and black—so black!

And with that knowledge came a thought. Out of the darkness. Out of the past. The knowledge that comes when one is faced with a sudden and inescapable fact.

That silky black—a black that almost looked blue—was just like his.

The features that marked her as a Native American were unmistakable. Just like his.

Her eyes were wide and tear-filled. Just like his.

The shade of her skin was a warm, rich brown. Just like . . .

He froze.

In that moment, Kathleen felt a shock wave ripple through Morgan's body, and fought back panic as he all but dropped her back on her feet.

He's seen Trish!

She looked up in time to see the disbelief spreading across his face. When he looked at her, she began to pray. *Please, God, help me find the right words.*

"Kathleen?"

She tried to smile and took a deep breath instead. She'd waited half her lifetime for this day, and now that it was here, she wondered why it should have had to be so painful.

Even Trish was beginning to panic. Kathleen tried to smile at her, but it wouldn't come. Instead, she took her by the hand and pulled her forward.

Morgan inhaled sharply, and the sound seemed magnified a hundred times in the sudden silence.

Abruptly, he grabbed Trish's arm and yanked her to within inches of his face.

"Who are you?"

When her eyes widened in fear, he regretted his tone of voice, but it was too late to take it back.

Kathleen touched Morgan's arm in a gentle but warning manner. "Morgan, any anger you have should be directed at me."

Eyes glittering darkly, he spun toward Kathleen.

"She's mine . . . isn't she?"

Kathleen's tears pooled and then spilled, a silent clue to the years of torment with which she'd had to live. And then she lifted her head and looked him straight in the eyes, unwilling to be afraid of the truth.

"No, Morgan, she's ours. Her name is Patricia Lynn, but I call her Trish."

He flinched. The knowledge was as sharp as the thrust of a knife. Stunned, all he could do was stare as he whispered, "Dear God." At the same time, something happened that he would have believed impossible. He found himself hating the ground Kathleen walked on.

Patricia Walkman had endured more trauma and upheaval than most people would endure their entire lives. And because she had, she saw the pain her mother was enduring at Morgan Tallchief's rejection and knew it could very well kill her.

On the verge of crying, Trish intervened. "Sir, you don't understand."

Sir? The word seemed so odd. He had a child and the only name she could call him was *Sir*? At that moment, he knew he had to forgive the girl. She was, after all, a part of him he had not known existed. And he had no doubt that she *was* his child.

His voice reverberated as he faced the fear he'd put on her face.

"No, girl, you're right. I don't understand. Maybe one of you would be kind enough to give me a reason that might make sense of this waking hell."

A coyote yipped in the nearby darkness and Trish jumped in fright, suddenly realizing that they were standing in the desert in the dark.

"Mom?"

Her voice was shaking as she slid beneath Kathleen's protective embrace.

"It's okay, sweetheart," Kathleen whispered. "It's only a coyote."

Morgan relented. There was a place and time for everything. He took the bags from the girl's slender shoulders, wishing he had the guts to touch her instead. But right now she didn't seem inclined toward such overtures, and he supposed he couldn't blame her. He'd hurt her mother. But was she old enough to understand how much her mother had hurt him? Could she even grasp his devastation?

He sighed inwardly. Probably not. He wasn't so sure he'd grasped it all himself. He squinted, his eyes piercing the darkness, longing for a more unfettered view of her face. He had a sudden and terrible longing to touch her. What would it feel like to hold his own child? He couldn't believe that a bit of his immortality had been living on this earth for the better part of fifteen years and he hadn't even known of her existence. Instead of giving in to his feelings, he turned them inward upon himself.

"Follow me," he said roughly. "I want answers, all right, but I don't suppose you need to have them scared out of you."

Without waiting to see if they followed, he hefted their bags onto his shoulder and turned, aiming for the single light cutting through the color of night.

"Come on, sweetheart," Kathleen urged, and held her daughter close. "It will be all right. You'll see."

"He hates you," Trish said, and felt her mother's pain as she flinched, then shrugged.

"He's hurt," Kathleen whispered. "Maybe in time he'll understand."

"I didn't think it would be like this," Trish whispered.

For the first time, Kathleen was a little angry with Morgan herself. She could take all the anger, and then some, that Morgan felt the need to dish out, but she wasn't about to have Trish caught up in his resentment.

"Neither did I," she said sharply, as she guided them both toward the beckoning light. "I suppose everyone changes. The boy I loved became a man. I don't know the man. I don't even know if I *should* love him. But I know that he's all we have right now and he's going to have to come to terms with that fact, just as I've had to come to terms with the disappointments in my life."

Trish took heart in the firm, no-nonsense tone of her mother's voice and relaxed. Her mother was right. They were safe here. For now, it was all that could matter.

Three

Morgan stood in the doorway, staring out into the darkness and waiting for them to follow. As they came closer to the house, he could just hear their voices, whispering secrets he couldn't share. He felt like an outsider and resented the fact. Everything within him railed at the injustice of what he'd been told. At that moment, he almost hated God for handing Kathleen back to him in this manner. She was alive, but everything he'd known and loved about her had been based upon deceit.

His fingers curled angrily. Just when he thought he was prepared to face them, they stepped onto the porch and he found himself backing up. When they came through the door hand in hand, the realization hit him head-on. His mind wasn't ready to accept the fact that less than thirty minutes ago, he had still been mourning a girl named Kathleen Ryder, and now she was standing in his house with their child at her side.

What was worse, Kathleen's physical appearance hadn't changed enough to make him forget the girl he'd known and loved.

He was so damned angry with the situation he didn't know where to start. He wanted to hate her. He resented the fact that she'd been able to keep him alive in her mind, when he'd had to bury her in his. Yet at the same time, he wanted to take her in his arms and cry for the both of them and everything that they'd lost.

He shuddered and then swallowed as his gaze slid from Kathleen to the girl. Now there was no denying what he'd already accepted as fact. Looking at her was like looking into a mirror and seeing a younger and feminine version of himself.

Daughter . . . this is my daughter! For the first time, a smile tilted one corner of his lips.

Kathleen saw it and went weak with relief. The smile. His smile. She'd known it and the boy who'd worn it so well. If that hadn't disappeared, then maybe . . . just maybe . . . some of the boy hadn't either.

"Don't be mad at her, Morgan. None of this mess is her fault."

"I'm not mad at her," he said gruffly. "I'm overwhelmed." His features softened and his voice shook as he reached out and touched her face in wonderment. "In fact, she's so damned beautiful it takes my breath away."

Trish had been determined to remain faithful in her mother's defense, but when her father's hand brushed against her cheek, joy surged through her. She felt like a traitor, and instinctively looked to her mother for guidance.

And when the look passed between them, Morgan

got angry all over again. The obvious bond between mother and daughter made him realize what he had missed. All those years of watching her grow and learn and love were impossible to recapture. She was of his seed, but not his heart. He didn't even know what her favorite color was or what she liked to eat. He didn't know what she was afraid of or what demons she had already conquered in her young life.

He wrenched his gaze from his daughter's face to the woman who'd borne their child.

"Goddamn it, Kathleen! Why make me think you were dead?" When she reeled from the viciousness of his attack, conscience made him relent. "Help me understand."

Her chin tilted bravely as she accepted the blame, but her voice was shaking as she began to search the room for their belongings.

"My bag, where's my bag?"

"I see it, Mom. I'll get it."

Trish darted past Morgan and dropped to her knees to dig through the contents, well aware of what it was that her mother needed.

"Here it is," she cried, and hurried back across the room, handing her mother a slightly crumpled legal-size envelope.

"Give it to your father," Kathleen said, and turned away, willing herself to a calmness she didn't feel as Morgan tore into the contents with a frown.

Moments later, he tossed the newspaper clipping aside. The frown on his face had deepened.

"What the hell was that supposed to mean?"

"It's my father's obituary. He died less than a week ago."

"Like hell. It's your father's picture, but that's not his name. The name under that picture says Maurice Walkman."

Kathleen dug in her pocket, and seconds later, handed him a Washington State driver's license.

Morgan looked, and then frowned and looked again. "Julie Walkman? Why have you been living under an assumed name?"

He could have said that she almost smiled, but the expression was a shade too bitter to qualify as joy.

"We've lived under a lot of names to stay alive."

His mouth twisted as he slapped the license in the palm of her hand. When she might have moved away, he grabbed for her wrist.

"Alive? You were worrying about staying alive? You picked a goddamned funny way of showing it, considering the fact that everyone in Comanche saw you and your parents die."

"But we didn't die," she whispered.

His eyes darkened, and there was so much anger in his voice that Kathleen wanted to run, but his grip tightened with each word that he spoke.

"Goddamn it! I *saw* you die. I *heard* your screams. I *watched* you burn. Can you even grasp what that did to me?"

The horror of the situation was not new to her, but hearing it from Morgan's lips made it somehow harder to bear. Without shame, she started to cry. "You don't understand. You saw what they wanted you to see. Up until my father's death, they controlled everything."

She looked at her daughter, then back at Morgan. "I thought it would be over when he died, but I was wrong. They'll come after us again, just like before. And I'm so tired—so tired of running."

Ignoring her tears, Morgan grabbed her by the shoulders, more forcefully than he'd intended.

"They? You keep saying *they*. Who, Kathleen? Who was in control, and what the hell was supposed to be over?"

"The FBI. Years ago, my father testified against a man he used to work for. Afterward, we were put in the Witness Protection Program. The stupid Federal Witness Protection Program that's supposed to give people a new start on life. Only for some reason, our start never seemed to take root." She choked on tears as she jerked out of his grasp. "We were like lambs that stayed one jump ahead of the slaughter, and everywhere my daddy went, the wolves were sure to go."

Morgan went still. The truth was staring him in the face and he wouldn't accept it. "But if you were being protected, then why the need to fake deaths?"

"They said it was because we'd been found—again. They said that it was the only way they could protect us from the people Daddy testified against. They said that everyone had to believe we were dead." Her voice weakened and her shoulders slumped as she looked up. "Even you, Morgan. Even you."

With that, she walked outside, unable to bear any further interrogation. The darkness was a welcome cover for heartache as she slumped against a wall and covered her face with her hands. In spite of the fact that she and Trish had made it safely to Morgan, she was experiencing defeat. She'd endured over the years by convincing herself she would be able make Morgan understand—that he would forgive and forget. It would seem she'd been mistaken.

Damn this world! Damn this man! Damn them all to hell!

Inside, Morgan was immobile. FBI? Witness Protection Program? He struggled with what she'd told him, trying to absorb the shock of it all. And then Trish touched his arm, and he was reminded he was not alone. Taking a slow, painful breath, he refocused his thoughts and looked down, once again, struck by a vague image of his own face looking up at him.

"Please," Trish pleaded. "Don't be mad at us. You've got to understand."

On the one hand, he wanted to be jubilant about Kathleen's reappearance, and on the other, he couldn't get past the lies that had ruined their lives. Looking at this girl, this child of their hearts, he felt sick that he'd been the one to put the pain and uncertainty on her face and in her voice.

"I'm not mad at you, girl. As for your mother . . ." His dark eyes glittered dangerously as he glanced over her shoulder to the woman standing outside on his porch. "You can't know how damned hard I'm trying to understand."

"She taught me to love you," Trish said softly, and then looked away, afraid that her admission was going to net another rejection.

Morgan's last wall shattered as he cupped his daughter's face and tilted her chin. Their gazes locked.

"She did what?"

A fragile smile broke the solemnity of her expression.

"I know all about your parents and your grandmother. You have five brothers and two sisters. I know that when you were growing up, you lived to run. Mother always said if you hadn't quit, you would have been the best in the world. I know that you like the scent of lilacs, and that old Laurel and Hardy movies make you laugh, and that you like hot, spicy foods. I know—"

"I'm jealous," he said softly, as he dared to test the silky softness of her hair.

Trish thought his interruption was odd and unexpected. "Why?"

"Because you know about me and I know nothing about you."

Her grin widened, and Morgan's breath caught. In the instant between her hesitation and her smile, he'd seen a shadow of his grandmother's face. At that moment, the full implications of having fathered a child sank in. Not only had he helped create a new life, but in doing so, he'd kept the circle of the Tallchief family intact. Grandmother hadn't died after all, at least not completely. A part of her still lingered in the daughter he'd unknowingly fathered. Emotion overwhelmed him as he braced himself for a refusal.

"I don't know whether you're ready for this or not, but I'd give a whole lot to know what it feels like to hold my own child in my arms."

Trish's heart soared, but she remembered her joy was at her mother's expense. She glanced over her shoulder. Her mother looked so small—and so alone outside in the dark.

"Well, Patricia?"

She sighed, unable to ignore his request any more than she could ignore the love she had for her mother.

She turned, tears brimming as she admitted to an old childhood dream.

"Dad . . . Daddy . . . I've been waiting for this moment all my life."

Dad? My God . . . my God. He opened his arms, imagining himself ready for the impact, but when she stepped within the circle of his embrace, he realized he'd been wrong. Her head fit right beneath his chin, and when she laid it upon his chest, the swell of emotion that swept over him was almost staggering. *His. She was his daughter!*

And then he amended the thought. *His child . . . and Kathleen's.*

Her body trembled against him, and she stifled a sob as he tightened his hold. Her hair was warm and heavy across his arms, and the tender curves pressed so intimately against him were a vivid reminder that his daughter was teetering on the verge of becoming a woman. Uncertainty daunted him. She was mere years away from becoming an adult. Would he ever be able to find a place for himself within her world before she was gone?

And as they stood, something began niggling at his memory. Something Kathleen had said about being wrong in thinking her father's death would end their years of running. He tilted her chin until their gazes met.

"Patricia?"

She looked up and smiled. "You can call me Trish."

He nodded, trying not to sound so abrupt. "What did your mother mean when she said it wasn't over?"

Her smile faded. "Mom thinks we're still in danger."

The thought of losing what he'd so suddenly gained

frightened him, and in turn, made him angry. His grip tightened.

"How so?"

Trish shivered. "You better ask Mom," she said, and then glanced wearily around the room. "Is there someplace I can wash . . . maybe get a drink of water?"

Morgan gave himself a mental kick. Once again, he'd missed the obvious. He had no idea how long they'd been walking, but regardless, they had to be exhausted. He picked up their bags, and the formality with which he spoke gave her the space she needed to recoup.

"I'm sorry, Patricia. Please, this way."

Too tired to remind him again to call her Trish, she followed without complaint.

He paused at the end of the hallway where two rooms faced each other. "Take your pick. Both bedrooms have their own baths. My room is up the hall on the right. When you've unpacked, feel free to prowl through the kitchen. I'm not going to guarantee there's much of anything cooked, but as soon as I—"

"I can cook," she said quietly. "And I was third in my class, and I can sew, and do laundry, and change flat tires, and I'm pretty good with computers."

Morgan got the message. "She did a very good job raising you by herself, didn't she?"

Trish nodded.

"And I know you love her very much."

She nodded again.

For a long moment, they looked at each other without moving. Finally, Morgan reached out and gently pushed her toward the nearest empty room.

"Get some rest, little girl. It will be all right."

Trish took him at his word. Because she had to. Because she couldn't face it if he was wrong. She walked into the room, closing the door behind her as her father walked away.

Lost in memories, Kathleen stared up into the dark, moonless sky, shivering from the unexpected chill of a desert night.

Morgan stepped outside in time to see her shudder. The urge to hold her was overwhelming. The knowledge that she was within arm's reach seemed impossible to grasp, and yet the truth of it all was right before his eyes.

A lingering breeze lifted her hair just enough for him to see the fragility of her neck beneath. The delicate curve of her cheek was barely visible, but he knew it as well as he knew his own. When she sighed, he heard her breath catch on a sob. The sound hurt his heart. He reached out, wanting to test the shiny surface of her hair with his hand, but hesitated, letting it hover just enough above her that he imagined he could feel the energy of her being, instead.

Something alerted Kathleen to his presence, and she spun, her eyes wide.

He dropped his hands to meet her gaze head-on. "Why don't you come inside? You must be tired."

"You startled me," she said, and then looked away, unwilling to let him see her tears.

But he'd seen them all the same, and hated that he'd been the one to make her cry. In spite of his belief that he was the one who'd been wronged, he felt oddly at fault, and because he did, his words came out all wrong. They came out angry all over again.

"Damn it, Kathleen, I'm not the one who hurt you."

She glared, her chin tilting, her eyes glittering in the darkness. There was little satisfaction in her voice as she threw the fact back in his face.

"Oh, I don't know about that. Right now, I'd say we're just about even."

With that, she walked past him and into the house, leaving him to think what he chose. No sooner had she entered than she spun, pinning him with a quick, nervous stare.

"Where's Trish?'

"Lying down."

Kathleen seemed to wilt as she ran a shaky hand through her hair. "Oh, God, will I ever quit being afraid?"

Morgan frowned. He didn't like what he was hearing one damned bit. He didn't want them in danger. He wanted—

His thoughts froze. What did he want? This woman was not the Kathleen he remembered. But then, he was no longer the boy he'd been, either. So much had changed. But they'd made a child together. Could they make a new relationship? Should they even try?

He took her by the arm and pulled her into a better light. He wanted to see her face when she answered. Only then would he know if she was telling the truth.

"Talk to me, lady. Tell me what the hell's going on. Why have you chosen to break the secrecy of the Witness Protection Program now?"

Her lower lip trembled, but her gaze never wavered as she met his stare.

"Technically, the government's need to continue protection ended when my father died. In fact, they have indicated to me that we are no longer in danger."

"So?"

She took a deep breath and, for the first time since her arrival, begged. But not for herself—for Trish.

"I came because day before yesterday we walked into our house and found it had been ransacked." She shuddered, recalling the horror.

He frowned. "People get robbed all the time. That doesn't necessarily mean anything. If they've been after you all these years, why weren't they there waiting for you to come home? If they didn't find what they were looking for, it seems to me they would have just waited for you to return."

She looked up. "No, but they called on the phone. The man on the phone was very blunt. He said, 'I want what's mine or I'll take it out of your hide.' "

"But what—"

She laughed bitterly and threw up her hands in defeat. "Damn it, Morgan, if I'd known what it was he was talking about, don't you think I would deliver it on a silver platter? Anything would be worth getting these people off our backs."

"What did the feds say?"

"I didn't tell them."

"Why the hell not?"

"Because I have a letter in my possession that clearly states we are no longer of consequence to them." She shrugged. "I know I could have called, but what would that have served? Another location? Another name? I'm sick to death of it all."

He sighed. "Okay, okay, but what about the local authorities? Surely they had an opinion on the break-in."

"I didn't call them."

Sarcasm thickened his voice. "Now why am I not surprised?"

An angry red flush stained her cheeks. "Damn you, Morgan! You can't possibly understand what our lives have been like. I don't even know if I want the police to know about us. I've lived my entire life being taught to trust no one but my parents—and they're dead. As for the FBI, they have declared us no longer in danger. I believe they are wrong, that the danger still exists. That's why I took our daughter and ran without looking back. That's why I came here. I believed that even if you couldn't forgive me, you would love your child enough to keep her safe." She exhaled on a slow, shaky breath as the room began to spin. "I'm sorry to get you involved in the hell in which we live—but I had nowhere else to turn."

Before Morgan could find the sense to answer, Kathleen fainted in his arms. He caught her as she slumped, and when he lifted her off her feet, her head lolled against his biceps. In this light, the stress under which she lived was plainly etched upon her face and body. He not only saw but felt her fragility, from the faint purple shadows beneath her eyes to the lack of substance to her weight.

"My God, what have they done to you?" he muttered, and then thought, *What have they done to us?*

He cursed beneath his breath as Trish came out of her room in a panic.

"Mother?" She grabbed Morgan by the arm and followed him into the other bedroom. "What happened to my mother?"

"She just fainted." He laid her down on the bed. When he saw the dust on her shoes and the cuffs of her slacks, he remembered the sandstorm.

"Trish, how long were you two on foot?"

"I don't know. Most of the afternoon. Our car quit on us just outside of Santa Fe." She tried to crawl onto the bed beside her mother.

Morgan channeled her panic into something useful. "How about bringing me a wet washcloth and a glass of water?"

Trish darted into the bathroom.

As Kathleen started to regain consciousness, she groaned, then began pushing against Morgan's hands.

"No, no," she moaned. "Let me go. Let me go. You can't make me go."

Stunned by what he was hearing, he stared down at her face, watching as she lay caught in the nightmare within her mind. And when she suddenly screamed his name and sat straight up in bed, her eyes wide and startled, her skin covered in a thin film of perspiration, he jerked back in reflex. The sensation was that of having been visited by a ghost. Right before the explosion she'd been screaming his name. Just like now. With the same degree of panic. With the same degree of loss.

Jesus! He stepped back, resisting the urge to gather her close. Had she struggled that fiercely before? Before the explosion? Before the world as he'd known it had gone up in a ball of flames?

Kathleen shuddered as her gaze began to refocus, and when she realized her mind had been somewhere in the past, she collapsed with a slow sigh of relief.

"Oh Lord, I haven't done that in years," she said softly.

"Mom? I heard you scream."

Morgan turned. Trish stood in the doorway with a washcloth dripping water onto the floor.

"She's all right," he said shortly. "I think I'd better

leave you two alone. When you're up to it, follow your nose to the kitchen. I'll fix us something to eat."

"Morgan?"

Kathleen's question halted his exit. He took a deep breath and then turned. He knew what she was waiting to hear, and she had a right to know.

"No matter what your reasons, you did the right thing in coming to me. Tallchiefs take care of their own."

Kathleen nodded, swallowing the lump in her throat as the sound of his footsteps slowly faded. She could accept the fact that she'd forfeited her rights to his allegiance, but Trish would be safe. That was all that could matter.

The lingering scent of fajitas from their late-night supper was still detectable as Morgan walked through the house, checking windows and locking doors for the night. The hallway leading toward the bedrooms was in darkness, the same as any other night. But for Morgan, the world as he knew it had somersaulted. Down the hall, mere yards from the bed in which he slept, lay the woman of his heart—and, dear God, the mother of his child.

Somewhere outside the house, a loose shutter banged against a wall. He had half a mind to ignore it until he remembered how Kathleen had reacted to the unfamiliar sounds during their meal and how her gaze had darted from shadowy corners to curtainless windows. If he let that shutter thump, she probably wouldn't sleep a wink. A few seconds later, he slipped out the back door, leaving it standing ajar.

When he came back inside, he realized he'd made a mistake in leaving the door open. Kathleen was standing in the kitchen, wearing nothing but a thin cotton gown. The gun she held was aimed straight at his heart, and the terror on her face was too real for calm conversation.

He froze, and she was the first to waver. Her shoulders slumped as she lowered the gun.

"I thought . . ."

He pointed with his chin toward the darkness. "Loose shutter," and then eased the door shut behind him. The click of the lock sounded loudly in the silence that enveloped them.

"I'm sorry." She started to shake. "It's just that I've been so afraid."

"Go to bed, Kathleen. I promised you, here you have nothing to fear."

For a long moment, they stood without moving, staring at each other and remembering while Morgan ached in a way he would never have believed possible.

Mere feet separated them. They were breathing the same air. Touching each other with nothing but looks. They were together, and yet had never been farther apart.

Finally Kathleen flipped the handgun onto safety and walked out of the kitchen without looking back. When Morgan could no longer hear the sound of her bare feet on the red clay floor tiles, he slumped.

"Jesus H. Christ," he muttered, and wiped a shaky hand across his face.

For a moment, he'd been as close to dead as a man can get and still be breathing. Kathleen would have pulled the trigger, and both of them knew it. At that moment, with knees weak and hands trembling, Morgan Tallchief accepted the last of the truth. Fact or fiction, Kathleen believed that she and her daughter were running for their lives.

He stood in the kitchen, listening to the sounds of the house settling for the night, and knew that tonight he would not sleep. He had questions that needed answers and no patience to wait for morning. With grim-lipped determination, he headed for his study.

The desktop was neatly organized, the surface clean and smooth to the touch. Morgan dropped into the chair and then opened a drawer, pulling out a flat leather-bound notebook. He laid it before him without opening it, considering the implications of what he was about to do. And then he thought of Kathleen, and the gun, and picked up the phone. It was time to resurrect some past of his own.

Dawn came, spilling sunlight onto the flat desert floor and warming the sand in a vast cover of heavenly heat. Morgan stood on the porch with a steaming cup of coffee in hand, wondering where honor had gone—if there ever had been such a thing as honor, or if it existed only within the minds of the gullible and the weak.

High overhead, jet trails were being sewn through the sky in neat white seams while miles away, Julie Walkman's abandoned rental car sat by the side of the road—the last visual reminder of a woman's frantic race for life.

If Morgan chose to believe what he'd learned during last night's calls, then everything she'd told him, and then some, was true. He had called old friends and claimed favors he'd never planned to use. But he'd found out what he needed to know.

Julie Walkman and her child were no longer of any interest to the FBI. The file was officially closed.

As he took a slow sip of coffee, he wondered, if the file was officially closed, then why would they still be in danger? Was there something Kathleen wasn't telling him—or was she telling the truth? Did she simply not know?

Four

"**B**reakfast is ready."

Morgan spun, cup in hand, and then smiled at Trish, who stood in the doorway, holding the screen open for him to come inside. This morning his daughter seemed younger, more vulnerable, and he wondered if she looked this way every morning or if he was seeing her in this light only because everything about the situation was so new. A thick black braid hung over her shoulder, and she was wearing a faded T-shirt and cutoff jeans. Her long brown legs were smooth and firm, her feet bare. She seemed so young, and at the same time, on the verge of becoming an adult.

"Hurry," she urged. "Mom's making pancakes. They're my favorite."

He smiled slowly. "So you like pancakes, do you?"

She nodded, and then grabbed him by the hand and began hurrying him toward the kitchen. "You'll like them, too. They're the best."

Kathleen looked up as they entered the room and tried not to stare at the sight of them holding hands.

"They're getting cold," she said, waving toward the pancakes on the table. "Don't wait for me. Go ahead and sit down."

Trish needed no second prompting. She slid into place at the table and began buttering the short stack on her plate.

But Morgan hadn't moved. He was watching the intense manner in which Kathleen was letting water run over her wrist, and when he saw her wince, he followed his instincts and moved to the sink instead.

Unaware of his approach, she shifted nervously when he grasped her arm for a closer look. "What happened?" he asked.

She shrugged. "Oh, nothing. I just burned my wrist a bit. It's not bad, but you know how burns are. The least little thing seems to hurt like blazes."

The half-moon brand was raised and already blistering. The sight of that burn, however small, made him remember the night he thought she'd died, and the horror he'd had to accept that she'd burned to death before his eyes. Even though he now knew that to be false, the thought of a burn upon her person, however small, was abhorrent.

"You need ice on that. I'll get you some."

"That's not necessary," she said. "Sit down, your food is getting cold."

"I've eaten cold food before."

She sighed, and leaned against the cabinet as he opened the freezer. One thing certainly hadn't changed about Morgan Tallchief—he was as stubborn as ever.

"Mom? Are you okay?"

Kathleen grinned wryly. Trish's concern was wrapped around a mouthful of pancakes and syrup.

"I'm fine. I just caught the edge of my wrist against the hot skillet. It's no big deal."

Satisfied that all was well with the anchor in her life, Trish forked another bite.

Morgan turned her hand palm-up and gently set the ice cube on top of the burn. Several seconds of relief passed before she realized that Morgan was still holding her arm, but that his grip was tightening. She glanced up. When she saw the path his gaze had taken, she froze. *Oh no.*

Breath caught in the back of Morgan's throat as he tried to get past the jagged white scar on the inside of her wrist. The implications were too horrible to accept. With shaking hands, he grabbed her other hand, turning it palm-up as well. The matching scar on the other wrist was for Morgan the proverbial nail in her coffin.

"Son of a bitch."

He dropped her hands as if he was the one who'd just been burned, and stalked past the table and out of the kitchen, leaving behind a distinct bang as the front door slammed shut.

Kathleen went limp. The pain on her arm was nothing to the one inside her heart.

"Lord help me," she muttered, swiping a shaky hand across her face.

Trish looked startled. "Mom, what happened? Where did Dad go?"

"Finish your breakfast. Your father and I have something to discuss."

Kathleen hated to have been the one to ruin what

was meant to have been their first act as a family. She could see Trish was fighting tears, and when the girl's lips began to tremble as she gazed at the empty places at the table, Kathleen regretted her hasty words. Once again, Trish was forced to accept the complications of their crazy life. She knew her daughter had counted on this meeting for years, even fantasizing about Morgan Tallchief. In her child's eyes, her father was as close to an earthbound God as man could be.

Kathleen paused beside Trish's chair and then bent and kissed the crown of her head. Reality was always a painful lesson to be learned.

"Don't worry, sweetheart. This, too, will pass."

Trish leaned her head against her mother's breast, accepting the comfort for what it was, and when she was alone, started clearing the table. It was obvious that no one else was going to eat.

Kathleen stepped out onto the porch, but Morgan was nowhere in sight. The sound of something breaking led her across the covered breezeway to an adjoining building where the door was standing ajar. She slipped inside, and then forgot her purpose as she stood in silent awe at the paintings inside. Color surrounded her, and the images they created were so alive that she shuddered. The war cries of Cheyenne dog soldiers coming from the images on canvas were almost audible.

Her gaze shifted to another painting, where women wailed for their dead, and when the wind suddenly whistled through the half-open door, she jumped in fright. The thin, high-pitched whine was all too similar to a woman's openmouthed shriek of despair. The distant sound of drumbeats seemed to emanate from another canvas, echoing within the four walls until her heartbeat began to keep rhythm.

Her gaze continued to move from painting to painting, and the sounds they evoked in her mind left her stunned. A horse neighed wildly as it plunged down the steep walls of a canyon, while its rider clung to its back by sheer will alone. Dust boiled up around the horse's hooves, coating the young warrior on its back as both plunged into what seemed a certain death. But then her gaze was drawn to the mounted soldiers who sat atop the canyon wall, watching in disbelief the young warrior's daring descent. There was something in the expression on the warrior's face that told the rest of the story. Whether he made it down the canyon alive or not did not matter. What mattered to him most was that he had eluded capture. He'd chosen his own path to glory.

Her attention shifted to the man across the room— the creator of all this emotion. He stood so alone. Impulsively, she reached out, sweeping her fingertips lightly across the surface of the nearest canvas. Closing her eyes, she traced the sure, bold brushstrokes, remembering that he'd traced her body in much the same way. She'd wanted to wail like those women in the paintings. Kathleen had already lost Morgan once. She couldn't bear to lose him again. Her breath came out on a shudder as she opened her eyes to the stunning beauty of what surrounded her.

Oh, Morgan . . . Morgan! What a gift! What a God-given gift!

He stood with his back to the door, staring out through the wide glass wall to the desert beyond. Pale green and earth red shards from a broken clay pot were strewn on the floor between them. Kathleen inhaled slowly, absorbing the knowledge of what must have driven him to destroy something he found beautiful. His anger frightened her. It was a side of him she'd never known.

"Morgan."

His shoulders stiffened, but he spoke without turning around.

"Get out."

"No! Not until you listen."

He spun, but she wasn't prepared for the viciousness with which he spoke.

"Damn you, Kathleen, you wanted to die!"

That she'd quit on herself—and on him—hurt more than he could say. For Morgan, that knowledge was all the more painful because he'd waged the same war with himself and won.

His accusation hurt. Her eyes blazed and her voice shook as she spoke. She was through taking criticism without giving back a little of her own.

"That's not true, at least not in the beginning. My parents monitored my calls, so at first, I just ran away. Five times, to be exact. I was so certain that if I could get to you, it would be all right."

Morgan tilted his head, unconsciously offering his chin for the blow of the truth, and was surprised by the underlying rage with which she continued.

"But that was my naïveté showing. I actually thought I would outwit my parents. The first three times I ran, they caught me. The next time, they had an agent pick me up. I was livid. I was stupid. I was young. I actually thought I had a right to my own life. They set out to prove me wrong."

Guilt was starting to replace Morgan's anger. "Look, I didn't—"

Her fingers curled. "Shut up! Just shut up, and for once, listen to me for a change."

He gritted his teeth and did as he was told.

"The fifth time I tried to run away, my father found me hitchhiking on the road outside of Seattle. When he got me in the car, he started to cry. He said if they found me, we would all be killed. He said I was being selfish. He said I had to understand that we'd all given up something to stay alive, and that I couldn't do any less."

The telling of it brought back memories Kathleen would have sooner forgotten. "I heard him and hated him. At the same time I felt so helpless—so alone. By the time we got home, I guess I'd put myself mentally out of reach. I don't remember. They said I went into my room and didn't come out. Not for school. Not for food. Not for anything. They would have taken me to a psychiatrist, but for that to help the psychiatrist would have to know what was wrong. And no one could know, right? Every damned thing about our lives was a secret and a lie."

"Kathleen, I'm sorry. I didn't—"

She looked up, her eyes blazing, her body trembling with an anger he couldn't understand.

"I'm not finished."

Once again, he acquiesced.

She smiled, and his belly turned. There was so much pain in the expression it made him sick.

"It's ironic, but in a way, you saved my life."

The words slapped him in the face. He didn't understand. He'd long since accepted the fact that when it had mattered most, he hadn't been fast enough to save her. Now she was saying he'd saved her life?

Kathleen held out her wrists. "Exactly seven days after the last time my father brought me home, I . . ." She closed her eyes and swayed on her feet as the memory swamped her. "Did you know if you hold your wrists under really hot water that you won't feel a thing?"

Dear God. Morgan couldn't stand it any longer. Seconds later she was in his arms. His voice was shaking as he held her close.

"I'm sorry. I'm so damned sorry. You don't have to say any more. I accept that it was neither one of our faults. Just for God's sake stop."

Kathleen took his embrace for the comfort it was. Nothing less. Nothing more. When she could think without wanting to cry, she remembered she still had to finish her story. She pushed herself out of his arms.

"When I came to in the hospital and realized I wasn't dead . . ." She shook her head. "It's just that I was so young . . . and so much in love. I didn't think I could go on . . . and then a doctor told me I was pregnant." She looked him straight in the eyes. "If we hadn't made love . . . if I'd walked off the bus that night and gone home alone . . . If you hadn't given me a child, I might have tried again. So, you see, in a way, you saved my life. You gave me something to live for."

He said nothing, overcome with emotion. She took another step back.

"I didn't come here expecting anything from you that you weren't willing to give. We don't know each other anymore, and I accept that. All I want—no, all I need from you is what you've offered, and that's protection. I've given up too much of my life to quit now. Help me keep our daughter safe. After that, I'll ask nothing more of you than you're willing to give."

Before he could answer, she turned and walked out, leaving him standing in the midst of broken pot shards with an anger that had suddenly refocused.

He glared after her, wanting to shout—wanting to rage. Hell, yes, he'd keep Patricia safe! How could she even suppose he wouldn't? What hurt him most was that she hadn't asked to be included in his protection. It was almost as if she was willing to sacrifice herself to whatever came next. He glared, and in that moment, if there had been another pot to kick, it would have gone the way of the first. Damn her to hell, how dare she assume she was expendable?

"Kathleen!"

She flinched at the shout, then turned to see him stalk out of his studio, slamming the door behind him.

"What?"

"Wait!"

She sighed. "I think we've said enough for one day."

He paused, and she could feel the control he was exercising over his own emotions. The very air about him seemed to tighten and bend to a will not of this earth. His eyes glittered, a black fire in a face without expression, as he took her by the elbow and aimed her toward the house.

She flinched at his proprietary manner. "Where are we going?"

"To breakfast. After that, we'll see to your car and then drive on to Santa Fe for groceries."

Her mouth dropped. It was the last thing she expected him to say.

"But you—"

"I can't remember the last time I ate someone else's cooking," he said. "And I don't intend to miss my chance, but something tells me we better hurry or that long-legged teenager will have cleaned her plate and ours."

After what had just passed between them, the last thing she wanted was to sit across the table from him and watch him eat. She started to pull away.

"You go ahead. I'm not hungry."

His eyes narrowed warningly. "Then get hungry. You're too damned thin."

She struggled with anger, refusing to let him know that she cared what he thought. Her voice was just past sardonic as she glared back at him.

"I don't know how on earth I will ever find the words to express my gratitude for your kind compliment and concern."

He grinned, and in that moment, Kathleen felt weightless, just as she had years ago on the day she'd met Morgan Tallchief. That day, he'd smiled, but only slightly, and then his face had become expressionless—like now. It was only later, when she'd come to know him so well, that she'd learned he wore his heart in his eyes. Everything he thought was there. One only had to look to see his passion or his pain.

This time, she looked away. *Oh, no you don't,* she thought, as he grabbed her hand and started through the house. *You can't just smile at me and expect me to accept that as an apology. No sir! Not this time, mister.*

She was still struggling when they entered the kitchen. Morgan ignored her and took a deep breath, focusing on Trish instead. "Hey, kid, did you save any for us?"

Trish spun. The look on her face held rapture, utter joy.

"I didn't think you guys were coming back."

Morgan pretended great incredulity. "Why not? Was it my inscrutable expression, or something I said?"

She giggled, and began dragging the platter of pancakes out of the refrigerator while Morgan set syrup and butter back on the table.

He pointed toward the microwave. "Nuke 'em for us, honey. Your mother and I are starving—aren't we, Kathleen?" He glanced at her only once, but there was enough warning in the gaze to dissuade Kathleen from arguing.

"At this time, I have nothing more to say," she muttered, and plopped down at the table.

Morgan winked at Trish and then remarked in a deadpan drawl, "I'll bet you don't hear that very often."

Anger moved the rest of the way up Kathleen's neck and over her face like a blast of hot desert wind, putting life in her eyes and color on her face that hadn't been there in years.

That did it! She didn't care how many times he turned his emotions on and off like some damned light switch. She was a grown woman. She no longer lay down for sweet smiles.

Morgan Tallchief drove like he ran, all out and without heed for anyone else, chasing after heat waves that hung in suspended animation just above the land

through which they passed, while dust boiled up behind them, marking their trail with a comet's tail of
New Mexico sand.

Trish sat in the backseat, engrossed in a book, unaware that with a little luck, they could very well become airborne at any given moment. On the other hand,
Kathleen sat tight-lipped and white-knuckled, refusing
to admit that he was scaring her half to death. This Morgan was so far removed from the boy she'd known that
she didn't even know where to start looking.

And it wasn't just the physical aspects of him that
had changed. She didn't know this man of many
moods, but dear God, she wanted to. The only thing
that kept her from beginning an all-out search was the
knowledge that having begun, she might not like what
she found at journey's end. What would she do if she
and Morgan Tallchief could not love in the now, as
they had in the past? She looked at him and then back
at the road as a wave of new fear washed over her.
They had to find a way to reach each other again. God
wouldn't be this cruel.

Morgan kept glancing down at the odometer and
then back up the road, expecting at any moment to see
a parked car. But when three miles, then six, and then
eight had come and gone, he was stunned. "Kathleen?"

She glanced up.

"Have I missed it?"

"Missed what?"

"Your car. We've already driven eight miles. I hate to
suggest the possibility, but it could have been stolen."

"No, we just haven't gone far enough."

His eyes widened. "How the hell long were you two
on foot?"

She shrugged, and glanced back at Trish. "Trish, how long do you think it took us to get to Morgan's house last night?"

"All afternoon," she said, and then returned to her book.

The Blazer swerved as Morgan remembered their exhaustion last night with new regret. "Please tell me you weren't in that sandstorm."

Kathleen shook her head. "No, we waited in the car until it passed, then we started walking."

He glanced at her, tracing her slightly upturned nose and that sweetheart of a chin with his gaze, struck once again by the unbelievable sight of her in the seat beside him. It took several long seconds before his thoughts focused enough for him to continue. "How did you know where to go? Weren't you afraid?"

Her gaze never wavered as she faced him head-on.

"I've always known where you were. And yes, I'm afraid. I've been afraid since the day I turned fourteen, but not of sandstorms."

There was nothing to say that would change what she'd said, and so he drove, accepting her life as a truth he could only imagine. It wasn't until they were a half a mile farther down the road that something she'd said dawned on him.

"Fourteen? But you didn't move to Comanche until you were seventeen."

Kathleen stared out the window, trying to follow his train of thought along with the scenery flying by. "So?"

"Then you were already in the program when you moved to Comanche."

She nodded, not understanding the odd expression on his face.

Considering all that had gone before, it was a small thing that bothered him, but given what he'd had to accept in the last twenty-four hours, he needed the whole truth and nothing but. His hands tightened around the steering wheel.

"Then Kathleen Ryder wasn't your real name, either, was it?'

"No, it wasn't."

Without warning, Morgan slammed on the brakes. The Blazer slid sideways in the road, spewing up dust and spitting it out from under the wheels like a bad taste.

Trish grabbed onto the seat as her book slid out of her lap, her eyes wide as she looked up to see what had happened.

Kathleen braced herself against the dash as the seat belt tightened around her breasts and waist, yanking the breath out of her body. She groaned as they finally slid to a stop.

"Morgan! For pete's sake, what are you trying to prove?"

"I'm not moving an inch until I know the name of the woman who gave birth to my child."

Fear melted, leaving nothing behind but remorse. *Oh, Morgan, Morgan . . . how do I make you understand?*

Trish pulled herself upright, suddenly embarrassed to be caught in the midst of such an emotional outburst.

"I'm just going to go sit on that rock over there," she announced, and bolted out of the car before either one of them thought to object.

Kathleen winced as the door slammed behind Trish. Her gaze raked the shocked expression on Morgan's face. Searching for the right words to explain, she reached out and gently brushed her hand across the knot of muscles in his forearm.

"In my heart, I will always be Kathleen Ryder, because that's who I was when we fell in love. And because you loved me, you gave life to Kathleen Ryder that no amount of federal protection could have done. But Morgan, I don't think you understand yet. Until you, I had ceased to exist."

He cursed beneath his breath and looked away. The silence between them lengthened.

"Does it matter that much to you?" she finally asked.

Morgan turned. Fixing a dark, hooded gaze upon her face, he mentally retraced the familiar heart shape, the clear blue eyes, the curve of her lower lip. His inspection was silent—almost frightening. The only sign of his emotion was the intermittent jerk of a muscle along the cut of his jaw.

"Morgan . . . does it?"

He took a deep breath and then blinked. When his gaze refocused, the flat, black expression in his eyes made her stomach turn.

"For all intents and purposes, the name under which you were born—or the girl you were—no longer exists, does she?" he asked.

She sighed. Finally, he understood.

"No, she doesn't."

"She has no family, or ties to a past, because that past no longer exists."

"That's right. All she has is her daughter—and you."

Reality hit him. Swiftly. Painfully. Then numbingly. At least he still mattered to her in some way.

"So okay, then. We go on from here."

Unexpected tears blurred Kathleen's vision. "From where?"

His hand shot out as he gripped her chin, forcing her to look and listen.

"From this moment, that's where. I've spent nearly half my life wishing I could turn back time. Today, that's no longer necessary. We go on from here."

A single tear spilled out the corner of one eye and slid down her cheek. He wiped it away with the palm of his hand and ached to be able to touch her more.

"There's just one thing," he added.

She looked up, a little nervous, a little bit afraid. "What's that?"

"I refuse to call you Julie Walkman."

Tension slid out of her body in a smooth, fluid movement as she smiled. "That's fine by me."

Embarrassed that he'd let emotion get to him, he looked away, then started the car.

"Better get the kid in here before she fries her brain. We've got a dozen things to do before sunset."

Kathleen opened the door and shouted at Trish, who'd wandered a short distance away.

Morgan shifted in his seat and then looked out the window, saw his daughter coming back toward the car, and forgot what he'd been about to say.

She was running back toward the car in a stride that could only be called fluid motion. Her legs stretched out before her, one then the other, hitting the ground with perfect precision. Her chin was up, her arms pumping, and there was a look on her face he recognized all too well. If he hadn't been sitting, he might have staggered, so great was his shock.

"Oh, my God."

Kathleen looked startled, and then realized that Morgan had not known his daughter could run.

"She's just her father's daughter."

A sharp pain pierced him as Trish slid into the seat, slamming the door behind her with a sharp thunk.

"It's about time," she grumbled. "It's hot out there, you know."

Morgan tried to smile past his shock. "Buckle up, girl. I think there's a pizza waiting for us down the road."

"All right!" Trish cried, and slumped back into the seat with a sigh as the air-conditioned interior began to cool her skin. "Let's hurry, okay? I'm starving."

Kathleen rolled her eyes, and then grinned. "And what else is new?"

Five

A few miles later, he saw a glimmer of sun against chrome. Although it was little more than a speck on the horizon, he knew before Kathleen pointed that they were about to come up on her car. When he looked down at the gauges, he whistled softly beneath his breath. She and Trish had walked almost twelve miles to get to his house.

"There it is," Kathleen said.

He nodded. Moments later, he pulled to a stop and then, in a break of traffic, turned around so that her car was facing his back bumper. Kathleen grabbed him by the arm as he opened the door.

"What are you doing?" she asked.

"We're going to take the car to Santa Fe, leave it at a garage, and go eat pizza, remember?"

She frowned. "But how will you . . . ?"

"Tow bar," he said, and slammed the door behind him.

Kathleen swiveled where she sat, looking out the

back window as Morgan knelt, disappearing from her view.

Trish looked up, only now aware that they'd stopped and that Morgan was no longer inside the vehicle.

"Where did he go?" she asked.

Kathleen pointed toward their abandoned car.

"One thing hasn't changed. He says what he has to in fewer words than any man I ever knew, unlike you, I might add," Kathleen said, and then grinned at her daughter's giggle as she returned to her book.

Kathleen rolled down the window and leaned out. Heat slapped at her skin, then licked at her cheeks like a taunting lover. She squinted her eyes against the white-hot glare and wished she hadn't left her sunglasses back at his house.

"Need any help?" she called.

She heard a grunt, one indistinct curse, and then the sound of a tool hitting pavement before he answered. "No."

She made a face at his terse remark before rolling up the window and flopping back down in the seat. *Okay, fine.* With a sigh of relief, she leaned back and closed her eyes, blocking out everything but the fact that, for once in her life, someone else was taking care of business.

The pavement was griddle-hot, the south wind messing with Morgan's hair, even hotter. It whipped the thick black strands across his forehead. Impatiently, he brushed it back with his forearm as he tightened the bolts on the hitch.

But his hair wasn't what was really bothering him. It was the woman inside his car. He still remembered the way her mouth conformed to his when they'd kissed, the way she'd flinched and then sighed all those years ago when he'd pushed his way inside of her—the feel of her arms tightening around his neck, and her breasts flattening against his chest, as the throes of passion had taken them both over the edge. He thought he'd known her as well as he'd known himself—but he hadn't.

Even then, Kathleen Ryder had been little more than a figment of the FBI's imagination. She had no past, and the way she was telling it, little hope for a future—and yet she'd given birth to his child.

What, he wondered, was he going to do about her? Better yet, what did he *want* to do with her? There was no denying he wanted to take her to bed, but was it to regain something he thought he'd lost, or was there something more—something new and different about the woman that was intriguing him?

While he was dealing with his tangled thoughts, an eighteen-wheeler began rolling to a stop on the opposite side of the road. Morgan looked up just as the driver jumped down and ambled across the near-empty highway to where they were parked, then squatted down beside him.

"Howdy. Name's Easter, Ned Easter, but my friends call me Bunny. Need any help?"

In the space of seconds, Morgan had given the trucker a thorough assessment and decided that the most ominous things about Bunny were a thin trickle of brown liquid leaking from his dip and out the corner of his mouth and the bulge of white flesh protruding between the waistband of his jeans and the tail of his T-shirt.

"I'm just about to hook up this tow bar," Morgan

said. "There's no ball on the bumper so I thought I'd try chaining it to the frame."

Bunny nodded. "It might work. I've got a couple of extra chains in my truck. If you need 'em, let me know."

Morgan nodded. Giving the man a last, careful look, he scooted beneath Kathleen's car with the end of the tow bar in his hand. Within minutes, he had it firmly fastened to the frame, and within that same frame of time, he'd heard more of Bunny's life story than he cared to know. The man's voice rose and fell with the ebb and flow of wind, neither pausing for inflection nor waiting for Morgan to comment.

Morgan gave the tow bar one last jerk, satisfied that it was safely in place, and started to push himself out from under the car. It was none too soon. Bunny was deep into relating the facts of his third divorce. Right in the middle of the details regarding the settlement he'd been forced to give "the bitch," Morgan felt something odd beneath his fingers—something that didn't belong. The shape was familiar, but somehow out of place. He craned his neck, trying for a better view, and gave up when he bumped his forehead against the underside of the frame. Again, he traced the shape of it with his fingertips, and as he did, a surge of adrenaline left him breathless as something clicked inside his mind.

No way! He had to be wrong. There was no reason for anything like that to be there.

But it was there all the same, and when he pulled, it came loose in his hands.

Squinting his eyes against the glare of sun on pavement, he held it toward the light for a better view and knew that he hadn't been wrong after all.

Son of a bitch!

He knew them well, even covered in dust. He knew how they worked. He'd even used them more than once himself. But why, if Kathleen was no longer important to the FBI, was there a tracking device on her car? A thin film of sweat broke out on his body just as Bunny Easter yelled.

"Hey, buddy, how's it looking?"

The shout startled him. Instinctively, Morgan made a fist around the device and pushed himself out from under the car.

"I think that's got it," he said shortly, and yanked his T-shirt over his head, using it to wipe his hands and dust off the back of his Levi's.

Bunny nodded, dusting his own hands as if he'd worked as hard as Morgan, when all he'd been doing was talking.

"If you don't need no more help, I guess I'll be hittin' the road," he said, and started back across the highway to his truck.

Morgan looked down at the device in his hand and then made a sudden decision. He followed the trucker across the highway.

With every step, his mind was racing. If he crushed the bug beneath his feet, the signal would stop sending, and whoever was on the other end of this mess would know. They might not know where Kathleen was, but they would have a fixed position from which to start, and twelve miles from his house wasn't any distance at all. Not for someone as determined as this.

The moment he thought it, he wondered why. Why did he believe her location needed to stay secret? He was nearly positive that the device he was holding was government issue. That meant FBI, and they'd been protecting her for years, so why did he feel this instinctive distrust?

In the middle of the highway, he paused, then turned. Just as he'd suspected, Kathleen was watching him through the window, mapping his every move with those wide, all-seeing eyes. He couldn't tell what she was thinking, but the look on her face was so tense and strained, he wondered if she ever relaxed. And then he remembered what he was holding and cursed beneath his breath. It would seem she had good reason to live on the edge.

His fingers tightened around the bug. None of this made sense. They'd told her the case on her father was closed and that she was safe. If that was true, then why the need to keep track of her whereabouts? His eyes narrowed angrily as he jogged to catch up with the trucker.

"I appreciate you stopping to help," Morgan said, and offered his hand.

The trucker grinned, then nodded and spit to one side before accepting the handshake.

"No big deal. I see a lot of stranded motorists on the road."

Morgan's smile didn't quite reach his eyes as he tested the curve of the tractor cab with his fingertips.

"Nice rig," he said.

"Yeah, and it's all mine," Bunny offered.

"You take real good care of it, too," Morgan said, and polished at a piece of chrome with his T-shirt.

Bunny puffed with importance. "I take good care of her, she takes good care of me."

Morgan's eyebrow arched. "She?"

Bunny cackled and spit. "Hell, yes, she's a she. I spend more time in her lap than I did my old lady's. Reckon that's why number three split. It's why they all split."

It was exactly what Morgan had been waiting to hear. "So, you're on the road a lot, are you?"

This time Bunny grinned before he spit. "I reckon you could say that. I'm on my way to L.A., then up to Seattle before running a straight shot back to Dallas, and then home to New Orleans."

Morgan smiled a little wider and ran his other hand along the edge of the cab and then beneath the curve above the fender, as if testing the strength of the metal. The magnetic connection the bug made with the underside of the cab was silent but firm.

"Yes, this is one fine truck," he said quietly, and gave the cab a last, comforting pat before stepping back. "Well now, you have yourself a real safe trip, Mr. Easter, and thanks again for stopping."

"You're real welcome," Bunny said, and then hitched at his pants before hoisting himself up to gain a toehold on the high-water running board.

Morgan stood and watched as the truck belched a puff of black smoke that dissipated above the cab like so much bad breath. Bunny ground at the gears and then started to roll, pulling from the shoulder of the road and into the lane of traffic while Morgan stood with his hands on his hips, his T-shirt dangling from one pocket and his feet slightly apart, watching as he drove away. A few moments later, he started back across the highway with a calmer frame of mind.

Now, you sneaky bastards. Follow that bug and see where it gets you.

Kathleen's breath stilled. Watching him lope back across the highway in that long, easy stride was difficult, but it was his bare upper body that made her weak. She remembered all too well the night that had changed both their lives forever.

Lost in muse, she was slightly startled when he opened the door and leaned inside. Right before he spoke, their gazes locked. Something quiet—almost reverent—passed between them and then it was gone as he tossed his dirty T-shirt into the backseat near Trish.

"Kathleen, I need your car keys. I've got to put the car in neutral before it can be towed, okay?"

She dug in her purse and handed him the keys.

The door slammed shut, and for her own peace of mind, she refused to look at him again. It was too much like playing with matches.

Seconds later, he was back. He tossed her keys on the seat beside her, and this time aimed his demand to the girl in the backseat instead.

"Trish, honey, hand me that clean shirt from the seat behind you."

Trish looked up and wrinkled her nose at the dirty shirt in the seat beside her.

"Phew!" she said, and lifted it up with thumb and forefinger, dropping it onto the floorboard before retrieving the clean one. "What do you say?" she asked, dangling the clean shirt just out of his reach.

Her playfulness surprised him, and then he grinned. "Pizza?"

Trish waved the shirt just out of his reach. "Is that the Cherokee word for please?"

Kathleen felt strangled between jealousy and joy. In

less than twenty-four hours, Morgan and Trish were bantering with each other like old friends while she was still fending off bitter accusations she couldn't explain away. She pretended a lack of interest.

"Girl, you're pushing your luck," Morgan muttered, and leaned a little farther inside.

Trish laughed as he grabbed it out of her hands while Kathleen tried to focus on something besides that flat, brown, muscle-rippled belly. As he pulled the shirt over his head, she looked away, pretending great interest in the hem of her shirt as he slid into the seat beside her.

Morgan gave Kathleen a long, contemplative look and then started the engine.

He would tell her about the bug when he thought she was ready to hear it. But not now. Not until she quit reacting to every sound as if it were a gunshot.

He shifted into gear and carefully eased off on the clutch. The car behind them jerked once as it began to roll, and then they pulled slowly onto the highway toward Santa Fe.

The constant drizzle outside Lester Bryant's office only added to the crap his day had become. Normally, he could see the tip of the Washington Monument from his desk, but today it was totally encased in a cover of low-hanging clouds. Traffic on the streets of D.C. was even busier than usual. Cabs came and went with rapid regularity. No one wanted to walk on a day like this.

Lester paced from window to wall and back again with a portable phone held close to his ear, his well-modulated voice low in keeping with the confidentiality of the conversation.

"Look, Benini, I'm telling you what I know. We were only miles behind her until that damned sandstorm hit."

He caught a glimpse of himself in the window's reflection and absently rubbed the bald spot on his head, combing what little hair was still growing toward the gleaming pate. Frustration was in his every move as he shifted the phone to his other ear.

"I didn't *say* the tracking device failed because of the sandstorm. I *said* we lost her because of it." He sighed, considering withholding the last bit of information, and then knew it would be foolish. This man always knew everything. "Truth is, my man didn't see the sandstorm coming until it was too late. And . . . he wouldn't have had the wreck if he could have seen where he was going."

Verbal recrimination flowed from the handset and into his ear. Lester's face was getting redder by the minute.

"No, he didn't injure anyone . . . or the car. It's fairly indestructible, but the accident *was* his fault. The mistake came in arguing with the cops." He took a deep breath and spit out the last of the news. "They put him in jail."

The screams at the other end of the line got louder.

"Hell, yes, he's out, but I had to be careful of how it was done. I can't go flashing my badge and expect to get results without some questions being raised that we'd rather not answer, remember? And, you should also remember that Julie Walkman and her daughter are on the run because of you. I told you where she was. All you had to do was pick her up. But no! You just tore the place up and then left without her or the goods." Lester knew he was taking chances by assigning blame, but he was sick and tired of taking all the heat. "And then you pulled that cheap Hollywood stunt and threatened her over the phone. My God! What did you expect her to do, have a candlelight dinner waiting for your return?"

Footsteps paused outside his office door and he frowned, holding his breath until they had passed.

"Look, don't worry," he continued. "My man should be able to catch up with them sometime tomorrow. They'll have to sleep. When I know something, you'll know something, okay?"

Lester hung up, satisfied that for now, they were back on track. He swiped his hands across his face and then dropped into the chair behind his desk. His round, little pig eyes narrowed as he leaned forward, staring intently at the open file upon his desk.

Shuffling the papers, he read with the absent skill of a man who deals with mountains of paperwork on an hourly basis. As he moved a report, an elderly man's face suddenly stared up at him from the page. It was a copy of Maurice Walkman's obituary.

He leaned back in the chair, letting his thoughts run back to a night long ago. A night when he'd waited impatiently within the small frame house in southern Oklahoma for a young girl to come inside. A night when he'd come close to letting her go up with the explosion that soon followed. He hadn't expected her to argue, let alone struggle as she had. When he'd tossed her over his shoulder in a fireman's carry, she'd inadvertently kicked him in the belly, then the balls. He'd lost his breath and his ability to walk at the same time. The only thing that had kept him moving was fear. Gut fear. He knew the house was wired to go.

What he didn't understand was why the Bureau persisted in continuing to relocate the family. For that matter, he didn't even know why Marco Benini wanted them found. All he knew was, he got paid a hell of a lot more for the information he'd fed Benini's old man over the years than anything the government paid him. He looked down at the file.

From a federal standpoint, Walkman's death had closed the file, although his testimony years ago had resulted in the incarceration of Paolo Benini. Even from jail, the old man had persisted in the pursuit of the man who'd testified against him. But Benini died before his goal was realized. When that had happened, Lester had assumed that would be the end of it all. To his surprise, Benini's son had merely picked up where father left off. His pursuit of the Walkmans had never let up, and his intermittent contact with Lester Bryant for information as to their whereabouts seemed to increase with the passing years. The way Lester figured it, Walkman had to have held something back the feds didn't know about. Something Marco Benini wanted. And unless Julie Walkman knew what it was, Maurice had taken the secret with him to the grave.

The copy of the obituary taunted him. Maurice Walkman's expression was in repose. He didn't look like a man with secrets, but Lester knew only too well they must still be there, or else the man on the phone would have quit years ago.

He glared at the picture. "Well now, old man. You won't do any more talking, will you? You went and died on us before you should have, and whatever Benini wants is still out there somewhere—isn't it? Maybe that's where your baby girl is going. Maybe she's making the move you never made, hunh? Is that it?"

In a fit of disgust, Bryant slapped the file shut, then tossed it into a lower drawer, which he promptly locked. Sometimes he hated himself. Sometimes he wished he'd never gotten caught up in this subversive mess. But everyone had an agenda. Everyone had priorities, even Lester Bryant. Only three more years and he could put in for retirement. He grinned, thinking of the little nest egg he'd made of someone else's greed. *And what a retirement.*

He glanced back out the window, picturing Joaquin Candelero hot on Julie Walkman's trail. Then he remembered the sandstorm—and the wreck.

"Mess up again, Candelero, and you're history."

Having issued the impotent warning, he pushed away from his desk, grabbing for his umbrella as he headed out the door.

Morgan stood in the shadows of the hallway, listening to the lighthearted sounds of female chatter and wishing he had the guts to enter Trish's bedroom and join them. If she'd been alone, he wouldn't have hesitated, but Kathleen was there. That meant he couldn't go in. If he did, she would find a way to make herself scarce, just as she'd been doing for the last three days. Somewhere between their confrontation in his studio and the day they'd gone into Santa Fe, she'd turned herself off to everything and everyone but Trish.

It was his fault and he knew it. Even now, the depth of his anger at her had surprised him. What Kathleen didn't understand—what she wouldn't let him tell her now—was that he'd finally channeled his anger to its proper place. He no longer blamed her for the deception, but he blamed himself for hurting her. But she didn't understand the man that he'd become.

The last tears he'd shed had been the night he thought she'd died. The last time he'd laughed, or known joy, had been earlier the same night, when they'd made love. The last time he'd known pleasure in drawing breath had been right before he'd heard her scream. Everything, every day, every year since had been nothing but an existence. He'd turned life off. Turning it back on was more difficult than one might assume.

The past three days seemed surreal. First she was dead, and now she wasn't. She'd come back to life. As yet, Morgan hadn't figured out how to do that.

He listened to the soft undertones of Kathleen's laughter and shuddered with a longing he couldn't name. Not once in his entire life had he shared his bed with a woman. He'd slept in theirs, but never taken one to his. He hadn't wanted to—until now. Now he lay awake at night with a longing that had less to do with sex than it did with possession. He'd had Kathleen's body—once. Yes, he wanted it, and her, again—and again—and again. But even more, he wanted that look in her eyes to turn soft. He wanted the distance she kept between them gone. He wanted to know that he could touch her, kiss her, hold her, whenever, wherever, and not be judged. He wanted those lost years back, and he didn't know how to make it happen.

Grandson, a man does not walk through life by looking over his shoulder.

A muscle jerked at the side of his jaw as his grandmother's words intruded upon his thoughts. He knew what they meant. He had to look to the future, not the past. Somehow, he and Kathleen had to create a new love without blame or regrets. He sighed. He had to make it happen . . . somehow.

A door opened, and he shifted deeper into the shadows, watching as Kathleen came out of Trish's room and started across the hall. Just as she was about to enter her own room, she paused, then turned.

Morgan stood without moving. By all rights, she shouldn't be able to see him, but somehow she'd known that he was there. Why, he wondered, did she have this sixth sense where he was concerned, when he'd lost every sensation he'd been born with except the basics that had kept him alive?

"Morgan?"

He took a deep breath and moved out of the shadows.

"Is everything okay?" she asked.

Hell no! "I'll be gone for a while," he said shortly. "Didn't want the sound of my coming and going to frighten you."

The thought of his absence scared her. She took a step forward.

"Come any closer, and I'll not vouch for what happens to you," he warned.

She froze. The growl in his voice didn't frighten her. But she wasn't prepared to make love to a man who didn't trust her.

"I'm not afraid of you," she said quietly.

"You should be."

Having stated the obvious, he disappeared, leaving Kathleen to savor the warning alone.

Somewhere in another part of the house, a clock chimed, striking the eleventh hour. Moments later, she heard the front door open, then shut. Impulsively, she followed the sound through the shadows, slipping out of the darkened house and onto the porch, letting herself become one with the night.

For a moment, she heard nothing but her own ragged breath. She inhaled slowly and then closed her eyes, concentrating, instead, on all that was around her. It was then she heard it, fainter than her own heartbeat, but just as recognizable; the rhythmic, repetitive thud of foot to ground. She opened her eyes and stepped off of the porch, searching the darkness for proof of what she'd heard.

There! Silhouetted by the glimmer of a faint quarter moon, she saw him. Breath caught at the back of her throat, and tears quickly blurred what little she'd seen, but she didn't need to look any further to know. He was running! She watched until he disappeared from sight and then waited for another hour past that. Finally, exhaustion claimed her, and she went back inside and crawled into bed.

Hours later, he entered her room. She was unaware that he stood inside the doorway, staring at her asleep on the bed. She didn't see the muscle working in his jaw, or the way his fists clenched as he struggled with himself and a longing he couldn't deny. She never knew he walked to the side of her bed and stood in the darkness, staring down at her face and at the way her hair splayed out across the pillow as well as the way her breasts shifted with the flow of her body. Nor did she know that long into the night, he sat in a chair at the side of her bed, watching her as she slept.

The next morning when she awoke, everything was

just as it had been when she'd gone to bed, except for a chair slightly out of place against a wall.

Candelero was nervous. Ever since the sandstorm and the wreck, he'd been at least a day and a half behind his target. No matter how hard he drove, he couldn't seem to make up the time. Granted, there were two of them and only one of him, but they hadn't stopped for more than four hours at a stretch. That surprised him. He hadn't expected two females to have such endurance. He thought about calling in for some help of his own and then discarded the notion almost as quickly as it had come. He didn't share anything, including money, with anyone except his *abuela*. Certain that it was only a matter of time before he caught up with Julie Walkman and her daughter, he kept driving, stopping only when he had to for food and fuel, catching catnaps in roadside rest stops and truck stop parking lots.

The only problem with that plan was Lester Bryant. Bryant was getting antsy. Candelero knew that meant someone higher up than Bryant was turning the screws. He shifted in the seat, angling for a more comfortable position, and glanced down at the sophisticated setup of computer equipment installed within arm's reach. With little more than the push of a few keys, he locked into a map of the state of Washington. A small but distinct blip appeared. He grunted in satisfaction. Using a couple more keys, he focused in on the area until he was staring at a city map of Seattle. The blip was at the lower edge of the screen, moving ever northward and into the city proper. Julie Walkman lived in Seattle. It was easy to assume where she was going.

"On your way home, aren't you, *chica?*"

Certain that he'd guessed his quarry's destination, he eased up on the throttle and stretched back in the seat, letting his mind wander toward a clean bed and some decent food.

It wasn't until the next day that Candelero realized he'd guessed wrong. By then, he was cursing beneath his breath as he sat in his motel room, staring at the phone. It wasn't so much that he'd been wrong. Hell, he'd been wrong before. It was answering to a man like Lester Bryant that made him nervous.

His belly growled. With a grimace, he reached for his pills and tossed them dry into his mouth, crunching them between his teeth. The acrid taste of man-made chemicals pulled at the skin inside his mouth, drawing out the natural moisture and leaving him with nothing but a mouthful of bitter powder, which he promptly swallowed.

With a grunt, he levered himself from the bed. Tossing the room key on the dresser, he left without looking back. His report to Bryant could wait. This morning, he was not eating breakfast served in microwavable plastic from some quick-stop vending machine.

Six

It was late the next afternoon when Kathleen wandered through the house, looking for something to do that would allay the sense of impermanence she'd felt since their arrival in Morgan's home.

She glanced into the living room and smiled at her daughter, who was sprawled on the floor with one of her ever-present books, happy to be indulging herself in her favorite pastime. Morgan was absent from the house, which meant he must be in his studio working. From something he'd said to Trish during breakfast, Kathleen had learned that a gallery in Santa Fe was about to have a show of some of his most recent works. That he was so blasé about the event told her a lot. He might put his heart into the paintings, but not his soul.

She paused in the doorway, looking out across the breezeway to the studio beyond and wondering if there was anything left of his spirit, or if she'd ruined that part of him forever. For all intents and purposes, Morgan had removed himself from everything and everyone he'd loved, and all because of her—and a lie.

Far in the distance, a jagged line of blue that was the mountains marked the line between the earth and heaven. To her untrained eye, there was nothing to see but a vast empty space between here and there. One had to look close to see a sense of balance, of life that existed in this desert that was his home. She thought of Comanche, the town in which he'd been born, and of the pasture land and the subtle but ever-present roll to the countryside. She remembered the pond on his grandmother's land and the fish he loved to catch—and the close-knit family he'd left behind him.

Why, Morgan? Why did you turn away from everything and everyone you'd known? People lose loved ones all the time, and somehow they find a way to go on. What was it that made you different?

Shading her eyes, she squinted into the sun's glare. Unshed tears blurred her vision of his world. It was all too obvious that this place of isolation and desolation mirrored the man that he'd become.

Quietly closing the door behind her, she paused in the breezeway. Warm air licked at the skin on her bare arms and legs, tickling the edge of her short, flared skirt and imprinting the matching white knit top firmly against her breasts. The pressure of fabric against flesh was light, like the touch of a hand to body—shaping, stroking, stoking slumbering fires.

Wrapping her arms around herself, she shuddered. She had to find something to do before she lost what was left of her control. The closed door to Morgan's studio beckoned. It was a small but definite barrier to her own brand of heaven.

There was only one thing left that might save her sanity, and that would be going back to work. It would be her salvation. Yet until her car was fixed, she was at the mercy of Morgan's goodwill. Once again, she would have to ask for his help.

When she entered his studio, he stood facing her with his back to the light, his gaze completely focused upon his canvas. His eyes mirrored the intensity with which he was working. The length of his legs was accentuated by dark blue denim. The breadth of his chest was all the more remarkable for the sleeveless, open-front leather vest that he wore over a bare upper torso. He was brown and barefoot, and the sight of that much skin left her weak. The breath that she'd taken slipped out on a sigh.

Say it now, you fool, before you forget why you came.

"Morgan, I want to see about getting a job."

Startled by the sound of her voice, he looked up, the paintbrush suddenly dangling from his fingers.

How long has she been standing there?

His gut twisted as he struggled to keep his voice even. "Job? What kind of job?"

"I guess the same as before. The skill serves me well."

He frowned. He just realized he'd never asked what she'd been doing with her life—other than lying to him and running. To give himself time to think, he dropped the brush into a jar of cleaning solvent and then knelt with a rag in his hand, pretending great interest in wiping up a spot of paint on the floor that had been there for the better part of a year.

"And that would be?"

"I'm a CPA."

He looked up, the spot and the rag forgotten. "But you always wanted to be a teacher."

A bitter smile came and went. "Wishful thinking. Can't leave in the middle of a school year with no explanation. They tried it with my father, remember. There are only so many times a person can die. I guess the Bureau decided the occupation was too much trouble."

Morgan picked at the paint drop with his fingernail. It was hard and dry, immersed within the porous tile like a burr in a horse's tail.

Damn. Do I let her go, or tell her? Morgan was anxious to tell her about the tracking device he'd found on her car, only he knew that would scare her even more. And then he thought, *To hell with the spot. Stand up and take this like a man.* He gave Kathleen a studied, sidelong glance. What he saw didn't give him any encouragement to confess. Her face was closed, almost emotionless. He could almost believe she had little on her mind except the obvious until he looked into her eyes. The fear that was always with her stared back at him through a clear, morning-glory blue.

Don't tell her.

The warning came out of nowhere, and he wondered if it was his grandmother once again intruding upon his thoughts or his own instincts warning him to tread carefully.

"I don't know, Kathleen. You came here believing you and Patricia are still in danger. At this point, we have no reason to suppose anything has changed. I think you should wait."

Having said that, he tossed the rag onto a table and

looked away, pretending he didn't notice her chin tilting stubbornly or the frown that slid in place.

Kathleen was stunned. How dare he dismiss her so lightly! She didn't care whether he liked what she said or not. He didn't understand that she'd lived with fear most of her life, and she didn't just *believe* they were in danger, she *knew* they were in danger. It was ironic that while Morgan had quit the thing he'd been born to do, for her, running had become a way of life. But damn it, no one was paying her to be afraid. Working was the only thing she could do and maintain some sense of control. If she didn't have that, she would go crazy.

The determination that had carried her this far was waning fast. She needed someone else to lean on who shared her world, her fears. For the first time, she began to understand what her parents must have felt. They'd had each other. She had no one, and now she felt like a burden Morgan hadn't been able to refuse.

"Wait for what? Death? Taxes? None of the above? I only wanted one thing from you, Morgan Tallchief, and it damn sure wasn't charity. I have to get a job, or staying here will be impossible!"

This time, the fear inside him won. He pivoted, moving too quickly for her to retreat. His fingers dug into her arms, holding her fast.

"You don't leave me again!"

Shocked by the unexpectedness of his anger, she forgot what she'd been about to say. She looked into eyes black with fury, slowly realizing she didn't know this man at all.

"You're hurting me," she said.

His voice was low. The words he uttered slipped out painfully from between tightly clenched teeth. "Damn it, Kathleen, you're hurting me, too." His voice was shaking as he loosened his grip and slid his hands up her arms to cup her face, instead. "I'm having a hell of a time living with the fact that you're not dead. That the woman I kept alive in my heart is now in my house, but not in my bed!"

His words created a need in her that drilled a hole in her belly, leaving her drained and aching.

"Kathleen."

Her name was at once a question and a prayer, but she had no answers he would like.

"Morgan, I can't change the past, and you don't want to forgive me for it, so where does that leave us?"

Frustrated, he wanted to shake her. "I don't know where you are, but I can tell you where I am—right where I've been for the past sixteen goddamned years—alone and hurting."

Her tears began to spill without warning. He groaned, then lowered his head until their foreheads were touching. His voice was quiet, his hands gentle, as he swiped at the tears with the balls of his thumbs.

"I didn't mean to make you cry."

"And I didn't mean to deceive you."

For a long, silent moment, they stared into each other's eyes, judging the depths of each other's pain. Neither spoke. Neither moved as they remembered another time, long ago when they'd stood just so and said nearly the same thing. Back then they'd made love afterward. Now they were little more than strangers with nothing between them but lingering tears and carefully drawn breaths. They'd reached an impasse.

He was drowning in her eyes and going down for

the last time when she spoke, and it was so far removed from what he was feeling that, for a moment, he couldn't think.

"Morgan?"

"What?"

"Don't hate me. I accept your resentment, but I couldn't bear it if—"

His kiss was unexpected, but the flash fire of longing that came afterward was not. Stranger or not, it was no longer possible to deny what she was feeling. Kathleen slid her arms around his neck and leaned into the embrace. When he groaned and pulled her between his legs, he could not hide what he felt—what he wanted. But it was broad daylight, and Trish was just across the breezeway. Kathleen tore her mouth from his lips, and then clutched at his vest, trying to steady herself on shaking legs.

"Morgan, we shouldn't be . . ."

He lifted his head. There was a look on his face she'd never seen before. She wasn't sure whether she should be excited or afraid.

"What is it?" she whispered.

"Shut up. Just shut up and kiss me."

She did, tasting his anger. When it softened, turning to a wild hunger with nowhere to go, she shuddered. The kiss ripped through years of empty nights and lonely days, filling her with an intense desire to belong. At that moment, she didn't care what he thought of her or how he felt about what he viewed as her betrayal. All she wanted was this man inside her, slamming his body against hers in a hot, mindless rush.

She thrust her fingers into the hair at the back of his neck and sighed when he cupped her hips, pulling her closer and grinding himself against her. One step led to another, and then another. Before Kathleen knew it, he had her pinned between himself and the wall, thrusting his hands beneath her top.

Morgan was nearly blind with longing, using instinct to guide him. The need to be inside her was upon him in a most terrible way. Breathing hurt. It came out in short, harsh grunts between the kisses he swept across her face and down her neck. He tasted tears and heard her soft, indistinct cries for satisfaction. When her breasts fell heavy into his hands, he groaned. And when she cried out, arching against his palms and begging him in the only way she knew how, he lost control.

This time, there would be no pain with the act, only the aftermath of sex without love and promises, and neither one of them was looking to the future.

Kathleen's hands were all over his chest, then his waist, then his belt, then struggling with the button fly of his Levi's when Trish's voice rang out loud and clear from the house across the way.

"Dad! Telephone! It's some lady about your paintings."

They froze with their hands on each other's bodies, their gazes locked into the other's face. Morgan lowered his head and tore a kiss from her mouth. Then, with a curse, he pushed away, pausing only once, to look back. Her lips were swollen, her face flushed. Her hair was tousled, her clothes undone. The look in her eyes was one of disbelief, and of a loss she couldn't name. He knew that the moment was gone. That if he came back now without answering his daughter's summons, it would not be the same. She'd let him past her defenses once. He doubted it would happen again, but he had to ask.

"Will you wait?"

The question ripped at her conscience. Her lips trembled as she struggled between sanity and salvation, and she cared too much to lie. There was nothing to be said but the truth.

"I'll wait before taking a job . . . but this shouldn't have happened."

He'd known it was coming, but hearing it aloud still hurt. Hiding his pain behind a blank expression, he turned and walked away.

Kathleen pressed trembling fingers against her lips and slid to the floor as her legs gave way. Unaware that her actions mirrored those of the woman in the painting above her head, she wrapped her arms around her body and began swaying to and fro upon her knees. That woman was in mourning. So was Kathleen.

Dear Lord, dear Lord, what have I done?

If Trish hadn't called out when she had, he would have taken her where she stood and she would have begged him for more. But it had happened, and the lust had passed, leaving more than distance between them.

There were no answers for Kathleen, nor had there ever been. She was who she was, a woman on the run. Until she discovered who wanted her dead, she had no future, just as she had no past. The only tie she had to reality was Morgan Tallchief and the child she'd borne him. She prayed to God she didn't lose them, too.

Lester Bryant was sweating. His nest egg was starting to stink. Marco Benini was through making threats and was down to promises Lester didn't want to consider.

"Look," Lester muttered, eyeing the half-open door to his office and lowering his voice even more. "You've got to quit calling me like this. I gave you my cell phone number, and this is the third time you've called me on the office line. This is FBI headquarters, for God's sake. For all I know, every phone in the place is bugged."

He winced, holding the phone a distance away from his ear, letting Benini vent while giving himself a rest.

"I know what I promised," Bryant finally answered. "I haven't let you down yet. But you have to remember, I haven't been directly involved in the program for years. Up until Walkman's death, all my information was old news. Hell, if that newspaper hadn't printed Walkman's picture with the obit, he'd still be lost to us." Bryant shifted the phone to his other ear. "And like I said before, I'm not the one who ransacked her home in Seattle and scared her into running. You should be glad I had the foresight to have her car bugged after I located them. My man is on her tail; when she lands, we'll know it, okay?"

He paused, then paled as Benini promised things to his body parts that he didn't want to consider. Before he could argue, the line went dead in his ear. He dropped the receiver back into the cradle, then dropped into the chair behind his desk, staring at a photo of his family. Connie, his childhood sweetheart, had given him a son and a daughter. The perfect, all-American family.

I did it for you, he thought, and then shame made him lay the photo facedown. He could lie to himself, but not to them. He'd done it for the money, and that was the truth. It had been too good to ignore, and the job too easy. He'd had access to so many records. Finding one small family hidden within the program had seemed simple. It hadn't been as easy as he'd assumed. More than once he'd asked one too many questions and spent days afterward in constant fear, certain that he'd be found out. And each time, he'd been so relieved to be wrong that he'd made vow after vow to quit while he was ahead. And then Benini would call, offering more money, and then more, until Lester Bryant was so caught up in the scheme that he couldn't quit. Not even if he wanted to. And oh God, how he wanted to.

Needing to hear a voice of reason, he thought of Connie and picked up the phone, yearning to hear the innocence in her voice, and then suddenly, he changed his mind.

"By damn, I'm going home, instead."

With grim-lipped determination, he set the photo upright and pushed himself out of his chair. It was past time for that south-of-the-border snake to call in, but he'd had enough of bad news for one day. He was going to catch the early train home and take Connie out to dinner. He couldn't remember the last time he had gotten home before midnight.

The door shut behind him with a distinct click as he ambled down the hall, toying with the notion of having Italian food for dinner, or maybe Chinese. Halfway to the elevator, a phone began ringing somewhere back down the hall. He turned, staring at the closed door to his office. A fresh wave of sweat broke out beneath his shirt. It was Candelero. He just knew it. *To hell with it all*, he thought. His face was grim as he turned and continued his march to the elevator to the tune of Ma Bell.

In the middle of the fourth ring, the elevator doors opened and Lester found himself face-to-face with the deputy director.

"Evening, Bryant, going down?"

Lester wavered. On the sixth ring, he suddenly pivoted, startling himself as well as the deputy director when he began to run. For a fat man, he moved with some degree of grace, his body mass shifting comfortably with each long stride, reminiscent of the days when he'd first carried a badge.

He hit the door with the flat of his hand, loping at an all-out stride. In three long leaps, he'd reached his desk. When he picked up the phone, it seemed as if it had been ringing in his head for days. Sweat totally saturated the shirt beneath his jacket, and his breathing was short and jerky as he gasped, "Bryant here."

"Lester, it's me. I know it's getting late, but there's a little matter I think we need to discuss. Why don't you come down to my office while things are slow. I don't want any interruptions after we begin."

Lester paled. He closed his eyes and inhaled slowly, trying to calm a frantic pulse. It was the director! He couldn't remember the last time the boss had called him. In fact, he didn't think it had ever happened. At least not like this. There had always been memos, never phone calls.

"What's up?" he asked, putting interest in his voice that wasn't really there.

The director's pause was too long for Lester's peace of mind. In the vernacular of the perps he'd spent his life bringing down, he feared he'd been made. When his boss finally spoke, he was certain that he was right.

"No, Lester, this isn't something I want to discuss

over the phone. I prefer face-to-face. Tell Ruth to buzz you right in. I'll be expecting you."

Once again, the line went dead in Lester's ear, only this time, Lester Bryant was about to follow its lead.

The sweat that had been pouring down his body suddenly ceased. His skin went clammy, then cold. Vision blurred as his belly lurched. Nausea warred with an oncoming blast of pain that shattered his control and the wall of his chest. To his surprise, a thin stream of warm, wet liquid suddenly ran down the inside of his pants. In a panic, Lester Bryant grabbed at himself, then the phone, then cursed as his legs gave way.

He hit the floor thinking of all that money he was never going to spend and wished he'd called Connie after all. It would have been nice to hear her voice once more before going to hell.

Candelero strutted past the cashier as he exited the café, pausing on the doorstep to survey the half-empty parking lot. The cinnamon-flavored toothpick on which he was sucking hung from a corner of his mouth. The ache in his belly had eased, and the phone number in his pocket only added to his swagger as he headed for his car. He'd been right. The waitress would have been an easy mark. She'd served him his food, but the side dish had been her phone number written in bloodred lipstick on the napkin.

He grinned to himself. He was no fool. He was looking for a woman, all right, but not one to fuck. He'd find Lester Bryant's woman for him and deal with personal matters later.

Just thinking of Julie Walkman made him angry. He'd been so close, so many times. It pissed him off royally that he'd had such a run of bad luck—and, truth be known, it made him a little nervous. Joaquin Candelero was not accustomed to bad luck.

A night moth swooped across his line of vision as he opened the door and slid into the driver's seat, locking the doors behind him. Although the darkened windows of his gray sedan were nearly impossible to see through, caution had been with him too long to ignore. He needed to check his location, but couldn't see anything without a light. His lifestyle precluded a simple act such as turning on the dome light. It would make him too much of a target.

Lifting the lid of the console, he pulled a small penlight from inside, then aimed it toward the control panel. But when he pushed the switch, it didn't come on. He shook it once, twice, then cursed when it slipped from his fingers and onto the floor.

"To hell with this," he said, and reached for the dome light just as a couple walked past his car. He paused in the act, listening to their laughter, even bits of their conversation. Once again, caution won. Instead, he bent down, feeling in the dark until his fingers connected with the slim metal tube, trying it once more for good luck. When nothing happened, he unscrewed the top, tilting it so that the tiny battery fell into his hands. He took out his pocketknife and began scraping at the points of contact, every so often wiping off the ends with a tissue.

It would have been simpler if he'd just started the car and driven away. Then he could have stopped somewhere later on and turned on all the interior lights he needed. But Candelero was a single-minded, methodical man. He'd made the decision to check

Julie Walkman's location now, and now it was going to be.

Satisfied that he'd done all he could do to improve the battery's function, he wiped it completely clean, then picked it up and slid it back into the miniature flashlight. One last screw of the cap and he was ready to try it again. This time, when he pressed the button, a small beam of light cut through the murky shadows of the car's interior. It gave him satisfaction to know he'd defeated the mechanics of the faulty light.

"Ha!"

Aiming the narrow beam toward the control panel, he quickly found the buttons he needed. With a flick of his wrist, he activated the computer and punched up the program, grunting with satisfaction as the tiny blip on the screen came into focus.

It looked as if Julie Walkman had finally stopped running, at least for the night. Her location hadn't changed in more than two hours, and in his opinion, it was about time. The way she'd been driving, the woman had to be a zombie by now. He glanced at his watch, mentally calculating the difference in time zones, and then shrugged. Bryant was like a bulldog. He would still be waiting for the call.

He tossed his toothpick into the ashtray, dropped the penlight back into the console, and picked up the cell phone from the seat beside him, quickly punching in the numbers to Bryant's office.

He counted one, two, and three rings, and then lost count. A frown creased his forehead, deepening with each unanswered tone.

"Come on . . . answer the phone, you fat bastard,"

Candelero said, and then choked on his own spit when someone suddenly did just that.

"Lester Bryant's office. May I help you?"

Candelero was speechless. It was a woman. Not once in their entire association had a woman *ever* answered Bryant's phone. Within the space of a split second, he'd debated with himself about hanging up and decided against it.

"I need to speak to Bryant. Is he in?"

She gasped, and the sound cut a nervous trail through his mind and reactivated the pain in his belly. What? What the hell had he said?

"Never mind," he said nervously. "I'll call back later."

"Oh, but sir, you can't! I mean . . . I don't know how to . . ."

Candelero braced himself to ignore the twist in his gut as she continued to stammer.

"We've all been . . . I mean, it was so . . ." She took a deep breath, as if reminding herself of why she was there. "Sir . . . are you family?"

Candelero frowned. "No. Never mind. I'll call back tomorrow."

And then he could have sworn that he heard her sob. His hand tightened around the phone.

"I'm sorry to have to tell you, but Mr. Bryant died of a heart attack this evening. If you'd like to leave your name and number, I'm sure someone else will be able to help you."

Madre de Dios! Candelero disconnected on a groan. It was over! His paycheck had come to an abrupt end. Cursing his luck and Lester Bryant's fat heart, he dropped the phone and stared blindly at the blip winking on the screen.

His mind raced as he sorted his choices. On the one hand, he was free to go home, which pleased him. On the other, he would return without a dime of the money he'd been promised. His payoff had depended upon the delivery of information on Julie Walkman's whereabouts to Lester Bryant. She was all but in his lap and now there was no one who cared. Oh, he knew there was someone else who wanted to know, but Lester Bryant had been the middleman, and Candelero had no way of connecting with the man for whom Bryant had been working.

And then another thought struck, and he cursed low and long, thinking of the revelations that were bound to come from Bryant's death. Bryant's wife would audit a will. Bryant's cases would be reassigned to someone else. Somewhere within all the shifting of paperwork, it was bound to come to light that one government-issue sedan, complete with enough computer equipment to track satellites, had been assigned without permission to Lester Bryant and was now nowhere to be found.

Candelero's eyes narrowed as the olive cast to his skin turned a sickly yellow. The thought of being discovered in this car sent him into a panic. Suddenly, the car that had been his bed on more than one occasion now became a ticking time bomb. He switched off the program, nodding with satisfaction as the blip disappeared from the screen. When he drove from the parking lot, he headed toward Denver, his decision already made.

A couple of hours later, he walked out of airport parking toward the terminal and never looked back. The car was wiped clean. When they finally found it, and he had no doubt that they would, there wouldn't be a shred of evidence left to connect him to one Lester Bryant, currently residing on some mortuary slab. Let the government boys figure out how Bryant's car wound up in Denver, Colorado, while he was dying in D.C. It made no difference to Candelero. He would be safe at home in Guadalupe when it happened.

Morgan walked through the darkened rooms of his house, listening for sounds that would indicate to him that someone was awake. When he heard nothing but his own heartbeat, he pivoted and headed for the front door, flipping on the porch light out of habit as he exited. Today in his studio, he'd been as close to taking a woman without her permission as he'd ever been in his life. The knowledge shamed him. He'd been taught better. But lying in a lonely bed tonight with guilt for company would gain him little—not even rest.

No man is perfect.

A bitter smile broke the sternness of his expression as the thought intruded.

"Sorry, Grandmother, but you're a little too late to help me now."

Running away will solve nothing.

"I'm not running away, Grandmother. I'm just wearing myself out so I can rest. Even an imperfect man has to sleep."

This time, no reminder from the past intruded as he knelt to check the ties on his running shoes. When he stood, wearing nothing but a pair of black nylon trunks and the shoes on his feet, his mind was already flowing into the run.

As always, the darkness of a desert night engulfed

him. The faint slice of moonlight was all that he needed to see by. He knew this land like he knew the back of his hand. He also knew one wrong step in the dark could break a leg. One wrong turn could kill.

He stepped off the porch and jogged a ways into the desert, looking back once just to center himself within the land and the light that beckoned from the porch beyond. Satisfied that all was as it should be, he lifted his head, focused on a landmark only he could see, and started to move. And as he did, his soul flew free, moving out ahead of him like a wind racing before a storm. He was unaware that he was not as alone as he'd believed.

Kathleen stood within the shadows of the house, watching until the desert night claimed him. Then she turned away, feeling an odd sense of jealousy. The land held him in a way she could not. He turned to the darkness instead of turning to her. He chose solitude when she could have offered so much more.

With an aching heart and empty arms, she crawled back into her bed and cried herself to sleep.

Seven

Although the day was almost over, the sun setting behind them was doing its best to show off. Color washed the western sky like the paints on Morgan's palette, mixing with the thin, streaky clouds low on the horizon and giving them the appearance of rich, colorful yarns spilled upon the air.

As Morgan drove them ever closer to Santa Fe, distant majestic buttes as well as the occasional odd-shaped boulders marked their position upon the terrain with elongated and impermanent shadows. The strange, almost mystical appearance of the desert at dusk made Kathleen think of spaceships and men walking on the moon. All she needed to complete the fantasy would be to look up into the sky and see the earth above her rather than the semitransparent shape of a new quarter moon.

Instead, she looked to her side and tried not to stare at the man behind the wheel. On any given day, Morgan Tallchief was hard to ignore. In a tuxedo, he was breathtaking, but he wore it with the same casual aplomb that he did blue jeans. He was a man comfortable within his own skin, and Kathleen didn't know whether that was good or downright dangerous. But his clothing did not reflect that of a man whose livelihood encompassed the colors with which he painted. Like his persona, it gave nothing away of what lay within.

Black was the color of his tuxedo—and of his hair— and of his eyes. In stark contrast, the white of the fine linen shirt he was wearing enticed the onlooker to wonder what was beneath, taunting like an empty canvas waiting to be filled.

The only bit of color upon his person was his tie, a bright and unmistakable hue on the muted landscape of his clothing. Like the color of a hot summer sky, like the color of Kathleen Ryder's eyes, the turquoise stone in a simple bolo tie rested neatly between the points of his collar. It was a symbol of the warrior who'd made peace with the land from which it had come.

With shaking hands, Kathleen smoothed at the skirt of her dress, lightly fingering the sheer, white gauzy material, trying to pretend that this was just an ordinary evening. But the exhibit to which they were going was no small event, nor was the fact that Morgan was the star attraction. Except for yesterday's shopping expedition to purchase the clothes that she and Trish were now wearing, it was the first time they'd gone out in public since last week when they'd towed her car in for repairs.

And, like her car, Kathleen's life was in limbo. The mechanic was waiting on parts. Kathleen was waiting for the other shoe to drop, yet Trish was flourishing beneath Morgan Tallchief's smile.

"Are we almost there?" Trish asked.

Kathleen hid a smile as Morgan looked at Trish in the rearview mirror. It was a typical question a parent hears many times during his child's life. She'd heard it so many times over the years that she usually tuned it out, but Morgan, as a brand-new father, was hearing it for the first time.

"Not too much farther," he said. "What's the big hurry? It's just an art show."

In teenage fashion, she rolled her eyes at the denseness of his remark.

"But it's your show," she said. "That's why it's so exciting."

Morgan glanced at Kathleen for her reaction as well, and tried not to despair at the emotionless look she gave him. He had an overwhelming urge to shake her, to make her react to him, even if in a negative way. He'd take anything but that bland, untouched expression on her face.

Then, if it hadn't been so damn painful, he could have laughed. Kathleen untouched? Hardly! He hadn't just *touched* her. He'd had her in a way he'd never had another woman. When they'd made love, she'd given him her virginity and a child, and he'd given her his heart and his everlasting soul.

Stifling the urge to pick a fight just to stir a reaction, he took a deep breath instead, then looked away, glancing back to the rearview mirror and focusing on Trish.

"So you're excited, hunh?"

She nodded.

"Why?"

Trish was almost twitching with delight as she met his gaze.

"Because you're my dad, and I've never been able to say that before. Because you're famous. And because you look so hot, the women are going to die when they see you walk in."

Morgan was speechless. Embarrassment left behind a slight red stain on either cheek as he quickly turned his attention to the road ahead. He imagined he could feel Kathleen's eyes upon him. It was obvious she didn't share Trish's opinion. She'd barely looked at him.

"I'm not famous." It was all he could think of to say.

"But you *are* my dad."

Reluctantly, he grinned, then glanced at Kathleen, unaware she was trying to maintain a cool exterior. To his delight, she, too, looked more than flushed when she met his gaze.

"There's that, all right," he drawled.

Kathleen knew that in spite of Morgan's teasing, he was floundering. She would have liked to keep her distance from this conversation, but didn't have it in her to leave him hoisted on his daughter's colorful opinions.

"Trish, that's enough," Kathleen said, glancing over her shoulder and arching an eyebrow at her daughter.

Trish caught the look as well as a warning tone in Kathleen's voice. She rolled her eyes and then grinned, satisfied that for the time being, she'd sufficiently stirred the waters.

Relieved that he was no longer the subject of conversation, Morgan started to relax. Just as the lights of

Santa Fe began to appear in the distance, Kathleen turned and looked at him.

His spiked black hair was almost tamed. The hard edges of his cheekbones were softened by the slight smile hovering around his mouth. But his eyes still glittered somewhere between daredevil and dangerous.

Kathleen couldn't suppress a slight chuckle. "You know, she *is* right about the look."

The glare he gave her was somewhere between "I can't believe you said that" and "I'll get you later."

Seeing Morgan slightly embarrassed and at a loss for words brought back the image of the boy with whom she'd fallen in love. Kathleen leaned back in the seat with a smile. It would have been in her best interest to keep her thoughts to herself, but the opportunity had been too perfect to let pass.

A short time later, he turned left at a busy intersection, aiming for an address halfway down the block. The lights pouring out through the windows of the sprawling adobe building spotlighted the arrival of Santa Fe's rich and passionate patrons of the arts as they got out of their cars. In the midst of it all, bright but intermittent bursts of light could be seen upon the street, and Morgan suddenly cursed beneath his breath. Cameras! He should have realized the press would be in attendance. A showing at a prestigious gallery such as this one always warranted a mention on the society page.

"What's wrong?" Kathleen asked.

"You shouldn't have come."

The panic on Morgan's face was enough to send her into a tailspin. Before Kathleen could ask why, Trish reacted in anger.

"Why not? Are you ashamed of us?" Then her voice broke as she blinked back tears. "Are you ashamed of me?"

He slammed on the brakes and suddenly turned down an alley, coming to a sliding halt near a Dumpster. Even in the shadows, the fierce glare in his eyes was evident as he looked over his shoulder to the girl in the backseat.

"Damn it, Patricia, don't *ever* let me hear you say that again!"

Kathleen's hand upon his arm stilled the fury within. Expecting to face her anger as well, he was relieved that she seemed willing to wait for his explanation. He exhaled slowly.

"The press. I forgot about the press."

Kathleen paled. The implication wasn't lost on her. Not after all these years, and especially not after what had happened after they'd printed her father's picture with his obituary.

"Oh, God . . . oh, God." Her voice began to shake as she glanced nervously over her shoulder to the street behind them. "It's not your fault. I'm the one who should have realized."

"Mom . . . I don't get it. What's the . . . ?"

"Pictures, Patricia. They'll be taking pictures. We can't have our faces plastered all over a newspaper and expect to stay hidden from whoever's after us."

To Kathleen's surprise, Trish exploded in rage. Tears began to flow, washing away her carefully applied makeup—and her last bit of hope.

"I hate this, I hate this!" she screamed. "Why can't my life be normal? Why do we have to be the ones to live on the run? It isn't fair! It just isn't fair!"

There was nothing Kathleen could say. Trish *was* right. It wasn't fair, and no amount of talk was going to change the facts.

Morgan silently cursed his lack of planning. This was all his fault. He should have remembered, then hopes wouldn't have been dashed and tears wouldn't have been shed.

"Look," he said. "Maybe we can salvage this evening after all, okay?"

Trish hiccuped on a sob and flopped back onto the seat, gulping dramatically as she fished in her purse for a tissue to repair the damage she'd done to her makeup. Kathleen was less optimistic. She'd long since passed the days when she could assume an adult kept every promise made.

She shook her head and reached for the door latch. "No, Morgan. This is your evening. We'll get out now and find something to do until it's over. Maybe we could meet later at a—"

He grabbed her arm before she could move. "Don't even think it," he growled. "I'm not letting you out of my sight. Not even for a minute."

Kathleen sighed. She should have known he'd react this way. "I'm sure we'll be fine. Trish and I can go to a movie. Maybe get a bite to eat."

Tell her now.

Morgan stiffened. Whatever voice it was he kept hearing, whether it be conscience or his grandmother's spirit, he could no longer ignore the truth.

"There was a tracking device on your car."

Trish's fit dissolved into a quiet fear while Kathleen went from shock to disbelief.

"There was a what?"

Morgan looked away, staring at the shadows of the alley rather than into the horror on Kathleen's face.

"A bug. A beeper. A homing signal. Call it what you will, but someone wanted to know where you were going."

To his surprise, she punched his arm.

"But you didn't tell me! Why didn't you tell me? Our lives are the ones at stake!"

"I wasn't actually keeping it a secret," he grumbled, knowing full well that's exactly what he'd done.

"Then what the hell do you call it?"

Trish shifted nervously and reached over the seat, touching her mother's shoulder in gentle comfort.

"Mom, don't. He was just doing what we asked him to do."

Kathleen spun, her eyes blazing. "And that was?"

"Protect us. He was just trying to protect us."

Kathleen went limp. Trish was right. Her breath slid out in a long, helpless sigh as she covered her face with her hands.

"Then they know where we are."

Morgan lifted her hands from her face, tugging at them until she was forced to look up. He grinned.

"I doubt it."

"Of course they do, Morgan. You don't know this life like we do. Even if I don't have my car, they have our last location."

His grin widened, and for a moment, she got so lost in the beauty of it she forgot to be afraid.

"Actually, they don't. If my guess is right, about now they think you're in New Orleans."

Her eyes widened. "New Orleans! But how? Why?"

"Remember the trucker that stopped to help me the day we towed your car?"

She nodded.

"I slipped the bug under his fender while we were talking. It was stuck like a tick on a dog when he took off for points west. If he kept to his route, then I'd venture to say someone's real confused about now, and it's not Bunny Easter."

"Who's Bunny Easter?"

"The trucker."

In spite of the ominous news she'd just received, Kathleen couldn't stop a smile. "You've got to be joking. That's not really his name?"

"No joke. Mr. Ned Easter, Bunny to his friends, stopped to offer his help. He just had no idea how much help he was going to be."

"Then that's that," Trish said, satisfied that her father had thrown their followers off the trail.

Kathleen wasn't as easily convinced, but was willing to accept the fact that the deception had probably worked—this time.

"No, that's not that," she said shortly. "It still doesn't get us past tonight. We can't risk having our pictures appear in a newspaper . . . any newspaper. And if we walk inside that gallery with the guest of honor, I can guarantee that's exactly what will happen."

"But that doesn't mean you can't go in before me. I'm a loner, remember? No one's going to expect me to come any other way. All I have to do is back out of the alley, let you two out, and wait until you've gone inside before making my arrival."

Kathleen frowned. "But we don't have an invitation, and this is a private showing, remember?"

He thrust his hand inside his jacket pocket and pulled out a card. "You do now."

Kathleen's eyes widened as the thick, embossed envelope slid between her fingers. It just might work after all!

"Okay, we'll do it," she said.

"All right!" Trish echoed from the backseat.

Kathleen looked back at her daughter, a warning in her voice that was impossible to miss.

"We stay together . . . and away from Morgan."

Trish nodded, trying to pretend that her dream of walking in on her father's arm didn't matter.

"It's cool, Mom. I understand."

Morgan knew she was disappointed. "I'm sorry, Trish. Someday I'll make this up to you, okay?"

Trish managed a smile. "I know."

Kathleen sighed. If only she could be as certain that he could make up for her disappointments as well.

"Then let's get this show on the road," Morgan muttered, and backed out of the alley.

Moments later, Kathleen and her daughter exited the car with invitation in hand, quickly blending in with other passersby upon the street. He watched without moving until they were safely inside the gallery, then proceeded toward valet parking at the front entrance.

Zora Chivas was working the crowd like the pro she was, plying them with champagne, coaxing interested buyers to particular paintings, doing the thing that she loved best: creating an event.

The gallery had been part of her divorce decree. Rather than being the lead weight around her neck her husband had hoped it would be, it had flourished, and her ability to spot and showcase new talent was part of the reason why.

She'd been hanging Tallchief pieces for more than a year and a half, but this night was special. There wasn't a piece on display that didn't have Morgan's distinctive signature on it. Sales tonight were already double what she'd hoped, so everything from here on out was icing on the cake.

And speaking of icing, the couple at her side could be considered pure sugar. Donald Seguro and his latest wife, Trixie, were seriously interested in one of the larger pieces. At least Donald was interested. If Zora didn't miss her guess, Trixie was more interested in the artist than the art.

If it took a personal introduction to the artist to get it sold, then they could have it. And even though she knew Morgan was going to give her hell for it later, he was going to have to play nice at least one more time tonight.

Zora gave her salt-and-pepper locks an extra tousle, ignoring the fact that the hairstyle did nothing to detract from her long, rather horsey, features. She didn't care. She played up her bohemian appearance to fit the artsy role in which she'd been thrust. Bracelets jangled and clanked against each other as they slid toward her elbow then back down her wrist as she waved to get Morgan's attention. She wore a yellow, sand-washed silk jumpsuit, a green leather vest, and red clogs, strutting in the ensemble as if it were the height of fashion. Nothing matched. Nothing mattered. Nothing but the pursuit of business and the sale of fine art.

Zora cornered Morgan between a lamp and a wall.

Squeezing his arm lightly, she thrust the Seguros into his space and saw him take a mental step back. She sighed. Darn that Native American soul. He was so good-looking. If he'd only be a little more social, her life would be easier.

"Morgan, darling! I'm sure you remember Trixie and Donald Seguro. I'm sure I told you of his interest in the North American Indian. If you remember, he did his doctorate on Chief Joseph of the Nez Perce."

While Morgan was wondering where to go from there, Seguro's wife made a strategic move by sliding between him and her husband. The pout on her lips was practiced, as was her slightly breathless whisper. She traced the shape of the turquoise stone in his tie with a bright red fingernail and looked up at him through a shadow of false eyelashes.

"Oh, Mr. Tallchief, this is so exciting!" Trixie said, playing with the ends of his bolo tie.

Morgan's nostrils flared. Without answering, he gave Zora a cool, calculated glare. She returned the look with a warning smile. To her relief, he held his ground.

His cold demeanor should have put Trixie off. Unfortunately, it only added to the excitement of her imagined conquest as she gave him a slow, calculating look. To Morgan's relief, her husband stepped to one side and extended his hand.

"Mr. Tallchief, it's a pleasure to meet you. I already have one of your paintings. It gives me great pleasure on a daily basis."

Morgan relaxed. At least this was a conversation he could deal with. He nodded at the compliment.

"So, which piece interests you tonight?"

"I think you call it *Corn Dance*."

"Ah, yes, that one. It came from one of my grand-mother's stories."

Donald looked pleased, while Trixie fidgeted. She had a fantasy of making love with a noble savage. Morgan Tallchief more than fit her expectations. Slowly, she licked her lips and sidled back into Morgan's line of vision, daring him to ignore her again.

"So, Mr. Tallchief, you seem much too much the warrior to be an artist. I'd venture to say you're more like Cochise." And then she giggled. "I don't suppose you're related."

It was one of the more stupid questions Morgan had ever been asked, and everyone but the blonde knew it. To his credit, he barely reacted.

"Related?"

"To Cochise, of course."

"I'm Cherokee."

Trixie pouted and frowned. "And . . . ?"

"He was Apache."

"Umm, yes, I knew that. But I thought since you're an Indian . . . and he was an Indian . . ."

To Zora's surprise, Morgan smiled. But she saw the brittle edge of it mirrored in his eyes and held her breath as he answered, praying that he didn't insult the Seguros and lose the sale.

"So, Mrs. Seguro, are you trying to tell me we all look alike?"

Trixie blinked, uncertain where to go from there. She leaned forward, playing her last card, and gave him a better-than-average view of her ample cleavage.

"You're just too cute for words." Then she leaned back against her husband, letting him feel the full weight of her hips against his pelvis. "Isn't he, Donald? Isn't he just too cute for words?"

Donald was manfully trying to ignore his wife's unexpected sexual offering and still concentrate on the task at hand.

"Mr. Tallchief, it's been a pleasure," he said quickly, and grasped his wife by the elbow. "Zora, *Corn Dance* is mine. I want it shipped to our chalet in Aspen."

Morgan nodded, then moved away before he got himself in any more trouble. *Damn you, Zora, you owe me one,* he thought, and began moving through the crowd, searching once again for Kathleen's and Trish's whereabouts. He knew they were here somewhere. He could feel Kathleen's presence as clearly as he heard his own heartbeat.

In spite of the unfortunate beginning to the evening, Kathleen found herself enjoying the show. Not only was she surrounded by the stunning evidence of Morgan's skill, but she could eavesdrop among the guests to her heart's content. Their remarks about his skill, about the emotion within each painting, were music to her ears. And as the evening progressed and she and Trish wandered in and out of the rooms where his work was on view, she began to realize a truth about herself.

She felt the same sense of pride when hearing Morgan praised as she did when someone praised her child for a task well done, and right in the middle of the foyer, she suddenly understood why.

It was because she loved him enough to share.

Tears burned the backs of her eyes. She hadn't meant for this to happen again. At least not this soon—

not before she knew for sure how he felt. She'd had full intentions of keeping her heart and her feelings to herself until she was certain that all danger had passed. She had no time to agonize over a man who no longer wanted her.

And yet I've gone and done it again.

She looked around with a nervous glance, imagining that everyone could read what was in her mind, and as she did, realized that Trish was nowhere in sight.

Fear spread in the pit of her stomach as she clutched at her purse. Turning in place, she tried not to panic as she searched the crowd. Just as she thought of going to Morgan for help, Trish came flying around a corner, grabbed her mother by the arm, and began dragging her back into the main salon.

"Mom! You've got to come see this!"

"Don't ever do that again," Kathleen hissed.

"Do what?" Trish asked as they made their way through the crowd.

"Disappear like that! You scared me to death."

Trish rolled her eyes. "I did not disappear. I stood right there beside you and told you where I was going and you nodded okay." She paused, her voice lowering as she ended her explanation with a dramatic sigh. "I assumed that meant you were listening."

At that point, Kathleen vaguely remembered doing just that. Regret came quickly.

"Oops, sorry, darling. Guilty as charged."

Trish grinned. Role reversal was interesting. "Just don't ever let me hear you say I don't listen to you, okay?"

"Okay."

"Now come on. It's just over here. You won't believe this painting."

Trish had been right. One look, and Kathleen hadn't been able to look away. He had called it *Half a Man*.

"It's you and Dad, isn't it, Mom? He put your faces on those people. Wow! This is too cool!"

Kathleen couldn't speak. The image on the canvas said it all.

It was quite obvious to the onlooker that the warrior's lover was dead. The warrior's grief was palpable. One had only to look at the abject disbelief with which he was standing before the young woman lying in state on a burial platform to feel the pain of his loss.

And while the young woman's face was calm in deathly repose, her spirit had yet to move on. Instead, her ghostly image was lingering in the air above her body. Her arms were extended, as if reaching toward him, yearning to give comfort to her grieving warrior, while her face was twisted with despair, knowing that her soul must go on, leaving her lover behind.

Not for Sale.

The small pink tag on the corner of the frame said it all. The painting had been Morgan's way of saying what her death had done to him. *Not for Sale* could mean only one thing. He still held the grief too close to his heart: She felt sick. The room swayed beneath her feet and it was all she could do to stay standing.

"I did this. I did this to him!" she whispered.

Trish looked startled. She hadn't expected her mother to react in this manner. She slipped her arm around her shoulders and hugged her lightly. "But that was a long time ago, Mom, and it wasn't your fault."

"Tell that to Morgan and make him believe it."

To Trish's horror, a quiet but steady stream of tears began flowing down Kathleen's face.

"Mom! Don't cry! Someone might see!"

Kathleen was immobile. She couldn't tear her gaze away from the painting. Now there was no longer any way of ignoring the grief Morgan had suffered when he thought he'd witnessed her death. All his shock, all the pain, all the disbelief was on the young warrior's face.

A couple strolled by, pausing to look at the painting, and then stared at Kathleen instead. Embarrassed, they hurried away, whispering beneath their breath about her odd behavior.

"Mom . . . Mother?"

Kathleen shuddered, almost swaying on her feet.

Trish was in a panic. She glanced around the room, trying to locate her father in hopes she might signal him in some way. To her dismay, he was nowhere to be seen. They were supposed to be keeping a low profile, and this public display of emotion wasn't going to help.

"Mother, please, you've got to stop. People are staring."

But Kathleen didn't respond, and short of making a scene, Trish didn't know what to do. Off to her left, a waiter was circling the floor, competently balancing a tray filled with glasses of champagne. Maybe if she got her mother something to drink she'd snap out of it.

"Mom, wait here, okay? I'll be right back."

Trish left her behind, darting into the crowd after the waiter, and wondering what she could possibly say that would persuade him to give a glass of champagne to someone who was obviously too young to drink.

Still struggling with her composure, Kathleen wasn't prepared for the sound of Morgan's voice or his arms suddenly encircling her from behind, holding her close against the strength of his body.

Her pain was his. He felt her grief, knew her shock, saw her disbelief, and for the first time since he'd put brush to canvas, regretted what he had done.

"Kathleen . . . sweetheart . . . my God, please don't cry."

Kathleen went limp as his arms tightened around her. Her voice was low and shaking, the picture blurring before her eyes as she blinked away tears.

"I'm sorry. I'm so, so sorry," she whispered. "I knew I'd hurt you. I just never knew how much."

Morgan cursed beneath his breath as he glanced up at the painting. He'd completely forgotten Zora had coerced him into including it in the show. She'd been after him for years to let her sell it, but to no avail. It was only after she'd set up the show that he finally gave in and agreed to let her hang it along with the others. How was he to know that the ghost in the picture would come back to life between then and now?

Kathleen was shaking. He could feel her body trembling as he held her close, and when he looked down, his gaze fell on the thin, tiny scars across her wrists, hard proof of her own brand of suffering.

He lowered his head, gently pressing his lips against the crown of her hair and then whispering against her cheek.

"You're not the only one who's sorry," he said softly, lifting her wrists to his mouth and pressing a kiss against each small scar.

His presence, more than anything else, brought her slowly to her senses. But by her actions alone, she'd done the very thing they'd sworn not to do, and that was cause a scene.

A woman's voice, low and concerned, came, seemingly, out of nowhere. Kathleen jerked back as Zora Chivas touched Morgan's arm.

"Morgan, is something wrong? Is this woman ill? I saw you holding her up as if she were about to—"

Zora paused, suddenly reassessing the scene before her. Morgan looked fit to kill, and the woman in his arms was pale. Zora frowned. There was something about her face . . . something that seemed familiar. She peered closer, wishing she'd worn her glasses.

"Do I know you?" she asked.

Kathleen shook her head and pushed her way out of Morgan's embrace, glancing around the room and praying that the reporter covering the event was nowhere in sight.

"No, of course not. I was just looking at the painting when I felt—"

Morgan put his hand on Kathleen's shoulder. "No, Kathleen. No more lies. Not about us. Not anymore."

Kathleen panicked. "But what about the . . . ?"

"Zora's a friend. She owns this gallery, and when she has to, she knows how to keep quiet." He looked at Zora and then grinned slightly. "Besides, she owes me one."

Zora frowned. Kathleen? That didn't ring a bell. So they hadn't met. But why . . . why did her face look so familiar? And then she knew! She spun around and fixed her gaze on the painting upon the wall.

"Oh, my God!"

She looked at Morgan, then Kathleen, then back to the painting again.

"Morgan! That warrior has your face. All these months and I never noticed. All I ever saw was her face . . . etched in such grief. It's her! It's you!"

Morgan sighed. "For pete's sake, keep it down, will you? It's no big deal, okay? Every artist has to have at least one self-portrait, right?"

"But that doesn't—"

Trish burst into the group carrying a glass of champagne and a wet paper towel. There was panic in her voice and fear on her face.

"Mother, are you all right? It took forever to get that man to let me have this champagne. I told him it wasn't for me, but—"

Zora gasped. This time, she didn't have to study long to decide where she'd seen this girl's face. Except for the eyes, she was the feminine version of Morgan Tallchief. Things were beginning to fall into place, and the concept staggered her. All this time, she'd believed him to be as near to a hermit as a man could be, and now this? She pointed at Kathleen.

"Mother? This woman is your mother?"

Kathleen groaned, and Morgan swore again, this time not nearly as quietly as before.

"Damn it, Zora, keep it down!"

"Mr. Tallchief, if I could have a moment of your time."

They turned, each one in a different state of shock, to see the reporter and his cameraman heading their way.

"Son of a bitch!" Morgan grabbed Zora by the arm and pointed to Kathleen and Trish. "Get them out of here." When she might have argued, his fingers tightened painfully. "Now!"

She didn't wait to ask why. There was an expression

on his face she'd never seen before. It was the first time she'd ever understood the meaning of the phrase "if looks could kill."

Without hesitation, she grabbed the champagne out of the young girl's hands.

"Give me that. I think I need it the most." She downed it in one gulp and handed the empty glass back to Morgan without missing a beat. "Follow me to my office, ladies. I've got some etchings in there that you just won't believe."

Morgan pivoted toward the reporter with the empty wineglass in his hand and turned on a hundred-watt smile. Somewhere in another part of the building, he heard a door slam with a loud and abrupt thump. His handshake was firm, his voice cool and confident as he fielded the reporter's questions like the pro that he'd become, but inside, he was reeling from the closeness of the call.

Eight

Zora slammed the door shut behind her. For several long minutes the three women stared at each other without speaking. Finally it was Trish who broke the silence. Her voice was shaky and weak as she sidled up to Kathleen and laid her head on her shoulder.

"Mom . . . did I do something wrong?"

Kathleen hugged her close. "No, of course not, sweetheart. None of this is your fault. It was just that reporter that caused all the panic." She sighed and hugged Trish a little bit tighter. "I should have followed my instincts and not come at all."

Trish's face crumpled. Everything they planned seemed to be destined to take a bad turn.

"Don't worry, darling," Kathleen said. "I'm sure Morgan will take care of everything."

Zora tunneled her hands through her hair, mussing it even more than usual. None of this was making a damn bit of sense.

"Okay, somebody better start talking," she muttered. "What's the big deal about that painting? I know what I saw and it's more than obvious that you two have a history. Morgan had his arms around you, but you weren't sick, you were crying, weren't you?"

Kathleen refused to answer.

"Look," Zora said. "I'm not asking just to be nosy, it's just that I consider him my friend."

Morgan entered the office just in time to save Kathleen from further cross-examination.

"Why, Zora, I didn't know you cared."

The elder woman spun, a startled expression on her face. She hadn't heard Morgan come in, but now that he was here, she wanted an explanation. Shaking a finger in his face, she let her social graces fly.

"You listen to me, Morgan Tallchief, I did as you asked and whisked this pair away before your interview took a nasty tabloid turn. Now damn it, I want some answers! This is my gallery. I sank a bundle of money into this night. Don't you think I deserve—"

Trish shrank even closer against her mother, cringing at the angry shouts. Only then did Morgan notice she'd been crying. His reaction was as sudden and explosive as Zora's complaint.

"Damn it, Zora, did you make my daughter cry?"

Zora paused in midgrip, then turned and pointed toward Trish and Kathleen.

"I knew it! I swear to God, I knew it! Except for her eyes, she's you all over again." She glowered indignantly at Morgan. "And I certainly did not make her cry." The look she gave Kathleen was long and considering. "You, of course, were the inspiration for *Half a Man*, which makes no sense, since you're obviously not dead."

Kathleen paled. "Morgan, what on earth have you done?"

There was a closed, mutinous look on his face that she recognized all too well.

"Nothing that shouldn't have been done the night you walked back into my life," he said. "Keeping your whereabouts a secret is one thing, but denying who you are to me is another. In fact, in all this confusion, we might have been overlooking the obvious."

Learning that Morgan Tallchief had a past didn't really come as any surprise to Zora Chivas. He was more man than most, but learning of it in this odd, almost subversive manner made absolutely no sense. In spite of the fact that she had yet to get a direct answer to even one of her questions, she couldn't help but ask another.

"Secret? Why does it have to be a secret?"

"Not now," Morgan said, waving her and her questions away as he drew Trish into his arms. "Poor little girl," he whispered softly. "Too much confusion . . . always too much confusion."

Zora slumped quietly into a chair, aware that they'd all but forgotten she was in the room. It didn't really matter. None of what they were saying made sense.

Kathleen persisted. "What do you mean, we've been overlooking the obvious?"

He gave Trish an easy hug and then pretended to turn his attention to Kathleen, although she'd been in the periphery of his vision since he'd walked into the room. It was fear of what he was going to say that kept him from looking her squarely in the face. Judging by her expression, he wasn't sure she was ready to hear what he had to say, but she and their daughter were more important to him than his own life, and he wasn't about to lose them. Not now. Not ever again. Carefully he chose his words.

"I think the best way to keep you two safe is to do what you've been doing all along."

Kathleen was aghast. "Morgan, you're not making sense. We've been running all our lives. You cannot be suggesting we start that again?"

Trish stiffened. She couldn't believe her hero was about to toss them out on their ears.

Morgan shook his head. *God, please don't let me mess this up.* "Hell, no, I'm not suggesting you run."

"Then what?" Kathleen said.

"I'm just suggesting you change your names."

If Kathleen hadn't been so miserable she might have laughed. "Again? And to what? What magic name could you possibly choose that the feds didn't, that would guarantee our safety?"

A pregnant pause hung silently within the space of four walls as he gauged her mood, hoping for a positive reaction. Finally, there was nothing to do but just say it.

"Tallchief."

Trish gasped. A quick smile came and went as she glanced nervously at her mother, afraid that her joy would be premature.

In that moment, Kathleen could have gladly wrung Morgan's neck. He'd put her in a position where she could hardly refuse his offer. There was nothing Trish wanted more on this earth than to be known as Morgan Tallchief's daughter. Without warning, he'd handed her the opportunity.

And, for all it was worth, Kathleen had to admit

she was no different. She had wanted the boy—and she wanted the man and his name. Yes, she wanted him in lust, but she wanted him in love with her more, not just as a means of keeping them safe. Yet how could she refuse? In all honesty, it could very well be the answer.

She bit her lower lip for courage and looked into dark, fathomless eyes. *Damn you, Morgan. You don't make this easy.*

"I need to know something first," she finally said.

"Know what, Kathleen?"

"Is it only to keep us safe?"

There was a long and heavy silence as he matched her, look for hungry look. Then he shook his head.

"No."

She nodded, shuddering as her body went limp. It wasn't exactly the proposal of her dreams, but then her whole life had been nothing but nightmares. Why, she wondered, had she imagined it would ever change?

"Then okay," she said quietly, and when her daughter flew back into his arms, she could not hide her pain.

Morgan held his child, but ached for Kathleen. She wasn't the only one who was disappointed. Before his dreams and his world had come to an abrupt and painful end, he'd had his own plans for marriage, and they'd never included anything as calculated as this. His voice was quiet and full of regret.

"I promise you'll never be sorry."

Kathleen grimaced through a wall of unshed tears.

"Haven't you learned by now you should never make promises you can't keep?"

The pain in her voice was his undoing. Grabbing her

by the hand, he pulled her close, then closer, until she had nowhere to go but into his arms. "Hush, woman, and come here to me."

When he made a place for her beside Trish, she gave up the fight. In spite of an internal warning system going on the alert, she wrapped one arm around him, the other around her daughter. As twisted as the reasoning was, they were finally going to be together, in the truest sense of the word.

Satisfaction filled Morgan's soul. He was through worrying about the past. What kept him sleepless on a nightly basis was fear of keeping them safe in the now. When Kathleen came into his arms, however unwillingly, he knew a sense of validation. This woman belonged to him, and he to her. Even though she didn't believe him, now they would have time to work through the mistakes of their past.

Mine. This is my family. God help anyone who comes between us again.

Zora's mouth was agape, her guests completely forgotten. There was no telling how many sales she'd missed while witnessing this real-life melodrama, but for the life of her, she couldn't tear herself away.

"I will be damned," she said. "You people are weird, even for Santa Fe. First we were crying. Then we were hiding. And if I didn't just misunderstand, now we're getting married. So, do we order the invitations, or turn out the lights and do this in the dark?"

Morgan looked up. His eyes narrowed, his voice lowered. "What *we* do is keep *our* mouths shut."

The warning was too real to ignore. "That was going to be my next choice," she muttered, as she headed for the door. "Please, pretend I'm not here. In fact, you don't have to pretend, because I'm not really here. I'm out there, selling your paintings for exorbitant amounts of money, and I think I'd better get back to work. It looks to me as if the size of your household has suddenly increased."

The door slammed behind her. No one moved until Morgan began issuing orders.

"Come with me," he said.

For Trish, the night had been too full of surprises. She hesitated, needing reassurance before she took another step. "Dad, where are we going now?"

He winked at his daughter, then kissed the top of her head. A moment of satisfaction came and went as Trish relaxed in his embrace. At least for her, the trust was already there.

But Kathleen was a different matter. It was easy to read her wariness. It hurt him to know he'd been the one to put it there. His breath escaped in a single, heartfelt sigh as he lifted his hand toward a strand of hair sticking against her cheek, caught fast in the tracks of her tears. He brushed it off her face, gently smoothing it back into place.

Kathleen died in his touch and was reborn by the answer he gave their child.

"Home, Patricia. We're going home."

The air was still, the night sky dark and cloudless. Light came only from the broken chunk of moon hanging high above the earth. It was all Morgan needed to see by. He ran with no aim, feeling little more than the ground beneath his feet and the sweat running down his back. A coyote's warning yip from a nearby ridge went unnoticed. There was nothing

within his mind but the sound of his heart, beating . . .
beating . . . beating.

Somewhere back there, his woman and his child
slept soundly within his house, assured by the promise that he'd made to keep them safe. And although
Morgan had meant every word he'd said, he was trou-
bled as to how to keep it. He would lay down his life
now if that's what it took, but then who would take
care of them when he was gone? Why was someone
dogging Kathleen's every step? What had her father
known that his death couldn't erase? What had he
done that couldn't be forgiven? What had he taken
and never given back?

Questions—questions, but never an answer. And no
matter how far he ran, the ghosts were always right
behind.

Somewhere within the instincts of a man who
knows his limits, Morgan began to circle homeward.
Time had become nothing but the beat of footstep to
ground. Each stride became slower and slower, shorter
and shorter, and when his foot finally touched something other than the sand on which he'd been running,
he knew that he was home. He stopped, dropping to
his knees on the flagstone patio, and then on all fours,
gasping for breath and welcoming the arrival of a
night breeze as it began to dry the sweat upon his skin.

When he could move without falling, he entered
his studio, choosing the shower in there rather than
the one inside the house. He kicked off one shoe,
then the other, and walked out of his shorts and
under the water, welcoming the cold needles of
spray against his heated skin.

Minutes later, he went into the house with a bath

towel as his only garment. He moved through the darkened rooms like the warrior he'd long ago become, walking with stealth, measuring each breath to match the tick of a clock at the end of the hall.

His room was near, the bed beckoning, but the need to know those he loved were secure overcame the need to sleep. A drop of water fell from his hair and onto his shoulder, a remnant of his recent shower. He swiped in absent fashion, his mind already on the doorway to his left. It pushed open without complaint.

His daughter! The syllables rolled in his mind like thunder in a storm, powerful by their sound alone as he measured her presence in an artist's increments. Her black hair was spread out across the pillowcase like spilled ink. A slender arm outflung from beneath the covers curved like the broken wing of a dove. A half smile upon her face gave her features a sense of peace. Her face was his face. The sight struck him anew, and he was humbled by the miracle of a birth he had not witnessed.

Satisfied that all was well, he stepped back, silently closing the door behind him before turning to the one across the hall. This bed check would not be as simple. Looking without touching did not come easy to a man who wanted as badly as he did. And yet he could not turn away from Kathleen's door. He took two steps and one deep breath, and when he opened the door, knew that he had quit the run too soon.

His heart jerked, his gut pulled. He hadn't known a man could want this much and still be able to think, but he did, and it all flowed into memories.

He watched her and remembered a night long ago, and the way she'd come undone beneath him. He clenched his fists, remembering that he'd been her first, and then he closed his eyes, remembering that she'd been his last. The women who'd come afterward had been nothing but a means to a release. He'd had sex many times, but he'd made love only once.

She stirred, and he held his breath, unwilling to look away. When she settled, he exhaled slowly. A weary muscle jerked in the calf of his leg, reminding him that it was way past the time to rest. With a hand on the doorknob and full intentions of doing just that, he started backing out of the door. If he'd been a few seconds faster, and if Kathleen hadn't tossed restlessly in her sleep before rolling onto her back, he might have made it out the door. But he wasn't, and she had, and now it was impossible to miss the tears on her cheeks. Even in sleep, she suffered. It was more than he could bear.

Quietly, he came inside, closing the door behind him. Bare feet made silent work of the distance between the door and her bed. The knot in his towel began to give way as he eased himself beside her, angling his long, lean body until they were lying side by side. Now there was nothing but a thin covering of cloth that separated him from the woman of his dreams, and it was not enough to keep his mind from moving into places it should not go.

Outside, a lone, dark cloud moved between earth and the face of the moon, but Morgan needed no light by which to see. Her presence was as real to him as his soul. His fingers brushed the boundaries of her hair, then her cheeks, pausing on the damp tracks and carefully wiping them away. While he was here, she would not suffer pain. Not in any way. Not if he could help it.

Kathleen stirred. The touch on her face was firm but light. She inhaled slowly, catching the faint but lingering scent of an herbal soap that was not her own. Turning in her sleep, she was cognizant of a resistance that was of flesh rather than covers. In that moment between rest and realization, she knew she was no longer alone. She came awake with a jerk.

"Sssh, it's only me," he whispered.

She went limp. Another second and she would have known that for herself. Only me? Since when was this man an *only* anything?

"Morgan?"

His voice wrapped around her senses like a heavy fog, leaving her weak and drained, unable to move, awaiting whatever he chose to do.

"You were crying," he whispered, and she felt his breath upon her face, and then his lips upon her cheeks. "Go back to sleep," he said quietly. "I just need to hold you. I will take nothing from you that you cannot give."

And when he slid his arm beneath her head and turned until they were lying spoon-fashion, her back to his front with little more than trust between them, she started to relax. She hadn't realized she'd been crying, but when the weight of his arm became the anchor that her life had been missing, an old pain began to lift. She shuddered, then sighed. The quiet between them lengthened and then eased. *God, please let this be right.*

"Kathleen?"

His whisper cut her to the quick, and it was a vivid reminder of the flesh-and-blood identity of the man in whose arms she lay. The heat of his breath stirred a yearning within her that she had to deny. They would make love. Sometime. Somewhere. And soon. But surely not like this. Unable to hide her anxiety, her voice shook as she answered.

"What?"

"I didn't ask because I had to."

She closed her eyes. The pain was back.

"Then why?" she whispered.

His fingers splayed across her belly, confirming his right to be there.

"Because right or wrong, dead or alive, you belong to me. You always have. You always will."

His words were balm to a badly bruised heart. This was what she'd come to him needing to hear. This was why she'd endured all these years—for the chance to make everything right.

"Oh Morgan, you will never know how long I—"

She started to turn within his arms, yearning to give back something that in some way matched what he'd just given her. But he sensed her intent, and held her immobile until he was through.

"No, Kathleen, not like this. Someday we will find a way to belong to each other, but for now, giving you my name is my way of keeping you and Patricia safe, if anything should happen to me, you will inherit all that I have, including family that will protect and cherish you. You will never be alone again."

Fear ricocheted through her, leaving her weak and breathless. *If anything should happen?* What did he fear? What did he know that he wasn't telling?

"Without you, I am always alone," she whispered, her voice breaking.

His hold eased. She felt his mouth upon her neck, then the side of her face. His whisper stilled her fears.

"Then rest . . . I am here."

Somewhere between heartbreak and dawn, they slept, wrapped in each other's arms. When Kathleen awoke the next morning, she was alone. She could almost convince herself that she'd dreamed the whole thing except for a slightly damp towel on the floor beside her bed.

The fax was spitting out a message that Special Agent Robert Caldwell didn't like. But it was to be expected. Ever since he'd been assigned Lester Bryant's files, nothing had gone right. There wasn't a single thing he could put his finger on that would explain his uneasiness, but instinct had been warning him that there was a possibility Lester Bryant hadn't been as squeaky clean as one might have hoped. This fax was just the latest bite of lemon.

He read it, then read it again.

"Oh, shit. The director isn't going to like this one stinking bit," he muttered.

Caldwell knew that promoting Bryant had been the director's idea. He'd voiced his regrets long and loud about the fact that Lester had died before he could give him the news. And now this? He cursed beneath his breath.

"May as well get this over with," he said, angling his long legs out from under the desk and ejecting himself from the chair in one smooth motion.

He left the office, heading down the hall with the gait of a man who was comfortable in his own skin, uncaring of the fact that he was probably going to be bald before his fortieth birthday. Just shy of skinny, his angular features somehow fit the length of his face, although his expression could change from drawn to droll with nothing more than a smile. He was a good man. A fair man. And he hated to be the bearer of bad news.

He hit the door with the flat of his hand.

"Ruth, is he busy?"

The director's secretary looked up from her desk. She'd been in this business too long not to know need when she saw it, and Caldwell definitely needed to get something off of his chest.

"Just a minute, Bobby, I'll ring."

She picked up a phone, her voice low and indistinct to anyone but the person on the other end of the line.

Caldwell grinned. Ruth knew her job. She never gave anything away, including expressions.

She looked up. "You can go in."

Caldwell winked as he walked past. "You look good in pink."

"And you don't," she said calmly.

He chuckled as he entered, then decided that a smile was not in keeping with the news that he brought.

"Sir. I believe you need to see this."

Caldwell laid the fax on the director's desk and then watched his face turn a bright, bloody red. So, his instincts had been right! Obviously, no one had officially issued Lester Bryant use of one of the star cars, so called for the Star Wars technology they contained, although it had been signed out in his name.

The director began cursing in three different languages and then, in the next breath, made a snap decision.

"Caldwell, you're on the next plane out, do you hear me? I want to know what the hell one of my star cars is doing in a Denver airport, and I want to know who's had it!"

The order came as no surprise. Caldwell nodded.

"Yes, sir, and after we're through going over the car, what do you want me to do with it?"

The director leaned across his desk, his voice loud and angry.

"You dust that baby for everything from bad breath to stinking farts and then you personally bring it back to D.C. I want to know who's been driving it all over creation, because it damn sure wasn't Lester Bryant. According to this fax, it was parked on the same day he died, and even Lester couldn't be in two places at once."

"Yes, sir."

He was on his way out the door when the director added a last command.

"Caldwell!"

"Sir?"

"Don't get any speeding tickets, either, or I'll dock your damned pay."

Caldwell grinned. "No, sir, I won't."

The way Caldwell looked at it, the architects who'd designed Denver's new airport had sold Denver a big bill of goods. To hell with moving sidewalks. The concourse seemed as if it were at least three miles long. And while he wasn't averse to a little exercise, he didn't like it forced upon him, especially at this time of night.

But Robert Caldwell had not become the agent he was by complaining of insignificant things. By the time sunrise had come and gone, he had a full investigation under way. Every car within a fifteen-foot radius of the abandoned vehicle had been moved. The yellow crime-scene tape blocking off the area drew more curious stares than he might have liked, but Caldwell had his orders. Local as well as airport authorities were taken aback by the presence of the FBI, but Caldwell had smoothed over the question of who was in charge with as little fuss as possible.

Since the car had been parked in a public area for some time, dusting for prints on the outside was almost a waste of time. The fingerprint of a wanted individual might be found on the outside, but that would be no proof that the individual had been inside the car. Dozens, even hundreds, of people had surely walked through the parking garage during the time of the vehicle's abandonment. Any number of them could have had reason to touch it in passing. But there wasn't an inch of surface in the interior of that car that missed being dusted. Unfortunately for Caldwell, it seemed to be clean—too clean.

Now and then, there was the minute bit of paper to be found, and oddly enough, whoever had left the car had thoughtfully left the keys beneath a mat. But there was nothing to tell them who it had been or why it had been abandoned.

And then they found the flashlight. It was tiny, as flashlights go, little more than a penlight. A penlight that was as spotless as the day it had come off the assembly line. The slim triple-A battery fell out into the investigator's hand. The same battery that Joaquin Candelero had cursed for not making the connection. But when they lifted a thumbprint from the surface of the battery, it made Caldwell's day.

When the technician handed him the print, he took

it on the run. "Keep looking," he shouted. "I'm going to start this through the system."

It took a while. Seventeen hours, to be exact. But when it spit out a face and a name, there was a smile on Caldwell's face that made him almost handsome. Not quite—but enough to make the receptionist at his motel take second notice of him as he was checking out.

"Sir, will you be needing a cab to get to the airport?"

"Yes, please," he said, as he fished through his wallet for a credit card.

"And what airline will you be taking?" she asked, her finger on the dial.

"None. I'll be driving, thank you."

He yanked the card from his wallet and presented it to her with a flourish. He grinned mischievously, amused at her confusion.

He signed his receipt, pocketed the card and picked up his bag. "I'll wait for the cab outside."

A short while later, he arrived at airport parking. The crime scene tape was gone, as were the people he'd called in from the crime lab. As he walked toward the car with the keys jangling in his pocket, he had a strange sense of déjà vu, as if he'd put himself in the place of the man who'd parked the car and walked away.

He slid into the seat and then sat quietly, staring at the accumulation of electronic technology within the car.

"Shit," he muttered, as he put the key in the ignition. "No wonder the director was nervous."

Just thinking about being responsible for returning this multimillion-dollar baby to its rightful home was sobering, but by the time he got to the outskirts of Denver and headed east, all his thoughts were focused on the investigation in progress. Robert Caldwell was the kind of man who hung on to a clue until it fit the puzzle on which he was working. And when they found Joaquin Candelero, another piece of the puzzle would be in place.

Nine

Kathleen sat slumped on the steps of Morgan's house with chin in hand, staring intently down the road in front of the house. Although the warmth of the sun felt good on her bare arms and feet, she squinted against the white-hot glare. A hinge squeaked on the door behind her, and when it did, her heart hit an extra beat. Morgan!

She hadn't seen him since he'd crawled into her bed last night, and part of that was her fault. She hadn't exactly been avoiding him, but by the same token, hadn't gone in search of him, either. The reason? She didn't know what to say.

You belong to me. That's what he'd said. And oh, God, had he ever been right. She did belong to him, more than he would ever know. But he'd restaked a claim for all the wrong reasons, and too many hurtful words had been said between them to pretend it didn't matter. Kathleen sighed, then bit her lip, pretending to concentrate on the road beyond and not on the man who was standing behind her.

Morgan muffled a sigh of his own. She knew he was there, he realized, and she wasn't going to do a thing about it. It was too late to take back the harsh words that had tempered their reunion, and he wasn't so certain he could have changed his reaction, even if he'd tried.

But the tilt of her chin made him smile. After all she'd endured, she still gave as good as she got. She was tough, his Kathleen, and he realized as he watched her that it was probably that very personality trait that had helped her survive.

The sunlight brought out the chestnut colors of her hair, burning browns to a dark rich caramel, turning the reddish tints to fiery auburn. A faint flush of perspiration gave a silken sheen to the smooth, even texture of her skin. Devoid of makeup, she didn't look old enough to have a daughter who was nearing sixteen.

Damn you, Kathleen, turn around and look at me. At least acknowledge that I am here. But she didn't, and he settled for what he could get, namely her presence.

His tennis shoes made little noise as he came nearer. Dropping a wide-brimmed sombrero on top of her head, he squatted down behind her, his quiet, noncommittal tone belying mixed emotions.

"You can go blind in this sun without protection."

Kathleen blinked as the wide expanse of brim instantly shaded her face.

"Thank you," she said quietly, readjusting the hat upon her head.

He leaned forward, and when his breath brushed her neck, she shifted nervously where she sat.

"What are you looking at?" he asked.

"Trish."

His eyes narrowed as he focused on a faint dust trail in the distance.

"What the hell is she doing out there?" he muttered.

"Running."

He stood abruptly. "In this heat? How long has she—?"

"Calm down," Kathleen said. "She's been cooped up in this house too long as it is. Besides, she's in good shape. She ran track for her high school back home."

There was a long pause between her explanation and his next question. Mainly because Morgan didn't know how to put what he felt into words, but he wanted to know badly enough to still ask.

"I know she's good, but . . ." He paused, uncertain how to explain what he meant.

Kathleen turned and looked up. "But what?"

"Does she like it?"

"Like what, Morgan?"

"To run."

An odd expression crossed Kathleen's face. "What do you think?"

His interest piqued, Morgan walked off the porch, unaware that Kathleen's gaze moved with him. The sun's rays turned the brown of his skin to burnished teak, the thick, black length of his hair to shiny jet, casting shadows beneath the sharp jut of nose and cheekbones, defining a body that was beyond description. So powerful was his physique that he could have posed for his own paintings. Morgan Tallchief was, in every respect, a modern-day warrior.

Words failed her as she thought back to the night before, when he'd crawled naked into her bed, promised things to her she would never forget, then held her while she slept. While he did not see, she looked her fill, tracing the breadth of his shoulders, the length of his legs, marveling that the boy she'd known had grown to such a man. But in remembering their past, she had to also remember that by loving him once, she had nearly destroyed him. What if coming back to him like this, with nothing resolved, only made things even worse? If something happened to him because of her, it would, quite literally, kill her. Fear shattered her practiced calm. She stood, caught in a sudden need to make him understand.

"Morgan . . ."

"I'm going after her," he said, and before Kathleen could argue, he'd moved from a walk to a jog. By the time he was on the road, he was in an all-out run.

She sank back to the steps with her heart in her mouth. She dropped her head to her knees and covered her eyes. It hurt too much to watch. The last time she'd seen him run in the bright light of day, he'd been eighteen years old and on top of the world. But then, so had she.

The phone began to ring inside the house. With a sigh, she dragged herself up, tossing the hat into a deck chair as she went inside. Life, she thought, could be a real mean bitch.

A short while later, Kathleen looked up as Trish bolted into the house with Morgan not far behind.

"Wow! Mom! You wouldn't believe how Dad can run! He caught up with me, and I was more than two miles down the road. You were right. He's the best!"

It hurt to see the pleasure on Morgan's face and know that but for her, the world would have also known what her daughter had just proclaimed. Trish's praise was a miserable reminder to Kathleen of what her lies had done to his life. It did nothing but add to her guilt. There was nothing she could say that wouldn't make things worse, so she changed the topic of conversation.

"The man from the garage called while you were gone. It's going to be several more days before my car is ready."

Morgan was not surprised by the coolness with which she spoke. In fact, it was little more than a repeat of the way she'd behaved during breakfast. He didn't know why she was so damned uptight. It wasn't exactly a typical morning-after meeting, since they hadn't made love. He couldn't figure out what had her in so many knots.

"It doesn't matter," he said. Still no response. "How would you like to go into Santa Fe? I need to check with Zora about a couple of things at the gallery."

Trish bounced across the floor on tiptoes, sensing a treat. "Are we going to eat out?"

Morgan grinned. The urge to give her everything she asked was overwhelming, but he remembered he wasn't the only parent in the room. He looked at Kathleen, waiting for her to voice an opinion.

Kathleen hesitated. No one seemed bothered by Trish's innocent remarks except her. She told herself she'd have to get over this guilt before she ruined their future as well as their past.

"Sounds like a plan to me," she said.

"It won't take me long to clean up," Trish said, and bolted from the room, leaving her parents to deal with what was left of the conversation.

When Kathleen turned away without a word, the

smile on Morgan's face stiffened. He'd had just about enough of her silent treatment. *He* was supposed to be the inscrutable savage, for God's sake, not her.

"Goddamn it, Kathleen. I want to know what's wrong with you. If I didn't know better, I'd think you were afraid of me."

The startled expression on her face made him sick. It was all he could do not to shake her.

"My God! That's it, isn't it? You *are* afraid of me."

"Of course not!" she sputtered, and then quickly looked away.

He stared at her in disbelief. "Like hell, Kathleen. You can lie to yourself, but don't lie to me!"

She spun, her hands in sudden fists, her cheeks hot with fury.

"You . . . you . . ." At a loss for anything but the truth to describe what she was feeling, she lashed out. "You're such a . . . a . . . man! It's the only excuse you could possibly have for being so dense. I'm not afraid of you! I'm afraid for you."

"Well, hell."

She glared. "My sentiments exactly."

"Why?"

"Why what?" she asked.

"What is there to be afraid of?"

"How can you ask me that? My father lived in fear until the day he died that he would be found. And although he'd willingly gone into the program, he never completely trusted the government to be able to keep us safe." She grimaced. "It would seem that he'd been right. He wasn't cold in his grave when they started after me, and I don't know why. I know nothing about anyone or anything. I was thirteen years old when they arrested Paolo Benini and fourteen when Daddy testified against him. Soon after, we went into the program."

"What did your father have on Benini, anyway?"

"He was a CPA for the Benini Corporation. By accident, he discovered a second set of books. When he found out that Benini was laundering money for the syndicate in a very big way, he went to the police."

"Then what happened?"

Kathleen began to pace the distance between window and door, ticking off a sequence of events upon her fingers.

"There was a trial. Benini went to prison. We went into hiding. About seven or eight years ago, Benini died, still behind bars. Six months ago, my father suffered a stroke and died only a couple of weeks ago. Ironically, they both lived out the last half of their lives under government control."

Morgan picked up the story. "So you bury your father, then someone tears up your house and threatens you. Add to that the tracking device I found on your car." He frowned. "You know this makes no sense, don't you?"

"Dear God, yes, I know that," Kathleen shouted, and then shook her head in disbelief. "I'm sorry. Sometimes it gets to me in a very big way."

Morgan ran his hand down the length of her arm in an easy, gentling motion. He hated that they seemed to constantly be at each other's throats.

"Look. I'm no detective and don't pretend to be. But there's got to be a reason other than revenge."

She moved away. "Like what?"

"I don't know. Maybe . . ."

He reached out and took her by the hand, and as he did, she paused.

"Don't run away from me, girl. I'm not the enemy, okay?"

She'd hurt him again, and that was the last thing she'd meant to do.

"I'm sorry," she said quietly. "I don't mean to be so defensive, but—"

His finger grazed the curve of her lips, silencing what was left of her apology.

"Let it be, love. Just let it be."

She nodded, shamed that it was always Morgan who was put in the position of being the one to forgive.

He tried another tack. "Did your father ever say anything—anything at all that referred to that time, or to Benini, himself?"

"No, not that I can—" She paused, frowning as she remembered something her father had said only days before he'd died.

"What?" Morgan asked.

"I didn't know what he meant, and his speech was so slurred from the stroke that I wasn't sure I'd heard him correctly, but Daddy did say something before he died that I didn't understand."

"What did he say?"

"He said he had a tiger by the tail and didn't know how to let go."

Morgan sighed, then pulled Kathleen into his arms. "Do you know that this conversation is the longest we've had in sixteen years?"

"Our reunion was hardly grounds for chitchat," she muttered, trying to ignore the fact that there was nothing between her lips and that wide brown chest but a thin white T-shirt.

He grinned. Once again, she was on the defensive, but he couldn't blame her. He'd asked for that one.

"I know, I know, but if you were more willing to communicate with me, we wouldn't keep having these misunderstandings."

She snorted delicately. "Coming from you, that's rich."

His grin broadened as he lifted her from the floor, leaving her feet dangling inches above the floor. "Stop wiggling or I'll get you all sweaty," he chided, holding her close against him until she did as he asked.

Everything slowed, including their heartbeats, as eyes met, dark black to clear blue, still hiding secrets neither had the guts to share. When she'd quit struggling, he set her back on her feet, taking care not to let go until he got the answer he wanted to hear.

"So you're afraid for me, are you?"

"And what if I am?"

His eyes softened as he traced the lower edge of her lip with the tip of his finger. Soft. She was so damned soft. With a groan, he cupped the sides of her face with his hands, tilting her chin until she had nowhere to look but at him.

"Say it, Kathleen."

Her heart skipped a beat, and then another and another.

"Say what?" she asked, mesmerized by that hot, dark gaze.

"You still love me, don't you?"

She gasped. Then he lowered his head. "Never mind," he whispered. "I'll find out for myself."

Kathleen groaned. His mouth on her lips was like the first taste of honey. So smooth. So sweet.

Insistently, Morgan pursued their pleasure, lingering until she was gasping for breath and clinging to him in mute desperation. But this time, he didn't forget that his daughter was just down the hall. With a groan, he was the first to break contact.

Still staggering from unspent passion, Kathleen reeled as Morgan took her hand, placing it in the center of his chest so that she could feel the thunder of his heartbeat for herself.

Her fingers curled upon the tender vibration beneath muscle and skin. "You are making me crazy," she said softly.

"The feeling, sweet lady, is entirely mutual." He kissed her once more, swiftly, urgently, groaning beneath his breath when he finally let her go.

She stood without moving as he walked out of the room. When she heard the door to his room open, then close, she lowered herself into a chair and leaned back and closed her eyes, reliving that moment of mouth-to-mouth connection. While lingering sensation throbbed beneath the surface of her lips, one of Trish's favorite songs suddenly came to mind. She didn't remember the exact words, but there was something in the lyrics that had to do with a man saying it best when he said nothing at all.

Special Agent Caldwell was stuck in traffic, cursing road construction and the cattle running willy-nilly all over the Oklahoma City roadway, compliments of a jackknifed bull-hauler. Paramedics were dodging wild-eyed steers in an effort to get the injured driver loaded into a waiting ambulance, and from what Caldwell could see, the man was in no shape to help round up his load.

Caldwell stared through the windshield, the look on his face one of comic disbelief.

"If only I had a video camera," he said. In his opinion, some of the men he worked with were full of bullshit, and he thought it most fitting that they should have access to the real thing.

However, there was nothing available except the space-age technology mounted within the dash. So he sat and watched the roundup in progress, and the longer he sat, the more he fidgeted. More than once, his gaze lingered over the maze of screens and access panels within arm's reach. It boggled his mind to think what this must have cost. Running his fingers across the buttons, he wondered absently how many of his tax dollars had gone into this setup, and with the thought came curiosity.

Without second-guessing the wisdom of messing with something this vast, he punched the power button. It was hard to say what he'd expected to see, but it wasn't what came up on the screen.

"Well, I'll be a . . ."

He slumped in amazement, wondering how they'd missed something this elementary. They'd checked the car for prints, but to his knowledge, no one had checked the equipment. They'd been so elated to get the star car back in one piece, they'd missed the obvious. Lester Bryant had gone to a great deal of trouble to get this car for a reason, and here it was, blinking back at him from a bright blue screen. The fact that a map of the North American continent had come up on the screen was no big deal, but the blinking blip in the state of Louisiana was.

"Holy cow," he muttered, wincing at his choice of words when a wild-eyed steer suddenly ran past.

Manfully ignoring the pungent scent of fresh manure just outside his window, he punched another button, and then another, each time zeroing closer in on the activated blip. When he had the location narrowed down to a definite area of New Orleans, he reached for the phone. This was something the director needed to know.

Trying not to gag from the smell outside, he counted the rings while deciding how best to break the news that he'd missed something so basic the first time around. But when the director answered, in typical Caldwell fashion, he blurted it out, minus the sugar-coated excuses.

"Sir, we got ourselves a little quirk in the situation."

At the other end, the director frowned. He didn't like quirks. They pissed him off.

"What kind of quirk?"

"The system in this car is active. There is a target on-screen as we're speaking, and the location is on the lower east side of New Orleans, Louisiana."

"Son of a . . ."

"My sentiments exactly, sir."

The director paused, readjusting his plan to accommodate this latest bit of news.

"Okay, change of plans. I want you to follow up on this and detour to New Orleans. Stop by the Dallas office on your way. Someone will be there to meet you. From there, you will both proceed to the target location. I want to know who's been marked, understood?"

"Understood."

"Oh, and Caldwell . . ."

"Sir?"

"Do not approach. This is strictly observation only. Until I know what Bryant was into, I don't want anyone knowing they've been made."

"Yes, sir," Caldwell said, and disconnected.

Although his window was still up, he dodged instinctively when an overweight man wearing a T-shirt, blue jeans, and a baseball cap came running past, swinging a lariat over his head and sidestepping cowshit with remarkable precision. Caldwell rolled his eyes at the untimely delay, and started looking along the roadway for a gas station within walking distance. From the way things appeared, it was going to be a while before normal traffic would resume, and he needed to pee.

Sunlight died in a burst of color, washing the desert below and beyond in a temporary rinse of grapefruit pink and tangerine orange. The evening star was already out, showing a heavenly twinkle with glittering persistence. Kathleen leaned against the porch post, watching the aerial display with the deference it so richly deserved, and wished she truly belonged here. Instead of hating the isolation in which Morgan had chosen to live, she found something peaceful about the absence of civilization. A coyote yipped, and another answered. In spite of the familiarity of the mournful sound, she shivered.

Morgan wrapped his arms around her, pulling her back against his chest and holding her safe within the shelter of his embrace.

"Cold?"

Startled by the unexpectedness of his voice, she gasped. "You scared me. I didn't hear you coming."

He grinned and nuzzled a spot below her right ear. "My ancestors would be proud."

Kathleen smiled and leaned against him. This was so like the Morgan of old, always teasing about the white man's misconceptions of the Native American.

"Where's Trish?" she asked.

He nipped at her earlobe, then splayed his hand across her belly, pulling her closer against the ache in his groin.

"In the shower." His voice lowered seductively. "And you know what that means for us."

She spun within his embrace, preparing herself for a confrontation she wasn't sure she could handle.

"What?"

"No hot water."

Morgan was waiting for a smile, but when she broke into peals of unrestrained laughter, he froze. It had been years since he'd heard that sound somewhere other than his dreams. A shiver ran up his spine, giving him an overwhelming urge to throw her over his shoulder and run off into the night, far away from people, and danger, and lies.

She was still chuckling when his voice cut through the sound.

"Kathleen."

His fingers tightened around her arms. In the moonlight, she could see the tension upon his face.

"I'm taking you home."

An odd little laugh came out with her remark. "But we're already here."

"No. I mean, home to Oklahoma. When I marry you,

it will be before God and everyone I hold dear. I want no misunderstandings about why it's happening, do you understand?"

Her breath caught, and her eyes suddenly glistened in the moonlight from unshed tears. All she could do was nod.

The pain on her face hurt his heart. The tears in her eyes hurt his soul.

"Don't," he begged, and pulled her closer.

"How can I not?" she asked. "What am I supposed to do, laugh because I've forced you into a corner with no way out? You've done the noble thing and asked, Morgan. I just wish to hell it hadn't been shoved in your face."

His chin tilted dangerously as his voice deepened. "Damn it, Kathleen, I thought you knew me better than that. No one forces me to do anything I don't want to do."

"Oh, really? Then what would you call it?"

He bent down, whispering against her cheek. "An answer to a prayer?"

Hope lifted the burden she'd been carrying alone. "I wish I believed that."

Unutterable sadness swept over his face. "I wish you did, too."

An uncomfortable silence extended until Kathleen pushed herself out of Morgan's arms.

"Where are you going?" he asked.

"Inside. Someone has to tell Trish to pack. It may as well be me."

He threw up his hands. "Okay, Kathleen, you can run, but you won't get far. I'm always going to be right behind you."

"I know," she said quietly. "It's what gets me through each day."

It wasn't much in the way of encouragement, but it was enough to get Morgan through the night.

By midmorning, they were on Interstate 40, heading east with the sun in their eyes, and as far as they knew, no one was at their back.

Kathleen was keenly aware of the significance of where they were going. More than sixteen years ago, she'd nearly killed herself trying to get back to Oklahoma and to Morgan. Now, she was on her way, and being driven there by the man himself. Somehow, it all seemed fair and right.

Ned Easter was a careless man about some things, but not about his truck. It was his unwritten rule never to start a new haul without washing it down. And when he took his pride and joy to the car wash, he did a very thorough job of knocking off grease and grime.

This particular trip to the Little Dixie Dip was no different from any of the others he'd made throughout the years—except for the fact that this time he knocked off more than grime when he aimed the pressure spray toward the underside of the fenders. The tracking device that Morgan had secreted beneath the cab caught the full force of the hot, soapy water. It clattered to the pavement, slipping unnoticed between the grates in the drain. By the time Bunny Easter had his baby all shiny and clean, Lester Bryant's bug was drowning in the New Orleans sewers, along with several dead rats. The waterproof casing wasn't as waterproof as the company had promised. It was deep underground and seeping, well on its way to the Gulf of Mexico via the mighty Mississippi.

No one was more aware of its imminent disappearance than Special Agent Caldwell. The on-screen blip ceased blinking when he was right in the middle of Loop 12 of the Dallas freeway. It startled him so that he missed his exit and was headed the wrong way. Trying to read a city map and stay alive in freeway traffic was hopeless. Before he knew it, Fort Worth had come and gone. By the time he'd worked his way to an outside lane to exit, he was sweating profusely. He pulled into a gas station, stopping at the full-service island. While he was waiting for an attendant, he glanced through the windshield, squinting as he read the street names in the distance, then laid his map across the steering wheel, trying to figure out where he was.

A young man sidled up to the driver's-side window and leaned down.

"Fill 'er up, mister?"

Caldwell looked up and nodded. When he looked back, he realized he'd lost his place on the map. Before he could relocate himself, the attendant leaned in the window again.

"Y'all need to punch the button," the man said, pointing to the door over the gas cap.

Caldwell grimaced. Once again, he'd lost his place. He opened the console and pressed a small white button, hoping to hell it did what it claimed and didn't do something audacious instead, like ejecting him from his seat. To his relief, a small, distinct click could be heard as the latch released on the fuel door.

Several minutes went by while his tank was being filled. In that time, the attendant washed the windshield twice, each time lingering longer and longer at each corner, unable to tear his gaze away from the vast array of instruments on the dashboard of the car. Caldwell pretended he did not notice.

"That'll be eighteen-fifty," the attendant said.

As Caldwell fished for his wallet, the attendant leaned down again, gazing into the car's interior with unfeigned awe.

"Man! That's one hell of a stereo system you got there, mister. I'll bet it pumps out the decibels."

Caldwell grinned as he paid for the gas. "You're right about that, boy. This baby rocks clear to the stars."

The attendant shook his head in amazement as he stepped back. "Yes sir, I can believe that."

Caldwell drove away with a smile on his face. It slowly disappeared while he came to terms with the fact that the director had to be notified. The blip's sudden disappearance had changed everyone's plans.

Ten

They'd driven as fast as the law allowed, and Kathleen had long since faced the fact that they would still not reach Comanche before dark.

When they'd driven into Oklahoma City via I40 eastbound, a flutter of nervous tension tied her stomach into knots. And when they took the southbound H. E. Bailey Turnpike, and then Highway 81 south at Chickasha, her hands started to sweat. The longer they drove, the closer they got to the place where she'd ostensibly died. How on earth would she explain her resurrection to a town full of people who'd watched her and her family go up in smoke? On the other side of the same coin, should they even know?

Kathleen glanced at her daughter, who was sprawled on the backseat sound asleep. The book Trish had been reading lay just beyond her fingertips where she'd dropped it. With a sigh, Kathleen turned back around, still worrying, as she had ever since they'd left Santa Fe, about arriving at James Tallchief's house without notification. James had a large family. What if there wasn't any extra room?

"Morgan, I feel funny about arriving without notice. I still think we should have called ahead."

He shook his head without moving his gaze from the roadway.

"No. It would only complicate our arrival."

"I doubt that," she muttered. "It's pretty complicated already."

He reached for her, his fingers curling around her hand, then pulling gently, insistently.

"You're too far away."

"But my seat belt . . ."

He finished her sentence for her. ". . . will unbuckle."

"That's not what I was going to say," she argued.

"I know," he said, urging her closer to his side. "That's why I said it for you."

When her leg was pressing against his, her arm resting against his rib cage, and her hair brushing against his shoulder, he relaxed.

"That's better, don't you think?"

She looked up at him, studying the strength of his features, the exotic cast to his skin, and the stubborn cut of his jaw, and had a sensation of déjà vu, remembering a bus ride home on a night long ago, when she'd watched him in this same light. Back then, she'd been in love enough to ignore the unknown future. Now the unknown made her cautious about admitting her love. But by the same token, she couldn't lie to him then, any easier than she could lie to him now. She rested her head against his shoulder and slid her hand across his leg, letting her fingers rest just above the bend of his knee.

"Yes, Morgan, it's better."

A quiet smile broke the tension between them. He winked, then returned his attention to the road. A half hour passed with nothing more being said. However, Kathleen could tell by the covert glances he kept giving her that something was on his mind, and she'd had all of the surprises she could endure. If there was something that needed to be said, she wanted to hear it now.

"Don't you think it would be better if you just spit it out now before we got any farther down the road?"

Morgan frowned. He wasn't prepared for her perceptiveness.

"Like what?" he asked.

"Whatever it is that you've been thinking about since we left Oklahoma City."

He sighed. "Well, damn, Kathleen, I think I've just lost what was left of my privacy. I didn't know you read minds, too."

She smiled slightly, then shrugged. "I'm a woman, not a psychic."

He slid an arm around her shoulder and squeezed lightly. "From where I'm sitting, that's one and the same."

"Morgan . . ."

"Hmmm?"

"I'm waiting."

It was obvious she wasn't going to give up until he confessed. "Okay. I've been thinking. It will take a few days to get a marriage license as well as the results from our blood tests."

"So?"

"So what if, during that time, we leave Patricia with James and Mary and go to Seattle?"

She frowned. "I have never left Trish alone with anyone other than my parents, not since the day she was born. Besides, they're all total strangers to each other."

"Then it's about time you did," he said. "But this hinges on her agreement, too, so don't panic. If she's uncomfortable with the idea, it won't happen."

Kathleen relaxed, but only slightly. "So, why leave her behind, and why go to Seattle?"

What he was about to say would suggest the possibility of her father's betrayal, and he didn't know how easy that was going to be for her to accept. It took him a while to decide where to start.

"For starters, your things are still there. We could pack it all up, maybe, hire some movers to bring what you want to keep out to Santa Fe."

"I suppose so, but why leave Trish behind? She could help with the packing, right?"

A muscle jerked in his jaw. "Yes, that's true. It's just . . ."

"Why do I sense there's more?"

His hands tightened upon the wheel. "Because you're reading my damned mind, remember?"

"What is it, Morgan? Please, you're frightening me."

He sighed. There was no easy way to say it. "I want to search your father's property, and I guessed you would not want Trish around when we do it."

Kathleen was shocked. "Search it? What on earth for?"

"I'm inclined to believe he hid something from the feds."

"Hid what?"

"Maybe something that belonged to Paolo Benini. Something he never told anyone about."

"No! I don't believe you," she cried, and started to pull away. He wouldn't let her.

"Damn it, Kathleen. Think about it! It's the only thing that makes sense, and you know it! Remember, your father said he was afraid the FBI couldn't keep him safe. What if he was holding a hole card of his own on the off chance that Benini ever did catch up with him? What if he was saving it to barter his family free?"

She went limp. Long, telling minutes passed while years of memories played through her mind. The whispered conversations between her father and mother that ceased whenever she entered a room. Her father's initial trust, then disgust, and finally, his disbelief in the system that had promised to be their salvation. His admission of having a tiger by the tail that he couldn't turn loose. What if Morgan was right? What if they'd been running all these years with something that didn't belong to them?

When she finally looked at Morgan, he could tell she'd bought into the theory in more ways than one.

"So, what do you think?" he asked.

The cold, even tone of her voice betrayed her true feelings.

"I think if you're right, I may never be able to forgive my parents. That's what I think."

"Then you'll come with me?"

"Yes."

They drove the rest of the distance in silence. It wasn't until they topped a small, rolling hill that everything changed.

An orange glow lit up a portion of the horizon. Kathleen gasped and sat up in the seat, transfixed by the light shining through the dark.

Morgan reached for her hand. "Honey, what's wrong?"

Her voice was shaking, her gaze unfocused, almost blank.

"There's a fire!"

"It's probably just someone burning a brush pile."

She clutched at his arm as the years fell away in her mind. "Remember the night you thought I died . . . ?"

Her voice faded, but her gaze stayed fixed upon the glow, and suddenly, the skin crawled on the back of his neck. He had a feeling he knew what she was going to say.

"Get rid of it, Kathleen. Get rid of every bad memory, or there'll be no room for the good."

A low moan slipped out of her mouth. Her hands curled around the edges of the seat as she swayed back and forth to a memory he could not share. Seconds later, he pulled to a stop at the side of the road and turned to her, his face in shadow, his eyes burning with displaced anger.

"Say it, Kathleen. Say it!"

She went limp as the words began to spill.

"I was fighting them, crying and begging them to let me go back. They wouldn't stop. Miles later, they let me up. When I looked behind us, that's what I saw on the horizon. It was our house, burning to the ground."

Her voice broke as she covered her face with her hands. "I knew you were there, watching me die, and I had no way to tell you it wasn't so."

Her voice caught on a sob as he opened his arms. She fell into them without hesitation. Her skin was soft beneath his lips, her hair mussed and slightly tangled as he dug his fingers into its warm brown depths. He kissed her face, tasting the salt of her tears, and gave up the last of old pain.

"Let go of it, love. Let it go. You're here now. I've got you, and I swear to God, I will never let anyone hurt you again."

She shuddered, then sighed as his mouth centered upon her lips, shattering what was left of her resolve.

"Ah, Morgan, Morgan," she whispered, and wrapped her arms around his neck.

He lifted his head, his nostrils flaring as he cupped her face with his hands.

"Say it, Kathleen! I see it in your eyes, but dear God, I need to hear it from your lips."

In the backseat, Trish stirred, and Morgan cursed softly before letting her go.

"Soon, Kathleen, there will come a time when you can no longer deny what's in your heart." He put the car in gear and pulled back onto the highway.

Kathleen refocused her gaze on the light in the dark and thought about what he'd said. He knew her better than she knew herself. Hiding her feelings *was* no longer possible. The truth was all about love. Pure. Simple. Overwhelming. She loved the man with a depth of passion she could never have given the boy.

* * *

When they drove into Comanche a short while later, nothing seemed familiar. She could almost believe she'd never been here before. And then they passed a street sign, and her gaze automatically turned to the left. Only four houses down at the end of a cul-de-sac, Kathleen Ryder had lived and died. A great sadness swept over her as she grieved for what might have been.

"Never mind," Morgan said quietly. "That's our past. We deal with the future and nothing else, okay?"

Words failed her. All she could do was nod as they passed through the small southwestern town. A short while later, Morgan began slowing down. Kathleen started to take notice.

"Isn't this where you used to live with your grand-mother? I thought we were going to James's house?"

"He moved into Grandmother's house after she died. It's a larger house than the one in which he and Mary had been living, and no one in the family wanted it sold."

"Oh."

The driveway was short, and except for a light shin-ing out of a window in the central part of the house, it was in darkness.

Kathleen began to fidget. "What if they're already asleep?"

"Not at seven-thirty. They're probably just watching television."

"Oh, God, help me get through this," she muttered.

Morgan parked and turned off the key. The sudden silence within which they sat seemed to resonate with tension.

"You don't need God for this one, sweetheart; you have me."

The poignancy of his claim touched her in a way nothing else possibly could.

"I know," she said quietly. "It's just hard for me to remember that I'm no longer alone in all this mess."

Morgan leaned over. Kathleen met him coming. They paused, mouth to mouth, taking issue with the fact that all they could share was a swift, brief kiss. Trish was rousing in the seat behind them. She sat up, rubbing at her eyes and smoothing down her hair.

"Are we there yet?" she asked.

Morgan broke away from Kathleen with a grin. "I'm starting to get the hang of this parent business. There are two general questions the kids always ask, right? Is it far? and, Are we there yet?"

Before Kathleen could respond, an outside light came on. As she watched, a tall, heavyset man exited the house and walked to the edge of the porch.

Morgan squeezed Kathleen's hand and then glanced at his daughter in the backseat.

"Rise and shine, sleepyhead. We're home."

"You go ahead," Kathleen told Morgan. "We'll be right behind you."

Morgan got out of the car and started toward the house, and as he did, was moved by an unexpected sensation of nostalgia, of having walked this way so many, many times before.

A loud shout of surprise and then one of delight came from the man of the house as James Tallchief bounded off the steps and across the yard. Within moments, he was hugging and laughing and yelling at the top of his voice.

"I don't believe it!" James shouted, thumping Morgan wildly upon the back. "I never thought I'd see this day. Welcome home, little brother, welcome home."

Morgan looked down into his older brother's eyes. "Little brother?"

James laughed. "So you're taller. It still does not make you wiser."

Morgan grinned as James gave him a final thump on the back and then grabbed him by the arm. "Come into the house," James said. "I can't wait to see the expression on Mary's face."

"Wait," Morgan said. "I didn't come alone."

James paused and looked past Morgan to the car that sat in darkness.

"Who came with . . . ?"

James never finished his question. His smile disappeared, and even in the darkness, it was easy to see his shock, then spreading fear. He turned loose of his brother, and took a quick step back, mumbling something in his mother tongue.

Uncertain of their welcome, Trish slipped up behind Morgan and slid her hand in the crook of his elbow.

"Dad, I can't understand him. What is he saying?"

Morgan gave her a hug, smoothing sleep-tousled hair away from her face. He gave Kathleen a look of apology before answering Trish's question.

"It's Cherokee, honey, and he just said . . . 'A ghost walks beside me.' "

Kathleen sighed. This was worse than she'd expected. She had expected her appearance to be a shock to James, but she hadn't expected to frighten him.

"James, it's okay," Morgan said quietly. "Believe me, my reaction was worse. It *is* Kathleen, but she's not a ghost."

"Kathleen Ryder is dead," James said, and then glanced nervously into the shadows, as if expecting to be struck down for uttering the name of one who was deceased.

Morgan nodded. "In a way, you're right. At least, that's what the FBI wanted us to believe."

James didn't budge. "FBI? What does the government have to do with this?"

"You've heard of the Witness Protection Program."

James's mouth went slack with surprise. A long moment of silence hung between them as he digested what Morgan was saying. The longer he stood, the better he felt. Finally, he nodded.

"Kathleen and her family have been in it since she was fourteen years old," Morgan added.

James's gaze moved from Morgan to Kathleen—and then to the young woman who was leaning against his brother. For the first time, he looked straight at her, studying her face and remembering what she'd called his little brother.

Morgan smiled, and took her hand. "James, this is my daughter, Patricia. Patricia, meet your uncle James."

James shook his head as a slow, bewildered smile broke the somberness of his expression. "Leave it to you, little brother, to scare me out of a good year of my life, and then hand me such a wonderful surprise."

Trish began to relax when James smiled. It was then that his resemblance to her father was most obvious. And when James reached out in wonder, touching her hair, then the side of her face, she knew it was going to be all right.

Kathleen stood to one side, accepting that she was

part of the conversation, but not of the family. Tallchief blood ran in her daughter's veins. Patricia bore her father's face. She had even inherited his athletic skill. Kathleen had no legal or moral claim upon Morgan other than an enduring love. How his family felt about that remained to be seen.

James Tallchief winked. "It is good to know you, Patricia."

Trish smiled. "Everyone usually calls me Trish."

James nodded, and then looked again to the woman who stood alone in the dark.

"So, Kathleen Ryder, your life has not been easy, has it?"

Unexpected tears sprang to Kathleen's eyes. She hadn't prepared herself for the compassion and understanding he showed so quickly.

"Come here, sweetheart," Morgan said softly, and held out his hand. "We're in this together, remember?"

James frowned. "In what together?"

Morgan gave his older brother a long, telling look. "Inside. We'll explain everything else inside."

James led the way.

The ten o'clock news played mutely in the background as James Tallchief leaned back in his chair with a thump. The look that passed between him and his wife was swift, but each understood the other without words.

"So, you will stay here with Mary and me," he announced. "No one will know to look here."

Morgan shook his head. "No. That's not why we came."

James frowned. "Then explain yourself, brother. I'm not as young as I used to be. I need my sleep."

Morgan looked around the room and could almost see his grandmother smiling back at him from her chair in the corner. And then he blinked, and there was no one there.

"I came home to get married. Kathleen has no family—except our daughter, and me. I figured I had plenty to share."

Mary Tallchief rocked to her feet, her round face beaming as she took Kathleen by the hand.

"A wedding! Why didn't you say so sooner? I'll have to let everyone know. Come with me, Kathleen, we'll make a list."

Morgan flinched, his voice louder than he'd meant it to be. "Mary, wait!"

She paused, a look of surprise on her face.

"Tell no one but family, okay? And make sure they keep it to themselves. The fewer people who know, the easier it will be to keep my ladies safe."

She dropped back to her seat. "I didn't think," she said. "I'm sorry."

"Don't apologize for being happy," Kathleen said. "We've had little of that to go around."

Mary nodded, her gaze falling on the teenage girl who sat silently at her mother's side. And then the front door flew open and four young men came into the room—dark hair flying, black eyes questioning, each wearing expressions of avid curiosity.

"Dad, whose car is . . . ?"

James grinned. His sons were home.

"Boys, meet your uncle Morgan."

A look of wonder spread over their faces. The tallest one spoke, the tone of his voice just shy of reverent.

"No way! You don't mean the one who was a runner?"

Trish reacted with indignation on her father's behalf.

"The one who *is* a runner," she said shortly, and then flushed when everyone suddenly looked at her and grinned. "Well . . . he is," she said, and slumped back into her seat.

James's eyes twinkled. "Patricia, meet your cousins. The skinny one is Everett. The mouthy one is Winston. The fancy dresser is Douglas."

Everyone chuckled at James's description of Douglas. The teenager's jeans were clean but torn, his T-shirt old and faded, the Eskimo Joe logo barely visible on the front.

"And," James said, "the pretty one is Michael. If you don't believe me, ask him. He'll tell you I'm right."

The boy called Michael smiled at his father's teasing remark, and as he did, Kathleen couldn't help but stare. He was so like Morgan had been at that age, it was eerie.

James pointed at Trish. "This is your uncle Morgan's daughter, Patricia. She's going to be staying with us for a couple of days until the wedding."

"Wedding! What wedding?" they echoed.

James continued as if they had never interrupted. His voice dropped in tone, his teasing manner disappeared. "Patricia and her mother need our protection. Someone has been trying to hurt them. I am counting on you to help me make sure they stay safe."

It took exactly ten seconds for the news to sink in,

and when it did, even Morgan was stunned by the seriousness of the young men's behavior. Douglas was the first to speak, and Morgan would later learn that, although he was third in birth order, he was also the brothers' unspoken leader.

"You can count on us, Uncle Morgan. Besides, we always wanted a little sister." And then he grinned at Trish. "It will be good to have someone in the house who's prettier than Mike."

Everyone laughed, including Michael, who took the teasing about his handsome face in stride. Trish looked around her, absorbing the similarity in faces, and had the sensation of having finally found where she belonged. She leaned against Kathleen's shoulder and whispered in her ear.

"Mom, it will be okay. I don't mind staying here while you and Dad go to Seattle." Her voice softened, trailing wistfully into near silence as she finished. "Maybe if you do, you'll find a way for the running to be over."

Kathleen's heart was too full to speak. She could do nothing but nod. Last week, they'd had no one. Only days ago, she'd found Morgan, uncertain whether he'd accept them or toss them out on their ears. And now she sat, surrounded by people who had taken her and her daughter in on Morgan's word alone. It was almost more than she could believe, and they needed to know how much she appreciated what they'd done.

She stood up, aware of Morgan only inches away. Her voice was quiet, almost hesitant, but her intent was soon obviously clear.

"I have something to say." Everyone turned to her. "I—" She looked at Trish and amended her words.

"*We* appreciate you more than you will ever know. I—
we have lived alone, and in fear, for what seems like
forever. Thank you for accepting us." Her glance fell
on Morgan as she added, "And for protecting our
daughter. I promise we will not outstay our welcome."

James crossed the room until he was standing eye to
eye with his brother's woman.

"That is not possible," he said quietly. "Family is always welcome."

Kathleen didn't know whether to laugh or to cry.
When Morgan stood up and shook his brother's hand,
all she could do was watch. *Please, God, don't let this all
be a dream*, she thought.

Douglas broke the solemnity of the moment. "Come
with us, Patricia. You can sleep in Michael's room. It's
the cleanest."

Michael grinned and winked as he took Trish by the
hand and pulled her up from where she was sitting.
"You're welcome to my room," he said. "But I'm not
sleeping with Douglas; he snores."

They squabbled all the way out of the room, but it
was nothing more than brotherly love.

Kathleen leaned against Morgan, grateful that the
ordeal was over.

"See, I told you it would be all right," he whispered.

James was all business. "Our couch makes into a
queen-size bed. Mary and I will take it, and you can—"

"No," Kathleen said quickly. "We'll take the couch. I
insist."

James smiled, and Mary jumped to her feet. "I'll just
get some clean sheets. It won't take long."

Morgan caught her by the hand as she was hustling
past. "Sister, take all the time you need. I'm going to

drive Kathleen back into town. She needs to lay a few ghosts to rest of her own."

Mary paused, a look of understanding in her dark brown eyes.

"That's a good idea," she said. "By the time you get back, everyone will surely have bathed. Maybe you will actually have some hot water."

Morgan grinned and then crossed the room, pausing at the entrance to the hallway.

"Trish!" A door opened down the hall. Seconds later, she appeared in the doorway.

"I'm going to drive your mother into Comanche for a little while. We'll be right back, okay?"

"That's cool," she said, and withdrew, closing the door behind her.

Morgan turned to Kathleen. "It's cool. We have her permission."

James's great laugh boomed out within the confines of the room. "So, little brother, you catch on to this parenting stuff pretty fast."

Morgan grinned. "We won't be long."

James dug into his pocket, then tossed a ring of keys across the room. "Come back when you're ready. Take my keys so you can let yourself in."

Morgan caught them in midair. "Thanks, James."

James nodded. They were halfway out the door when he remembered to add, "Hey, Morgan."

Morgan paused and turned.

"There's a key to the gate of the old Delroy place on there, too."

There was a thoughtful expression on Morgan's face as he looked down at the keys, then followed Kathleen outside, quietly closing the door behind them.

The security light was still on outside, casting a pale glow onto Kathleen where she was waiting for him.

"You didn't have to do this," she said.

He went to her. When she stepped into his arms, he sighed.

"Yes, I think I did." His arms tightened briefly before he guided her toward his car. "You're not the only one with ghosts."

Eleven

For Kathleen, going back to Comanche was like reentering a bad dream. The closer they got, the more rapid her heartbeat. An odd, misplaced sense of panic had her on the edge of the seat, as if by coming back, she might unearth the demons that had originally stolen her away.

The trip was difficult for Morgan as well. It was a reminder of murdered innocence, of having been thrust into a lifetime of grieving within the space of mere seconds.

"Oh, God, Morgan, this is harder than I'd imagined."

He pulled her close, giving her a quick, reassuring hug.

"Grandmother had a saying: 'Anything that comes easy is not worth the salt it took to cure it.' I was never sure if she was talking about the prairie chickens I used to hunt or some monumental crisis." He grinned. "I'm inclined to believe she purposefully left her words of wisdom broad enough to cover any given situation."

Kathleen leaned her head against his shoulder in thoughtful silence, watching as the minuscule town of Comanche suddenly appeared out of the darkness.

"It hasn't grown much, has it?" she asked, eyeing the single row of lights down the main street and the few scattered throughout the small residential part of town.

Morgan shook his head. "I'd venture to guess it's dwindling, not spreading. Not enough industry to keep the young people here, and not much chance of one coming to change it. It's just another small Oklahoma town trying not to blow off the map—but it's home."

Kathleen heard a rare and unexpected tenderness in Morgan's voice. Sentiment from the hard man that he'd become seemed out of character. She glanced up at him in the darkness, wishing she could read what was in his mind. And then she set the wish aside and began searching the silent and darkened rows of buildings for familiar landmarks. Few remained. So many changes had come and gone within the last sixteen years, it only stood to reason that Comanche, Oklahoma, would be affected by time, as well.

Morgan suddenly pulled into a curb in front of a small café and parked. The dim yellow glow of the streetlight under which they'd parked was driving a small swarm of June bugs into a frenzy. High above the street, they alternately circled and dived at the burning bulb, tiny kamikazes bent on self-destruction. Without hesitation, he took Kathleen by the hand, pulling her across the seat and out of the door on the driver's side.

"Let's walk awhile, okay?"

Her eyes were wide and fixed upon the gentleness in his voice as he held her fast against the night.

"Giving the ghosts time to slip up on us?"

He sighed and leaned down, grazing her lips with a kiss. "To hell with ghosts, Kathleen." He took her hand and pressed it near the center of his chest where his heartbeat thumped with vital regularity. "This is what matters. You. Me. We're real. We're here. Ghosts are nothing but old memories."

Before she could answer, a police car turned a corner down the block and slowly eased its way up the street, coming to a stop behind the bumper of Morgan's car.

The uniformed officer inside gave both Morgan and Kathleen a slow, considering look.

"Having trouble, mister?" the officer asked.

Morgan tensed, and then suddenly started to smile. "Jake? Jake Ramsey, is that you?"

The officer squinted in the half light, giving the tall Indian a closer look. A wide grin suddenly split his face as he put his cruiser in park and got out, his hand already extended in welcome.

"By God," he said, pumping Morgan's hand vigorously. "Morgan Tallchief! I never thought I'd see the day when you'd be back on the streets of Comanche. Where have you been all these years, and what on earth are you doing out here at this time of night?"

Morgan grinned. He hadn't expected to ever see any of his classmates behind the wheel of a law enforcement vehicle, especially this one. As a teenager, Jake Ramsey had spent more Saturday nights in jail than he had making time with the girls.

"I guess you could say I've been a little bit of every-where," Morgan said. "I did a stint in the navy and mustered out as a SEAL. Now I'm living in Santa Fe."

Jake nodded, his face still creased in smiles. "Yeah, that's right! I did know you were in Santa Fe. The local paper did a piece on you a while back. Showed you standing beside some of your paintings." His gaze moved to the woman who stood in the shadows. She looked vaguely familiar.

"Who's the lady?"

Kathleen turned away, giving Jake Ramsey little but a shadowy profile at which to look, although he con-tinued to watch her, his lawman's mind focused on the contours of her face. Finally, he shook his head in be-wilderment.

"She reminds me of someone. . . . I just can't put my finger on who it is," Jake said.

"She's just a friend," Morgan said quickly. "I thought I'd show her the sights. We're going to walk around a bit. It's easier to see the sights on foot. Remember what we used to say? 'Blink while driving through Co-manche and you'll miss the whole damned town.' "

Jake chuckled. "That's for sure. Well, you be careful now, y'hear? Don't hurt yourself in the dark."

Jake stood to one side, still eyeing the woman who stood in the shadows. Intrigued by her quiet behavior, he kept trying without success to remember where he'd seen her face. Just as Morgan started to walk away, it dawned on him.

"Hey, Tallchief!"

Morgan paused, and turned.

"I just remembered who your lady friend reminds me of. Do you remember Kath—"

The words stuck in his throat. All too late, he remembered that the woman on his mind had been Morgan Tallchief's sweetheart—and that she'd died in that awful fire just before their graduation. His mouth dropped as he stammered and stuttered, moving backward toward his cruiser.

"Uh, I, uh . . . never mind," he mumbled. "You two have yourselves a real good time. Tell James I said hello. Maybe I'll see you again before you leave."

He jumped in his cruiser and sped away, leaving Morgan and Kathleen behind with the ghost he'd inadvertently resurrected.

Morgan slid his hand beneath the fall of hair on Kathleen's shoulders, gently squeezing at the tension in the back of her neck.

"Come on, sweetheart, I have a need to move."

Her smile was bittersweet as she gazed up at him. "Just don't start running, or you'll leave me far behind."

"No, Kathleen, I would never leave you."

That's right. We both know I'm the one who left. But she never uttered the words that would mark the guilt she carried. It would serve no purpose. She was determined that tonight should be the beginning of a whole new chapter in their lives.

Two blocks down and one block over exhausted what could be considered the business section. Upon turning a corner, they entered into the residential part of town.

Frame houses, brick houses. Old houses, new houses. Neatly kept yards, yards that were sorely in need of attention. Fences varied from chain-link to white picket to hedgerow. Some were neat, some hung by little more than a promise to be fixed.

The scent of charcoal briquettes and cooking meat filled the air. A dog barked. A cat squalled in response. Music from a stereo drifted out of an open window somewhere down the street, adding to the resonance.

Kathleen absorbed it all, reveling in the warm night air upon her face and the familiar sounds of small-town living. On impulse, she grabbed Morgan by the arm, urging him to stop.

"Wait," she said, and then closed her eyes.

"What is it?" he asked.

"Peace. Just listen to the peace."

My peace comes from being with you, Morgan thought as he looked at her, studying the shadow and shape of her face as she tilted it to the moonlight. Certainty filled him. They'd done the right thing by coming back to where it all began.

Moments later, she opened her eyes and sighed, a small, relaxed smile upon her face.

"That was nice," she said softly.

Too moved to speak, Morgan took her by the hand as they began moving through the quiet streets of Comanche. It wasn't until they'd turned another corner that Morgan paused, staring intently down a sidewalk devoid of lights. At first, Kathleen thought he was only being careful about walking into the dark, and then she started to take notice of where they were. It was the shortcut to her old home, a familiar path they'd taken many, many times before.

With a start, she wondered if he was aware of their location, but when he neither spoke nor looked in her direction, she let it slide. The only contact between them was the firm but gentle grip he had on her hand.

A short distance away, she suddenly stopped, surprised by what she saw.

"Morgan, look! Someone put up a fence around the old Delroy place." She leaned across the padlocked gate, peering into the thick, murky shadows. "That's odd. I don't think anyone lives here, so why would they want to fence the place off?"

He dug in his pocket, pulling out the ring of keys James had given him before they'd left the house. Within moments, he'd dropped the padlock into her hands, then opened the gate and walked inside the yard, pulling her in behind him. He turned.

"The place is mine, Kathleen. I bought it years ago. James and his boys fenced it off for me. They keep it mowed and the hedge clipped so it won't overtake the whole property." He waved a hand toward the rose of Sharon hedge, more than six feet high and heavily laden with sweet, flowering blossoms.

"But the house—"

He interrupted. "—is empty. Just like me."

No. Oh no. Please don't say that to me. Not here. Not now. "Morgan . . . I don't know what to—"

He brushed his mouth across the surface of her lips, neither asking nor demanding a thing from her except her presence. Then he smiled. It was a small, slightly crooked smile, but it nevertheless broke her heart.

"Ssh," he said. "It doesn't matter. Not anymore. Regardless of the reason, we're together again."

He took the padlock from her hands and threaded it back through the chain, locking the world out and them inside, then led her along the edge of the thick, impenetrable hedge until they were deep inside the yard with nothing but a sliver of moonlight by which to see. By the time they stopped, Morgan's gut was in a knot. He wondered if she remembered the place as vividly as he did. He'd been here a thousand times in his dreams, and oddly enough, coming back hurt less than he would have believed.

He pointed at the thick carpet of clover on which they were standing. "This is where it began, Kathleen. Right here. You lay down in sweet grass and gave me the world." Then he turned away, unable to look at her. "Did you know that the town had a memorial service for your family?"

Kathleen could only whisper. "No, I didn't."

"I didn't go. I came here instead."

She reached out, wanting to take away the pain that she'd unintentionally caused.

"Why, Morgan? Why did you shut yourself off from everyone who cared for you? Why did you stop running? You could have been famous. And the Olympics . . . they were already talking about—"

He spun around, grabbing her by the shoulders and trying not to shake her.

"What would I have wanted with a medal when I couldn't have you? Winning wouldn't bring you back, and there was no way in hell I could take a prize for running, when I hadn't been fast enough to save the person I loved most."

Kathleen looked up at the man who held her. He was so tall. So proud. And he'd been so hurt. Tonight, she'd been given a second chance to heal what she and fate had done to him. She stepped back and out of his arms. As he watched, she began to unbutton her shirt.

The ache in his heart took a nosedive south. Every muscle in his body went on alert. He got the same feeling he had during his years in the SEALs, right before someone yelled "duck."

"Kathleen . . . what the hell are you doing?"

"Starting over."

She took his hand and guided it beneath the opening on her shirt.

He jerked as the soft, smooth globes of her unbound breasts filled his palms. Breath hung at the back of his throat, caught between a sigh and a moan. Sixteen years rolled away as if they'd never been, and Morgan found himself as helpless to exert caution now as he had been before. With a grunt, he pulled the shirt away from her body, giving himself a full and unfettered view of the woman she was, but looking wouldn't be enough for the man he'd become.

The world in which they stood began to shrink until there was nothing before him but the ivory body of a woman in wait, bathed in a glimmer of moonlight.

One of them moved, but neither would remember who'd taken the first step. There were no words, no promises, no thoughts of control, only the sensation of cool, thick clover against suddenly bare bodies, soft gusts of warm air, melting them to each other. Urgent kisses, slow breaths. No longer the children they'd been, man took woman, body to body, attuned to an inner rhythm only they could hear.

He burned, his manhood fully extended as it thrust against the soft planes of her belly, waiting for an invitation. When his head dipped toward her breast and his tongue encircled a hard, brown peak, she gasped, then dug her fingers into his hair, trying, without success, to hold on to the dark, spiky strands.

Her invitation had come, and there was no need for

a response, because he was already there. One swift thought of what he was about to do suddenly swept through his mind.

"No protection," he gasped, as he slid deep inside.

"No need," she whispered, and wrapped her legs around him.

And then there was no time to dwell on what she'd meant. Cognizant of nothing but what he was feeling, Morgan rocked within her, testing the unexpected tightness, remembering before, and the way she'd taken him in and pulled him under. And, just like before, he lost everything but his mind in the sweetness of Kathleen.

His voice shook and his body burned as he buried his face in the curve of her neck and himself inside her. It had been so very, very long. The sensation overpowered him as he whispered near her ear.

"Oh, God, oh, God . . . just like before."

Kathleen soared within his arms. She felt light, weightless, driven to take all that he gave and give back all that she was. Her hands moved across his back, tracing the power of the man, following the ebb and flow of his muscles as they bunched and then released. Over and over, like water lapping at a shore, he came and went within her until her body began to tense and her mind began to whirl.

She'd almost forgotten the sensation of loss of self. That moment when love spills, one into the other. The mindless pleasure of climax with him still deep inside. When it came, she thought she was ready. She was wrong. She gasped, clutching at him in sudden fear as her shameless body overcame her sane mind.

Morgan knew when she lost control, and savored

the knowledge that he'd been the one to bring her joy. Moments later, he followed, riding the high all the way down. He had no idea how long he lay within her arms. But when he could think without wanting to cry, he became aware of Kathleen's hands on his face and her words flowing past his ear.

"No one but you. No one but you."

He levered himself up, resting upon his elbows as he gazed down at the woman he loved.

"There's no one but you in my life, either," he said softly, and moved a misguided strand of her hair from the corner of her lips.

She shuddered, still stunned by the power with which he'd swept her away.

"No, you don't understand," she said, and laid a palm against his cheek, forcing him to look at her until he fully understood. "For me, there's never been another man . . . ever. You were my first. Tonight was the second time I've ever made love."

Her admission stunned him. He hadn't wanted to think about it, but he'd assumed that somewhere within the last sixteen years, there had to have been . . . His thoughts ended abruptly.

"Are you serious?"

She nodded, trying to smile through tears.

"My God," he muttered, and started to look away, suddenly shamed by her faithfulness when he had not done the same.

Kathleen read his reaction clearly. "Don't!" she said, and made him look at her again. "For you, it wasn't the same. I had a reason to stay faithful, Morgan. You weren't the one who died. I was. I didn't expect you to become a monk. You were only eighteen years old." Her smile bathed his face, healing what was left of his guilt. "Besides, when you've had the best, there's no use settling for less. I figured you'd be worth the wait." She pulled him down until their lips were only inches apart. A swift, tender kiss was exchanged. "And I was right."

A grin broke the stark angles of his face, changing it from handsome to nearly beautiful.

"I suppose you're going to expect miracles."

"Only small ones," she whispered, encircling his neck with her arms. "Only small ones."

A brisk wind whipped down the prairie and around the eaves of the sturdy old house, whistling through a half-open window somewhere down the hall. Morgan lay on his side without moving, absorbing the familiar sounds. Kathleen slept close beside him, one arm outflung, the other clutching his hand that rested on her belly.

For him, sleep was impossible. If he'd been at home, he would have been out in the desert, running for all he was worth. But not tonight. Not after what he and Kathleen had shared a few hours earlier. He needed to know that she was close. He needed to know that she was safe.

Every so often, he would lean down and listen for the sounds of her breath, just to make sure that she was all right. Asleep, she looked fragile and helpless, but he knew the appearance to be deceiving. She was one tough lady. And she might be afraid, but she would never let him see it. She'd done all the right things to keep herself and their daughter alive. Even now, by coming to him on little more than trust, she was still waging a war with an unknown adversary, desperate to stay one jump ahead of a crumbling wall of terror. He hated not knowing the face of the man who dogged her life. In the SEALs, the enemy most often was known to them—if not by face, at least by name or that of the country in which they lived. Here, it was like being afloat on a river without benefit of raft or boat while a current swept them farther and farther away from the shore. Helpless. He felt helpless, and it made him mad as hell.

She sighed in her sleep and Morgan shifted, pulling her closer, holding her tighter. He dropped back onto his pillow, letting his gaze roam the shadows of the house that had once been his home.

A dreamcatcher hung above the doorway leading down the hall. Family pictures placed in orderly fashion upon the wall were to his right, and even in the darkness, Morgan could see the white, even smiles of James's sons as they looked back at him from a handmade frame.

His last year's Christmas gift to James and Mary hung in a solitary place of honor above the mantel over the fireplace. He smiled to himself, remembering the difficulties he'd had in shipping it. It was the only actual portrait Morgan had ever done. Even though most of it was in darkness, he could see it as clearly in his mind's eye as if the room had been bathed in light.

So, Grandmother, I came home.

She smiled back at him from the canvas. He could almost hear her say, *I've been waiting.*

A floorboard creaked down the hall, and all of his senses went on alert. It only stood to reason it would be one of the family, but his instincts wouldn't let him assume.

He raised up on one elbow, peering through the

darkness, waiting for another sound. The wind whistled again like the long-lost wail of a motherless child. Another board creaked, and then another.

"Who's there?" he asked, his voice low and demanding.

"Dad? Daddy?"

It was Trish.

"I'm here," he said softly.

"Where's Mom?"

He hesitated only briefly. It would be the first time she saw them together, but it damn sure wouldn't be the last.

"Here . . . beside me."

He heard her hesitate, then he heard her sigh.

"What's wrong, honey?" he asked.

"I think I'm a little bit afraid."

He smiled. His daughter wasn't such a grown-up after all. His voice was just above a whisper as he eased himself away from Kathleen and sat up in bed. As he moved, she stirred restlessly, somehow sensing that he was no longer as near.

"Do you want to sleep in here with your mother? If you do, I'll take Michael's bed. It won't be the first time my feet have hung over the end."

"No, don't leave," Trish begged, as she tiptoed to the side of the bed.

It didn't take Morgan long to discern her intent. He leaned over Kathleen and pulled back a corner of the quilt. Trish crawled in quickly, a little afraid that the offer might be rescinded.

Morgan rearranged the covers, and then moved a bit to the side so that there was enough room for the three of them.

"Is that better, honey?"

He heard her sigh. "Yes, thanks."

Quiet enveloped them, and Morgan thought she had drifted off to sleep when one last whisper broke the stillness of the house.

"Dad?"

"Yeah?"

"Is that your grandmother?"

He realized she must be looking at the portrait over the fireplace.

"Yes."

"I wish I'd known her," she said softly.

Ah, God, I wish that you had too. "You have her smile."

"I do?"

Kathleen stirred, and he could tell that their whispers were beginning to wake her.

"Go to sleep," he whispered.

"Dad?"

He grinned to himself. "What?"

"Good night."

"Night, honey."

"I love you," she added softly.

In the quiet of the night, in the darkness of the house in which he'd been born, his world rocked for the very last time, coming to rest in a very safe place.

"I love you, too," he answered, and closed his eyes before the tears began to fall.

Trish savored the words, letting them roll through her mind over and over like chocolate over her tongue. The wind played another mournful note, but this time, she didn't mind.

Tonight had been a milestone for Patricia Walkman. She'd finally come to terms with who she was. No longer did she wonder about her brown skin and dark hair. No longer did it matter that her face was so different from her mother's.

She looked like these people. She even smiled like them. As she absorbed the knowledge, the strangeness of her surroundings no longer seemed to matter. Here, in the house where her father had once lived, she began to feel safe. These were people who cared about her.

Trish glanced toward the opposite side of the bed to the man who lay beside her mother, then she sighed and smiled, shifting within the nest she'd made for herself and savoring the fact that they belonged to each other. Her father's eyes were closed, but his arm was reaching out to her mother—and now to her. She sighed again. The next time the wind whistled throughout the rooms, she didn't even hear it. Her nervousness was replaced with a vast sense of peace. As she drifted to sleep, a maverick thought was the last to leave her mind.

So this is what family is like.

Twelve

The sun was not shining the day of Lester Bryant's funeral. A cold gray mist dappled the shiny surface of his coffin as mourners gathered beneath their umbrellas to hear a minister extol his attributes one last time. Fellow agents who'd come to pay their respects stood out from the crowd like raisins on rice. They wore matching expressions and matching suits and took more than the normal interest in the people around them. Distrust and suspicion had, for them, become a way of life.

Marco Benini watched the ceremony from behind the tinted windows of a nearby limousine, secure in the knowledge that his presence might be noted but not his identity. He was awash with anger as he wished Lester Bryant a happy journey to hell. Thanks to Lester's untimely death, Benini's search for justice was over, unless a miracle occurred. Somewhere out there was a man who, more than likely, knew where

Julie Walkman was, but Benini had no way of knowing who he was or how to contact him. Only Lester had known.

There was an old saying, "You can't take it with you." Benini cursed beneath his breath as he watched two soldiers fold the flag that had been draped over Lester Bryant's coffin, then hand it to his wife. Unfortunately for Benini, Lester was the exception to that rule. He *had* taken one thing with him: Julie Walkman's whereabouts.

Blood gathered beneath the surface of Benini's skin as frustration came to a boil, making the smooth, olive cast dark and ruddy. The years of listening to his father berate the system and everyone in it had instilled an unparalleled passion and hatred for any authority other than his own. Thanks to Lester Bryant's death, there was no one left to threaten. He felt helpless.

The last conversation he'd had with Bryant kept rolling around in his head, and Bryant's accusation stung now, more than ever. It wasn't easy to accept the blame for giving Julie Walkman a reason to run. But he *had* made that call—not because he really believed she'd knuckle under to his demands, but because he'd wanted to hear the fear in her voice. He cursed again, only louder, and motioned for his driver to move on. He'd seen all he'd come to see.

Caldwell entered the director's outer office. Ruth, his secretary, looked up.

"He's waiting for you, Bobby."

"Just like I'm waiting for you," Caldwell quipped.

One of her eyebrows arched. Not much, but enough to give Caldwell hope. He leaned forward, bracing the flat of his hands on the front of her desk, and gave her his best bird-dog smile.

"So, Ruthie, is there anything you'd like to tell me?'

She swiveled her chair, returning to the ever-present work on her computer screen. "Your fly is undone."

He flushed, then grinned as he pushed away from her desk and reached for the zipper, telling himself this might very well be considered progress. At least she'd looked.

He pushed his way into the director's office, swaggering as he went.

"So, we're back in the saddle, so to speak," Caldwell said, and dropped the keys to the star car onto the boss's desk. "I got your message. I hear we got a match on the fingerprint we lifted from the flashlight battery."

The director nodded, then pointed. "Turn off that light, will you?"

Caldwell did so, then took a seat. A click and a whir signaled the onset of the slide show. The director's voice rose and fell in cadence with each picture that appeared on the blank wall opposite his desk. When the first picture appeared, Caldwell stared intently, measuring the enemy.

"This is our man," the director said. "A gun for hire named Joaquin Candelero. Age forty-two. Born and raised in Guadalupe, Mexico. Parents drowned trying to cross the Red River during flood stage when he was three. Wetbacks in the true sense of the word."

Caldwell frowned. Making light of people's deaths, no matter how ironic, didn't set well with him. He made no comment, nor did the director expect one. Their eyes were locked upon the swarthy but handsome face of the man in the picture, studying the secretive set of his expression as well as taking note of the shoulder holster just visible beneath the edge of a windblown jacket. The projector clicked, the motor whirred softly. Another slide moved into place.

"After his parents' death, Candelero was raised by his maternal grandmother. This picture was taken during a *Cinco de Mayo* celebration in Guadalupe about three years ago. That's her on the right of Candelero. The taller woman on his left is unknown, but we think it was probably just his woman of the moment. He fancies himself quite a ladies' man."

"What do we know about him?" Caldwell asked.

The projector whirred. Another picture slid into place.

"Just that he's for hire to anyone with the money, and that he's been picked up more than once but never charged. Do you recognize the man on Candelero's left?"

Caldwell squinted. The man was in profile, but the face was too familiar too miss.

"Holy sh— Is that Fidel?"

The director nodded. "Either him or a double. We have no idea what the two were doing together, but we do know that soon after this picture was taken, one of Miami's loudest Castro opponents was shot down in cold blood just outside his office in Little Cuba, and that a week later, Candelero bought his grandmother a new house. Understand, I'm not saying Castro paid for a hit, I'm just saying that the timing is more than interesting."

Caldwell's eyebrows arched as he absorbed the fact that a hit man would spend money on someone other than himself. Knowing a bad boy's weak spot always helped.

"So, he loves Grandma, does he?"

The director nodded. "With a passion. There was a rumor a while back that someone insulted Candelero's grandmother by insinuating that she was living on blood money. The man wound up being buried with a Colombian necktie as an accessory."

Caldwell shuddered. Just thinking about the act made him wince. He'd only seen it done once, but once was enough. It was hard to forget a man whose throat had been cut and whose tongue had been pulled through the slit and left hanging on the outside of his neck like a bloody red tie.

"Damn," Caldwell muttered.

"Turn on the lights, will you?"

Caldwell did as he was told. He walked back to the desk, lightly rubbing at his eyes as they adjusted to the stark white illumination of fluorescent lights. The director's anger was obvious as he braced his hands upon the desk and leaned forward.

"Caldwell, I want to know what in hell a man like Joaquin Candelero was doing in one of my cars. And . . . I want to know what his connection is, or rather was, to Lester Bryant. You've got a starting point. The grandmother in Guadalupe. Go pay a visit to your Company golfing buddy. See if they can't get some men on this right away. If Candelero is anywhere in Mexico, I want him picked up and questioned. And tell them I want some answers. If I had a dirty agent working under me, I want to know before the god-damned media gets news of it first, understood?"

Caldwell nodded. Using the resources of the CIA to

investigate outside the territories of the United States of America was protocol. The FBI had no jurisdiction outside of the fifty states, but that was where a Company man's jurisdiction began.

"Yes, sir," he said, and made a quick exit. A short while later, he walked out of a different office with a satisfied smile on his face. One phone call, and wheels were set in motion. If Candelero was anywhere within the boundaries of Mexico or points south, they would soon know it.

For now, all they could do was wait.

Midmorning sun beat down upon the hood of his car as Morgan loaded their bags into the trunk. He glanced at his watch, making note of the time and calculating how long it would take them to drive back to Oklahoma City to catch their flight.

The front door opened, and he looked up. Kathleen came out with Trish at her side. They were both trying hard to be brave, but the fear on their faces was evident, and there was little he could do to make it better. The resolution of their parting had to come from them. He gave them a thoughtful glance, then busied himself with the baggage, wincing as he accidentally bumped the inside of his arm against the edge of the trunk. He pushed up his sleeve to look.

Earlier this morning, Morgan and Kathleen had gone for blood tests. All that remained of the trip was a small, dark puncture on the inside of his arm—that and the marriage license stored safely inside James's desk.

They'd waited for the results within the quiet confines of the doctor's office, giving one another silent but telling glances. Later, they'd stood before the Stephens County court clerk, waiting again while she prepared the application for their marriage license, and found themselves at a loss for words. Morgan knew Kathleen was hurting, but there was little he could do to make this better. This should have been a day of joy, but no one was smiling. He cursed beneath his breath and slammed the trunk shut.

Kathleen turned at the sound, focusing on the expression on his face and then looked away, trying not to imagine what he must be thinking. Their arrival had turned his life upside down. This morning in the court clerk's office, she'd wanted to cry. After what they'd shared last night, applying for a marriage license should have been easier. Instead, it seemed to have made it worse. Making love with him again had been a reminder of too many years gone wrong.

Once, a long time ago, she'd believed she would one day marry Morgan Tallchief, and now that it was happening, it should have made her happy. She wasn't. She still couldn't get past the idea that it was for all the wrong reasons. His offer had been genuine, but it had not come out of undying passion. It had come out of fear of losing her and their daughter. A marriage should be based on love, not necessity or panic.

Trish shuffled beside her, and Kathleen took a deep breath, unable to think about Morgan right now. Leaving Trish behind was scaring her to death. The girl was clinging to her tightly and Kathleen was valiantly trying to hide her own emotions. If her daughter knew how panicked she really was they'd never be able to leave her behind. So she turned and hugged her, trying to be calm while coming to terms

with the fact that Trish was going to be out ot her sight
for two whole days.

"Are you sure you don't mind?" Kathleen asked,
nervously brushing at a flyaway strand of her daughter's hair and fiddling with a button on her shirt.

Trish was worse than nervous. She'd never spent a
night away from her mother, ever. Although she felt
safe enough here within family boundaries, the
wrench was more than a little frightening, but she
wouldn't let on. She'd overheard more of her parents'
conversation on the way to Comanche than they'd believed. If going back to Seattle might help their cause
in any way, she was willing to do her part to make that
possible. She glanced past her mother to Morgan and
took heart in the easy wink he gave her as he walked
up. It gave her the strength to smile.

"Relax, Mom. I swear I don't mind. Uncle James and
Aunt Mary are great, and so are the guys." Then she
suddenly threw her arms around Kathleen's neck, trying valiantly not to cry. "Besides, I want to get better
acquainted with everyone. At least with Dad's family,
I don't look out of place."

Kathleen was stunned by the offhand remark. She'd
never known that Trish even thought like that. While
she was struggling with something to say, Morgan
stepped in before more than feelings got hurt.

"Hey, girl, that's no way to talk," he said lightly,
smoothing at the same wayward strand of hair that
had been bothering Kathleen. "Pretty women are
never out of place."

Trish beamed, and the uneasiness of the moment
was broken as James came outside.

"Are you ready to leave?" he asked.

Morgan exchanged a look with Kathleen before he answered. "As ready as we'll ever be."

Still, Kathleen couldn't let go. "James . . ."

He turned, his attention completely focused on what she'd left unsaid.

"I will take care of her. While she is in our care, she will be like our daughter. And day after tomorrow, you will come back to get ready for your wedding."

Kathleen managed to smile. She was still struggling with composure when Mary Tallchief came out of the house with Douglas and Michael at her side. The boys went toward the garage to get the family car as a brisk, Oklahoma wind lifted the hem of Mary's skirt, then flattened it against her legs. Mary seemed to ignore it as well as both men as she walked straight toward Kathleen. Impulsively, she hugged her. The show of affection surprised Kathleen.

"We will take good care of her," Mary said quietly.

This time, Kathleen's smile came easier. "I know you will. It's just that . . ."

Mary's touch was light, but her words were not. "You are a mother. I am a mother. Just because our children grow older does not mean we worry less."

Kathleen nodded as the knot in her belly began to unwind. They really understood!

Then Mary turned to Trish. "Patricia, we're going into town. Do you want to go with us?"

"Do geese fly south in the winter?" Morgan drawled, as Trish bolted toward the house to get her purse.

James laughed. "Women are all the same, no matter what age, right, little brother? Mention shopping, and they are ready and waiting."

Morgan grinned as Kathleen and Mary pretended great indignation.

A couple of minutes later, Trish came out with her hair pulled back, a clean shirt on, and a small purse on a long strap slung over her shoulder, bouncing against her hip to the sway of her walk.

She gave Morgan and Kathleen one last, quick hug. "Have a safe trip." Then she turned. "I'm ready, Aunt Mary."

At that point, Douglas pulled up behind her and honked. Mary jumped in fright, which was the reaction he'd hoped for. He was grinning broadly as she spun toward the car, a disgusted expression on her face. Before she had time to complain, the wind caught her grocery list, yanking it right out of her hand and sending it skipping across the prairie.

"My list!"

Trish's reaction was instinctive. "I'll get it," and she went from standing still to an all-out sprint.

Trish ran with her chin up and her legs outstretched, focusing entirely upon the list as she ran with the wind, unaware of the stunned expressions of James Tallchief and his family. Both Douglas and Michael crawled out of the car, disbelief etched upon their faces as she flew past them.

"Whoa!" Michael said beneath his breath. "Look at her go!" He looked first at his dad, then at his uncle Morgan. In typical Michael fashion, he said exactly what was on his mind. "Man, oh man, Dad, if you'd been the runner in the family instead of Uncle Morgan, who knows what I might have been."

James gave his youngest son a long, considering look, then drawled, "Boy, you should be thankful you got my good looks, instead. Morgan had to be fast because he was so ugly."

Morgan burst into laughter. Even as a child, he'd had to endure family comments about his handsomeness. The old remark had been his brothers' way of keeping him humble.

By the time Trish came back with her aunt Mary's list, Douglas and Michael were looking upon their cousin with newfound respect. She had a skill they both coveted.

Hours later, Morgan and Kathleen's plane landed at Seattle-Tacoma International. The cab ride from the airport was almost silent. Only now and then did Kathleen bother to point out a place of interest. Morgan had the feeling that although she and her family had lived here for years, she'd never really put her heart into the city, and then at the same time, remembered why. At any given moment throughout her life, she could have been yanked from her surroundings and been forced to assume another new name and identity. She didn't dare care about where she lived, because she never knew if they would stay.

When the cab pulled up in front of the house, Morgan looked at it through an artist's eye and, in spite of its Victorian charm, found it somehow lacking. Even the house had a sense of impermanence. It was set at the top of a hill, with the nearest house several hundred yards to the south. The lawn was a vast, smooth green, but slightly in need of mowing. The shrubs were orderly and clipped. But there were no lawn chairs on the spacious veranda that encircled the house on three sides, no colorful hanging baskets of impatiens that seemed to abound everywhere else in Seattle. No toys, no bikes, not even a mailbox on the street with the inhabitants' name.

Kathleen paused at the curb and looked up as if waiting for an invitation to proceed.

Morgan touched her arm, his voice low and even. "Are you all right with this?"

There was no way she could forget how she'd felt walking into that house and finding everything they owned in disarray. And then the phone call had come and changed the way she'd been living her life. After that, her decision had been clear. There would be no more lies, no more secrets, only an overwhelming need to get to Morgan.

She looked up. "I can face anything with you beside me."

She humbled him. He took her hand, and together they made their way up the walk.

Kathleen thought she was prepared for the sight, but when she opened the door, instead of walking inside, she caught herself backing up, stumbling into Morgan, instead. It was like seeing it again for the very first time. And, as before, her skin crawled as an overwhelming sensation of nausea left her mute and shaking. So she hadn't yet come to terms with the violation of her world.

Morgan caught her before she fell, and then looked over her shoulder into the room beyond. He could almost feel the lingering terror they'd left behind.

He stepped past her and walked inside, unable to believe the total devastation before him. The walls had been stripped of pictures, the shelves denuded of knick-knacks and books. Furniture had been overturned and gouged open, springs and stuffing alike spilled out of frames and cushions like the guts of a disemboweled animal. Pages had been ripped out of books; broken glass poked up and out of the thick pile carpeting like uncut diamonds growing in grass.

"Son of a bitch!"

Kathleen followed him inside, then grabbed at his arm as he started around a sofa that was lying on its back.

"Watch out for that cord!"

Morgan sidestepped an overturned lamp, then set it upright. He'd believed Kathleen's story almost from the start, but here was glaring proof of what had sent her running. This was no ordinary burglary. It was textbook search and seizure.

His mind slid back to the time he'd seen them coming down his road in the dusk. They'd been running from this! He remembered the reception he'd given them and silently cursed himself even more. What made this even worse was the knowledge that when this had been happening to them, he'd been blithely unaware that they'd even existed—that his women had been in danger and he'd been safe in his house, painting some goddamned picture.

"Is anything missing?"

Kathleen paused in the act of picking up a broken photograph.

"Just my peace of mind."

His eyes went flat. The rage within him spilled as he crossed the room and took her in his arms. "I won't let them hurt you." He tilted her face, making her look at him as he spoke. "Last night, you trusted me with your heart. Today, I'm asking you to trust me with your safety. I know coming back here was rough, but I wouldn't have asked if I didn't think it mattered."

She looked past his anger. It wasn't directed at her, but at the situation. What she focused upon was his fear for her, and took heart in the fact that it came because he cared. With a sigh, she relaxed.

"I know that, Morgan, or I wouldn't have come."

He groaned, then lowered his head, catching her slightly off guard. His lips were still hard and angry when they centered upon her mouth, but they softened as she gave herself up to the kiss.

Moments later, they broke apart, desperate for more, yet well aware that this was neither the time nor the place.

Kathleen flattened her hands upon the breadth of his chest, lightly smoothing the fabric of his shirt as she tried to put a mental distance between them.

"Where do you think we should start?" she asked.

In a bed. On the floor. Any damn place but upright, because my legs are already shaking. But Morgan knew that she wasn't thinking of what he was thinking. He caught her hand, lifting it to his lips and pressing one quick kiss on her palm, instead, before he let her go.

"Where we're standing, I suppose. Try to look at everything with new perspective, because whatever it was your father might have concealed had to have been simple enough to remain undetected over the years and small enough to hide through all of your moves, right?"

She turned in place, trying to find a good place to start. Her voice was shaky as she glanced back up. "Everything's such a mess."

Morgan drawled, "Look at it this way. They've saved us the trouble of digging through drawers."

She laughed, slightly surprised that she remembered how. "You always did have a way with words."

A sardonic grin spread across his face. "It's not necessary to resort to flattery, Kathleen. I'm already putty in your sweet little hands."

His teasing broke the tension of the moment. Soon they were deeply involved in their search. It was a difficult task, one that took time as well as patience. What made it all the more frustrating was the fact that while they were going through everything within sight, it was like looking through a haystack without knowing if the proverbial needle even existed.

The glow from a streetlight came through the living room sheers, reflecting off the glass shards imbedded in the carpet and glittering like the moon on dark water. Kathleen stood in the hallway at the edge of the carpet, gazing back into the room with an expression of defeat. She and Morgan had been through this house twice and hadn't found a thing out of the ordinary, let alone worth killing for. It only stood to reason the thieves hadn't found whatever it was they'd been looking for or she would never have received that call.

What was it, Dad? What do they want? Why didn't you tell me before it was too late?

Morgan called out to her from the kitchen, pulling her back into the present.

"Want any more pizza?"

"No thanks," she said, wondering if Trish was all right, then wondering if they would ever be all right again.

A cabinet door thumped shut. The sound of running water came from the room behind her. She turned away from the devastation before her and walked back into the kitchen.

Morgan was standing at the sink with his back to the door. She looked at him for the longest time, noting the breadth of his shoulders and the length of his legs, and letting herself remember the power with which he'd taken her, remembering the fresh scent of sweet clover crushed beneath her body as he'd given her all his weight. Her spirit ached for a renewal of the passion he'd shown. She was so tired of being afraid. She wanted to forget everything but the way it felt to come apart in his arms, and then be reborn in the love she saw deep in his eyes. She wanted Morgan Tallchief in a way she'd never wanted before.

Long minutes passed before she realized he was no longer moving but was standing at the sink staring out the window before him, into the darkness beyond. It took a while longer before she realized he wasn't looking into the night, but at her reflection instead, using the dark beyond the glass as a mirror. Her breath caught, then released as she exhaled on a slow, anxious note.

He hadn't even known she was there, not until he'd absently looked up and seen her reflection behind him. Then he'd been unable to tear his gaze away from the changing expressions on her face. His hands shook as he braced himself against the counter, remembering when he'd seen her look like that last. She'd been flat on her back beneath him, and he'd been far enough inside of her body never to want to come out. Without waiting for her to speak, he shut off the faucet and turned.

Kathleen swayed on her feet as she realized what

he'd seen. Water dripped from his hands. Fire burned in his eyes. He started toward her, unsnapping his shirt as he came.

At the same moment he reached her, she flipped off the light, leaving them bathed in nothing but the after-glow of streetlights beyond these walls.

His hands centered at her waist, then moved up-ward, mapping her contours, with a gentle but per-suasive touch. When he got to her face he paused, tracing the tilt of her nose, then the shape of her mouth with a fingertip.

"Your face, your beautiful, beautiful face."

She sighed and leaned forward, giving herself up to the inevitable. Her hands spread the edges of his shirt open, then slid to the smooth, tight flesh beneath. Her palms flattened before moving downward from the breadth of his chest to his belly, lingering longest on the belt buckle that kept him out of her reach.

"Make love to me, Morgan. I don't want to think. I just want to feel."

Moments later she was in his arms. His voice rum-bled against her ear like distant thunder. "Where?"

She wrapped her arms around his neck, holding tight to the only anchor she had left. "Anywhere, Mor-gan, just as long as you're there."

Seconds later, he laid her gently upon her bed, toss-ing pillows aside as he followed her down.

A long time later, the quiet sounds of a woman's soft laugh and a man's low groan drifted throughout the house, only to be swallowed up by the darkness. To any passerby, the house seemed at rest, like the people who would soon sleep within.

But outside on the street, another set of circumstances was developing. Private detective Autrey Griggs couldn't believe his eyes. Tonight, he'd seen lights inside the house on the hill. There hadn't been lights in that house for nearly a week. He sat in his car, halfway down the block from the house, debating with himself as to the wisdom of calling his boss now or waiting to ID the people first.

What if they're just relatives? What if they're nothing but house sitters? What if Julie Walkman already sold the house and it's someone totally unrelated?

Just thinking about giving Marco Benini false information made him shudder.

Resolving to wait, he settled down in the front seat, pulling his jacket a little tighter around him and searching for a comfortable spot in the compact's tiny interior.

Thirteen

Consciousness came to Morgan without warning. One breath he'd been sound asleep with Kathleen in his arms, and the next, he was wide awake and searching unfamiliar shadows inside the room for a reason.

It hadn't come from Kathleen. She was sleeping peacefully, tucked into the curve of his body. For a moment, he lay without moving as he listened for something that would signal an alarm. Although he heard nothing, too many years of experience warned him not to ignore his instincts.

Careful not to awaken Kathleen, he slipped his arm out from beneath her head and rolled out of bed. Within seconds, he'd pulled on his jeans and was starting out of the room when he looked down at his bare feet and remembered the glass still imbedded in the living room carpet. He went back for his boots.

He walked through the house, quietly reorienting himself with the layout as he searched for a sign of intruders. Moving slowly and without sound, he made a thorough sweep, finally satisfied that nothing was amiss. Still disturbed by the suddenness with which he'd come awake, he went to the living room window and started to look outside when caution resurfaced. Glass crunched beneath the soles of his boots as he stepped to one side and then shifted the curtain ever so slightly.

The hill upon which the house was sitting gave Morgan a bird's-eye view of the city beyond. In the distance, the never-ending traffic on the highway beyond was little more than a ribbon of lights. Closer, the Space Needle rose above the Seattle skyline, a modern-day monolith pointing the way toward heaven. Along the block, streetlights burned in orderly succession.

Morgan stood without moving, watching the area with studied intent, looking for something that seemed out of place.

At the foot of the hill, a car turned a corner, the engine accelerating as the driver started up the steep incline. In the time it took for the car to pass, Morgan had noted year, make, and model, as well as an out-of-state tag. From where he was standing, the license number had not been readable, but he could catch a glimpse of the driver. She was young. Too young, he decided, to be a part of what was happening to Kathleen.

Tension dissipated as he started to step back. He might never have noticed the parked car about a hundred yards down the hill if it hadn't been for the faint glow on the end of a cigarette coming from inside.

His lips thinned as he noticed it was very conveniently parked beneath the only streetlight with a missing bulb.

At the sight, his senses went on alert. Everything he'd learned about Kathleen and Patricia's life came rushing back. Living the lies, existing under the guise of new names and places, the break-in, the phone call, the tracking device on her car. Instinct warned him this was not an innocent incident.

A quick rage moved him. Before he thought, he was out of the door and off of the porch, moving toward the car with single-minded intent. He wanted a name—and a face. He, by God, wanted an end to this dance.

Autrey Griggs was half asleep. His head lolled intermittently, rolling forward, then snapping back as he came and went within the boundaries of being awake. The cigarette he'd lit several minutes ago was hanging from his lip and dripping ashes in his lap with messy irregularity. The windows were up against the chill of night air, while the smoke from his cigarette drifted and swirled around his head like clouds around the distant Mount Rainier. His backside alternated between numb and aching as he shifted uncomfortably in the seat. Right in the middle of a cognizant moment, he remembered how much he hated stakeouts, and then his mind went blank as he drifted off once again.

When his head hit the headrest, the lit cigarette dangling from his lips fell into his lap. A dull pain ricocheted from one eyeball to the other as he opened his eyes and groaned.

Rubbing at the back of his head, he happened to glance up.

Oh, man! The front door is open! And before he could react, he saw a man come down the steps. Intent on getting a look at his face, Autrey never felt the heat until the lit end of the cigarette had blistered his leg.

"Oh, shit!" he yelped, and began slapping at his crotch, desperate to put out the fire before it did damage to something personal.

When he looked up again, he turned pale, but not from the pain of the cigarette burn. The man had already crossed the yard and was halfway down the street, coming toward him. From the way the man was moving, it appeared he could have mayhem on his mind.

In a panic, Autrey quickly twisted the key in the ignition. Twice the engine sputtered, coughed, then died while he continued to grind on the starter and pump the accelerator, all the while cursing General Motors in succinct and colorful terms. Gas fumes filtered through the ventilation system as his hands began to shake. It was flooding.

He looked up. The man was nearer, and Autrey could see his face—and his build—and his rage. He groaned, then went weak with relief when the engine suddenly caught and fired.

Within seconds of putting it in gear, Autrey stomped on the gas. Only feet from being had, he made a U-turn in front of the man, gunning the engine and speeding down the hill in a wash of fumes and black smoke.

When the car suddenly came to life and spun out in front of him, Morgan actually thought of giving chase. Instead, he watched in disgust as the taillights of the car disappeared out of sight.

"Damn it."

A chilling gust of wind blew into his face, curbing his anger and reminding him of where he was. He took a deep breath as if coming out of a trance, then looked around and couldn't believe what he'd just done. Not only had he disobeyed every rule of covert activity he'd ever learned, but he'd put himself in imminent danger with no means of self-defense. Walking out of the house without a weapon was bad enough, but he'd done it with no backup and without notifying a soul. He thought of Kathleen, asleep in the house behind him, of Patricia, waiting for them back in Oklahoma, of all the wasted years and sleepless nights he was just starting to reclaim. He started to shake.

Lifting his head to the night sky, he inhaled slowly, deeply, reminding himself of who he was and why they'd come.

A brave man is a cautious man.

Morgan wiped a shaky hand across his face as he looked up at the heavens and grimaced.

"Yes, Grandmother, and where were you a while ago when I needed a swift kick in the butt?"

As usual, there was no answer for Morgan other than the one he already knew. Tonight he'd been lucky. Next time—and he had no doubt there'd be a next time—he wouldn't make the same mistake. Next time, they'd never see him coming.

He turned and went back to the house. Only once did he look behind him. The streets were clear, the neighborhood quiet. The bottom step gave slightly as he stepped up on the porch, popping, then creaking, as he headed for the door.

At the sound, he thought of Kathleen and winced.

When he looked up, he realized it was too late to worry about being quiet. She was standing in the door with her gun dangling from the ends of her fingertips, and he was reminded of another night, when she'd met him at his own kitchen door with a gun pointed at his head. Her fear was palpable.

Another persistent breeze off the ocean lifted the hair from her face, outlining her pale, thin gown against her body and giving her a ghostly, sculpted appearance. She staggered, then started to sway.

"Morgan?"

He caught her as she fell. When he lifted her into his arms, he saw she was barefoot and remembered the glass. With a curse, he kicked the door shut behind him as he hurried through the house, desperate to get her into the light and see what damage she'd done to her feet. He laid her down on their bed, switching on the lamp and searching her face for signs of pain. His voice was rough, but his hands were gentle, as he knelt by her side. With dismay he saw small but distinct blood drops seeping from the soles of her feet. "Kathleen, sweetheart, what the hell were you thinking?"

Her huge eyes were fixed upon his face as he inspected the damage she'd done to herself.

"That you might be in danger."

He picked up the gun she'd dropped on the bed, hefting it lightly in the palm of his hand and then staring intently at the expression on her face.

"What were you planning to do with this?"

"If I had to—shoot to kill."

Once again, her courage overwhelmed him. Too moved to answer, he managed a nod, then got to his feet and went to the bathroom in search of tweezers to pluck out the few bits of glass. When he came back he sat down beside her and handed her a handful of cotton balls and a bottle of alcohol, then pulled her left foot across his lap.

"Morgan?"

He paused and looked up.

"Was that man watching the house?"

He dropped a piece of glass on the bedside table. "I wasn't sure, but that was going to be my first question."

Kathleen jerked, but from anger, not pain.

"What the hell were you thinking? He could have killed you."

He looked up with menace, and the cold tone of his voice sliced the air between them.

"Not if I got to him first."

Quiet filled the room as each took the other's measure, both finding strength in knowing they were no longer alone. Finally, Kathleen sighed, and dropped back onto the pillows behind her.

"Okay, Doc, do your stuff."

Morgan lifted her foot for a closer view and then cursed beneath his breath at the task before him.

"I won't cry," Kathleen said softly.

He looked up. "But I might."

Those three simple words delivered the last of her old guilt. She searched his face for a reason not to say what she carried inside and could find nothing.

"I love you, you know."

His hand tightened around her ankle as the words warmed the cold in his heart. She'd said it! She'd finally admitted what he'd known all along!

"I love you, too, girl, and as God is my witness, you might make a good man of me yet."

Devils danced in her eyes, changing dark blue to clear and bright.

"I don't know, Morgan—it's hard to believe you could get much better."

The double entendre was so delightful and unexpected that for a moment he was speechless. And then he grinned.

"One can always· hope," he drawled, and then winked before returning to his task.

She˙bit her lip as he yanked a fragment of glass from between her toes, then sighed as the pain began to recede.

Morgan glanced up, wincing along with her and then breathing easier when she, too, could relax.

"I'm almost through," he said, moving from her left foot to her right.

"Promise?"

His eyes were dark and filled with regret. "God, yes, woman. Anything you want."

"You. I want you."

Lust warred with a level head as Morgan tried to work through her request without losing his mind.

"But sweetheart, your feet . . ."

"Morgan . . ."

"What?"

"I don't plan to stand."

It didn't take him long to finish.

For the first time in a long, long time, Autrey Griggs took a gun to bed. He knew it was a stupid act. The man he'd left behind was half a city away and there was no way Griggs could be traced. As always, he made a point of removing his license tag before starting a stakeout. At this moment, it was lying on the floor of the backseat, conveniently within reach should he have been stopped by the Seattle police.

Still, the cold, hard barrel of the snub-nosed revolver felt good in his hands as he slid it beneath the pillow. When he crawled into bed and pulled up the covers, instead of relaxing, he suddenly kicked at the end of the bedclothes in frustration. Stupid cleaning woman. She always tucked his sheet in at the bottom. How many times had he told her he didn't want his toes squashed?

The notion was a holdover from his childhood. A memory of always having to wear hand-me-down shoes. The damn things never had fit right. To this day, he hated anything tight on his feet.

When the covers were the way he liked them, he began to relax, lying wide-eyed and sleepless as his thoughts returned to the task at hand. What should he say to Marco Benini? He had to tell him something. Granted, he hadn't actually seen Julie Walkman, but someone had been in her house, and he'd gotten a better-than-average look at his face. Marco would want to know.

He shuddered, remembering the rage on the big Indian's face and how close he'd come to being caught in the act of spying. Oh, he'd had a good excuse to use if he'd been caught. Autrey was a man who always planned ahead. But something told him that the Indian wouldn't have waited to hear what he'd had to say. He had a very distinct feeling that he'd come real close to extinction tonight, and he didn't like the thought.

He rolled over in bed, squinting at the clock on the wall, then calculating the time difference between here and New York. Too late here. Too early there. Good. He'd have time to catch a short nap.

He jammed the pillow beneath his head, rolling it and scrunching it until he had it just right, then wished he'd thought to shave before he'd gotten into bed. Three-day-old whiskers itched. But the notion passed as weariness overcame him. By the time he awoke, it was long past noon.

Sunlight streamed across the bed, warming the skin on Kathleen's arm, invading the dark peace beneath her eyelids as she slowly awoke. For a moment, she lay without moving, absorbing the fact that she was in her own bed but no longer alone. She stretched slightly, wincing as a tender spot on her foot brushed against the covers. Then she remembered last night and turned to watch the man who slept on his side with his face turned toward her.

The sunshine resting upon the side of his cheek gave it the appearance of having been bronzed. She looked her fill, mesmerized by high cheekbones, a proud nose, and that wide, sensuous mouth. Her gaze fixed upon it as she shuddered with longing, remembering the feel of his lips against her skin.

His broad shoulders rose above the covers, partially shading her from the sun's early-morning rays. Pinned to where she lay by the long, strong arm thrown across her body, Kathleen welcomed the weight, taking comfort in the anchor he'd become in her life. He stirred, and she felt the length of his leg against her body and thought of his grace, of how he moved when he walked—and when he ran.

Dark eyebrows arched naturally above matching thick lashes. Hair as black as jet radiated a heat she yearned to touch, but again, she remembered last night and relented. They hadn't slept much after he'd removed the glass from her feet. Not wanting to disturb him, she let herself be satisfied with just looking.

God, how she loved him!

She sighed, momentarily closing her eyes and settling deeper into the mattress. A few seconds later, she blinked and looked up. He was staring down into her face. Silence grew as she watched his eyes grow dark, then darker still. His mouth firmed, his nostrils flared. She heard him whisper her name and then he rolled, coming to an uneasy stop atop her body. Once more, her name left his lips, and when it did, she lifted her arms and opened her legs and made room for him to come in.

He did, but with a groan, then a sigh.

They moved, one unto the other; with love, but also with a certain sense of desperation. Last night their union had been gentle and easy, a slow-building passion that took time to catch fire. This morning they burned like the sun beaming down on their faces as they gave up to the lust, slamming their bodies against each other with selfish intent.

Kathleen moved with the ride, her eyes closed as she concentrated on the hammer of flesh against flesh, of a stringy, jerking pulse trying to find rhythm inside a swiftly fading mind, of his breath on her face, his sweat on her brow.

Climax hovered at the edge of insanity, teasing, taunting. Blood raced, swelling within her and pushing at walls that were bound to give way.

And then he tensed and Kathleen knew the end was near. Clutching at him with both hands, she wrapped her legs around his waist and lifted herself to the thrust. It was, for both of them, the final stroke. He buried his face beneath her chin and groaned.

Walls gave. Sense shattered. Honey flowed.

Morgan felt stunned. It wasn't the actual act of making love that had scared him, it was the fact that for a short while, he'd lost his sense of self. Just at the point of climax, he'd imagined his soul spitting out with his seed. The sensation had been overwhelming, and for a moment, he actually believed that he'd died. He hadn't been prepared for his next breath, but when it happened, it came with a groan.

Surprised to find himself still of this earth, he encircled Kathleen with both his arms and rolled, taking her with him.

His words were broken—disjointed bits and pieces of himself as he smoothed her hair from her face and his hands across her skin. "Love you . . . love you so damned much. So much it hurts."

He heard her sob.

"Ah, God . . . don't, baby, don't."

She couldn't stop.

"Sssh," he urged, sweeping his broad strong hands down the length of her back, soothing her as he would have a child. "Sssh," he whispered again. "It's okay, it's okay."

"No," she sobbed, as she held him tight. "No, it's

not. This feeling between us is so strong . . . so right, but I have the most awful sensation that it can't last. Something or someone is going to take me away from you again. I just know it."

He shoved his fingers through her hair as he rolled again, coming to a stop when he was fully atop her body. His eyes went flat, expressionless. A muscle jerked near his jaw. When she had nowhere to look but at him, he spoke, and the words sent a chill to her heart.

"Then heaven help them—and me—if it happens, because I will kill the man who touches you, so help me God."

The moving van sat at an angle on the high, steep hill, the movers coming and going as they carried what was left of Kathleen's possessions to the truck. Morgan stood watch upon the porch while she dealt with the men inside, pointing out what could be salvaged for them to pack, casting aside what had been irrevocably ruined during the break-in.

It wasn't much, but considering her lifetime on the run, it was all she had, and Morgan insisted it move with her to Santa Fe. Inside the house, the phone began to ring, and Morgan spun instinctively, remembering the phone call before that had sent her running. He was inside the house before she could answer. When he saw her face, he knew she was remembering it, too.

Kathleen answered, then held her breath.

"Ms. Walkman?"

"Uh . . . yes, this is she."

"This is Ron, from Frames and Games. We have

your painting ready to be delivered. May we bring it out?"

She sighed in relief, smiling at Morgan to let him know the call was legitimate.

"Yes, please. Actually, I'd almost forgotten about it." And then she looked at her watch and frowned. "Can you bring it within the hour? I'm in the process of moving. I'd like to take it with me."

"Yes, of course," he said. "We'll be glad to package it for you for moving, at no extra charge. Give us about thirty-five minutes, okay?"

"That will be fine. We'll be waiting," Kathleen said, and turned to Morgan as she hung up the phone. "How fortunate. I'd almost forgotten."

"Forgotten what?"

She started to explain when one of the movers walked past her with a box in his hands. She gave Morgan a long, considering look and then shrugged. "Dad bought me a, uh . . . picture. He was having it re-framed when he died. In all the confusion of the funeral and then this . . ." She waved at the mess in which they stood. "I completely forgot. I only saw it once, but it's not something I would have wanted to leave behind. It's being delivered ready for shipping. If they drive up while I'm inside, just have the movers pack it right into the truck, okay?"

He nodded, wondering about the odd, almost secretive expression in her eyes, and the hesitation with which she'd explained. But then she turned and winced, gasping as she stepped down too hard on one of the cuts on her feet, and he forgot about everything except her well-being.

Seconds later, he had her in his arms and was carrying her toward the kitchen. The broken barstools were already bundled and ready to be discarded by the real estate agent's cleaning crew, so he put her down on the open counter separating the two rooms, leaving her legs to dangle freely down the side.

"Sit! If the men have questions, they can come find you."

Kathleen did, slumping in place and staring around with a slightly dejected air.

He saw her reaction and frowned. "Honey?"

She looked up.

"Are you sorry . . . to be moving, I mean?"

"No! Oh no! It's just . . ."

His hand cupped her cheek. "Just what?"

"My life. It's just like this house. What isn't broken is in a really big mess. Sometimes I wonder if it will ever be straightened out."

He stepped in between her legs and pulled her head to his shoulder, rubbing lightly at a tense spot he felt between her shoulder blades.

"How about concentrating on good things, like our daughter, and the fact that by day after tomorrow, you will be my wife?"

She pulled back, then looked up at him and smiled.

"Morgan . . . darling . . . that last little thing you mentioned won't do squat toward calming my nerves." Her voice lowered as she leaned forward, whispering only inches away from his lips, "I'm still reeling from the way you make love. I don't know whether to take heart in my good fortune, or resign myself to a great, but very short, life."

He grinned. "Remember what they say: 'What a way to go!' " Before she could argue, one of the movers stepped around the doorway. "Hey, lady, do you want us to pack that armoire in the east bedroom? It's only got a couple of scratches on it."

His question quickly broke their mood. Kathleen frowned, then sighed. "I don't know. It's got that long scratch, but it belonged to my mother. I sort of hate to—"

Morgan interrupted. "Pack it," he ordered. "If I can't fix it, I know someone who can."

Kathleen smiled, and for Morgan, it was all the thanks he needed to get them home. A car horn honked from the driveway outside.

"That's probably the man from the frame shop. Just have him set the package inside the van, okay?"

Both Morgan and the man from the moving company nodded at Kathleen's order, each going to complete their tasks.

As Morgan stepped off the porch and into the yard, a cloud suddenly passed between sun and earth, leaving him standing in shadow. It was startling but brief, as the cloud soon moved through the sky. But in that short moment, he froze, his spirit attuned to more than what had actually happened. His skin crawled as he did a slow, 360-degree turn, his gaze searching the unfamiliar landscape in which he stood. Unlike last night, he saw nothing amiss, but he knew it was far from over. He took a deep breath and said a quick prayer against the portent of dark days to come.

Autrey Griggs sat on the side of the bed, methodically picking at a sore on his left knee as he waited for Marco Benini to answer his phone. His stomach growled, reminding him of how long it had been since last he'd eaten, and he stood, taking the portable phone with him as he ambled toward the kitchen.

Six, seven, eight rings, and still the phone continued to peal. He picked up the coffeepot, measuring water and coffee with the absentminded skill of a man who's lived alone all his life, and put it on to perk.

Ten times, eleven times, the phone jangled his nerves.

"Answer, you bastard, or don't blame me if—"

"Hello!"

Expecting a servant to answer, Autrey let the threat die on his lips as he recognized the voice. "Mr. Benini?"

"Who wants to know?"

"It's me, Griggs."

Unmindful of the water dripping from his body, Marco Benini dropped into a black leather chair, cursing beneath his breath as he accidentally slid across the surface before coming to an unsettled stop near the edge. He swiped his beach towel across his wet legs and then gave it up as a lost cause.

Autrey frowned. "Look, if this is a bad time, I can call back."

"Hell, no, talk to me!" Benini growled, mopping at the chlorine-scented water from his pool that was puddling at his feet. "I need to hear some good news today. Everybody who works for me is throwing up their guts. Damn cook gave them food poisoning. It's a miracle I'm not puking right along with them."

Autrey sighed. At least he wasn't the cause of Benini's bad mood. But what he had to tell him might just make it worse.

"I've been watching the Walkman house here in Seattle like you told me," Autrey said.

Benini struggled to sit up. Something in the tone of Griggs's voice told him he was about to get news.

"And? Did you see her? Did the bitch come back?"

Autrey took a deep breath. "I'm not sure."

"What the fuck do you mean, you're not sure?" Benini screamed. "Either you saw her or you didn't!"

Benini's curse rippled through Autrey's eardrum and slithered painfully down his spine.

"I saw someone," he said. "But it wasn't a woman, it was a man. Actually, he was a great big Indian."

Benini frowned. "Indian . . . as in East, West, or Native American?"

Autrey fidgeted. He never had been good at geography. "Uh . . . Indian as in Geronimo, not Gandhi."

"Shit," Benini muttered, uncaring if Autrey heard him or not. "Fools. Everyone I hire is a fool." Then he took a deep breath, refocusing on the matter at hand. "Okay, so you saw this man . . . this Indian. What was he doing at the Walkman residence?"

Coming after my scalp. "I couldn't tell. All I know for sure is, he spent the night there."

"Is he still there?"

"Uh . . . I don't know."

Benini sighed. He didn't want to know, but had to ask. "And why don't you know?"

"Because he made me last night. I had to scram."

"Shit! Shit! Of course he made you. You're a fool! Remember?"

By now, Autrey was sweating. Even though he was on one side of the continental United States, and

Marco Benini in New York on the other, it was still too close to a man with a hair-trigger mind.

"What do you want me to do?" Autrey asked.

"Get back there! Find out who he is, what he's doing there, and if he leaves, I want to know where the hell he's going!"

Autrey rolled his eyes and opened a cabinet, stretching as he reached for an empty cup. "Right! I'm already on it."

"Listen, Griggs, don't mess up again. I'm running out of patience, understand?"

The underlying warning in Benini's voice unnerved him, and the cup slipped out of his hands and onto the floor, shattering at his feet. Autrey looked down in dismay. It was his last clean cup.

"Yes, sir. I understand."

The line went dead in his ear.

"What do you mean, they're gone?"

The cleaning woman stood at the edge of the steps, a mop bucket in one hand, a baseball bat in the other. She took a step backward, waggling the bat at Autrey in a warning fashion.

"Just what I said, mister. Now get. I've got my work to do. The real estate agent needs this place cleaned up by tomorrow, and it's a real big mess."

Autrey sighed. He knew that. He'd been responsible for that. It had been his second mistake. His first had been betting on horses with his boss's money. Getting in debt to a man like Marco Benini was scary. Getting out was proving to be worse.

He took a step back to prove he meant her no harm and grinned, trying persuasion rather than threat.

"Look, I didn't mean to come on so strong," he said, and winked just to show he was true. "It's just such a disappointment. Julie Walkman's old man and me were good buddies. I just heard about him kickin' the . . . uh, I mean, I just heard he died and all." He shrugged. "Little Julie was my goddaughter, you know."

The cleaning woman relented, but only slightly.

Autrey relaxed and gave himself a mental pat on the back. Sympathy. It got them every time.

"I came to pay my respects, and now I'm just sick about this move. I can't lose touch with little Julie. She's just like my own."

The cleaning woman was now leaning on the bat, resting her weight upon it as if it were a cane.

"Well, now," she muttered. "That's too bad." She kept staring at Autrey, taking his measure. A few seconds later, she seemed to come to a sudden decision by starting to explain. "All I know is, they moved everything out that ain't broke. I didn't talk to her myself. She was already gone when I got here."

Oh, damn. Benini is going to pitch a sweet fit. Then he thought. "If she was already gone, who let you in?"

"The agent gave me a key, but I didn't need it," she said. "The movers were still here when I came."

Autrey perked up. Movers? As in van? As in wonderful trucks with business logos emblazoned upon their sides?

"I don't suppose you noticed what company she was using?" he asked. "Maybe I could trace her that way?"

The woman brightened. "I sure did. It was one of them moving vans with the big ship painted on the side."

Autrey beamed, then pivoted, leaving the cleaning woman and her bat alone. This was manna from heaven. He knew a woman who worked for Mayflower. It might cost him a dinner and a night in the sack with the horny old bitch, but it would be worth it just to get Benini off his back.

Fourteen

On the road ahead of Morgan, a pickup loaded with watermelons swerved to miss a coyote running across the highway. As it did, the end gate came loose and the watermelons began to roll. They fell onto the pavement in front of oncoming traffic, bursting open and splattering upon impact, sending juicy red meat and sticky black seeds everywhere. The drivers in the oncoming vehicles began a mobile version of a country two-step, trying to keep from being nailed by the green torpedoes.

Morgan swerved twice, neatly dodging two oncoming melons as well as a jeep loaded with teenagers who seemed to be in hysterics about the entire event. As he bypassed the watermelon hauler who was braking to a stop, he glanced at Kathleen. She was still asleep—worn out from their trip and then the flight home. He grinned. She'd missed the whole show.

And then his mood changed as he thought of what

lay ahead. In less than an hour, they'd be home. By tonight he would be a married man. He thought of the phone call he and Kathleen had made to James just after they'd landed at the airport in Oklahoma City. His grin broadened.

"Hey, James, is Trish okay?" he'd asked his brother.

"She's more than okay, she's great!" had been the reply. "Mary and I are thinking of keeping her. My sons have not been this well behaved since they quit believing in Santa Claus."

Morgan laughed softly beneath his breath, and then glanced at Kathleen, resisting the urge to pull over and kiss her awake. Dear God, but he loved her. In the short time since she'd come back into his life, she'd become as necessary to him as his own heartbeat.

As if sensing she was the subject of serious contemplation, Kathleen moaned, then sighed, shifting restlessly as she slept. Morgan rubbed her shoulder, lulling her back into sleep, then pulled her close.

When she finally resettled, her head was resting on his leg, her bare feet tucked up in the seat. The tiny cuts on her feet were healing nicely. Only a couple of the punctures had been deep enough to cause her pain, but in Morgan's mind, any pain Kathleen bore was too much.

He returned his attention toward the highway, keeping one hand on her shoulder, the other on the wheel, then glanced at his watch, noting the time it would take to get back to Comanche.

He thought of Trish, waiting for them to return. She'd been in his life such a short time, and already he couldn't envision living it without her.

Again his gaze moved back to Kathleen. They had

made a beautiful child together. His gut clenched as he watched her sleeping, and a notion came out of nowhere. He hadn't used any protection when they made love. She'd claimed there was no need. He hadn't asked if it was because she was protected or if it was because she didn't care.

The car swerved as realization struck him. She could be carrying his baby—again. He took a deep breath and eased up on the gas, settling back into a safe, normal speed. Tears burned his eyes as he accepted the notion. When he looked down again, her sweet face was little more than a blur. He wanted to see Kathleen pregnant with their child. His jaw clenched as he looked back at the road. If it happened, at least this time it wouldn't be born without his name.

Many miles later, when they drove through Comanche, Kathleen was wide awake, anticipating the reunion with her daughter. Less than three days ago, when they'd driven this same stretch of road, their lives had been entirely different. He glanced at her and smiled easily.

"It's not so bad this time, is it, honey?"

"What's not so bad?" she asked.

"Coming home."

There was a light in her eyes when she smiled. "No, it's not. This time, I have a reason to be happy."

He reached out and took her hand, pulling her closer until her hair was grazing the edge of his shoulder. He could smell her shampoo as well as a faint whiff of perfume. It was enough to make a good man crazy with want.

"I know it was hard for you to leave Trish behind, but I think it probably did the both of you some good."

She looked vaguely surprised. "Oh, I more than agree with you. That wasn't what I meant when I said I had a reason to be happy."

"Then what?"

"When we marry, I will be shedding the last of a fictitious identity. No matter what the FBI said, I could never make myself believe that Kathleen Ryder, or Julie Walkman, or all the others in between ever existed. Being Kathleen Tallchief is different." She leaned against him, her hand brushing his cheek. "You didn't know when you offered me your name that you would also be giving me back my life."

His heart was full, almost to the point of pain. All he could do was smile at her admission. When he turned down the road leading toward his grandmother's old home, they saw Trish standing on the porch, watching, waiting for them to come home. Even though they were several hundred yards away, he saw the look on her face and the joy in her step as she leaped from the porch and started running down the road to meet them.

He braked to a stop and then sat and watched, marveling at the grace in her stride and the easy speed with which she ran. Emotion filled him. His voice was shaking as he spoke.

"Thank you, Kathleen."

"For what?"

His eyes were on their daughter, but he held fast to Kathleen's hand. "For keeping her, and for bringing her back to me."

"You're welcome," she said quietly.

Morgan cleared his throat, suddenly embarrassed that he'd let her see so far inside his soul. "Guess we'd better go meet her or she'll run her sweet self to death."

They got out of the car, and Morgan waited as Kathleen went to meet her child. By the time Trish made her way to him, he was ready and waiting. She danced into his arms in a whirl of dust and delight and he held her as if he'd never let her go.

Hold fast to those you love.

He tightened his hold as his grandmother's voice slipped into his mind. *I'm trying, Grandmother. I'm doing the best that I can.*

Morgan bolted into the kitchen, holding a string tie in one hand and a vest in another.

Mary Tallchief was standing at the sink. At the sound of his voice, she turned, then smiled. She'd never seen this man so rattled.

"Damn it, Mary, I can't make this tie look right."

She took it from him and dropped it onto the cabinet. "Then don't wear it," she said calmly, and took the vest, holding it out so that he could put it on. She stretched up on tiptoes as she brushed at his hair, trying without success to smooth the short, dark ends back into place.

"Your grandfather's vest is enough adornment. James wore it when we were married. It's good that you will wear it today. It will bring you luck."

Morgan sighed, then caught Mary's hand, squeezing it in thanksgiving and grinning. "Thank you, sister."

Mary arched an eyebrow, then smiled. "You're welcome."

Douglas opened the back door and leaned in long enough to shout, "Mom, a cop just drove up!"

Morgan spun around. His nerves were already on edge, and this didn't help.

"I'll go see who it is," he said.

Jake Ramsey was on his way up the steps when Morgan came out the front door.

"Hey, buddy," Jake said, pushing his hat to the back of his head and grinning from ear to ear. "I heard through the grapevine that you're about to get married. Why wasn't I invited?"

Morgan's gut clenched. *Oh, damn. Talk about a "need-to-know" basis!* Morgan was not yet sure whether he could trust him. He managed a smile. "As you can see, it's just a family affair."

Jake nodded, the grin still wide upon his face. "I was just kidding," he said. "Actually, I'm here on sort-of-official business.

Morgan froze.

"You got a telegram. I volunteered to bring it on out." *Have mercy.* "Thanks," Morgan said. "I appreciate it."

Jake handed it over, then waved as someone hailed him from the backyard. "Wow, looks like you're doing it up right," he said.

Morgan read the message, nodding absently as he absorbed the news.

"Good news?" Jake asked.

Morgan looked up. The smile was back on his face. "The best," he said.

Michael Tallchief came running around the corner of the house. "Uncle Morgan, the preacher needs to see the marriage license. He doesn't know Kathleen's full name. Where is—" At the sight of the policeman, he froze, the rest of the words dangling on the edge of his mind. "Uh . . . never mind, I'll ask Mom."

Morgan's stomach did a nosedive as he looked at Jake Ramsey's face. It was caught between shock and disbelief. For a long, silent moment, the men stared at one another, one waiting for an explanation, the other praying for a revelation.

Jake looked up, expecting Morgan to break into an easy laugh. But the wariness in his old friend's eyes was a red flag to the lawman's instincts. He thought back to the first night he'd seen Morgan, and to the woman he was with who'd stayed in the shadows, and to her face—the face of a girl long dead.

"Morgan . . . ?"

"What?" he growled. The warning was there for Jake to hear. Whether he heeded it remained to be seen.

"You're marrying a woman named Kathleen."

Morgan took a deep breath and then nodded.

"Odd coincidence, isn't it?" Jake asked.

"You could say that," Morgan answered.

Sensing that he was about to be given the runaround, Jake pressed the issue. "Is there anything you want to tell me?"

"Not really."

Jake chewed on the inside of his lip as Morgan Tallchief blatantly shut him out. After a bit, he decided he could accept that. After all, it wasn't against the law to get married. At the point of letting it rest, another member of Morgan's family added fuel to the fire. James's voice bellowed out from somewhere inside the house.

"Morgan! Your daughter is looking for you." Hushed voices came next, and then James uttered one last, succinct word. "Damn."

But it was too late. Jake was already hooked.

"Daughter? You have a daughter? I didn't know you'd ever—"

Suddenly his face got red and he stuffed his hands in his pockets and looked down, drawing his own conclusions about what he'd just heard. He started toward his cruiser.

At this point, Morgan realized that staying silent could make things worse rather than better. He wouldn't have people in his own hometown whispering behind Trish's back because of something he and Kathleen had done in love and in haste years ago. His voice rang out, stopping Jake in midstep.

"Jake!"

He turned. "Look, Morgan. I'm sorry as hell I didn't let this drop. I never meant to—"

"Can I trust you to keep your mouth shut?"

Jake's eyes narrowed suspiciously.

"It's not illegal, damn it," Morgan said "But it could be a matter of people living or dying."

"What the hell have you gotten yourself mixed up in?" Jake asked.

"Righting an old wrong."

Jake leaned against his cruiser and folded his arms across his chest. "I'm waiting."

Morgan glanced up at the house. When he looked back at Jake, it was obvious he'd come to some sort of conclusion.

"That was *my* Kathleen that you saw."

Jake's mouth dropped. "You're crazy! She's dead, Morgan, and don't try to tell me that woman is some crazy reincarnation of—"

"Shut up, Ramsey, and just listen. You're a lawman.

You've got to be familiar with the Federal Witness Protection Program."

Jake nodded. As he looked at the house, his mouth began to go slack. "Are you trying to tell me that . . . ?"

"Kathleen Ryder didn't really die. For that matter, neither did any of her family. They were being relocated, and it wasn't the first time. They'd been in the program since Kathleen was fourteen."

"Son of a . . ."

"My sentiments exactly," Morgan said.

"Then why is she here and not still in hiding?"

"Her father's dead. The man he testified against is dead. The FBI has closed the file. Supposedly, she's safe."

"Supposedly?" When Morgan answered, Jake began to accept the seriousness of the situation.

"They were living in Seattle. About a week after her father's funeral, they came home one day to find the house trashed. Nothing was missing, but everything had been searched. While they were still in shock, someone called and threatened her. That's when she took Trish and ran. She came to me. A couple of days later, I found a tracking device on her car."

"Well, I'll be damned. This is straight out of the movies. You know you could be up against something serious here, don't you, Morgan?"

Morgan nodded, then looked away. Moved by the telling, it took him several deep breaths before he could trust himself to speak.

"Up until a week ago, my life was in limbo. And then I got back a woman I thought I'd lost and a daughter I never knew I had." He looked down at the ground, and then back up at Jake. "I can tell you it's humbling to see yourself in another human being. Kathleen and I are getting married for two reasons. One, because I don't ever want to lose her again, and the other, because we're hoping the name change will throw whoever's after her off the trail."

"So that's why you're keeping this ceremony low-key. In a few hours, Kathleen will be just another Tallchief, right?" He grinned. "And God knows there's plenty of them."

Morgan smiled. "Exactly."

Jake straightened. "You can trust me. I'll keep this close to my chest. You've got my word on that. I assume you're going back to Santa Fe to live."

Morgan nodded.

"Well, if anything fishy happens down here, you'll be the first to know."

"Thanks, Jake. You'll never know how much."

Jake grinned and opened the car door, then watched as Morgan started back toward the house with the telegram in his hand. The man was big, much bigger than he'd been in high school, but he still moved with the natural grace of an athlete.

"Hey, Morgan."

Morgan paused, then turned.

"Your daughter . . . can she run?"

A slow smile broke the solemnness of Morgan's face. "Like a young deer."

Jake grinned as he crawled behind the wheel. It only stood to reason.

"Oh, Mom! You're beautiful!"

Kathleen took a deep breath, her eyes glistening

with unshed tears as she turned away from Trish for a last look in the mirror. The dress had been Trish's idea, and her welcome-home surprise. With James and Mary's help, she'd searched the malls in Duncan with one special style in mind, finally finding it at a boutique in Claridy Creek Mall.

And when Kathleen had opened the closet and seen it hanging inside, she knew her daughter had seen straight to her heart. It was exactly right.

The semisheer fabric was a soft, blue cotton, as pure a blue as the Oklahoma sky. A loose, off-the-shoulder ruffle floated above her breasts, moving with the sway of her body as she walked. The bodice was fitted, while the full, tea-length skirt flirted just above her ankles. She spun once before the mirror, watching with delight at the way the fabric drifted out, then fell into soft, loose folds around her legs. Morgan was going to love it.

As she turned away from the mirror, waning sunlight sliced through the part in the curtains and into her eyes. The day was nearing its end. Already the backyard of the Tallchief homestead was full of family, with more arriving with each passing hour. Mary had done what Morgan had asked. Except for the preacher, there wasn't a single outsider among those present.

Trish pulled a curtain aside and peeked out a window. Although Kathleen was on the other side of the room, her daughter's soft gasp still reached her ears.

"What is it, honey?" Kathleen asked.

Trish spun, her eyes wide with excitement. "Mom! Come look! There's a man out there who looks a lot like Dad."

Kathleen turned. "It's probably his brother, Reid. He and Morgan used to look a lot alike."

Trish savored the knowledge as she continued to look. "Oh, Mom, over by the lilac bush is the prettiest woman. Her hair is almost down to her waist, and it's so thick and black! And, oh, look at the little boy—there in a stroller by Aunt Mary's clothesline!" She giggled. "Just look at his hair. It's sticking up all over his head like grass. Have you ever seen such a cute baby?"

Kathleen crossed the floor, coming to a stop beside her daughter before smoothing her hand down the silky black lengths of Trish's hair.

"Yes, actually I have. Her name was Patricia. She had so much hair I had to braid it to keep it out of her mouth, and she laughed at just about everything except her wet diapers."

Trish dropped the curtain and turned. "I love you, Mom."

Kathleen opened her arms, sighing with satisfaction as Trish settled within her embrace. "I love you, too, sweetheart. So much."

For a time, they were still, satisfied just to be holding one another, but when Trish began to fidget, Kathleen could tell something was bothering her.

"Honey?"

Trish smiled, then looked away.

"What's wrong?" Kathleen persisted.

Trish shrugged.

"Patricia . . . talk to me."

When Trish looked up, her eyes were filled with tears.

"Everyone out there is either a Tallchief or married to one. In a little while, you will be, too. It isn't fair. I don't want to be Patricia Walkman. Morgan is my father. Why can't I have his name, too?"

Before Kathleen could answer, someone knocked on their door. Trish turned away, unwilling to let anyone see her cry. Kathleen was torn between needing to comfort her daughter and answering the door, when another loud series of knocks made the decision for her.

"Who is it?" she called.

"It's me, Morgan. Is Trish with you? I've been looking all over for her."

Kathleen rolled her eyes. "Yes, she's in here, but I'm not supposed to let you in. It's bad luck."

"That's a white man's superstition, not the Indian way. Open the door. I have something to show the both of you."

"Please, Mom?" Trish begged.

Kathleen threw up her hands and went to the door. She yanked it open, then stepped aside. "Just don't blame me if we're forever cursed."

Morgan stepped inside and closed the door. For a moment, all he could do was stare. They were so beautiful, and they were his. One hovering on the edge of maturity, the other waiting for her life to begin all over again.

"Have mercy," he said softly, and touched Kathleen's hair, then her face. His hands were shaking as he tested the soft blue fabric of her dress between his fingers.

"She's awfully pretty, isn't she, Dad?"

The wistfulness in his daughter's voice reminded him of why he'd come. He turned.

"Like mother, like daughter."

Trish lit from the inside out and began fiddling with her own new dress, ironing out imaginary wrinkles on the slim red skirt and fiddling with the spaghetti straps on her shoulders.

"You don't think it's too much?" she asked nervously. "Aunt Mary said it was me."

Morgan pretended to frown. "It makes you look too damned old."

Kathleen hid a smile when Trish turned once again to the mirror, as if testing her father's theory. Bless Morgan. It was the perfect answer.

While Trish was studying her reflection with renewed interest, Morgan leaned down and stole a quick kiss, whispering in Kathleen's ear as he did.

"Forgive me for not talking to you about this first, but somehow I didn't think you'd mind."

"About what?" she asked.

"This," he said, and handed her a telegram.

Leaving Kathleen to read it alone, he crossed the room, coming to a stop just behind Trish.

Trish's gaze shifted from her own reflection to her father's, and for a moment they stared at one another from the mirror. So much alike. Unknowingly, their thoughts mirrored their images. *Our faces are the same, but not our names.*

Morgan put his hands on Trish's shoulders.

"Patricia . . ."

Her gaze shifted. "What is it, Dad? Is something wrong?"

He nodded.

Her face crumpled as she spun around, clasping her hands to her ears in dismay. "Oh no! Please! I don't want to hear it!"

Morgan lifted her hands from her face, gentling her with his voice and his touch. "No, sweetheart, it's nothing like that."

She wilted. "Then what's wrong?"

"You. Me. This whole situation."

Her voice quavered. "I didn't do anything wrong, I swear.".

"I know," he said quietly. "But somewhere along the way, your mother and I did, and for that, you've had to pay a big price." He turned to Kathleen and held out his hand. "May I show it to her?"

All she could do was nod as she laid it in his hand. In turn, he gave it to Trish, waiting as she opened the single sheet of paper and started to read.

ADOPTION PAPERS READY AND WAITING STOP CAN
BE FINALIZED WITHIN DAYS OF YOUR RETURN STOP
SAVE ME A PIECE OF CAKE STOP GREGORY

She gasped, and the look she gave him was one Morgan would never forget. "Gregory is my lawyer," he explained.

Trish's eyes widened. "Is this about me?"

"Of course it's about you," he said gruffly. "I told you I was going to change your names, and I meant it. You're my daughter. I want the world to know it."

She threw her arms around Morgan's neck. "I thought I was going to be left out, but I should have known better. I should have trusted you like Mom trusts you." She squealed in his ear and spun out of his arms, dancing across the room with the telegram clutched tight in her hand. "Wow! This is the absolute best day of my life."

Before he could answer, Mary Tallchief burst through the door, glaring at Morgan in the same judgmental way that she did her four unruly boys.

"I should have known I couldn't trust you to leave them alone," she muttered, pushing and shoving until he was almost out the door. "It's bad luck to see the bride before the ceremony, and you know it."

"He told me Indians didn't believe in such stuff," Kathleen said.

Mary rolled her eyes and then hid a small grin. "Maybe they do, and maybe they don't. The point is, Morgan Tallchief, you never stuck to traditional ways before, and I see no reason for them to suddenly become a means to your ends." She shooed him the rest of the way out the door. "Get! Go find James. Don't let him spike my punch, and if he already has, keep him out of it until the ceremony is over. The last thing you want is your best man at less than his best."

Having issued her orders, she slammed the door in his face, then turned to Kathleen with a huff. "Men!"

The three women laughed. There was little else to be said.

Kathleen stood at the edge of the yard. Although there were dozens of people watching her, she wasn't aware of them. Her gaze was fixed solely upon the man waiting for her beneath a tall, spreading oak.

He stood a head above the rest. The slight breeze stirring moved the soft, sultry air among the crowd who waited with him. His pants were dark, his long-sleeved shirt pristine white and opened at the collar. As she came closer, she could see the detailed beadwork on the brown leather vest he wore over it.

Somewhere to her left, a small child wailed and was suddenly silenced by a yearned-for bottle. Far above them, a jet left its trail in the heavens. In the midst of all the normality, the clear, plaintive trill of an Indian flute suddenly broke the silence in which she'd been walking. She wasn't prepared for the music or for the depth of emotion that could be pulled from such a small piece of wood. The sound tugged at her heart, the notes rising and falling with each step that she took, hanging high on the wind, then ending abruptly, like a bird taking flight.

The melancholy music matched her spirit. By marrying Morgan, she was putting him squarely in the middle of whatever was wrong with her life. She so wanted this to be right, and she was so afraid it would go all wrong.

And still she walked, unable to stop, too much in love to say no. The flute player ended on a last, dying note just as she laid her hand in Morgan's outstretched palm. When his fingers closed around it in a strong, firm grip, she began to relax. All she had to do was remember the love, and everything else would surely be all right.

"Dearly beloved . . ."

She took a deep breath. The next thing she knew, the preacher was saying, "I now pronounce you man and wife. What God has joined together, let no man put asunder."

Kathleen looked up, focusing on the glitter in Morgan Tallchief's eyes. As she waited, he bent down. "Finally!" he whispered, then sealed it with a kiss.

Morgan always did have a way with words.

* * *

FBI headquarters was in quiet turmoil. The word was out. At some point during Lester Bryant's twenty-three years at the agency, he'd started selling out. What they didn't know yet was to whom.

Behind closed doors, discussions ranged from foreign powers to organized crime. Lester Bryant's worst fears had been realized. Not only had he been found out, but his family was having to bear the brunt of his shame.

That's what made Robert Caldwell's news important. Candelero had been located and picked up for questioning, and he had been more than forthcoming with information. For once in his life, he was telling the truth.

Caldwell burst into the director's outer office with a handful of files clutched tight to his chest.

"Ruth, is he busy?"

As always, the secretary gauged the importance of the question, as well as who asked, and made the decision on her own. She was well aware of the stink Lester Bryant had caused. Nothing would please her more than to have the status quo returned to her beloved agency. If this man could fix it, he could have all the time he needed with her boss.

"Just a minute, Bobby, I'll check." She picked up the phone. A few seconds later, she looked up. "You may go in."

Caldwell winked as he passed. "Killer dress, Ruthie. You should wear red more often."

"You have gravy on your tie," she said calmly, and swiveled her chair back to the computer screen.

Caldwell chuckled. One of these days he was going to find her weak spot, and when he did . . . The thought died as he shut the door behind him. The director looked pissed.

"If you have news, it better be good, otherwise get the hell out of my office. Everyone from the president on down has been on my ass and I'm in no mood for more bad news."

Caldwell grinned and laid the file folders before his boss. "They found Candelero. He was so scared of winding up in a federal penitentiary that his cooperation was almost pitifully easy to obtain."

The director leaned back in his chair, as if bracing himself for the worst.

"So, was he working for Bryant?"

Caldwell girded himself for the explosion he knew would come next. He nodded.

"Son of a holy bitch! Did he say why? By God, I want to know what makes a man like Bryant turn."

Caldwell pointed to the files. "It wasn't a hit. In fact, Candelero claims all he was hired to do was find a woman named Julie Walkman. That's why Bryant put him in the star car. It seems they'd bugged her car and Candelero was using the equipment to track her. When he found her, he was supposed to call Bryant. What happened after that was anyone's guess. Candelero claims he doesn't know anything more, and the boys believed him." Caldwell grinned wryly. "I'm sure they said pretty please when they asked."

The director rolled his eyes. He didn't want to hear the gory details. He wanted facts.

"Who the hell is Julie Walkman?"

Caldwell shoved the files nearer. "That's where it gets interesting. According to that neat little package I picked up from the Witness Protection division, that was the last name given to the fourteen-year-old daughter of a family they put in the program years ago."

The director frowned. "The hell you say? What would Lester Bryant be needing with a kid?"

Caldwell shrugged. "Julie Walkman might have been a kid when her parents went in, but she's past thirty now. And, according to that"—he pointed to the files he'd laid on the desk—"the file is closed. All pertinent parties are now deceased."

The director pinched the bridge of his nose, then stood with a curse.

"Damn it, I want answers to this mess, not more questions."

"I skimmed the case file before bringing it in. There's not much to go on. Because of the impermanence of their situation, they made few friends and left no ties each time they were moved. Seattle, Washington, was where they were living when her father died. About a week later, Julie Walkman simply disappeared, leaving everything she owned behind. She took her daughter and . . ."

The director turned, his face a study of concentration. "Wait a minute. Back up."

Caldwell waited.

"You said she was fourteen when they went into the program."

"Yes, that's right."

"And, you said they made few friends and left no ties when they were moved."

Caldwell nodded.

"So, where did the daughter come from? Fairies?"

Caldwell shrugged. "Who knows? A one-night

stand. An affair. Any number of ways. For God's sake, boss, she's a pretty thirty-something. Take a look for yourself."

The director opened the file, absently studying the picture before him. "How old is her kid?"

Caldwell checked his own notes. "Uh . . . fifteen, nearly sixteen."

"And what do you get when you subtract sixteen from thirty-two?"

"Uh . . ." Understanding dawned. "Sixteen! She was sixteen years old when she got pregnant!"

"Right. Now where was she living at that time?"

Caldwell slapped his forehead with the flat of his palm. "I didn't think of that angle."

The director grinned. "That's why I get the big desk and the big headaches." Then he picked up the folder and began sifting through the reams of paper. A few moments later, he looked up at Caldwell.

"She was living under the name Kathleen Ryder. Her father was teaching algebra in the Comanche public school system in Comanche, Oklahoma." He shifted a few more papers. "What's the significance of this clipping?" He held up a yellowed picture from an old newspaper called *The Comanche Times Weekly*.

Caldwell shrugged. "I don't know. There isn't any notation regarding it."

The director frowned. "It's got to mean something or else it wouldn't be in here." He looked closer. "Some Indian kid named Morgan Tallchief is pictured getting an award for setting a national track record." He looked up. "What's some high school track star got to do with the Ryder family?"

Caldwell continued to flip through his notes. "Wait, here's something."

The director dropped the file and turned his back to the desk, gazing pensively out the window toward the lawns below, thinking of the sixteenth hole on his favorite golf course as Caldwell began to recite.

"Directly after their resettlement in Seattle, Kathleen Ryder, then going by the name Julie Walkman, tried to run away. Four . . . no, five times, to be exact. The last time they brought her back, she tried to commit suicide."

The director frowned. Kids always got the raw end of their parents' mistakes.

"And . . . ?" he asked, wanting Caldwell to get to the end of the story.

Caldwell looked up. The light in his eyes hovered on the edge of excitement. "And nine months later she gave birth to a baby girl of ethnic descent."

The director turned around, a look of surprise on his face. "But she's not . . ." His forehead furrowed deeper. "What ethnicity?"

"Uh . . . they don't say. Wait! Here . . . there's a small notation. Maybe Indian or Mexican. Dark skin, straight black hair."

They both stared at the newspaper clipping. "There's your lead, Caldwell. Go to Comanche, Oklahoma. See if anyone there remembers a girl named Kathleen Ryder, then find out for sure if this Tallchief kid was her sweetheart. Looks like she tried pretty hard to get back to him once. Maybe when the program cut her loose, she figured this time it was okay to run. If we can find him, maybe we'll find her . . . and then maybe . . . just maybe, we'll find out what turned Bryant dirty."

Caldwell picked up the files and started out the door.

"Hey, Caldwell."

He turned. "Yes, sir?"

"Good work."

Caldwell grinned. "Yes, sir. Thank you, sir."

Fifteen

The sun was just about gone when Morgan turned off the highway toward home. Last night, he and Kathleen had spent their honeymoon at his brother's home, in the living room on the convertible couch while his grandmother's face stared down at them from the painting on the wall. It couldn't have been much worse if he'd planned it.

Some of the family had stayed on after they'd gone inside, partying in the backyard until all hours. The last to leave finally drove away around three in the morning. He remembered because right afterward, James had stumbled in through the front door, fallen over Morgan's boots, and then laughed all the way to his room.

Morgan grinned, remembering the scolding that Mary had given James behind closed doors for being tipsy in front of his sons. She could have saved her breath, because the boys were all sound asleep.

Their car had been loaded by sunrise, and soon afterward, they had started back to Santa Fe. There was no time to linger or travel the back roads. The moving van from Seattle was scheduled to arrive at his house sometime tomorrow.

Kathleen dozed, stretched out in the backseat alone while Trish rode in the front with Morgan. As usual, she was nose-deep in a book. She didn't even notice when they turned off the highway. Several miles later, Morgan began slowing down.

"We're here."

Trish looked up at him and marked her place in the book, then stretched and yawned. "It feels good to be home, doesn't it?"

It was so casual, he almost missed the significance of her remark. And then it dawned on him that she'd not only accepted him, but his home as well. He grinned and winked.

"Yeah, kiddo, it sure does."

He glanced in the backseat and then smiled at the way Kathleen had gone to sleep—on her stomach with her knees bent and her toes resting against the window. One arm trailed the floorboard, the other she'd tucked under her cheek for a pillow.

"Wake your mother up, honey. I'll go unlock the door. Don't bother with the bags. I'll get them later."

She nodded as Morgan got out of the car. When he opened the door and started inside, he thought of her house in Seattle and what it had felt like to walk into chaos. Even though all seemed in order, he started through the rooms, one by one. By the time Trish and Kathleen made it to the front steps, he'd done a thorough sweep of the house.

"Hey, wait a minute!" he shouted, and ran to the front door, stopping Kathleen before she could come in.

Still groggy from her nap, she was startled by his shout. She didn't know whether to run or stay put and wait for him to explain.

"What's wrong?" she asked.

He swooped her into his arms and then spun her around. "The bride is supposed to be carried across the threshold, remember?"

Trish groaned dramatically, and slipped past them. "Excuse me while I leave you guys to tradition. I'm starved." She disappeared toward the kitchen.

Kathleen looked up, loving the way Morgan's eyes crinkled at the corners as he laughed at their daughter's hasty exit.

"Don't feel bad. It's all a matter of age and priorities," she said.

His smile softened as he bent down and kissed her. "I know damn well where my priorities are. As for age, I think I've still got a few good years left in me."

Savoring the lingering taste of his mouth on her lips, Kathleen wrapped her arms around his neck and grinned. "Then take me home, husband. I don't want to waste a day."

He did as she asked and stepped over the threshold, pausing just inside the doorway.

"Welcome to my world, Kathleen Tallchief."

Her grin melted into tears. "There is a God," she whispered, and laid her head beneath his chin, taking heart in his strength as he carried her through the house toward their room.

*   *   *

Trish bounced into the room the next day, sidestepping a half dozen boxes as she made her way toward the front door.

Kathleen straightened up from the box she'd been unpacking. "Where do you think you're going, young lady? We're not nearly through."

"But Mom, I've unpacked all my stuff and put it away. I wouldn't know what to do with all this."

Morgan entered the room with a handful of hangers. "I do," he said, and handed them to her. "I just laid an armload of your mom's clothes on her bed. Why don't you be a doll and hang them in the closet for her?"

Trish was torn between arguing and maintaining her place as the princess in his life. The princess won out. She took the hangers and rolled her eyes as she passed.

"Okay," she said, trying hard not to whine. "But when I'm through, would it be okay if I watched one of your videos?"

Morgan glanced at his watch. "Sure. That'll be about lunchtime. We'll all take a break about then."

Trish wasn't sure, but it sounded to her as if she'd only been given a reprieve, and that when the movie and lunch were over, they'd be hard at it again. However, she knew when to fuss and when to shut up, and this was definitely a shut-up situation.

"Deal," she said, and danced out of the room, the hangers clinking as she went.

Kathleen grinned and then resumed her task, digging deep in the box and feeling her way through the packing paper for the next item to unpack.

Morgan figured he'd just been tested. "Well, was I had?" he asked.

She straightened. "Actually, you were quite good. I think you have her guessing. She isn't sure whether you cut her loose, or just let out more rope."

Pleased with himself, Morgan winked at her, then turned to study the assortment of things they'd unpacked, wondering what to put where, and how on earth it was all going to fit. As he looked, a large, flat package leaning against the wall near the front door caught his eye. It was the picture the frame shop had delivered as they were packing to leave.

When Kathleen saw him start toward the door, she panicked.

"Morgan, wait!"

He turned, startled by the sound of her voice.

Kathleen thrust a hand through her hair, disgusted with her own reaction.

"Never mind," she said. "It's okay. I don't know what I was thinking."

"I was only going to unwrap your picture, honey. Since it was a gift from your dad, I assumed you'd want to hang it."

"Yes," she said softly. "I definitely want to do that."

He hesitated. "Then you don't mind if I—"

"Of course not. You've given up your whole house to us. Be my guest," she said. "You can help me decide where it should go."

Strapping tape went, then the box, then the paper. But when he peeled the last sheet away and turned the picture faceup, he wasn't prepared for the jolt in his gut or the shock of recognition.

Stunned, he looked up. Kathleen stood a few feet away watching his face for a reaction. She didn't have long to wait.

"My God!" Morgan cried. "It's *Runner*. I painted it last year right before Christmas."

"I told you. Dad bought it for me last month for my birthday. When it was delivered, I was so overwhelmed I couldn't talk. Smiling and thanking him was the hardest thing I'd ever done. I wanted to lie down and bawl. It was like having you with me . . . but not being able to touch you or talk to you. He thought he'd done a wonderful thing by giving me something you'd painted. Instead, it only brought home to me how much I'd lost. I stood it against the wall for two days, unable to look at it without aching, and then one day he suddenly decided it needed a different frame. I didn't argue, but it wasn't until it left the house that I was able to draw an easy breath."

Morgan set the painting down. In a quiet voice, he held out his arms. "I'm here, sweetheart, and I'm not going anywhere. Touch all you want."

She walked into his embrace, sighing as his arms enfolded, then held her close. Her voice broke as she buried her face against the front of his shirt. "Every time I look at it, I feel the need to beg your forgiveness."

His arms tightened. "Don't, Kathleen. We've been all through this before. No one made me quit running competitively. I did it to myself." Together, they turned toward the painting leaning against the wall.

Three Indians from three separate centuries were caught in the moment of motion as they ran across the canvas. The one farthest back was little more than an outline. He wore nothing but a breechcloth and moccasins. Long muscular legs seemed to pound the earth as muscles clenched in his thighs. Thick black hair flew wildly out behind him as he raced toward some unseen goal.

The second figure, the one in the middle, had slightly more substance, yet his features, as well as his body, were still indistinct and obviously from a time long past. He, too, seemed to fly across the ground, and his hair and his clothing were nearly the same as the first. Long muscles corded in his arms and legs as he leaned forward in stride. The painted stick he held tight in his fist was extended toward the man in the lead—a symbolic passing of the baton to another generation of runners.

And it was the man in the lead, the man who seemed in imminent danger of running off the edge of the canvas, that dominated the painting. He ran leaning forward, while reaching back for the painted stick his ancestor was extending. He was a man of this century, but with a soul from the past. Long, black, shiny hair blew away from his face as he ran with the wind, looking forward—but never behind. He wore school colors instead of deerskin, and there were track shoes on his feet instead of moccasins, but the looks on each of their faces was the same, as if they could see something within themselves that no one else could see.

Kathleen looked up at him. "My father knew I never got over loving you, and he never got over feeling guilty. I guess he thought I would treasure something that you had painted." She sighed, her voice wavering as she looked back at the picture. "And I did . . . I do. But he'd aged so much. He was so forgetful. He didn't realize the runners were you."

"I never knew when it sold," Morgan said. "All I got was a check from Zora and a letter of congratulations."

She smiled. "And you had it coming. It's a magnificent painting, Morgan. Let's find a place to hang it."

"You don't have to. Not now."

She paused, then turned. "Oh, but I do. Now, more than ever. Trish needs to see this to understand that she's truly her father's daughter."

Kathleen's words touched his heart. His head dipped. Their mouths met, settling easily against the other's, lingering just long enough to strike sparks. She was the first to draw back.

"The painting," she said softly.

"Hold that thought," he muttered, then turned, grasping it by the edges of the new frame.

As he did, his finger accidentally poked through the backing. "Well, damn." He turned it around to inspect the damage.

"What's wrong?" Kathleen said.

"I punched a hole in the backing." He tilted it slightly, aiming it more toward the light. "But I don't think it's of any consequence."

"Here, let me see."

As he handed it over, an odd bit of color from inside caught his eye. "What in the . . . ?" He took it out of her hands and tilted it closer to the window, peering intently into the small tear. "There's something inside. Something red."

Kathleen leaned forward. "Maybe it's just part of the canvas, or maybe a sticker the frame shop put on."

He continued to look, alternately poking his finger into the hole, then tilting it up for another close look. "No, I don't think so. Besides, they wouldn't put one inside. See, here's theirs down on the edge, and I don't put anything on the back of my work, let alone something red."

Now Kathleen was curious. "Let me look."

He did as she asked, holding the painting while she bent down and thrust her finger inside the hole. A few seconds later she looked up, frowning in concentration as she continued to run her finger across its surface.

"It feels sort of like a . . ." She hesitated, as if searching for a definition just out of reach and then, in frustration, thrust in her hand. She ran her nails along the edge of the surface of the object, and when she found a loose corner, pulled.

"I've got it."

Beware of false treasures.

Morgan tensed. He hadn't been prepared for his grandmother's voice. Not at a time like this. And he sure didn't like the way it made him feel.

"Let me see," he urged, setting the painting aside.

She laid the object in his hand.

It was a small, flat booklet. The color was slightly faded, but Morgan sensed its power as he opened it up. For a time, all he could do was stare at the name, Paolo Benini, written on the first page. Tension curled a knot in his belly.

He turned to the next page. There was nothing on it but an odd sequence of numbers. He frowned, trying to remember where he'd seen something like it before, then when he did, their significance became clear.

"Oh, my God!"

The look on Morgan's face made Kathleen step back. "What? What is it?"

"If it's what I think it is, no wonder Benini didn't quit trying to find it."

"But Benini's dead," Kathleen reminded him. "As is my father."

Morgan handed her the book. "Just because you're an innocent party to a crime doesn't mean you're safe. One Benini is dead. There could be others."

What he was saying just didn't make sense. She looked down at the book. "But what is it? This can't have been worth all those years of fuss."

He didn't answer. Instead he bent down and picked up the painting and peeled off the sticker from the frame shop.

"What are you doing?" she asked.

"I want to know who put this in here, and why. You said your father suddenly wanted to change the frame. Maybe he just needed a new place to hide his tiger."

Kathleen froze. Morgan's allusion to her father's enigmatic words made her sick. Dear God, he'd been right. So her father *had* been hiding something, but at what cost?

She waited while he made his call. When he hung up and turned around, she could see that the news wasn't good.

"They said the small red book was already there when your father brought it in. He told them it was documentation proving the authenticity of the painting. At his instructions, they left it alone."

"But Morgan, it's just a few numbers. What possible significance could they have?"

"I've only seen a sequence like this once, and they were the key to getting into a numbered account at a bank in Geneva."

"A Swiss bank account? Are you saying my father held the key to Benini's Swiss bank account?"

Before he could answer, the phone began to ring.

Rain peppered the windshield of Special Agent Robert Caldwell's car as he drove south along Oklahoma's Highway 81, constantly watching the road signs between the squeaky sweep of wipers to make certain he was on the right route. The last thing he wanted was to get lost in the rain this far from nowhere.

According to his information, Comanche, Oklahoma, had a little over fifteen hundred residents. By all rights, a town that size would have few secrets. The way he figured, it shouldn't be too difficult to find someone who remembered an entire family's burning to death. All he had to do was find the right person, ask a few questions, and hopefully get a step closer to finding the elusive Julie Walkman.

A half hour later, he came to a stop inside the Comanche city limits. A single light at the junction of Highway 81 and Highway 53 was the extent of Comanche's public traffic system. When it turned green, he proceeded through, searching the signs on the buildings.

Comanche Times Weekly.

A newspaper office was always a good place to start. Even though the fire that supposedly killed the Ryder family happened over sixteen years ago, they were bound to have records. He started to pull to the curb when he saw the sign on the door. *Out to Lunch.* He glanced at his watch. It was thirty-two minutes after three in the afternoon. Either someone was having a long lunch or a late lunch, or the sign was the only one they had to indicate they were closed.

"On to Plan B," he said to himself, and began looking for the local police department.

He wasn't being careless. Robert Caldwell was never careless, but he *was* paying more than his usual attention to the buildings and a tad less attention to his driving. However, he did see the blur from the corner of his eye and slammed on his brakes just in time to keep from sideswiping what turned out to be a pig. It was big and pink, with a large, flat, upturned nose and a belly that came close to dragging the ground. In fact, it was the biggest pig he'd ever seen. And from the way it was standing, he didn't think it was going anywhere.

Caldwell peered through the windshield, staring in disbelief. The pig stared back at him through the rain. The only sounds were the constant squeak and scrape of the wipers on glass and Caldwell's uneven breathing.

And then the humor of the situation struck him, and he began to relax. He'd always feared one day to be caught in what might be called a Mexican stand-off. Now that it had happened, it was hardly as he'd expected.

He glanced in his rearview mirror. Since he was stopped in the middle of the street, it might be prudent to see if he was about to be rear-ended. There was nothing coming down the street behind him except rain. He looked back at the pig.

Just as he was about to honk his horn, a tall adolescent boy suddenly burst out of an alley on the run. He carried a long prod in one hand, a rope in the other.

Old, faded jeans and a blue checkered shirt were plastered to his lanky body, while water poured from the brim of a soggy old Stetson riding low on his ears. The kid looked wet and bedraggled and mad as hell.

Even though Caldwell dreaded the consequences, he couldn't bring himself to let the kid drown on his own. With a soft curse, he opened the door and got out, trying to ignore the sudden slash of rain against his dark summer suit.

"Need some help, boy?"

The youth was wild-eyed and almost too angry to speak. A long, imaginative string of curses rent the air as he stomped toward the pig. Caldwell was mildly impressed. The kid looked barely old enough to drive, and yet he knew words that Caldwell hadn't learned until a stint in the marines.

"Thanks, mister," the boy said, spitting rainwater and words. "But you'd best get on back inside your car 'fore Suey makes a move. That cussed old Duroc boar don't like strangers." Then he spit again, mingling a succulent curse with the rain spilling down from his hat. " 'Course, he don't like much of anything else, neither."

Caldwell stepped back, keeping the open car door between himself and the pig, and felt his socks squish inside his shoes. If the kid said Suey didn't like strangers, who was he to argue? Still, he felt slightly ridiculous watching from the sidelines while a boy did a man's job.

Ahead, a car turned the corner on two wheels, then came their way with red and blue lights whirling. Caldwell breathed a quiet sigh of relief. The patrol car slid to a stop only feet from the hog. A short, stocky man crawled out from behind the wheel wearing a uniform, a raincoat, and a big, wide grin.

It was all Jake Ramsey could do to hold back a laugh. "Damn it, Stanley, what are you doing with that sorry piece of bacon in town? The hog show was over yesterday."

Caldwell grinned. So the kid's name was Stanley.

"Yeah," Stanley mumbled, carefully circling the hog while dragging the rope and its noose behind his leg. "But Dad's trailer had a flat on it last night, and the ag teacher said I could load him up today, instead. I reckon Suey was pissed about having to stay in the barn by hisself last night. He ain't cooperated worth a damn."

And while Caldwell watched, the kid suddenly tossed the rope. The loop came through the air like a snake with wings, settling around the big hog's neck before the animal knew what was happening. The kid yanked, the rope went taut, and the hog tossed its head up, squealing like a runaway stallion. Right about then, Caldwell hit the front seat of his car and slammed the door, shutting himself in and the big hog out.

The kid had been right. Suey didn't like much of anything.

He was raising hell and then some, and trying to take Stanley with him. If the officer hadn't grabbed the rope and helped the kid hang on, the hog would have dragged him down the street.

As Caldwell watched, a pickup truck pulling a trailer came up from behind, then passed him by, stopping a few feet from where the impromptu rodeo was taking place.

He figured it was Stanley's father, as he watched the three men try to make a seven hundred-pound hog go somewhere it didn't want to go.

And as he watched, he remembered the last time he'd been in Oklahoma, stranded on an interstate in the middle of Oklahoma City and watching people rounding up steers from the overturned rig. Mean-ass pigs. Runaway steers. What, he wondered, was the deal with Oklahoma and runaway critters?

By now, there were several cars behind him, all watching the proceedings with undue interest. Caldwell could tell the locals from the people just passing through. To a man, every one of the residents got out to offer assistance, or at the least some advice, while the strangers stayed safely inside their cars.

Finally, it was over. The kid, the truck, and the hog were gone. The officer was slightly muddy, but seemed in good spirits as he stood in the street, motioning traffic to proceed.

As Caldwell inched forward, impulsively, he rolled down the window and leaned out.

"Officer, I'd like to talk to you."

Jake Ramsey frowned, then shrugged. "Pull to the curb, sir. I'll be with you just as soon as I get the traffic moving."

Caldwell did as he was told. After he'd parked, he dug his handkerchief from his pocket, using it as a towel to dry his face as well as the bald spot on his head. He was stuffing it back in his pocket when the officer knocked on his window.

"Yes, sir," Jake said. "How can I help you?"

Caldwell pulled out his badge. "Where can we talk?"

A spurt of adrenaline rocked Jake Ramsey where he stood. It was a little like the same feeling he used to get watching Roxie Lee Hindershot walk; somewhere between excitement and panic.

"Follow me," Jake said.

Caldwell did. All the way to the station, through the rain and into the building, past the dispatcher, and right into the office of the chief of police. When the officer closed the door behind him and motioned for Caldwell to sit down, he did so with relief.

Jake was more than curious about the arrival of a federal agent. It wasn't an ordinary occurrence for Comanche.

"Name's Jake Ramsey," he said. "I'm the patrolman on duty today. The chief's home nursing an ulcer, but I'll be glad to call him. He lives nearby. It won't take him long to get here."

Caldwell started to nod, and then paused, trying to be considerate of bellyaches and rain. "Maybe it won't be necessary," he said. "I'm just looking for some information. If I get what I need, we won't have to bother him."

Jake nodded, but his nerves were on edge. "If you don't mind, sir, I'll just call the chief and let him know you're here, all the same. He'd want to know."

Caldwell shrugged. "Suit yourself," he said, and as the officer picked up the phone, Caldwell asked, "Has he lived here long?"

Jake paused, the receiver in his hand, wondering what that had to do with the price of rice in China. "All his life."

"Then he would have known Nathan Ryder and his family, right?"

A cold chill went straight down the back of Jake

Ramsey's spine. Halfway through punching in the numbers, he stopped and quietly set the phone back on the cradle. Morgan Tallchief's warning was too fresh in his mind to consider this a coincidence.

"If you don't mind," Jake said, "I'd appreciate another look at that badge of yours."

Caldwell stilled. If he didn't know better, he'd think the look on Jake Ramsey's face was almost threatening.

He pulled out his badge, slightly surprised when Ramsey took it out of his hands and held it closer to the light.

Outside, rain continued to fall, hammering against the single window inside the office. Steam began to rise from their clothes, giving the room a slightly musty scent as each waited for the other to make a move. Caldwell was the first to call in his hand.

"Look, Officer, if you have a—"

"Ramsey, the name is Ramsey," Jake said, and handed back the agent's badge.

Caldwell sighed. Obviously he'd gotten hold of someone who considered himself a big duck in a little pond.

"If we're going to have a problem with questions, then maybe you should call your chief," Caldwell said.

Instead of arguing or blustering, Jake Ramsey sat on the edge of the desk and leaned forward.

"Why Nathan Ryder?"

"Why the fuss?"

Jake leaned back and folded his arms across his chest. "I asked you first," he said quietly.

Caldwell caught himself grinning. "So you did." He hesitated, but only briefly. "Let's start over, okay?" Then he pulled a small notebook out of his pocket.

Jake remained silent. He was of the school of thought that if you gave a man enough rope, he'd either hang himself or get himself out of his mess.

"Have you lived here long?" Caldwell asked.

"All my life."

"And that would be . . . ?"

"Thirty-four years."

So he was about the same age as Kathleen Ryder would be. He had to have known her. And if that Tallchief kid had been a track star, he would have known of him, too.

"So then, you would have been in school during the time Mr. Ryder was teaching here."

"Yep."

"Did you know his daughter, Kathleen?"

"Yep."

Caldwell made a quick notation. "She was very pretty. I suppose she was popular."

"I suppose."

"Probably had so many boyfriends she didn't know what to do, right?"

"Nope."

Caldwell paused, pen to paper, and looked up in surprise. "She didn't have any boyfriends?"

"Didn't say that," Jake muttered. "You said she had lots. She didn't. She wasn't that kind of girl."

"But you said—"

Jake suddenly stood. "Look, Galloway—"

"Caldwell."

"Whatever. Before I answer another question, I want to know why you're asking, and don't give me any bullshit, because I'll know it if you do."

Caldwell tensed. "Sorry, Ramsey. It's classified information on a need-to-know basis. And the way I see it, you don't need to know anything more than what I've already told you."

Jake glared. He had Morgan Tallchief's number in his wallet right now, and he had two choices. Either he told this stranger what he wanted to know, or the chief would do it without hesitation.

Suddenly, he walked behind the chief's desk and sat down.

"Calhoun, there's coffee in the outer office. Why don't you help yourself to a cup while I make a little call."

"Caldwell, not Calhoun, Caldwell."

"There's cream and sugar."

Caldwell knew when he'd been dismissed.

Trish bounded from the bedroom with a hanger in her hand. "Phone!" she yelled, but Morgan was already picking it up. Still locked into the book they'd just found, he sounded less than friendly.

Jake was slightly taken aback by the gruff-sounding voice. "Morgan? Is that you? It's me, Jake."

Morgan plowed his fingers through his hair in frustration.

"Yes, it's me. Sorry I was so abrupt. I had something on my mind." Then it dawned on him that Jake Ramsey probably wouldn't be calling to pass the time of day. "What's wrong?"

Jake glanced toward the door, then lowered his voice. "I've got an FBI agent in my outer office asking questions about Kathleen Ryder and her family."

"Son of a . . ."

Jake grimaced. It was just as he'd feared. This shouldn't be happening.

"What did he want to know?" Morgan asked.

Jake sighed. "Stupid stuff, like was she popular in high school, and did she have lots of boyfriends."

Morgan frowned. "That's all?"

"I swear, except for asking me if I knew Mr. Ryder, too."

The little red book was burning the proverbial hole in Morgan's hands. He glanced at it, judging the consequences of holding it back as opposed to getting rid of it now. His eyes narrowed. Maybe they'd just gotten an answer to a prayer.

"Let me talk to him," Morgan said.

Jake sighed in relief. At least, whatever happened now was out of his hands.

"Hang on," he said, and laid down the phone. "Hey, Cochran, telephone."

Caldwell came back into the room, nursing a burned tongue. "The name's Caldwell." He set a Styrofoam cup full of hot, steamy brew on the edge of the desk and picked up the receiver, glaring at Ramsey. "That stuff in that pot is close to being a lethal weapon."

Jake grinned. "Yeah, I know."

Caldwell knew he'd been had. He rolled the receiver close to his mouth.

"This is Caldwell."

"Why the questions about Kathleen Ryder?"

He froze. "Who am I talking to?"

Morgan hesitated.

Trust your instincts and you will be trusting yourself.

Forgetting that he was still on the phone, he said, "Okay, Grandmother, you win."

Caldwell frowned. "Who's Grandmother? Is this some kind of a joke?"

"No, sir, there's not a damn thing funny about this whole situation," Morgan said.

Caldwell took a seat. "Give me a name. I like to know who I'm talking to, buddy."

"Tallchief. My name is Morgan Tallchief."

Caldwell was extremely glad he'd been sitting down.

Sixteen

Morgan's years in the military had taught him one thing. Attacking was a hell of a lot easier than waiting in defense.

"You said your name was Caldwell?"

"That's right I'd like to ask you some—"

"No," Morgan said. "I'll do the asking. I want your full name, the name of your immediate superior, and a number where I can call you back."

Caldwell's jaw clenched. He never had liked being under the gun, even when it seemed inevitable.

"Look, Tallchief, all I need to know is—"

"My way or no way," Morgan said.

There was more than backbone in the man's remark. Caldwell recognized a promise when he heard it.

"Special Agent Robert Caldwell. Just call FBI headquarters in D.C. Ask for the director." He glanced down at the phone and then gave out the number. The line went silent. Morgan Tallchief was gone.

"What did he say?" Jake asked.

Caldwell looked up. "He said he'll call back."

Jake nodded. "Then he will."

"Damn it, Ramsey, don't you think it's about time to help me out here? I ask about Kathleen Ryder and I get Morgan Tallchief. What's their connection?"

"He'll tell you what he wants you to know."

"I could haul your ass for obstructing justice," Caldwell said.

Jake's face turned a slow, angry red, but he wouldn't be pushed. "Then haul away, Calvin, because the way I see it, your agency has meddled way too far into their business as it is."

"My name is Caldwell."

Jake didn't move. "And it's gonna be mud if your people mess them up again."

Ramsey's simple threat was more revealing than he might have believed. It told Caldwell two things. Not only had he found someone who knew Kathleen Ryder and Morgan Tallchief, but from what he'd just said, he knew more than a little about their history together.

"Freshen your coffee?" Jake asked, holding the coffeepot over Caldwell's cup.

Steam was still rising from inside the one he already had. Caldwell covered the cup with his hand.

"No thanks."

As Jake set the pot back on the burner, Caldwell peered intently into the thick black brew. "What do you make this out of, old tires?"

Jake grinned and, to prove he was the better man, downed a goodly portion of the cup he'd just poured for himself in one smooth gulp.

Unwilling to rise to the challenge, Caldwell set his cup down and glared. Minutes passed, then ten, then thirty. By now, he was starting to get nervous. What if Tallchief didn't call back? He began to pace from the coffeepot to the water fountain and back again, resenting the fact that he was not in control. He glanced at his watch, then at the clock on the wall.

"Come on, Tallchief, call!"

The agent's credentials checked out, just as Morgan had suspected, but that didn't make revealing Kathleen and Patricia's whereabouts any easier. As long as they were with him, he knew he could keep them safe, but he also knew that as long as they held that passbook, the hunter would never stop. All he had to do was make the call. He picked up the phone. When the agent answered on the first ring, Morgan knew there was no turning back.

"This is Caldwell."

"Why all the questions about Kathleen Ryder?"

A knot in Caldwell's belly began to unwind. It was the Indian. He'd called back, just as he'd promised.

"Look, some of this is confidential, so if you'll just let me ask the questions—"

Morgan interrupted. "No. Someone's been messing with me and mine, and it stops here."

Caldwell's eyebrows arched. Another veiled threat. What the hell was going on? "I'm one of the good guys, remember?"

"Not from where I'm standing."

Caldwell remembered Julie Walkman's file: the newspaper clipping, the baby born out of wedlock. If the kid was his, then he could understand why

Tallchief might be so bitter. He decided to come at him from another direction.

"Actually, I'm trying to locate a woman named Julie Walkman. Do you know her?"

Morgan frowned. Caution overcame curiosity. This was getting too intense to be dealt with over a phone.

"Sorry, Mohammed, if you want to talk, you're going to have to come to the mountain."

Caldwell squeezed rainwater out of his sleeve, taking some satisfaction in the fact that Jake Ramsey might have to mop it up later. "Meaning?"

While Morgan was fingering the red passbook he still held in his hands, he happened to look up. Kathleen was staring at him from the doorway. He winked, then slipped the small book into his shirt pocket, refocusing his attention on the man at the other end of the line.

"I'm not going anywhere. If you want to talk, you come here," Morgan said.

"Fine. Tell me where."

"Santa Fe, New Mexico. When you get there, call me at this number. I'll give you further directions."

"If you can promise no pigs or cows, you've got yourself a deal," Caldwell muttered.

Morgan grinned. Something told him Oklahoma hadn't been kind to the man from D.C.

Caldwell jotted down the number Tallchief gave him. What the hell. Another day. Another state. Maybe it wouldn't be raining out there.

"I'll be waiting for your call," Morgan said, and then hung up the phone.

"What's happening?" Kathleen asked.

"Come here," he urged.

She wouldn't budge. "No, Morgan. Tell me now."

"Jake Ramsey called. There was a man in his office asking questions about Kathleen Ryder."

"Oh, my God," she gasped, and instinctively glanced around to see where Trish was.

Morgan caught Kathleen just as she was about to bolt. "I talked to him, and then I checked him out. He's FBI."

Her gaze was fixed upon his lips, as if measuring each word Morgan spoke. He wouldn't lie to her. If he said it was so, then it had to be so. She swayed, suddenly weak on her feet.

He steadied her, and then held her, regretting the fact that he'd been the bearer of more traumatic news.

"I'm sorry, Kathleen, but this was bound to happen."

"I know." Her lips twisted bitterly as her gaze swept the room. "I should have known the fairy tale couldn't last."

He tightened his grip. "Damn it, this is no fairy tale, and it's not over. Not by a long shot. When the agent gets here, we'll talk, and then he can get the hell out of our lives." He patted his shirt pocket. "And he can take your father's tiger with him."

"Then will it be over?"

Morgan threaded his fingers through her hair, then pulled her close.

"I hope so, sweetheart, but only time will tell."

By the time night came, everyone was tense and anxious. Trish had cried a few tears and gone to bed early. Morgan understood her method. Sleep until the worst was over. Unfortunately, it had never worked for him.

Kathleen prowled the rooms with an armful of

folded bath towels, as if searching for a place to put them down. Her behavior was scattered and, Morgan suspected, so were her thoughts. Jake Ramsey's call had rocked their world. Morgan had invited a stranger to intercede on their behalf. It remained to be seen how successful that would be. All they could do was hope.

Later, Morgan stood at the window, measuring the desert by moonlight. Small clumps of sage gleamed white, dusted by a luminous glow. The horizon was black and uneven, broken by the silhouette of a distant mountain range. On the surface it appeared empty, but he knew looks were deceiving. The desert could be a killer, and there were a dozen ways to die.

A rhythm-and-blues song drifted into the quiet from somewhere down the hall. He smiled to himself. He was learning about his daughter. She always went to sleep with a radio playing.

The shower came on, and Morgan shifted his stance. It was Kathleen. She showered, Trish bathed. Again, another fact to store in his heart, along with the ones that were already there.

The thought crossed his mind to join her, and then he set it aside. There was not enough privacy for something like that.

Restless, he walked outside, leaving the front door open. A hinge squeaked on the screen door as he eased it shut and he made a mental note to oil it tomorrow. In his house, everything must move as it was meant to. It was a habit he'd picked up in the SEALs. Never let them hear you coming.

He paused on the top step, inhaling deeply as he lifted his head to the night. The solitude and the dark eased his mind. Gazing upward, he searched the heavens, absently orienting himself with the stars. As he watched, one suddenly streaked toward earth, then disappeared as quickly as it had appeared.

Make a wish upon a falling star.

Is that the Indian way, Grandmother?

No, but it is the way of a child. Now, Grandson, make your wish.

Morgan smiled, remembering the nights when, as a boy, he and his grandmother would sit outside long after dark and watch the wide Oklahoma sky. He always wondered why she'd been so fascinated by something unattainable. The night after her funeral, Morgan had stood outside their old house and looked to the stars and remembered again. Had she been looking all that time for her own place in heaven, or had she just been a stargazer and a dreamer?

He walked off of the steps and into the yard, moving a few feet farther out in hopes of catching the weak, shifting breeze. A faint gust moved across his face, and he had a sudden desire to feel the cool breeze upon his body as well. Before, when he'd been alone, it hadn't mattered how much clothing he wore. Now, he had Trish to consider, and he suddenly realized he missed the freedom.

He turned and looked back at the house. One small light shone through an uncurtained window. His gaze lifted, and a slow smile began spreading across his face. The roof! He hadn't been up there in over a year.

Within minutes, he'd pulled the old handmade ladder down from beneath the connecting breezeway and angled it up through the large square opening overhead. Anxious now that he'd begun, he climbed up the ladder and onto the flat, sprawling roof of his adobe house. For a moment, he just stood and looked up into the darkness. In a manner of speaking, Morgan Tallchief was on top of his world.

Only the night saw his shirt come off, then his boots, then his jeans. When he was down to a pair of black briefs, caution overrode need. He went down on his knees, then sat back on his heels. Letting his arms go limp, he closed his eyes and let his mind fly free.

Sometime later, reality returned with the squeak of the screen door. His eyes flew open, his mind, sharp and clear, his skin, cool and refreshed. He knew without looking that it was Kathleen. He felt her presence, could almost hear her breathing as she walked.

Slowly, he got to his feet and moved to the edge of the roof, then looked down. She was standing in the yard, searching the desert. She thought he was running.

The breeze pushed her gown against her tall, slender body and lifted her hair from her neck. His gut clenched as he watched her. *Look up, Kathleen. Turn around and look up.*

His unspoken thoughts were like a magnet. To his surprise, she did just that. He couldn't see her face clearly, but he could tell by the way she moved that he'd surprised her, maybe even frightened her.

"Morgan?"

His voice came to her on the wind. "Come up."

"How?" she asked. "Did you fly?"

He smiled, then motioned. "The ladder. Use the ladder."

Only after he'd pointed it out did she realize it was there.

He heard her bare feet on the patio tile, then thought of the rough-hewn wood on the rungs and feared it would hurt her. But before he could move, she was already there.

Kathleen paused at the edge of the opening through which she'd climbed and felt as if she was standing on the edge of a precipice. She was stunned by the beauty of Morgan's nearly bare body. From where she stood, he appeared to have been carved out of a single mighty oak. Moonlight delineated the hard contours and long muscles of his runner's body, shadowing his face so that he appeared more fantasy than fact. A white slash of dim light cut across his cheekbones and the bridge of his nose.

The faint breeze became a roar in her ears. She saw his lips move, but heard no sound other than the rush of blood through her own body. Yet when he held out his hand, her heart knew what he asked. She took a step forward, and then another, and then another. They met, then melded together, his dark to her light, his body to her gown.

"Off, take it off," he whispered, then did the deed for her by pulling her gown over her head. It fell to their feet, unheeded as he reached out and pulled her close. "Kathleen . . . my Kathleen."

She swayed, then moaned beneath her breath as his hands slid from the back of her neck down her shoulders, tracing the fragile span of her waist, then cupping her slim hips and fitting himself between her thighs.

The thin black fabric he was wearing was an insult to the flash fire of need that his touch had instilled. Her hands stroked his back, then moved downward, testing the hard, bunched muscles of his hips beneath his briefs as he braced them both with his strength.

She leaned back in his arms until she could almost see his face. "Off, take them off."

His teeth shone white in the dark as he did as she asked. When he came to her again, there was nothing between them but need.

His fingers traced the shape of her breasts, and then his breath caught and held as the peaks hardened against his palms. When she sighed, he smiled and cupped her face, instead. Tasting her lips, he caught the faint but lingering scent of soap and shampoo as he thrust his fingers through the thick, heavy length of her hair.

He was hard now, throbbing and heavy. Thoughts spiraled into one compelling need to find release. Kathleen pushed out of his arms, then caught his hand, tugging as she dropped to her knees, urging him to follow.

The surface of the roof was still warm from the heat of the day as he spread her gown and laid her upon it. He knelt between her knees, then laid his hands upon her legs, stroking the softness. The contrast of their bodies was as strong as that between daylight and dark.

She lifted her arms, beckoning, almost begging, and when he stretched full length atop her and pushed his way deep inside, the reason for their differences became clear. They fit like an arrow to a bow as Morgan began to move within her.

Kathleen arched, meeting him halfway. But when he began to move, she became lost to the rhythm and gave herself up to the man, letting him lead the way. His face was little more than a blur above her, but she could see enough to know that he was lost in the act.

His eyes were closed, his head thrown back to the night as he held himself above her so as not to crush her with his great weight.

They rocked to the rhythm of love, and when it became impossible to think, they rode the explosion all the way to the stars.

Kathleen had one brief flash of sanity in which she knew her time had come. She remembered looking up at the sky overhead as she started to come undone. Darkness magnified the pinpoints of starlight above them as heat spilled within her, coiling and uncoiling like a twisting serpent. Suddenly, Morgan leaned down and whispered something indistinct in her ear.

She shattered, and the sky above began to spin like a psychedelic light on black velvet. By the time it had stopped, and the world had ceased to roll, Morgan was lying on his back holding her safe in his arms.

"Morgan . . ."

He smoothed at the rough tangles he'd made of her hair, then kissed her forehead as he whispered, "What is it, Kathleen?"

"Earlier . . . I thought you'd be running."

He felt her shiver, and wrapped her closer within his embrace.

"I know. I saw you."

"Why?"

"Why what, sweetheart?"

"Why weren't you? Was it because of us? I don't want to ever again stand between you and something you love."

He looked up at the sky, absently studying the heavenly constellations as he searched his mind for a way to express what he felt. Again, as he watched, a star suddenly fell from the sky, burning out long before it reached the earth.

"I love you, so you can stand any damn place in my life that you choose," he said, then took a deep breath, allowing the truth an easy way out. "Before, I ran for a lot of reasons. Sometimes because I couldn't sleep. Sometimes because my body craved the activity my mind and my hands had already had. But most of the time, I was running away from ghosts."

"Oh, Morgan."

Her soft, indistinct cry hurt his heart. He blinked, shocked by a sudden blur of tears he would not let fall.

"It doesn't matter anymore. One little ghost who'd been lost came back. So . . ." He hugged her quickly, needing to break the somberness of the moment. ". . . the empty nights are gone. Now, let's get you dressed and down off this roof before you freeze. The desert gets cold at night."

She hesitated, unwilling to break the mood and the moment. "As long as I have you, I'll never be lost or cold again."

Her words stayed with him long after they'd gone to their bed, but for some reason, they didn't give the comfort that he might have believed. Instead, he felt an unnerving dread. Afraid to give way to the panic, he closed his eyes and made himself sleep.

Autrey Griggs had decided it was time to move on. When he delivered the information Benini wanted, he would be free of his debt. And being debt-free meant that he could do anything he chose. Autrey chose to get as far away from Marco Benini as humanly possible. He wasn't sure where he would go, but returning to his roots was looking more enticing with every passing day. It would be nice to live out the rest of his life on the Louisiana bayou. Years ago, he'd left because of mosquitoes and gators. Now they didn't seem nearly so bad. He'd grown up there. Dying there, which he hoped was some years down the road, wouldn't be so bad.

But before any other decisions could be made, Autrey had to give Benini what he wanted. He sat on the side of his unmade bed amid the few boxes containing his worldly possessions and picked up the phone.

By God, Benini had better be happy with this news, he thought. Lois Settlemeyer at Mayflower Moving and Storage had been a tougher nut to crack than he'd first believed. It had taken fresh flowers, a fancy dinner, and an obliging fuck to get the information out of her that he needed.

He counted the rings while waiting for someone to answer and tried not to think of Lois Settlemeyer's pale, spare body jerking and gasping beneath him. It was like making love to a blue-veined road map. Too flat and too marked to enjoy. Suddenly a familiar voice growled into his ear. Autrey shifted into an upright position.

"Benini, I've got what you need."

When Marco Benini cursed, then began to laugh, Autrey Griggs smiled. Damn, it felt good to be free.

"Dad, someone drove up!"

Trish's nervous shout brought Morgan out of his chair and Kathleen out of the kitchen where she'd been making some breakfast tea. It was barely seven A.M.

"Get out of sight. Don't come unless I call."

Kathleen took one look at Morgan's face and grabbed Trish by the hand, bolting without hesitation. No one had to tell her the seriousness of this meeting. It could be the difference between living without fear or looking over her shoulder for the rest of her life.

A loud knock sounded on the front door, but Morgan didn't make a move to answer until he was sure they were safely out of sight.

The second knock came. He went to the door and swung it wide.

"Yes?"

Robert Caldwell was momentarily caught off guard. He'd had a mental picture of a young man with long black hair who stood with easy grace. This man stood inches taller than the boy in the photo, was pounds heavier, and gave away nothing by his expression.

He glanced at Tallchief's hair. Like his eyes, it was an intimidating black. Short, almost spiky in style.

In spite of an urge to step back, he stood his ground. This man might not fit the old clipping, but he definitely fit the background information he'd gotten during the drive to Santa Fe. Ex-military. Ex–Navy SEAL. His eyes narrowed, gauging the closed, almost defiant expression on Tallchief's face. The man was trouble, and it showed.

"Morgan Tallchief?"

"Who wants to know?"

Caldwell pulled out his badge.

Morgan looked at it carefully, then looked past Caldwell, to his car and beyond.

"You came alone?"

"Yes."

Morgan stepped aside. When the agent entered, Morgan locked the door behind them. At the sound, Caldwell spun around, slightly surprised by the covert behavior.

"Okay, I'm here," he said, "Now can we talk?"

Morgan's gaze moved to the slight bulge he detected beneath the agent's jacket.

"Are you armed?"

Caldwell cursed, then opened one side of his jacket, revealing the gun and shoulder holster. "Hell yes, I'm armed. I'm a federal agent. I'm on the job. And I've danced through just about all the hoops I'm going to, mister. I want some answers."

"You can come out now," Morgan called.

Caldwell's pulse jerked. Tallchief had asked him if he was alone. He hadn't had the foresight to ask him the same question. Instinctively, he reached for his gun and then winced in sudden pain. Tallchief had hold of his wrist, just hard enough to make a believer out of him. He froze, then forgot what he'd been about to say as two women came into the room.

He didn't know the younger one, but he could guess who she was. It was the other woman's face he knew well, and it was the last face he'd expected to see.

"You're Julie Walkman!"

Morgan turned loose of Caldwell, then held out his hand to Kathleen.

"No, this is my wife, Kathleen Tallchief, and our daughter, Patricia. Kathleen, Special Agent Robert Caldwell, of the FBI."

"Your wife? But how . . . when . . . ?"

"It doesn't matter," Morgan said. "What does matter is why your people closed her father's file, then bugged her car. What the hell were you doing, using her for some sort of bait?"

Kathleen gasped. That aspect had never occurred to her. She suddenly felt angry at what she and Trish had been through. Her eyes flashed as she nailed Robert Caldwell with a question he hadn't been prepared to answer.

"Did you? Were you using my daughter and me for bait?"

Caldwell looked past her to Morgan. "Of course not," he said shortly, then added, "How did you know about the DTD?"

Disbelief turned to anger as Kathleen suffered being all but ignored. "Hey!"

Startled, both men looked at her.

"I'm the one who's asking the questions, not Morgan, and what's a DTD?'

Embarrassed, Caldwell tried to make peace. "A digital tracking device. DTD for short." He tried again, only this time, he directed his question to Kathleen. "How did you know it was there?"

She glared. "I didn't. If it hadn't been for Morgan . . ." Suddenly sickened by the ugliness of it all, she dropped her head and turned away, unwilling to let this stranger see her cry.

Morgan stepped in front of her, giving her the space she needed to compose herself out of the agent's sight.

"She didn't find it, I did. Now tell me why it was there," Morgan said.

Caldwell sighed. This was where it was going to get sticky. "We don't actually know."

Morgan took an angry step forward. "Don't lie to

me, Caldwell. Badge or no badge, you'll be out on your ass if you do."

Caldwell held his ground. "Don't threaten me, Tallchief. I'm telling you the truth. There was never an official order of any kind put out regarding your wife other than to close her father's file."

When no one disputed his claim, Caldwell began to relax. His gaze slid from Morgan to the young girl who now stood at his side. Except for the eyes, the likeness between father and daughter was uncanny.

"So, Patricia, I guess it's been rough on you," he said gently, trying to ease the tension in the room.

Like her father, Trish stood her ground. Her voice was only a little bit shaky as she answered. "Up until a couple of weeks ago, it wasn't so bad."

"What happened a couple of weeks ago?" he asked.

Kathleen answered for her. "After we received an official notification from the program that our file was closed, we assumed that meant we'd be safe. We assumed wrong."

Caldwell frowned. "I know it was an intrusion upon your privacy, but having your car bugged doesn't mean your life was in danger."

"No," she said sharply, "But finding our house ransacked, and the threatening phone call that followed it, does. Add to that a tracking device on my car, and I start to believe Santa Claus just might not make it to my house this year."

She tensed, then tried to relax as Morgan laid his hand upon her shoulder, squeezing gently as a reminder that he was still there.

Caldwell was stunned. This added a new dimension to what they already knew. What bothered him was that the obvious suspects, such as Candelero, were in custody, while the others were deceased, including Lester Bryant. He chewed at the edge of his lip, tugging at his ear in an absent fashion as he absorbed these new facts into the case.

"Why weren't we informed about the phone call and the break-in?" he asked. "You should have let your contact at the agency know."

This time, Kathleen made no attempt to hide her anger.

"Why would I do something so useless? So we could be moved again—so I could uproot my daughter and our lives all over again—or maybe so we could keep running? I think not! You people have had more than enough time to prove your worth to me. I'm sick of running, and I've changed my name for the very last time."

Morgan stepped in. "Look, Caldwell, I know government issue when I see it. I worked with the stuff for the better part of sixteen years, and that bug I pulled off her car was definitely one of ours. So if it wasn't FBI, then who?"

Caldwell looked away. "We don't know."

Morgan saw red. "Out!" he said quietly, pointing toward the door.

Caldwell looked up, startled by the sudden and unexpected order to evacuate, then remembered Morgan Tallchief's warning about lying.

"We aren't sure," he amended.

Morgan's stare didn't waver.

Caldwell sighed. "You take no prisoners, do you?"

"Never saw the need."

Caldwell shuddered. The cold, implacable tone in the Indian's voice came close to frightening.

"Do you mind if I sit down?" he asked.

When Morgan stepped aside, motioning toward an adjoining room, Caldwell accepted the grudging invitation to sit. As he entered the room, out of habit, he gauged his surroundings, taking note of all that was there. There was nothing he could see that was out of the ordinary. Just polished wood and overstuffed leather furnishings with a definite Southwest influence. And then he amended himself as he remembered Morgan Tallchief's roots. Maybe not Southwest, but more aptly, Native American. His eyes narrowed thoughtfully as he looked at the painting hanging over the fireplace.

Runner. The colors on canvas seemed to move with the three men caught in a moment of motion. Nerves suddenly danced beneath Caldwell's skin. They looked so real! From where he was sitting, he imagined he could almost hear the methodical sound of breaths inhaling and exhaling as feet pounded the earth.

He shuddered. Damn, that was spooky! And then he remembered the newspaper clipping. Morgan Tallchief had been some sort of athletic prodigy. That probably explained the choice of subject. Absently, he leaned back in his chair, wondering if Tallchief had given it up now that he was painting.

Morgan entered the room. "Can I offer you something to drink? Water? A soft drink?" Once again, a slight smile broke the seriousness of his face. "I promise not to poison it."

Caldwell relaxed. "No, but thanks." He pointed toward the painting. "Is this one of yours?"

Morgan looked up. The smile was gone when he

turned away. "It belongs to Kathleen. Her father bought it for her last month for her birthday."

"Whoever the artist is, he's good. Those men look like they're about to run off the canvas."

Morgan glanced up at the painting and then looked away. "Thank you," he said quietly.

Caldwell looked slightly startled. So Tallchief had painted it! His eyes narrowed thoughtfully. Why was that so hard for him to admit?

Out in the hallway, Kathleen was struggling to hide her own fears so as not to alarm her daughter. Gently, she tugged at the long, black braid hanging over Trish's shoulder, then brushed at a speck of lint on her shirt.

"Are you all right, honey?"

Trish nodded. "I guess so, but Mom, what does all of this mean? Did Grandpa do something bad?"

This was exactly what she'd feared might happen. "No, darling, of course not. Whatever he did, he did out of love for us. I suspect he feared that somewhere down the road, the FBI wouldn't be able to keep us safe. To him, holding back Benini's passbook was sort of like . . . insurance. As long as your grandfather had something they wanted, he believed they wouldn't kill him. Unfortunately, he didn't take everything into consideration."

"Now that you found it and we're going to turn it over to the authorities, will we be safe?"

Kathleen hugged her. "I hope so. But we'll have to wait and see. Just don't be afraid. Remember, we've got your father on our side."

Trish's expression lightened. "He's awesome, isn't he, Mom?"

Kathleen thought of last night and making love beneath the stars. "Pretty much." She gave Trish's braid one last, gentle tug. "You don't have to stay, you know."

Grateful for the reprieve, Trish made a swift exit for her room, leaving Kathleen free to join the men. She took a seat beside Morgan, who was sitting opposite Caldwell on a couch. At her arrival, Caldwell wasted no time. He leaned forward.

"Kathleen, did you ever know an agent named Lester Bryant?"

She frowned thoughtfully, missing the sharp look Morgan gave the agent as she searched her memory.

"No, I don't think . . ."

And then something surfaced—she flashed back to the moment when she was tossed in a van, when her world exploded in a ball of orange fire. She'd heard one man curse and another man yell, *Damn it, Bryant, you cut that too close!*

She looked up, but not at Morgan. "When we lived in Oklahoma, they blew up our house."

Caldwell winced as Morgan's expression visibly darkened. Compassion colored his answer.

"I know. I read the file."

She nodded. "Everyone else was already out of the house and waiting in a van in the alley when I got home, but I didn't know it until later." Once again, she forced herself not to look at Morgan. Instead, she took a deep breath, and continued. "Our school had been to a state track meet. An agent was waiting for me when I walked inside my house. I didn't know his name, but I might have seen him off and on during the years during some of our moves. Later that same night, I heard someone call him Bryant . . . but I didn't really know him. The agents were never the same. The only constant in our lives was some man who was my father's contact within the program, but I never knew his name."

Caldwell's pulse leaped. So Lester Bryant had known Julie Walkman, even if it had been in one of her other lives. That was a connection they hadn't had.

"Did you ever see this Bryant fellow again?"

"No. They took us to an airport. A different set of people went with us to Denver. From there we went to San Diego, then Seattle. Within a week, we had a different name and a different home. We never moved again after that."

"You never had any further problems?"

"No, not until after my father died. The paper printed his picture with his obituary. That's how they found us, I'm sure."

Caldwell frowned. "They? Who's *they* and what could *they* possibly hope to gain by harassing your family all these years?"

Morgan took the red passbook out of his pocket and tossed it into Caldwell's lap.

"Maybe this."

Caldwell opened it. When he read the name on the inside front cover, he tensed, then when he turned the page, he paled.

"Holy shit!" He looked up, embarrassed. "Pardon me."

"Is that what I think it is?" Morgan asked.

"Where did you get this?"

"We found it behind the framing on that picture yesterday when we were unpacking."

"Did you just move in?"

"Officially, yes," Kathleen said. "This was already Morgan's house. When we first arrived we had only what we could carry on our backs."

Caldwell persisted. "Then how did your stuff get here?"

"We went to Seattle, hired movers, and had them pack what hadn't been destroyed," Morgan said.

"It was Morgan's idea to go to Seattle," Kathleen said. "He believed there had to be a reason other than revenge for us to have stayed on the run." She glanced at the passbook in the agent's hand. "Obviously, he was right."

Caldwell shifted nervously. Someone could have been watching the Seattle location. For all he knew, they could already be on their tail.

"Someone was watching the house in Seattle," Morgan said.

Caldwell's opinion of this man's prowess grew a little bit stronger. Not only was the man just shy of menacing, but it was obvious he didn't miss much. And he'd just read his mind. Caldwell took out his notebook.

"Did you get a good look at his face? Could you identify him if you saw him again?"

Morgan shook his head. "No, it was too dark."

"Then what makes you think he was watching that particular house? Maybe the incident wasn't even connected."

"He was watching it, all right," Morgan said.

"How do you know?"

"Because when I went after him, he ran."

Caldwell leaned back in his chair, smiling slightly.

"Well, I'm not so sure I wouldn't have done the same. You're an intimidating man, Mr. Tallchief. In the dark, I would venture to say, threatening."

"He was watching the house."

The smile slid off Caldwell's face. "Then you know what that means, don't you?"

Morgan nodded. "Eventually, they'll wind up here."

Kathleen gasped, then turned toward Morgan, giving him a wild, angry look.

"Why am I just now hearing this?"

He shrugged. "Because it's just a theory. I could be wrong. There was no need to scare you unduly."

"But Morgan, I have to know these things! What if you're gone one day and I have no idea that—"

He touched her face. "I won't leave you alone—ever."

She sighed. "You're not being practical. You cannot live the rest of your life being my bodyguard."

"I'm already your husband," he said quietly. "In my mind, they're one and the same."

Suddenly, Caldwell felt like a voyeur. He cleared his throat and looked away. Pretending great interest in his notes, he began to go through the pages, checking to see if there were any questions he'd left unanswered. It was then he remembered to ask, "When were you in New Orleans?"

Both Morgan and Kathleen looked startled by the unexpected question.

"We were never in New Orleans," she said.

Caldwell frowned. "Oh, but yes, ma'am, you were. I know because I was tracking the DTD signal when it went off the map."

Kathleen grinned, then looked at Morgan. He was making no attempt to hide a smile.

"What?" Caldwell asked. "What's so damned funny?"

"You might have been tracking the DTD, but it wasn't on my car," Kathleen said.

Caldwell thought of all those wasted days and miles and stifled a curse.

"Well, then, who had it?"

Kathleen couldn't resist a smile. "As a matter of fact, I believe it was the Easter bunny."

Morgan laughed aloud, but Caldwell didn't see the joke.

"That's real funny," he said. "But I'd still like to know the truth. I wasted a lot of my time tracking that signal."

Kathleen continued to grin as Morgan answered.

"I slipped it under the hood of a trucker's rig. He said his name was Ned Easter, but that his friends called him Bunny. He never knew the bug was there, and I have no idea what happened to it."

Caldwell's eyes widened. "Tallchief, you have a very inventive mind. Have you ever considered a job in law enforcement?"

Morgan shook his head. "I've broken all the heads I care to in this lifetime. I'm satisfied just to paint." Then he laid his hand on Kathleen's knee without looking at her. "And to take care of my family."

At that point, Caldwell looked back at the painting. It was then that his focus moved from the act in which the runners were engaged to the runners themselves. Their faces were the same! His eyes widened. It was Tallchief! He'd painted himself in those men.

Once again, the old newspaper clipping came to mind. *College-bound Olympic hopeful sets national record.* But instead of winning medals, he'd learned how to kill. What must her death have done to him?

Caldwell looked away, but not at Morgan. Embarrassed, he didn't want to let on that he suddenly understood what was driving the man. Tallchief had lost her once. Obviously, Caldwell thought, Tallchief wasn't going to lose her again. He wasn't surprised when Morgan started asking questions.

"Why the interest in Lester Bryant? Do you suspect him?"

Caldwell frowned. "He's dead."

Morgan shifted in his seat. "Then why ask?"

Caldwell ignored the question, concentrating on the red book instead. He fiddled with his notebook, then made a decision.

"I'd like to take a look at Kathleen's car, maybe get a forensics team to give it a thorough going-over."

"Why?" she asked.

"We might lift some prints from it, other than your own, of course, that could be of use to us."

"I doubt it," Morgan said. "It quit her on her way out. We had it towed to a garage. It's still there. The mechanic is waiting on parts, and I'd venture to say half the county's had their hands on that car."

Caldwell frowned. "Still, it's worth a try. We've got ourselves a little puzzle, but there's still too many pieces missing to tell what's really there."

She shrugged. "Be my guest."

Caldwell flipped through the pages in the red book, then suddenly looked up. "Paolo Benini has a son. Did you know that, Kathleen?"

She gasped, startled. Only after Morgan touched her did she calm down.

Caldwell continued as if nothing had happened, as if he hadn't just dropped a small bomb into the conversation.

"Tallchief, I'd like for you to come with me to look at the car. I want you to show me where the DTD was planted, and I—"

"No."

Caldwell frowned. "Why not?"

"I'm not leaving my family alone."

Caldwell threw up his hands. "I didn't ask you to. They can come with us—or better yet, I'll get some of my men out here. I think we need to keep a twenty-four-hour watch until the recovery of this passbook is made public. After that, whoever has been after her will know it's out of her hands. How does that sound?"

Kathleen got to her feet, her eyes blazing. "Why do you two keep talking about me, but not to me? I'm still here. Don't I have a say-so in this mess?"

Morgan took her hand and pulled her back down beside him. "I'm sorry, and you're right. Ultimately, the decision should be yours."

"Fine then," she muttered. "Go do what you have to do. I just want this over with. I'm sure Trish and I will be safe with Mr. Caldwell's men."

"Mind if I use your phone?" Caldwell asked.

"If you need privacy, there's one in the kitchen," Morgan said, and pointed the way.

Caldwell jumped to his feet. At last something positive was being accomplished.

"I think I can have some here within a couple of

hours. Maybe by tonight, this will all be over," he said.

His words were prophetic, but not in the way that he'd intended. The only thing over would be the waiting.

Seventeen

Morgan glanced over his shoulder as he pulled out of the driveway. One FBI agent was standing in the doorway, another was making a quick survey of their surroundings. Both were within fifty feet of the house. Two of Uncle Sam's finest could surely take care of Kathleen and Patricia for the short time in which he'd be gone.

"I'll take you to Kathleen's car, but I'm not staying," Morgan told Caldwell as he returned his attention to the road ahead.

Caldwell shrugged. "Fine by me. My forensics team should be waiting by the time we get there."

Morgan stomped the accelerator. "It won't take long."

"Obviously," Caldwell muttered, checking to see if his seat belt was fastened, then glancing at the speedometer. He figured if they went any faster, they just might become airborne.

"Frustrated pilot syndrome?" he drawled, expecting Tallchief would get the hint and slow down.

Morgan never cracked a smile. "You mean man wasn't meant to fly?"

Caldwell chuckled. "Not without wings."

An easy silence passed between them, and for a time, each man stayed lost in thought. For Morgan, there were too many unanswered questions. The FBI knew something they weren't telling, and he had a sick feeling that it was bad.

"It's almost ten A.M.," Caldwell said, then yawned. "I feel like I haven't slept in a week."

"It was just after seven when you got to my house. What time did you get up?"

"Yesterday. I drove all night from Oklahoma."

The only sign of Morgan's uneasiness was a slight tensing of the muscles along his jaw.

"What was the big hurry? You've had over sixteen years' worth of Kathleen's life already."

Caldwell looked away.

"Why did you ask Kathleen about Lester Bryant? You never did say if your Bryant and hers was one and the same."

"No, I guess I didn't, did I?" Caldwell said, and fiddled with a loose thread on a shirt button.

For the moment, Morgan let it slide, but when they arrived at the garage, his suspicions intensified.

As Caldwell had predicted, the forensics team was waiting, having arrived only moments ahead of them.

"Sorry about this, buddy," Morgan told the mechanic in charge, who'd been shuffled out of his own garage with little explanation other than a flash of a badge.

"What's going on?" the mechanic asked.

Morgan frowned. "You don't want to know."

Before he could question Morgan further, another agent escorted the mechanic out of the way, leaving Morgan and Caldwell to watch as men and women in white lab coats swarmed the area.

"Where did you find the DTD?" Caldwell asked.

"Underneath."

"As in under the hood, or—"

Morgan shook his head. "No, underneath, on the right side of the transmission housing."

Caldwell made another notation in his book.

For several minutes, the men stood and watched. It was such a routine, repetitive procedure, that Caldwell was caught off guard by Morgan's question.

"You think Bryant was dirty, don't you?"

When Caldwell didn't answer, Morgan snapped. He grabbed him by the collar and none too gently pushed him against the wall of the garage.

"Damn you, I want an answer!"

Caldwell pushed him away, then stomped outside of the garage and into the sunlight, blinking rapidly as his eyes began to adjust. When he could see more than spots before his eyes, he looked up, fixing Morgan with a cold, angry stare.

"I know what you want," he said. "And for what it's worth, I don't blame you. But I've got my orders, and they don't include sharing confidential information with civilians."

Morgan's voice lowered until it was barely above a whisper, yet Caldwell felt the impact of the question as if Tallchief had shouted in his face.

"Was he the only one?" Morgan asked. "Or are there

others? Can you vouch for the two men you put on my family?"

Caldwell blanched, and Morgan saw it.

"Son of a bitch," he mumbled, and turned on his heel.

"Where are you going?" Caldwell yelled, as Morgan stalked toward his car.

"To call home."

"There's not a damn thing wrong with my men!" he shouted, but Morgan kept walking. Pissed at the big man's hardheaded attitude, he cursed beneath his breath, then followed Morgan to the car. He wanted to see the expression on his face when he found out he was wrong.

Morgan slid into the seat and picked up his phone. He punched in the numbers, then counted the rings. He hadn't expected Kathleen to answer on the first one, but when Trish, who usually raced for the phone, hadn't answered on the tenth, he started to worry.

"Damn," he said, disconnecting, then punching the numbers in again, convinced he had to have misdialed. The phone rang until Morgan lost count. His gut was in knots. Every instinct he had told him something wasn't right.

"What's the matter?" Caldwell asked.

Morgan looked up at him from where he was sitting. "You tell me," he said softly, and slammed the front door shut.

The car was already rolling when Caldwell jumped inside. Neither man made a sound until miles later when Morgan turned off the road and into his driveway. Then it was Caldwell, and all he did was groan.

The front door to the house stood ajar. One of his

agents lay faceup in what looked like mud. It took a second for Caldwell to realize it was the man's own blood. He drew his weapon.

As he got out of the car, he crouched behind the open door, his gun aimed at an unseen target, but his thoughts were on the man on the ground. Damn! Henderson's wife was going to make a very young widow.

Fear shattered what was left of Morgan's reserve. He was out of the car before it stopped rolling. He made a run for the side of the house, wanting to shout, yet afraid it could be the trigger to end a madman's patience.

Seconds later, he ventured a quick glance in a window and saw nothing—heard nothing. He motioned to Caldwell that he was going in.

"Damn fool," Caldwell muttered, then bolted out from behind the car, backing him all the way.

Morgan slipped inside, then into the shadows, remembering the sounds of his own house and listening for something that didn't belong. Seconds later, it came in the form of a moan from somewhere to his right, in the living room.

Kathleen!

He moved without making a sound, attuned to the harsh, intermittent gasps of someone trying to draw breaths. After what he'd seen in his front yard, he should have been prepared, but he wasn't. Not here, not within the sanctity of his own home.

It was the other agent. "Caldwell! In here!" he shouted, then leaned over and grabbed the agent by the arm. If it took the man's last breath, he needed an answer.

"Where are they?" he yelled. "Where's Kathleen? What happened to my daughter?"

Suddenly, Caldwell pushed him aside. "Let up, man! Can't you see he's in a bad way?"

Morgan turned, his voice slicing the air between them. "At least he's still alive," he said bitterly, taking the wounded agent's gun as he stood.

Caldwell grabbed for his phone and began calling for help, leaving Morgan momentarily alone with his thoughts. *Not again! Damn you, God, don't do this to me again!*

He got to his feet and began a sweep through the rooms, praying he'd find them, then amending that to finding them alive.

Hope faded and died as he stalked from room to room. Reason disappeared behind a wall of dark hate, and at that moment, Morgan knew that if it took him the rest of his life, he would kill the person who'd done this.

Throughout the house, there was no furniture upturned. No broken glass. Nothing missing—except his reasons for living. He moved on to the studio without conscious thought, taking note of little else but the fact that there was no one there, either. Wind from the desert whistled through a half-open window, and for a moment, before he cataloged the sound, he thought it was a woman's cry.

He turned in place, the gun hanging loosely in his hand. Faces stared back at him from the studio walls, mocking by their very silence. Suddenly, everything within him gave way.

"No."

He staggered, then let out one long, agonized scream.

"Nooo!"

Between blind rage and pain, he drew back, sending the gun through the air. It went through a window, cracking the silence like a burst of gunfire, followed by a waterfall of tinkling glass.

His gut twisted as his eyes went out of focus. Try as he might, he couldn't see past a thick veil of red. The same red as the blood spilled on his living room floor.

He had told Kathleen he would take care of her. He'd promised her he would look after their daughter, too. And in the end, when it had mattered, he hadn't even been here to try.

And then he heard Caldwell shouting his name, and there was something in the tone that sank past insanity to buried reason. Something that made him take a step back, and then another, and then another. Before Morgan knew it, Caldwell had him by the arm and was spinning him around.

"Look, man! Out there! Isn't that your kid?"

Morgan's head jerked as the red veil lifted, giving him a clear view to the direction in which Caldwell was pointing.

A young girl was running toward the house. Her hair was long and black, and as she ran, she was screaming his name.

"Oh, Jesus," Morgan whispered, and started to run. He didn't remember moving, only catching her in his arms as she started to fall.

Morgan's hands were all over her at once, checking for injuries. Physically she seemed fine; mentally she was about to break.

"She made me run," Trish sobbed, pleading for her father to understand. "I wouldn't have left her"—she gasped, trying to catch her breath—"but she made me go without her! Oh, God, Daddy! They killed the man in the yard. I saw him fall." She shuddered, and buried her face against Morgan's shirt. When she spoke again, her voice was weak and broken. "They took her, Daddy. They took Mom away and I'll never see her again."

Morgan swept her into his arms. "Are you hurt, baby?" he asked, his voice just shy of breaking.

Trish wrapped her arms around his neck and gave herself up to despair. Tears rolled as she tried to explain.

"No, just scared . . . so scared." Her voice trembled as she tried to explain. "I ran and ran without looking back until I heard the helicopter lift off, and then I hid in some sagebrush and waited until it was out of sight. I started back . . . and then I saw your car." She swallowed a sob and tightened her grip on his neck. "I was afraid you'd leave, too."

Helicopter! Son of a bitch, they could be anywhere! Morgan's heart clenched. He couldn't let Trish know how scared he was.

"No, honey, I promise you . . . I'll never leave you alone with strangers again."

She looked up at him with Kathleen's eyes and he felt sick.

"I want my mom."

"I know, baby, I know. So do I."

He picked her up, shifting her lightly within his grasp, then started walking. The sound of oncoming sirens met them as they finally reached the breezeway joining studio to house.

Caldwell was on the porch, a phone in one hand, his

gun still in the other. When he saw them, he disconnected instantly and went to Morgan's aid.

"Is she all right?"

Morgan nodded.

"Thank God," Caldwell said, and then glanced toward the house. "Don't take her inside," he ordered. "At least not yet."

Morgan looked at the man in the yard. His body had been covered with a sheet.

"What about the one inside?" Morgan asked.

"He just died," Caldwell said.

Trish sobbed, and turned her face toward Morgan's neck.

"I'm sorry, honey," he said softly.

Caldwell touched her shoulder briefly, his voice gruff with unshed emotion. "I'm sorry, too, Patricia. This is more than we bargained for."

"Agent Miller was a nice man," she sobbed. "He's the one who pushed me out the back door as they came in the house. He tried to make Mom go, too, but she wouldn't. She screamed at him to stop, and said that if she ran, they'd catch both of us. She was the one they wanted. She was going to stay." She shuddered. "If it hadn't been for Agent Miller, they might have seen me. I heard him start shooting, and then I heard my mother screaming for them to stop." She took a deep breath. "I ran away. I didn't hear anything else."

The sirens were coming closer. Caldwell looked over Patricia's shoulder, straight into Morgan's eyes.

"Miller did more than save your daughter's life," he said. "He just might have saved your wife's too. He heard them talking. We think we know where they took her."

Morgan froze, then slowly set Trish on her feet, where she stood within the shelter of his arms.

"Where?'

Caldwell hesitated a moment too long.

"Don't do this to me," Morgan warned.

Caldwell had heard Morgan's rage of despair. He'd also heard glass breaking, and then seen the life coming back in Tallchief's eyes with the reappearance of his daughter. He didn't have it in him to keep anything back. Not any longer.

"Teneca Air. Have you heard of it?"

Morgan frowned, searching his memory. "Private airport north of Santa Fe?"

Caldwell nodded. "According to my sources, abandoned over a year ago after the owner went bankrupt. We've already got a surveillance team on the move. I'll know within a couple of hours if anyone's there."

"When you go in, I'm going with you."

"Don't be a fool, man. I can't guarantee your safety. What if something happened to you—then who'll take care of your daughter?"

At that point, the ambulance pulled up in the yard, along with several county police cars. Although federal agents had been killed, local law enforcement would still be involved in the investigation.

"My family takes care of their own," Morgan said, and stepped aside as medical personnel ran past him and into the house at Caldwell's direction. Morgan gave Trish a swift look, then started toward his car.

"Where are you going?" Caldwell asked.

"To make a call."

"Here. Use mine," Caldwell said, and tossed his cell phone toward Morgan, who caught it in midair. "The bad boys are always allowed one call with the law's compliments. In this instance, it seems the least we could do is allow you the same."

"Thanks," Morgan said, and walked a distance away out of the noise of the crime scene now being processed. He glanced down at his watch as the phone began to ring. There was an hour's difference in time. In Comanche, Oklahoma, it was nearing noon.

James Tallchief was in the bathroom, drying his hands in anticipation of the fried chicken and new potatoes he'd already seen on the table. He grinned to himself as he hung the towel back on the rack. Mary sure knew her way around a kitchen.

"Smells good," he said, as he entered the kitchen and took his seat. Before he had time to drop his napkin in his lap, the phone began to ring.

"Wouldn't you know it?" he muttered, and pushed away from the table.

He answered curtly, but his annoyance disappeared when he heard his brother's voice. A wide smile broke the somberness of his face.

"Hey, Morgan, what's up?"

As he listened, his smile quickly died. His eyes darkened, and his face tensed as he began a mental countdown of available options for complying with his brother's request.

"Don't worry, little brother," he said quietly. "We'll be there."

He hung up, and when he turned, Mary was standing in the doorway.

"What's wrong?" she asked.

"Kathleen has been kidnapped."

Mary gasped. Sudden tears sprang to her eyes. "Oh, no!" And then she thought of Morgan's daughter, and how much she'd come to care for her in such a short time. "And Trish?"

"She's safe." He frowned, wondering how Mary was going to take what he was going to say, but aware that he would go regardless of how she reacted. "Actually, that's why he called. He asked me to come take care of her, and I'm going."

"I'll come with you," she said quickly.

James touched her face, and thought of how much she meant to him. In the same moment, he wondered if Morgan would survive a second time if Kathleen should really die.

"No, Mary. Morgan doesn't need baby-sitters, he needs bodyguards."

Her eyes widened in fear, but to her credit, she neither argued nor cried. "I'll pack for you," she said.

He glanced toward the kitchen. "Save some chicken for when I get back. I've got some phone calls to make."

Morgan's kitchen had become a field office for the ongoing arrival of federal agents. Two of their finest were dead, and a woman had been kidnapped while under their protection. It was no longer just another case; it had become personal.

Morgan listened without speaking as new information was spilled on a minute-to-minute basis. The only good news to come out of it all was they believed Kathleen was still alive. They'd come to that consensus because of the phone call.

As calls went, it wasn't much. The caller hadn't

even cared who he was talking to. It had been short and to the point. Kathleen was being ransomed, and all the kidnapper wanted for her life was one small red book.

"They wouldn't let us talk to her. You know what that means," one agent offered. "She could already be dead."

Caldwell glanced quickly at Morgan, afraid that he'd take the man's head off for the mere suggestion. To his surprise, Tallchief was just staring out the window. He didn't know Morgan was tuned in to a conversation all his own.

Believe and it will be so.

I do, Grandmother, I do believe.

Caldwell put his hand on Morgan's arm.

Morgan jerked, then spun around. "What? Is there news?"

He nodded. "And none too good," he said. "That damned airport is in the middle of nowhere, about eleven miles off the nearest highway. There's no way to get to it without being seen. If we rush it, they'll see us coming miles away. If we wait until dark, they'll see our lights. Although, *if* we wait until dark, we could parachute some men close by, but chances are the plane would still be heard and the men could be spotted. Tonight will be close to a full moon."

Morgan winced. Last night he'd made love to Kathleen beneath that moon. It didn't bear considering that she could die beneath it tonight.

Caldwell felt incredibly guilty. He'd promised Tallchief they'd be safe. "This is far from over," he said. "Remember what they said. They'll call back at midnight and give us a time and place to deliver the book." He glanced at his watch. "It's nearly four o'clock now. That leaves us . . ."

Morgan put his hand over the face of Caldwell's watch. "Very little time."

Suddenly, everyone inside the house began to shout. Men grabbed for their guns, taking a defensive position as the sounds of a helicopter could now be heard in the distance. Morgan flinched. That was the same sound Kathleen had heard. He started toward the door when Caldwell grabbed him by the arm.

"Where do you think you're going?" Caldwell asked.

Morgan pushed past him and stepped out on the porch, shading his eyes as he looked to the south. The chopper was little more than a dark spot in the sky, but as it came closer, it became obvious by the camouflage paint that it was military.

Caldwell poked his head back inside the house. "It's military," he shouted. "Are we expecting anyone?"

Morgan walked off the porch, shading his eyes from the sunshine as the chopper began to circle and then descended. When it landed, seven men spilled out of its belly. Morgan's heart surged and his vision suddenly blurred. He started to move.

Wind from the blades whipped sand and pebbles against his face and arms, but he didn't stop walking. His gaze was focused on the man in front—and the others who came behind.

Some were tall and slim, others shorter and broader, but their skin was brown and their hair was black, and they came with purpose in every step. He knew them. They shared the same name, the same faces, the same blood. Five brothers and two brothers-in-law, and they were all carrying guns. Morgan reached James first, and without pause, walked into his arms, accepting his brother's embrace.

Caldwell watched flabbergasted as the meeting played out. When the others circled, each in his own way touching and greeting Morgan, it was obvious the Tallchief family had arrived.

James gave Morgan a last, hearty hug, and then stepped back, observing the bleak expression in his youngest brother's face.

In spite of the ominous occasion, Morgan managed a slight grin. "Hell of an arrival, brother."

"Mary's brother is a colonel in the National Guard, remember? I told him this was a federal case. It was all he needed to hear to alleviate his conscience about using government property." He grinned slightly. "After all, what's family for if you can't use them in times of need?"

Morgan looked into each man's face, remembering other days and better times. Then they stood in a whirlwind of debris as the helicopter lifted off and swiftly disappeared.

When they could talk without eating dust, Morgan spoke to them all, measuring each brother's lack of expression as sensitivity to his own. "Thank you for coming."

"Tell us what you need," James said.

There was nothing between Morgan and his family but the truth.

"I need you to take care of my daughter tonight. And if something happens and I don't come back . . ."

James shifted his gun to his other hand and tried not to think of losing Morgan. "She's family, little brother. You don't have to ask."

Caldwell stood on the porch in openmouthed awe as the phalanx of armed men came toward him. Lost in his muse, he jumped as one of the agents walked out of the house and then stopped abruptly, about to reach for his gun.

"Who are they?" the agent asked.

Caldwell frowned, remembering Morgan's phone call. "Baby-sitters . . . I think."

The agent gauged the men's somber expressions, as well as their odd assortment of guns.

"Get their number for me, will you? My wife and I could use someone like them. I've got a four-year-old who suddenly decided last month that he's now the boss."

Caldwell laughed. It didn't last long, but for the moment, it felt good.

Morgan stood alone outside his house. It was nearing dusk. Within the hour, the sun would set. Inside, the house was a hive of activity as the team of federal agents ran through their options of retrieving Kathleen Tallchief alive from the kidnappers' hands. The nervous tension with which Morgan had gone through the day had moved to a dead calm. It was the same feeling he'd always gotten before going out on a mission. Back then, they'd had a target and a plan, and to a man, everyone was trained to do his job. That's the way it was tonight. He had a target. Kathleen. He had a plan. Get her back. What Caldwell didn't yet know was how Morgan was planning to do it.

Once again, the screen door squeaked. He turned. It was Patricia, followed by James and Reid, the brother closest to Morgan in age. As promised, at least two of his family dogged her steps at all times. She came off the porch toward him.

"Dad?"

Morgan wrapped her in his arms. Resting his chin upon the crown of her head, he closed his eyes and said a small, silent prayer. To his dismay, Trish started to cry.

"Honey . . . don't," he begged, and gently kissed her forehead and then wiped at her tears.

"I'm scared," she sobbed. "What if you can't get Mom back? What if you don't come back, either?"

Ah, God. There was no way he could lie to her, not now. "I'm scared, too," he said.

"You are?"

"More than you know. I've spent my adult life alone. Then I found you and your mother, and you made living worthwhile. Earlier today, when I thought you were dead, I wanted to die with you. When I knew that you were okay, and that your mother could still be alive . . . it gave me reason to care. I love you two very much, you know."

"I know," she sobbed. "But I heard Agent Caldwell say it was going to be impossible to get to Mom without being seen."

The screen door squeaked. Caldwell was standing on the porch. Morgan could tell by the look on his face that he regretted Trish's having heard him.

"No, it's not impossible. At least not for me," Morgan said, speaking more to Caldwell than to Trish.

The agent straightened perceptibly as he heard Morgan's words and saw the look on his face.

"But how?" Trish asked. "What can you do that a dozen special agents can't do?"

He tilted her chin, until she had nowhere to look but at his face.

"I can run."

Her eyes widened. "Dad!"

James looked at Reid, then shrugged, knowing it was out of their hands. Morgan might be their little brother, but he'd long ago become a man.

But Caldwell was floored. He came off of the porch in two bounds, grabbing Morgan by the arm and all but yanking him around.

"You're crazy," he growled.

Morgan shrugged out of his grasp. "No, I'm not. I'm a runner. I've run farther than that on any given night just to be able to sleep, and I have the . . ." he paused, searching for the word that wouldn't shock his daughter ". . . skills to do what must be done after I get there—and I'm going tonight."

Caldwell threw up his hands in frustration. "We're talking maybe eleven miles—in the dark. Who's going to take their call if you're not here? They're supposed to tell us where to deliver the passbook, remember?" He thrust his fingers through his thinning hair, then pivoted, staring off into the evening sky. When he turned back around, there was grit in his voice. "Given the fact that you could do it, you wouldn't be in any shape to take down the men if you actually got there before midnight."

"You're wrong," Morgan said quietly.

"You're not going alone."

"Kathleen is alone with God knows who. She believes I will come." He swallowed harshly, allowing himself no show of emotion. "That much I know. She's waiting for me, Caldwell. I'm going, with or without

your permission. Besides, your men can't keep up
with me and I have to get there before midnight."

"Oh, what the hell," Caldwell muttered, then spun
on his heel and started inside.

"Dad, is he going to let you go?"

"He has no choice," Morgan said. Then he looked to
his brothers. "Take care of her for me . . . until I get
back."

Morgan looked down at his daughter, then held her
close, telling himself it wouldn't be the last time he
held her. James nodded, while Reid looked away, but
Morgan had seen the fear in their eyes. To his surprise,
Trish quietly pulled away, then looked at him with a
near-calm expression.

"When you see Mom, tell her I love her, okay?"

He tried to grin. "You tell her yourself when we get
back."

Trish nodded, then let James lead her away.

Eighteen

"This is suicide, Tallchief, and I don't like it," Caldwell said, as Morgan stepped out of the car and knelt to tie his running shoes. "As it is, we've pushed our luck in getting you this close, and we're still more than eight miles from Teneco. It's not too late to change your mind. Say the word and we can go with our earlier plan."

Morgan stood, his words ringing with sarcasm. "You mean the one where we wait for the kidnapper's call, give him what he wants, and hope that he's a man of his word and turns Kathleen loose, unharmed?"

Caldwell looked away. Refuting what Tallchief had just said was impossible. It wasn't in him to lie.

"Okay, it's a long shot." Then he grabbed Morgan by the arm. "Every hostage situation is a long shot. You should know that better than most. What I'm saying to you is, you're only one man. We don't know for sure if it was Marco Benini who made the call, although our

sources are pretty sure that it was. Regardless of who
has your wife, we don't know how many men he has
with him. For all we know, the man who called could
be in one location and Kathleen in another."

Morgan buckled a fanny pack around his waist,
then readjusted the knife and scabbard that was hanging from the belt. An agent stood nearby, handing him
his gear, piece by piece. Morgan took the offered gun,
grunting with satisfaction at the silencer attached, and
slipped it into the pack. Old rules still applied. Never
let them hear you coming.

Finally, he looked up at Caldwell. "It's bound to be
Benini. He's the only one who has anything to gain.
And the man's a hunter. He's been after Kathleen's
family for years. He'll be there. He won't want to miss
the kill."

While Caldwell watched, Morgan thrust a finger
into some blacking, striping the bridge of his nose as
well as the arch of his cheekbones in a sort of camouflage. When Morgan turned, Caldwell almost shuddered. From the cold, hard glitter in his eyes to the
black paint streaking his face, Tallchief was as close to
warlike as a man could look.

Caldwell cursed beneath his breath, then handed
Morgan a small transmitter. "At least with this, we'll
have a way to track you. Here, put this in your
pocket."

"Don't have any," Morgan said, and patted the sides
of his shorts. The thin black fabric was designed for
optimum comfort when running. They weren't meant
for wallets and change.

Caldwell rolled his eyes. "Then put it in that fanny
pack."

"It will rattle against the gun."

Caldwell glared at Morgan, then gritted his teeth. "Donovan! Find a way to attach this damn bug to Tallchief." He glared at Morgan. "I still have some say-so in this matter, and I'm telling you, you're not leaving without it."

Morgan shrugged, then turned away, staring intently toward the direction in which he would go. In spite of the moonglow highlighting the desert before him, there were no familiar landmarks on which to focus. Running at night was risky. In the desert, even more so. He couldn't haul ass without something on which to fix his sights. He turned.

"Donovan, let me see that map once more."

The agent quickly complied; using the trunk lid of Caldwell's car as a table, he unfolded the area map and handed Morgan his flashlight.

Morgan took the map, then turned it so that it was facing the way he was standing. After pinpointing the abandoned airport on the map one more time, he looked up at the stars, aligning himself with one of his grandmother's favorite constellations. As long as the sky stayed clear, he had a heavenly map by which to run.

"Here," Caldwell said. "At least take the radio. If you need us, all you have to do is call."

Morgan pushed it away. "No. Those damn things pick up all kinds of signals out here. How would you like to be standing behind a man with a gun and have that thing squawk in his ear?"

Caldwell cursed and shoved it back in his pocket. "I've got an idea: Why don't you let me shoot you now and get it over with? At least you'll die a rested man."

Morgan grinned. Donovan approached, holding something in his hand. It was long and black, and it dangled from his fingers like feathers in the wind.

"Tallchief, how about a sweatband?"

Morgan took it, testing it for weight. The transmitter Caldwell had wanted him to carry had been inserted within the folds of the black cloth. He nodded his approval, then tied it around his forehead, unaware that the dangling ties looked like a warrior's feathers. Donovan thrust a small plastic bottle of water in Morgan's hand, then walked away. Morgan started to set it aside, then thought better of it.

"Happy, Caldwell?" Morgan asked.

"Ecstatic," he drawled.

"It's tracking," Donovan said, checking the computer system inside the van.

Caldwell walked to the vehicle and leaned inside. Moments later when he turned around, Morgan Tallchief was gone. Panic skittered through his mind, then receded.

He looked back inside the van. The signal was strong. "The least he could have done was say good-bye."

A few minutes later, a small cry went up from the men inside who were tracking Tallchief's movement across the desert.

Caldwell spun around, his gaze focusing on the flat screen before him. "What's wrong? Has it stopped sending?"

"Look, sir! Look at him go!"

Caldwell leaned forward, staring at the blip as it moved across the screen. "Are you sure that's our man?"

Donovan looked up. "That's Tallchief, all right." He grinned. "Unless we've got ourselves a UFO."

Caldwell thought of the old newspaper clipping in Kathleen Ryder's file. So Tallchief's skills hadn't been exaggerated after all. The man wasn't running; he was damn close to flying. Caldwell thought of the way Morgan drove a car and realized he should have known. The son of a bitch ran like he drove.

Nervously, Caldwell glanced at his watch, then out into the desert. In less than two hours, they would proceed toward the airport as Morgan's promised backup. And even though the plan was in motion, his nerves wouldn't settle back down. Tallchief hadn't given himself much leeway to be wrong.

Morgan ran, putting one foot after the other, moving faster than he normally did on a desert run. There was no burst of speed in easier territory and no slowing down when the going got rough. The air was cool, but he didn't feel it. Sweat ran, sticking his clothes to his skin, and he never knew. His body took him through one level of exhaustion and then another without hitting the runner's proverbial "wall." His mind wouldn't let his body give up.

Kathleen was out there somewhere, and he'd promised to keep her safe. And so he ran, a lone warrior, at home with the night.

Although Morgan was less than thirty miles from his home, the terrain felt ragged and different. South of Santa Fe, where he resided, the land was flat, with occasional sagebrush and cholla cactus, and once in a while, a piñon tree could be seen squatting in the distance. Here, the vegetation was thicker. In places, sagebrush was anywhere from ankle high to knee high. He recognized it by the sweet smell wafting in the air as the dry vegetation crushed beneath his feet. Somewhere beyond his circle of vision, evergreens grew. Their sharp, pungent aroma burned his nostrils as he ran.

On a particularly open space, he took time to glance up at the sky, assuring himself that he was still moving in the right direction. There above him was the same constellation with which he'd started. It was all he needed to know.

Keep me on the right track, Grandmother.

It didn't matter that she hadn't answered. Somehow, tonight, he felt her with him.

Overhead, a helicopter circled, and his gut clenched as he thought of the one that had taken Kathleen away. Chances were, Caldwell had been right. In a helicopter, they would never have been able to get close enough to the old Teneco building without being seen. If it was Benini's men standing guard by air, then he hoped they were merely looking for lights that didn't belong. If they had any type of night-vision instruments, especially those that searched by heat, he'd already been made. If he was lucky, it was just a pilot out for a ride.

The desert was cold, but Morgan was hot as he continued to run, burning up his energy—and the miles—as he moved ever closer to Kathleen. The small bottle of water Donovan had thrust in his hand was nearly empty. He tilted it as he ran, pouring the tepid fluid between his lips. A trickle of moisture ran from the side of his mouth where he'd spilled it. He didn't bother to wipe it away. Soon, it blended with sweat running down his jaw, then onto his shirt. Nothing mattered but getting to Kathleen.

*   *   *

A small trickle of dried blood dotted the corner of Kathleen's lip. Her jaw ached, her head throbbed, and more than once her vision had blurred. But she'd die before she gave Marco Benini the satisfaction of seeing her cry.

The chair in which she was tied was old and rickety. Once, while trying to ease the pressure from the ropes around her wrists and ankles, she had moved too sharply and gone tumbling sideways onto the floor.

At the sound, Benini had spun from his post at the old hangar window, his gun drawn. The glare on his face deepened as he waved at his cohort to set her upright.

Now, several hours later, Kathleen had another move she needed to make. There was the chance that asking could cause her more harm than good, but, she told herself, she'd never know until she tried.

"I need to go to the bathroom."

Marco frowned. Kidnapping the woman had turned into one big headache. She'd thrown up in the helicopter, then bumped her head and bled on his shirt. Now she wanted to pee. He had two choices. Let her go in her pants and then smell it for the next six hours, or untie her and give her the privacy she obviously needed. Instinct told him to tell her to go right ahead. Instead, he heard himself telling Amal to untie her. Just to make himself clear, he got down in her face and very slowly put the gun between her legs where she sat, angling it just enough to make his point.

"Mess with me, lady, and I'll deliver you to your lover in neat, tiny pieces."

Fear wrenched every muscle in Kathleen's body, but

she did little more than blink. Only after Benini had
backed up did she make the effort to stand. The man
he called Amal yanked her by the arm, hastening the
motion. Her stiff joints protested as Amal dragged her
past the helicopter they had parked inside the hangar
to the other end of the building. She guessed, by the
looks of the partitioned-off areas, that this was where
the offices had been.

Amal kicked open a door, then shoved her inside what
had once served as a tiny bathroom. The sink was missing, the commode cracked, but still standing. She stumbled and fell across it, bracing herself with outstretched
hands to keep from hitting the wall. Wood splinters from
broken paneling tore through tender flesh, piercing her
palms. Upon impact, cockroaches began slithering into
the cracks, while a lizard shinnied up the side of a wall.
It was all she could do not to scream.

She dragged herself up, then turned and looked at
the swarthy, ponytailed man standing but a few feet
away. With all the dignity she could muster, she
reached out and pushed the door shut in his face, then
held her breath. When she heard nothing but a shifting
of feet and an indistinct curse, she tried to relax as she
looked around.

Boy, had she ever gotten what she'd asked for! She
was in a bathroom, but it was the bathroom from hell.
The lid to the commode was closed, and after the cockroaches and lizards, she wasn't sure she wanted to see
what might be inside.

To her relief, it contained nothing but rusty water
stains and a couple of disintegrating cigarette butts.
The absence of water did not deter her. Within moments, she'd found the relief she sought.

"Get out here now, or I'm coming in after you."

Kathleen shuddered. Amal's threat was all too real. To a man, Marco's thugs had stripped her naked with their eyes more than once. All that stood between her and perdition was Benini himself, and she didn't think it was because he cared about her welfare. During the short time they'd been together, she'd learned one thing about her captor: If it wasn't *his* idea, it wasn't a good one.

She winced as she zipped up her jeans. Her hands were burning horribly, and when she looked, she went numb at the damage the splinters had done. Already the grooves were puffing up and imbedding the wood slivers deeper into her flesh. It would probably take a surgeon to get them all out. If she lived to have it done.

She glanced at herself in the piece of cracked mirror still hanging, and then gasped. Wiping at her face with the sleeve of her shirt, she managed to get most of the dirt from her cheek, but without cool water or ice, she could do nothing to ease the swelling on her lip and jaw.

It doesn't matter, she told herself. *They can carve their initials on my face if it will make them happy. Nothing matters if I just come out alive. I want to live to see my daughter grown. Someday, I want to watch her walk down the aisle with her father at her side.* Kathleen covered her face and willed herself not to cry. *I want another baby with Morgan. He deserves to see at least one of his children grow up. I want to grow old with him.* She looked up at herself, then closed her eyes. *I don't want my last breath on this earth to be drawn alone. Dear God, don't let me die.*

Amal kicked the door. It was his last warning, and Kathleen took it as such. She straightened her shoulders, tilted her chin, then stepped outside.

He grabbed her by the arm and began dragging her back the same way they'd come. Silently, she endured the abuse. This time, when he shoved her in the chair and began retying the ropes, she bunched her hands in such a way that when he was through, the blood at least had room to flow.

Hours passed as Benini paced, glancing at his watch, then the woman, then back at his watch. He couldn't figure her out. Most women would have been screaming their heads off, or begging for mercy. But not her. Something about the look in her eyes gave him the creeps. The expression reminded him of his Sicilian grandmother. She'd been a woman who'd known the meaning of revenge.

He scoffed at his fantasy and turned away. This woman was nothing to him. She couldn't hurt him. Her life was, quite literally, in his hands. He glanced back out the window. It was almost dusk. Only a few more hours and the book would be his. Anticipation made him antsy. The money—his father's money—it was his by birthright alone. It didn't matter to Marco that it was ill-gotten gains. His whole world revolved around taking, not giving.

Something clattered outside the hangar, and he leaned forward, peering as best he could through the dust-covered windows. He thought of the dead federal agents they'd left behind.

"Amal, make sure the men are in their positions. There's no way they could possibly know where we are, but just in case . . ." His voice trailed off, and as Amal went outside to do his boss's bidding, Marco turned to Kathleen. "I don't like surprises."

She did nothing but blink. Her lack of fear irritated

him. Suddenly, he was enraged at the thought of the years of hapless pursuit of this woman and her family. He thought of the money they'd spent and the men that they'd killed trying to find them. Damn her, the least she could do was appreciate who he was!

"What's wrong with you?" he growled. Once again, he used his gun for a finger, lifting her hair from her cheek, then pushing aside her blouse, absently inspecting a rough, angry scratch that angled toward her left breast. He traced her swollen lips with the tip of the barrel, pressing down upon the spot where it had bled just enough to get her attention.

"Are you on something . . . hunh? Is the pretty lady a little junkie? Are you spinning on a high and keeping it all to yourself?"

Kathleen's mind raged, but her voice stayed silent. Her only movement was to follow the motion of Marco's gun with her gaze. When he turned away, she tried to relax. Suddenly, he spun back around and, with a loud, angry grunt, caught the side of her face with the barrel of the gun. She never saw it coming.

She moaned, then gasped, shuddering as her face began to throb where her teeth had cut the inside of her mouth. In reflex, her eyes filled, and twin tracks of tears slipped down her cheeks.

"So, bitch, you *can* feel, can't you?"

Careful not to upend her chair again, she tilted her head and spit blood on the floor. It landed too near Marco's feet to have been an accident. He stared at the splatter near the toe of his boot, and couldn't believe his eyes. She was either the most gutsy woman he'd ever seen or she had a death wish. He stared at her with feral intensity, then he inhaled slowly, reminding himself of the plan at hand. Calmly, he smoothed his hands down the front of his shirt, tracing his slight paunch with pride. In the old country, a good belly was a sign of wealth. It meant he could afford to indulge himself to his heart's content. A cold smile broke the anger on his face.

"Before, I wasn't sure what I was going to do with you after this was over, but I am now."

Kathleen's heart was racing, but she wouldn't look up. It took every ounce of will she had left to keep from fainting.

"Look at me, bitch!"

She swallowed a groan, then lifted her head. When he leaned forward, she fought the urge to close her eyes.

"My men want you. I like to give my men what they want."

A shudder slipped past her resistance. Marco grinned. At last, a result he could appreciate.

"I'm told that women like Amal's looks." He was so close that Kathleen could feel his breath upon her eyelids. "Unfortunately, he doesn't much like women—and he doesn't leave his leftovers for other men."

It came out before she thought. Before she could stop her tongue from moving, before she could stop her mind from thinking it. Her voice was raspy and dry, but the emotion was there just the same.

"He will kill you for this."

Marco looked slightly confused. He straightened, then took a step back and stared. A cold, blue gaze looked back.

"Who?" he growled. "Another fed?" His bushy eyebrows arched playfully. "Surely you don't mean your boyfriend? What's he going to do—scalp us?" His harsh chuckle echoed within the walls.

But she didn't say anything more, and the longer she stared, the more uncomfortable he became. He sneered and walked back to the window. She was just talking.

Their only light inside the hangar came from a portable generator, so when Marco looked out, he was slightly surprised to see it was already dark. Instead of walking to the open hangar doors, he leaned closer to the window, presenting less of a target as he peered out through the thin, dusty glass. Moonlight bounced from nearby bushes, giving the place an eerie, otherworldly look. He thought of his beautiful New York City—of restaurants that stayed open all night and cab drivers that never slept. Of pretty women and easy money and power. Always the power. The absence of that here made him nervous, as if he didn't quite know where he stood.

Impulsively, he stalked to the door and yelled out to the night. "Amal, get your ass in here, and bring Tuley with you."

They came on the run and when they were inside, Marco felt himself calm. He'd given orders and they'd been obeyed. Now he was back in control.

"Are the men in place?"

Amal nodded. "Steiger's set up on the east lookout. Hamilton's on the west. I put Wainright on the south toward the mountains."

"Where's Ambrose?" Marco asked.

"He's out there somewhere, guarding the front door. He's gotta be point man, remember? Ever since Vietnam, Ambrose has to be point. He's sitting out beneath

some sagebrush, smoking those damned cigarettes. If
he doesn't set himself on fire, we'll be lucky."

Marco nodded. "I don't care where he sits, as long as
he does his job."

But Amal's attention had already refocused, as his
gaze slowly swept the bound woman's face, missing
nothing of the new blood and bruises on her face. "She
been giving you trouble?"

Marco sneered, then thought of his promise to Kathleen and started to grin. It wouldn't hurt to give her a
little something to think about.

"When this is over, she's your bonus."

Tuley moved into Kathleen's line of vision and
cupped himself rudely, grinning as she quickly looked
away. Amal, however, did nothing but stare. Kathleen
flinched.

*There is no way they'll find me in time. Oh, God, let me
die with some grace.*

Morgan's mind was on hold. Everything he did was
attuned to the movement of his arms and legs, to the
ever-present forward motion of the run, so when the
first sign of light suddenly appeared upon the horizon,
he almost stumbled. He hadn't been prepared for the
abruptness of its arrival.

Instinctively, he began to slow down to a lope. His
mind shifted gears, as it had been trained to do. He
began to circle slightly, unwilling to come straight in
on the light without reconnoitering the area. Gauging
his distance to be several hundred yards away, he gave
a quick glance heavenward, assuring himself that he'd
stayed on course.

This had to be Teneco.

His mind jumped to Kathleen, and he took a deep breath, forcing the emotion back where it belonged. First things first. Make sure she was there. If she was, he was well aware that to get her out, he would have to take the men out, one at a time. Killing was the easy part. Keeping her alive while it happened was where concentration came in.

He was close enough now to see the vague outline of a massive hangar looming upon the moonlit ground like a hulking monster. Its eyes were the windows through which weak light spilled out, its maw, the wide-open doors through which it swallowed its prey.

As he moved slowly eastward, the tail of a helicopter was just visible through the open doors. His pulse leaped. He'd found the right place.

He paused, stilling his breathing to a slow, even pace, then listening, hoping for the sound of a voice that would tell him that this time his run had not been in vain. He heard nothing but the occasional muffled laughter of men, coming from inside.

That doesn't mean a thing, he told himself. *She's probably bound and gagged.* Glancing down at his watch, he frowned. It was eleven-thirty. Whatever he had to do, it must be done before they attempted to make their midnight call.

His hand shifted to the knife at his belt. In a smooth, silent motion, it came loose in his hand. With his eyes trained to the night, he went into a crouch and started moving through the brush, circling the hangar. Seconds later, he got his first glimpse of Kathleen, and every thought in his mind went cold. Even from where he was standing, he could see her face—and what they'd done to her. Whatever it was within him that had brought him this far stopped and died. A single thought kept running through his mind. *They shouldn't have touched her.* His fists curled around the handle of the knife. The waiting was over.

Steiger was a city man. The coyote howling on a nearby ridge was getting under his skin. Even though he told himself he was in no danger, the high, mournful sound, followed by a series of sharp, quick yips, gave him the creeps. It was the last thing he heard.

A hand closed around his mouth and he felt himself being dragged backward against great·strength. His rifle slipped to the ground as he grabbed at the smothering hands on his face. He didn't feel the pain, only the twist as his head disconnected from his spine. Lights burst in his brain and then quickly went dark. No breath. No thought. No sound. He never felt himself die.

Morgan eased the man to the ground, taking no pleasure in what he'd done. All he knew was to remove the obstacles from his path to Kathleen, and Steiger had been in the way.

Morgan continued to circle, moving slowly, silently, staying within the outer perimeter of darkness surrounding the hangar. It was a big building. There had to be others. He would find them.

Wainright was taking a piss. His semiautomatic rifle lay on the ground near his feet as he aimed his water in the opposite direction. It hissed slightly as it struck the ground, and so did the air that suddenly came up his windpipe as the knife sliced a gash in his throat. Wainright threw up his hands, grabbing at his neck and staggering backward in shock. His eyes were wide and horror-filled as he gazed at the dark apparition before him. All he could see were fierce glowing eyes and the glimmer of moonlight on a big, bloody blade. He fell forward, dying in the puddle he'd made.

Morgan thrust his knife in the dirt to the hilt. When he pulled it out, it was clean. With no wasted motion, he picked up the gun as he stood. Several yards later, he shoved the weapon beneath some sagebrush, then thrust his hand in the fanny pack and pulled out his pistol, fingering the silencer once more, just to make sure it was intact. Satisfied with what he felt, he kept on moving. Now he was downwind.

Hamilton was indulging in his favorite solitary pastime. His dick was hard and his hand was busy. He felt no guilt for the act. The way he looked at it, it was Benini's fault for keeping the woman all to himself. A real man couldn't help being aroused by someone like her. But, since she wasn't available, he was taking the easy way out. At the point of climax, something cold was suddenly poked in his ear.

He gasped as his dick went limp. Something popped, like uncorked air coming out of a bottle. Leaving a neat round hole, the bullet went in one ear and out the other, just like his mother's warnings had always done. Dead before he could blink, he never knew when Morgan Tallchief eased him to the ground.

Morgan stepped over the body, his mind already ahead of his feet. He never looked back, and if he had, there would have been no remorse on his face. They'd been the ones to cross the line. All he was doing was putting them back where they belonged.

Now he was back at the front of the hangar, near where he had started. He glanced down at his watch. Fifteen minutes until twelve. He paused, then squatted, searching the ground ahead from a different angle. The air around him still felt tainted, as if by the presence of another human being. He lifted his head and inhaled. His eyes narrowed as the faint but unmistakable scent of tobacco came to him on the breeze.

Ambrose squatted among the knee-high sagebrush, secure in his position. From where he sat, he could see across the sage, but no one could see him. He took a last, long drag on his cigarette. As he exhaled, a slight shift in the breeze blew the smoke back in his eyes, causing him to squint. He stubbed the butt in the dirt, smashing it with his finger until all the fire was gone. Shifting his position, he moved his weight from one leg to the other while resting on his heels. Less than five minutes later, he began to fidget and put his automatic rifle across his lap as he dug in his pocket for another smoke.

Tapping the pack against his finger, he grabbed the ejected cigarette, then stuck it in his mouth, comforted by the feel of paper against his lip. In one smooth motion, he traded pack for lighter. The blaze flared, his smoke took fire. He took a long draw, inhaling the tar down deep into his lungs. As he rode the sharp jolt of nicotine high, the hair suddenly crawled on his neck, just as it had in Vietnam when Charlie had been nearby. But he was older now, and that had been a long time ago, and his reactions were no longer as quick.

He never saw it coming—only felt the cold blade of steel against his throat. He coughed, then sighed. The smoke never made it to his lips. Instead, it slipped out the new hole in his throat.

Once again, Morgan shoved the blade into the

ground, as if the removal of each man's filth was necessary before moving on. He glanced down at his watch, then back into the night toward the north. Once, he thought he saw a headlight bounce up, then disappear. They were on their way! That meant he didn't have much time left. There was no way of knowing how many were still inside or where Kathleen was in relation to what could be considered the line of fire.

His body tensed as he turned toward the hangar. The silhouette of a man moved between a dirty window and the light.

He went into a crouch and started to move.

Benini glanced at his watch, then smiled. It was time, but when he reached into his pocket, he came up empty. Frowning, he patted himself down, and when his cell phone was nowhere to be found, he started yelling at the top of his voice. He had a ransom call to make. How could he make it without his phone?

"My phone! Where the hell is my phone?"

Tuley scrambled up from his chair while Amal pushed away from the wall where he'd been leaning. Together, they began searching the area for Benini's missing cell phone.

Kathleen's heart jerked painfully. *Oh, God! What now?* Her gaze moved from Benini to Amal. The man was studying her body as one would a map. She lifted her chin, then looked away. *Don't let him see how scared you are! Don't give them the satisfaction!*

Benini looked up and noticed Amal's attention was not where it had been directed.

"God damn it, Amal, I'll kill her myself if you don't

get your mind in the game. Find my phone! You can
fuck her later!"

Amal blinked slowly, as if coming out of a trance.
He turned, his thoughts everywhere but on the man
who suddenly came through the door. All he saw was
a flash of black, and then his body jerked, his head
popping back on his neck from the impact of the bullet between his eyes. He went down like a poleaxed
steer, his gaze, though sightless, once again fixed upon
Kathleen.

From somewhere behind her, Tuley was firing his
gun. Instinctively, Kathleen ducked, screaming in
fright as the shots rang close to her ears and echoed
loudly within the high, empty hangar. As she moved,
the chair in which she was sitting went sideways,
dumping her back onto the concrete.

Tuley bolted toward the helicopter, firing as he ran,
then suddenly spun, grabbing at his chest as he fell.
The gun in his hand hit the floor and slid beneath the
chopper, out of reach.

Marco roared. The sound came from fear as much as
from rage. He'd watched both men die without knowing how it had happened, but when a tall, dark man
dressed in black stepped out of the shadows with a
gun aimed straight at his heart, his gut clenched, and
he remembered what Kathleen Ryder had told him.
He'll kill you.

Marco Benini's gun wavered, but he stood his
ground. The way he figured it, he still had the upper
hand.

"Drop your gun or she dies!" Benini shouted, his
gun aimed toward the floor, straight at Kathleen's
head.

In that split second when his gaze shifted from the man with the gun to Kathleen's face, a thousand thoughts went through Morgan's mind. He saw past her blood and bruises to her acceptance of their fate.

A silent weapon is often the best.

I hear you, Grandmother.

"Drop it, Cochise, or she dies now!" Benini screamed again, taking another step that brought his gun closer to Kathleen's head.

Morgan gauged Benini's fear from the tremor in his voice. The man had reached his limit of endurance, and that made him a very dangerous man.

"Take it easy," he drawled, and turned his gun sideways before laying it on the ground.

"No, Morgan! Don't! He'll kill you!" Kathleen cried.

Benini smiled. It was going to be all right after all. He didn't need backup to get one small book. All he had to do was make his call and then disappear, leaving no witnesses behind. Now that he had the Indian under his power, he changed the angle of his gun. It was no longer pointing at the woman. Now it was aimed squarely at the center of the man's chest—a target far too broad to miss.

Kathleen moaned under her breath. Once Morgan had watched her die. Now God was punishing her by giving her the same sentence. She kicked and struggled, trying to jerk free of her bonds.

"Benini . . . please! Don't!" she cried. Marco sneered and glanced down at her. This was too rich. Before she wouldn't talk; now she was begging. "Beg me, bitch, I like—"

Marco choked, then gagged, his words quite literally cut off from the source as a knife suddenly pierced his throat. Bile rose from his belly, then had nowhere to go. He staggered, dropping his gun and fumbling helplessly with the handle of the knife, trying in vain to pull the shaft from his windpipe. Pain racked him, sending him to his knees.

His eyes rolled back in his head as the room began to shrink within his vision. Rage and disbelief were on his face as he slipped to the floor. Only feet from Kathleen, he now reached toward her with outstretched hand, mouthing a word that had no sound.

Kathleen thought he'd called her a bitch. She looked away, stunned by how swiftly a life could end.

"Oh God, oh God," she whispered, and then closed her eyes and started to cry.

Morgan shuddered. The tone of her voice said it all. He didn't know how to behave. From the way she was trembling, if he touched her next, he feared she might come undone, yet leaving her alone on the floor was impossible. He took a deep breath and started toward her, aware that she'd seen a side of himself not meant to be seen.

And, to be truthful, it was a side of himself he never would have believed existed, but the military had found it and fostered it. And he'd run with the pack until it had nearly eaten him alive. How could he make her understand that he would have done this, and worse, if that's what it would have taken to get her out alive?

He touched the side of her face, and when she flinched, his heart dropped.

"Easy, sweetheart, I'm just cutting you loose."

A low, shattered moan came out of her mouth, but she stilled at the sound of his voice. He reached for the knife imbedded in Marco Benini's throat and then hesitated. He would not use it on her bonds. She'd been touched by their filth far too much already. Instead, he knelt at her side and began working the knots loose with his fingers.

He freed her hands, gently rubbing them to increase circulation, and as he did, once again touched her face, as if assuring himself that she was still in one piece. This time, he took heart in the fact that she hadn't withdrawn. He bent to untie her feet, and felt an urge he hadn't felt since he'd been a boy: He wanted to lay his head in her lap and just cry.

As he worked at the ropes, Kathleen's awareness of the quiet around them became stronger, and with it came calm. The adrenaline rush of believing she was going to die, and Morgan with her, had started to fade. Tremors racked her body, but it was little more than subsiding shock. When her hands were free, a deep sigh came up from deep inside. All she could think was, *Thank you, God.* She opened her eyes, searching Morgan's face for the promise she needed that it was really all over.

Slightly startled by his warlike appearance, she found herself without anything to say. Yet as she watched him working at the knots on the ropes around her ankles, his silence began to confuse her. She'd expected almost any reaction except the one she was getting. When he'd touched her face, his eyes had been full of fear. But why? It was over. He'd come, even when she'd been afraid he could not, and he'd saved her. What was there left to fear? Surely, it wasn't about Trish. She'd believed she was safe. The last sight she'd had of her daughter, she'd been running away.

"Morgan?"

He jerked, startled by the sound of her voice, then looked up.

"Trish . . . where's Trish?"

"With my brothers."

"But how? Where?"

"I called them, and they came."

Tears filled her eyes as he looked away, returning to the knots on the ropes around her ankles.

His head was so close to her hands. Impulsively, she reached out, ignoring the pain to her palms, and laid her hand upon his hair.

At her touch, his head dropped lower, and she felt him trembling. In that moment, she knew! He was no longer afraid for her; he was afraid of her—or at least, of her reaction.

"I told Benini you'd kill him."

Morgan stilled. For a long, silent moment, he neither spoke nor moved. Finally, he looked up. His voice was low, barely above a whisper. He stared at Benini, then back at Kathleen. "You did what?"

"I told Benini you'd kill him for what he'd done to me."

Morgan took a deep breath and reached out for her hands. When she winced, he looked down and, for the first time, saw the broken and bloody nails and the splinters. A dark, ruddy flush spread beneath the surface of his skin as he stared at Benini once more.

"He should have taken longer to die."

She sobbed once, then swayed.

He cursed beneath his breath, then pulled her to her feet and lifted her into his arms. With a muffled groan, he rested his cheek against her bruised and battered face and started out the door. They never looked back.

*   *   *

"Damn it, I told you we'd be too late," Caldwell muttered, as they sped toward the hangar. He glanced at his watch. It was ten minutes after midnight. Whatever had happened was probably already over. Several hundred yards away, the single light from somewhere inside the building was a faint but clear beacon in the dark desert night.

"Look, sir! Coming out of the door! Isn't that Tallchief?"

Caldwell stood up in the jeep, leaning forward as they bounced across the uneven ground. A smile began to spread from one side of his face to the other. Even from his uncertain perch, he could see Tallchief was carrying a woman in his arms.

"Son of a bitch! He did it!" He was out of the jeep, even as it was sliding to a halt.

"Is she all right?" he yelled.

Morgan paused by the jeep, then looked down at Kathleen as he sat her on the hood. "She will be. Has anyone got any water?"

Four nearby agents scrambled to be the first to bring her a drink. It was another small plastic bottle, like the one Donovan had given to him. Morgan took off the cap, trying not to shake as he held it to her lips. She took the water as a baby would a longed-for bottle, trying to breathe between long, hungry gulps.

"Easy, sweetheart," Morgan whispered.

She did as he asked. When she had finished, he handed it back.

Tears were already drying on her face as she leaned her forehead against Morgan's chest. "I want to go home."

Morgan picked her up and then got into the jeep, settling Kathleen into his lap without relinquishing his hold.

Caldwell leaned inside. "Kathleen, we can call in a helicopter if need be. This is a pretty rough ride."

Kathleen grimaced, then almost smiled. "No helicopters, please. I threw up in the last one."

A sideways grin parted the darkness of Morgan's face. Maybe it would be all right after all. If she could make fun of any part of this hell, there was hope for them yet.

"We need to stop in Santa Fe on our way through," Morgan said. "She needs some serious first aid."

"Already done," Donovan said, and jumped into the jeep, then glanced at Caldwell, who was the agent in charge. "With your permission, sir."

Caldwell waved them away. "Get them out of here," he said. "It looks as if the dirty work has already been done. There's nothing for us but the cleanup." Then he glanced at Morgan. "How many?"

Morgan focused his attention on the question and not the expression on Kathleen's face.

"Four out, three inside."

Kathleen closed her eyes, absorbing the information. *Four more! Dear God. At any point, he might have died and I would never have known until it was too late.*

Caldwell saw the expression on Kathleen Tallchief's face and almost wished he hadn't asked.

"Wait a minute," Morgan said, and eased Kathleen up from his arms. He unbuckled the fanny pack, then handed it, gun and all, back to Caldwell. "I won't be needing this anymore—or this," he added, pulling off the sweatband with the transmitter.

Kathleen shivered, then sighed, resuming her place within his arms.

"Move, Donovan. We've got a long way to go before we get home," he said gruffly.

At Morgan's order, they drove away, leaving the scene of destruction in the past, where it belonged.

The cool desert breeze whipped through their hair as Morgan wrapped her close in his arms, trying to shield her from any more discomfort. Just when he thought she'd fallen asleep, he heard her sigh, then sensed her look up. He looked down. She was staring at him through tears.

"Do I scare you?" he asked, thinking of the "war paint" still on his face.

She shook her head, sending silent tears streaking down her cheeks.

"Don't cry," he said softly, and for the first time since he'd found her, bent his head and grazed the side of her face with his lips, trying desperately not to touch anything hurt.

"Until tonight, I never really understood."

He frowned, then breathed a quick sigh of relief as they bounced out of the desert and onto smooth road.

"Understood what, sweetheart?"

"How hard it was to watch someone you love die."

An old, painful memory tried to resurrect itself. He resisted it by holding her close.

"It's over," he said. "It's all over. From now on, there's nothing ahead but the rest of our lives."

Kathleen cupped the side of his cheek. "Thanks to you."

He tried to look away, but she wouldn't let him. She

struggled to sit up, needing to see his face, and fought against the wind whipping the words from her mouth.

"Don't turn away from who you are, Morgan Tallchief, because you'd be turning away from me, as well. I love you—all of you."

Her words shattered him. She'd seen the darkest side of him and still it hadn't mattered. Then she kissed the edge of his chin and managed to grin.

"You did what you had to do for us, and for that, I will be forever grateful. Now take me home. I want to hold my daughter . . . and take a bath . . . and eat a horse . . . and . . ."

He lifted his head to the night, leaving his laughter behind as the lights of Santa Fe came into sight.

Just as he'd promised, Tallchiefs took care of their own.

Epilogue

Hannah was beginning to fuss. Kathleen glanced down at the dozing baby in her arms and smiled. Another Tallchief, right down to dark eyes and black hair. Only Morgan swore she was going to look like her, not him, this time. He said Hannah had her nose— her mouth—her chin. He didn't know it, but she also had her name. She'd never told him who she'd been, because to talk about the past still hurt him. And to Kathleen, it no longer mattered. What counted was the love that bound them all together.

Morgan heard the baby's soft wail and shifted on the bleachers where they were sitting. An outdoor track meet in Albuquerque's late March wasn't the best place for Hannah to be, but Kathleen had been insistent. She didn't want any member of the Tallchief family to miss Patricia's big event, including her baby sister. It didn't matter that, at barely thirteen months, Hannah Tallchief would not remember a thing. For

Kathleen, what counted was being able to look back on it in later years and include Hannah in the story.

Morgan touched Kathleen's arm. "Want me to take her?"

She shook her head, rocking where she sat. The bleachers were high, and they were a long way up. "Maybe she'll go back to sleep. If I move her, I'm afraid she'll wake up, then want to get down and play."

Morgan kissed the baby's soft hand, then brushed a swift kiss on Kathleen's cheek before straightening.

She smiled. He didn't have to say it. She saw it in his eyes every day of her life. He loved her. He loved his daughters. He worshiped the ground they all walked on. And the feeling was mutual.

The day was still, the sun hesitant to emerge from the clouds. People huddled together in the bleachers, their jackets pulled close against their necks, often stuffing hands inside pockets to keep them warm. Kathleen pulled Hannah's blanket a little closer around her, sighing with relief as the baby slipped into a quiet slumber. Her little mouth pursed, her cheeks working as she sucked in and out in her sleep.

Morgan leaned over to watch, in daily awe of every facet of the baby's growth. The loudspeaker in the announcer's booth suddenly squealed, momentarily diffusing his words. The announcement ended, with the crowd hearing only the last little bit of what he'd said.

". . . girls' hundred-yard dash."

Kathleen clutched Morgan's leg. "This is it! It's Patricia's event!"

An odd expression moved through his eyes. If she hadn't known better, Kathleen would have sworn it was regret. She looked away, unwilling to test her theory further. They'd long ago faced the fact that for them there was no going back. He'd forgiven her for the lies and she'd forgotten his darker side. Only now and then, something occurred that would bring it all home to them, and when it did, the unspoken rule was to pretend it had never happened.

He covered her hand with his own, but didn't speak, and when his grip absently tightened, she realized how tense he'd become.

"It will be all right," she said quietly, and leaned her head against his shoulder.

He sighed, moving from the place he'd been and back to his woman, where he belonged. He looked down at Hannah, then up at Kathleen. "It's already all right."

She nodded, then ducked her head to hide unexpected tears, pretending great interest in covering Hannah's left hand, which had escaped her covers.

The announcer's voice shattered the calm of the people in the stadium as he began to reel off names and schools the six young girls who were getting into position at the starting line represented. Although they all appeared to be fit, fine athletes, one girl seemed to stand out from the rest.

She was half a head taller than the others, and unlike her competitors, who'd bound their hair into various fashions to keep it out of their eyes, hers fell loose on her shoulders; thick, long, and very dark. The blue and yellow colors of her track suit contrasted sharply with her rich, brown skin. Again, unlike the others, who were dancing nervously from foot to foot, or stretching in order to loosen up, Patricia Tallchief stood without moving, staring intently ahead.

When Morgan looked at her face, he knew that she was already gone. In her mind, she was moving down the track. It was the way of a runner—letting the spirit go first, leaving the body to follow after.

"On your mark!"

The six contestants took their places on the line. Morgan caught himself holding his breath.

"Set!"

Their slim, young bodies quickly angled into starting positions, and even though he knew it was coming, when the starter pistol went off, Morgan jerked. Beside him, Hannah whimpered, and he was vaguely aware of Kathleen soothing her fears.

They came off their marks in irregular patterns, each runner moving at her own special pace. But it was Patricia who came off the line in the lead and never looked back. Ejected from a dead start like an arrow from a bow, she ran with legs outstretched, her head tilted back, her body moving in a perfect synchronization that comes to only a few. Even from where Morgan sat, he saw the expression on her face and recognized it for what it was—a runner's rapture.

The noise from the crowd began to strengthen. The announcer's voice rose octave after octave as the slim brown girl with long black hair took an unexpected lead.

With every step that she was taking, Morgan ran it right beside her. He knew the jolt of foot to ground, of moving within the air instead of against it. Her heartbeat was his heartbeat. Her breath was his own. He never knew when he stood up, but when she crossed the line, many yards ahead of the others, he was no longer alone.

The crowd went wild, and Kathleen had a sensation of déjà vu. She'd been here before. But unlike the others around her, she didn't need to stand to see. She'd already seen it happen through her husband's eyes.

Again, the announcer was trying to make himself heard over the roar of the crowd. Only bits and pieces of his voice made its way through the massive cheers, but what came through, Morgan already knew.

". . . tied . . . long-standing national record set by . . . eighteen years . . . Tallchief dynasty."

Kathleen took a deep breath and looked up. Dear God! Trish had just tied Morgan's record!

Morgan's heart soared as Trish circled the track to cool down. His gift hadn't been wasted! Impulsively, he reached down and took a fussing Hannah out of Kathleen's arms. Bundled against the cool March air, Hannah Tallchief waved fat baby arms in delight as her father swung her high and settled her safely upon his shoulders. She'd never known fear because he kept her from harm, and that was his gift to her.

"Look, baby girl!" he said softly. "Trishie is down there."

Hannah didn't see her beloved sister anywhere, but it didn't matter. She'd heard the name. For her, it was enough. She dug her fists in her daddy's dark hair and chortled.

Down on the track, Patricia Tallchief was still locked in the run. She knew it was over, but the feeling was still strong in her heart: that ultimate high that comes from knowing that if she tried, she could run forever.

Her teammates were shouting in her face and she thought, *It must have been a good run.* As she circled the track she continued to look up in the crowd, searching for her family, wanting to share this moment with them. And then from the sidelines, her coach suddenly appeared.

"Trish . . . Trish! You tied your father's record! You tied a national record!"

She paused, stunned by what he'd just said. Her heart leaped. She spun around, now frantic in her effort to find where they sat. *What will Dad say? Will he care? Will he be proud—or is it going to hurt him, instead?*

As if by instinct, she suddenly saw them, heads above the others and high up at the top. Hannah was straddling her daddy's neck and laughing as she clutched at his hair. There, beside them, Mom was grinning and waving. Trish lifted her arm and smiled back. And then, as if saving the best for last, she let herself look from Hannah to the man who held her, and in spite of the distance between them, was instantly pulled into her father's dark eyes.

In that moment, the noise and the people disappeared, and it was as if she stood face-to-face with the man who'd given her life. His eyes were crinkling at the corners in the way that they did when he was most pleased, and his mouth was quirked just a little to the right in that sarcastic, "I was right all along" smirk. Joy spiraled within her as she quietly accepted the torch he passed on.

The moment between Morgan and Trish came and went so quickly, he could almost believe it had never happened, yet when he looked down at Kathleen and saw the tears in her eyes, he felt content. It was finally true. The past no longer mattered. He winked at her, and then bent, holding Hannah tight as he leaned down and kissed Kathleen firmly upon the mouth.

"My God, Kathleen, did you see what she did? I do believe we've created a monster."

Hannah took the occasion to grab a larger handful of his hair, and Morgan winced as she squealed and then pulled.

Kathleen lifted the baby from his shoulders and then plopped her in his arms, grinning as she asked, "Are you referring to Patricia, or Hannah?"

He tilted his head back and laughed. Life was truly rich.

Everything comes full circle.

He hadn't heard the voice in such a long time now, and he knew it was because she hadn't been needed. Once again, he gazed down beyond the crowd to the field below. There had been others of his kind before him. He'd seen them in his mind and painted their picture so people would know. Now it had come full circle, from father to daughter, and so it would go. Peace settled within him.

Yes, Grandmother . . . I can see that now.

The World of Sharon Sala

When a man meets a woman in the books of Sharon Sala, there is no question that it is meant to be—that it is *fate*. For in the wonderful world of this bestselling author, who also writes as Dinah McCall, love is often left in the hands of destiny—threatening danger, the bonds of family, a terrible accident, or even just the whims of Mother Nature. Now, experience the romance for yourself, with these excerpts from a few of Sharon Sala's classic stories. Whether first love remembered or a new passion like no other, her stories will inspire your faith in destiny, and remind you that love is always around the next corner . . .

Dreamcatcher

Dreamcatcher, *a Dinah McCall book, melds reality and dreams into a world of passionate romance. Unable to free herself from her husband's brutal obsession, beautiful Amanda Potter retreats into her own dream world where a comforting lover adores her and keeps her safe. But can someone so intoxicating exist in her waking hours, too? Jefferson Dupree, a man searching for the woman he knows is his destiny, is determined to create for Amanda a reality more fulfilling than any dream.*

"Catch her! She's going to fall!"

Detective Jefferson Dupree turned at the shout just in time to see the young woman teetering at the edge of the makeshift stage set up in the center of the park.

He lunged, arms outstretched, and took the weight of her body against his as they both tumbled to the ground. There was little time for him to register her softness and the subtle scent of her perfume. Or how perfectly she seemed to fit within his embrace. There was only time to brace himself as he cushioned her body with his own.

Amanda had known she was going to fall. There was no time for shock or fear. Just the thought that it was going to be embarrassing as hell if she didn't die. Because only then would the fall have been forgivable.

Congressmen's wives did not fall from stages in front of crowds of voters.

But the expected pain of landing on the ground didn't come. Instead she found herself cradled against a broad, thundering chest, and held so gently that for a heartbeat she wished never to move.

"Oh my God," she whispered.

Forgetting to feel embarrassed, she found herself lost in gentle, brown eyes that were shot through with just enough gold to remind her of warm whiskey. His nostrils were flared slightly from the strength he'd exerted in breaking her fall. His upper lip was sharply chiseled, the lower, full and sensual, but at the moment, twisted slightly in a grimace of pain.

Everything about him that she saw came and went within a millisecond, and then she thought, *David is going to kill me.*

In the moment when they stared into each other's eyes, something passed between them. Something swift. Sudden. Urgent. But it was never voiced.

From the corner of his eye, Jefferson Dupree saw David Potter dashing from the stage. Before he could find the breath or impetus to speak, the woman was yanked from his arms. He would have sworn that for an instant Amanda Potter had clung to him as if dodging her husband's hands. The moment he thought it he told himself he was a fool. She was married to one of West Virginia's brightest and most charming congressmen. Her world had to be just about perfect.

"Oh, my! I'm sorry," she whispered, and looked up into her husband's face, searching the handsome perfection for approval.

Dupree wasn't certain whom she'd just apologized to, but he assumed it would have been to him.

"No need to apologize," he said, brushing off his jacket and slacks. "I'm just glad I was here. Are you all right? That was quite a fall." Out of habit, he started to check her for injuries.

But Amanda Potter wasn't allowed to answer. She was busy being engulfed within her husband's embrace. Jefferson Dupree was shocked at the odd shaft of resentment he felt when he saw it happen. Moments ago it had been *his* arms that had sheltered her. It had been *his* chest she'd laid her head upon.

Tallchief

In Tallchief, *a heart-wrenching tale of a passionate hero, Dinah McCall created Morgan Tallchief, a man who has lived with the loss of his one true love, beautiful Kathleen Ryder, for sixteen lonely years. Suddenly, he discovers that Kathleen is alive, and she needs Morgan's help to escape the danger she's run from for so long. But in return she—and only she—can help Morgan re-learn what it means to love.*

The steady roar of a motor had all but lulled them into an easy, sleepy silence. Nightfall had come and gone as the success of the day settled wearily on the shoulders of the young athletes who were on their way home. Many dozed as the Comanche Public School bus made its way south. A few, like Morgan and Kathleen, sat arm in arm in the back of the bus, stealing kisses when no one was looking and aching for more as only young lovers can.

Kathleen's gaze raked the stern profile of the young man she loved without caution, seeing past the solemnity of his expression to the gentleness she knew was within. She slid her hand across his thigh and felt the muscles contract beneath the fabric of his jeans as he acknowledged her and her right to touch. She held her breath, waiting for him to turn, for those dark, fathomless eyes to pierce her soul.

When he did, the slow smile on his face stilled her heart.

"You were wonderful today," she said softly. "I was so excited I thought my heart would burst when you crossed the finish line. Oh, Morgan, if you could only see yourself run!"

He smiled in the darkness, then slipped his arm across her shoulders and hugged her close. There was no way he could make her understand, but he *did* see himself when he ran.

But the run was in the past, and right now, there was nothing on Morgan's mind but this woman/child who'd stolen his heart. Slowly, he threaded his fingers in her hair and then began combing through it in a sensuous, repetitive stroke.

"Your hair feels like silk on my hands," he whispered, and feathered a kiss near the lobe of her ear.

Kathleen shivered, wishing they were alone, wanting those hands to touch her in other places, aching for that beautiful mouth to take her breath away. Instead, she sat motionless, letting him do what he chose. She loved him too deeply to deny herself—or him.

In the dim light, she could almost see the expressions changing on his face as he touched her hair, touched her cheek, traced the shape of her mouth with his hand. Eyes so dark they seemed bottomless suddenly blazed with a longing she recognized—and feared. Loving this boy was the center of her world. She dreamed of making love to him, of lying naked against his strong, brown body and feeling his long, dark hair cloak her face as they kissed; wondering what it would feel like when he was inside of her. Heat surged low in her belly. Her breath slipped out in a near-silent moan.

She shivered, and Morgan's hand stilled. When he heard the catch in her breath and felt her shift uneasily in the seat beside him, he knew what she was thinking. In that instant, his own body betrayed him. Blood surged through his veins as his nostrils flared. He sensed her longing as intently as he felt his own. Swiftly, he traced the fragile curve of her neck, feeling his way through the darkness to the place where her lifeblood flowed. Unable to deny himself or her, he lowered his head.

When Morgan's mouth slid across the pounding pulse threading down her neck, Kathleen closed her eyes. She gave herself up to the longing, leaning into his caress because she had to, and it was not enough.

Her pulse hammered beneath his mouth. Transfixed by the sensuousness of knowing her in this way, he traced her neck with the tip of his tongue and pictured them somewhere else, doing more—much more.

At the point of foolishness, he stopped. There was an ache in him that had no end, but he had to stop what he was doing before he got them both in trouble. Coach Teters let some things pass, but not out-and-out necking. The last thing he wanted was for the other guys to watch what he and Kathleen might do, even if it was nothing more than a kiss. What he felt for her was too special to share.

When he broke the contact, she looked up and then sighed. "We're almost home."

If she could have her wish, they would ride in the dark forever on a bus bound for nowhere.

Chance McCall

*In one of Sharon Sala's most emotional love stories,
amnesia takes* Chance McCall *away from innocent
Jennifer Ann Tyler, who has been secretly in love with
him for as long as she can remember. When Chance re-
turns to her father's ranch, remembering nothing,
Jenny knows it's up to her to help speed Chance's
recovery—and perhaps heal her broken heart at the
same time.*

Chance watched Jenny flit from one group of men to
the other, playing hostess one minute, and reverting to
"one of the boys" the next. She kept slipping glances in
his direction when she thought he wasn't looking, but,
true to her claim, she'd more or less left him alone. He
didn't know whether he was relieved or disappointed.
His fingers curled around the cold bottle of beer in his
hand and knew that holding that beer was not what he
wanted to do. Holding Jenny seemed much more necessary . . . and important.

"What's for dessert?" Henry asked, as Jenny
scraped the last of the potato salad onto his plate.

"Movies," she answered, and grinned at the men's
cheers of delight. "Roll 'em, Henry," she called as she
walked away from Chance. "And the first one to start
a fight has to clean up the party mess."

Chance grinned as the men muttered under their

breaths. Jenny knew them well. They'd rather feed
pigs than do "woman's work." And a cowboy does not
willingly set foot around a pig.

Images danced through the night on the beam of
light from the projector and jumped onto the screen,
bringing a portion of the past to life. It didn't take long
for the laughter to follow, as Henry's weathered face
and hitched gait filled the screen.

He was leading a horse toward Jenny, who sat
perched on the top rail of the corral. The smile on her
face kicked Chance in the gut. And when she vaulted
off the fence and threw her arms first around Henry,
and then around the horse's neck, he swallowed
harshly. It was a Jenny he'd never seen. This one
wasn't scolding, or wearing a continual frown of
worry. She was unconscious of her beauty, uncon-
cerned with her clothing, and looked to be in her teens.

Firecrackers went off beneath a bystander's feet,
telling Chance that it must have been a Fourth of July
celebration that was being filmed. A man walked into
the picture, and Jenny's face lit up like a roman candle.
Absolute and total devotion was obvious. When the
man turned around and made a face at the camera,
Chance caught his breath. *It's me!* He had no memory
at all of the occasion. Jenny was handing him a bridle
that he slipped over the horse's head. She was smiling
and laughing and clapping her hands as the crowd
around her began singing.

It took Chance a minute to decipher the song, since
this movie had no sound. Happy Birthday! They were
singing Happy Birthday to Jenny! His breathing quickened and he stiffened as he watched Jenny throw her
arms around his neck and plant a swift kiss on his

cheek before allowing him to help her mount the horse. Because he was looking for it . . . because subconsciously he'd always known it was there . . . he didn't miss the intense look of love that Jenny gave him before she turned to the horse's head and rode off amid cheers and birthday greetings from the crowd.

It was too much! Chance knew that the rest of the night would simply be a rerun of similar scenes and similar people. He didn't have to remember it to know that Jenny Tyler loved him. He'd felt it through the darkness in the hospital, when he had no memory at all . . . when there was nothing in his life but misery and pain.

What he didn't know, and what he couldn't face, was the depth of his own feelings for the boss's daughter, and memory of what, if anything, had ever happened between them. He turned and walked away, hidden by night shadows.

Jenny saw him go and resisted an urge to cry. It would do no good. And it would be too obvious if she bolted after him. *Damn this all to hell,* she thought. *Why can't you remember me, Chance McCall? Injury or not, I'd have to be dead not to remember you.*

Second Chances

Weather stranded both Billie and Matt in the same airport, but it was fate that made them meet in Second Chances. After disastrous holidays, Billie Jean finds herself trapped in Memphis on New Year's Eve. She is alone, until she meets a tall cowboy lingering in the shadows and passion takes over. What seems like a fluke is really the hand of destiny, changing Billie's and Matt's lives forever.

Matt sensed, rather than heard, her approach, as if someone had invaded his space without asking. Instinctively he shifted his absent gaze from the swirling snow outside to the reflection of the woman he saw coming toward him from the rear.

At first, she was nothing more than a tall, dark shadow. It was hard to tell exactly how much woman was concealed beneath the long, bulky sweater she wore, but she had a slow, lanky stride that made his belly draw in an unexpected ache. Just as he was concentrating on slim hips encased in tight denim and telling himself he'd rather be alone, she spoke.

"Would you like something to drink?"

Every thought he had came to a stop as her voice wrapped around his senses. Men called it a bedroom voice—a low, husky drawl that made his toes curl and his breath catch.

But when their hands touched, Matt wasn't the only one in a state of sudden confusion. Billie lost her train of thought, while the smile on her lips froze like the snow against the windows. There was a look in his eyes that she'd never before seen on a man's face. A mystery, an intensity in the dark blue gaze that she hadn't bargained for. Several staggering breaths later, she remembered what she'd been about to say.

"I thought you might like to . . ."

She never got to finish what she was saying. He took the can and set it down on the ledge without taking his eyes off her face. Mesmerized, she stood without moving as his hands lifted toward her cheeks. When his fingers sifted through the strands of escaping curls that were falling around her eyes, she caught herself leaning toward his touch and jerked back in shock. Then he grinned, and she felt herself relaxing once more.

He lifted a stray curl from the corner of her eye. "That face is too pretty to hide."

A surge of pure joy made Billie weak at the knees. Embarrassed, she looked away, and when she looked back, found herself locked into a wild, stormy gaze and dealing with another sort of surge. Ashamed of what she was thinking, she pretended interest in the storm and knew that she was blushing.

"Where are you going?"

I wish to hell it was with you. Wisely, Matt kept his wishes to himself.

"Dallas."

She nodded and looked down at the floor.

"I was in Memphis for Christmas vacation. I'm on my way back to California." When she got the nerve to look up, those dark blue eyes were still staring intently.

They shared a long, silent moment, then the noise of the crowd behind them broke the tension. It was obvious by the loud chanting voices that the countdown to midnight had begun.

"Ten . . . nine . . . eight."

Billie looked up. His eyes were so blue. So compelling. So lonely. She took a deep breath.

"Seven . . . six . . . five."

She bit her lower lip, then took a step forward. Just in case. Hoping—wishing—needing him to want what she was wanting.

"Four . . . three . . . two."

Matt groaned beneath his breath. He saw the invitation in her eyes as well as her body language. So help him God, there wasn't enough strength left in him to deny either of them the obvious.

The merrymakers were in full swing as they shouted, "Happy New Year!"

Matt cupped her face in his hands, then waited. If she didn't want this, now was her chance to move. To his utter joy, she not only stayed but scooted a hairbreadth closer to his chest until he could almost feel the gentle jut of her breasts against the front of his shirt. Almost . . . but not quite.

"Happy New Year, Memphis." He lowered his head.

Finders Keepers

Molly Eden thinks fate is not on her side. Ever since her chance at a baby was robbed from her, grief has only been a few steps behind. Then, on a warm summer day, someone comes toddling into her life to change it forever. Joseph Rossi's baby son, Joey, is that darling someone, and when Joey Jr. asks Molly to be his mother, he proves that children can be wise beyond their years and see love where there was only loneliness before in Finders Keepers.

"Isth you my momma?"

Molly didn't know what startled her more, the unexpected question or the touch of a child's hand on her bare thigh.

"What in the world?"

She spun. The food on her barbecue and her solitary picnic were forgotten as she stared down in shock at the small boy who waited patiently for an answer to his question. She was startled by the unexpected pain of his innocent question—it had been years since she'd let herself think of being anyone's momma. But the child's expression was just short of panicked, and his hand was warm—so warm—upon her thigh; she couldn't ignore his plight just because of her old ghosts.

"Hey there, fella, where did you come from?" Molly

bent down, and when he offered no resistance, she lifted him into her arms.

But he had no answers for Molly, only an increase in the tug of his tongue against the thumb he had stuffed in his mouth. She smiled at his intense expression, and patted his chubby bare legs. Except for a pair of small red shorts, an expression was the *only* thing he was wearing.

"Where did you come from, sweetheart?"

His chin quivered and then he tugged a little faster upon his thumb.

It was obvious to Molly that the child was not going to be any help in locating missing parents. She turned, searching her spacious backyard for something or someone to explain the child's appearance, but nothing was obviously different from the way it had been for the last twenty-two years when her parents first moved in—except the child.

"Are you lost, honey? Can't you find your mommy?"

His only response was a limpid look from chocolate-chip eyes that nearly melted her on the spot.

She frowned, patting his sticky back in a comforting but absent way and started toward the house to call the police when shouts from the yard next door made her pause.

"Joey! Joey, where are you? Answer me, son!"

Even through the eight-foot height of the thick yew hedge separating the homes, Molly could hear the man's panic. She looked down at the child in her arms and sighed with relief. If she wasn't mistaken, the missing parents were about to arrive, and from a surprise location. The house on the adjoining lot had been vacant for over a year, and she'd been unaware that anyone had moved next door.

"Hey! You over there . . . are you missing a small boy?"

"Yes . . . God, yes, please tell me you found him."

Molly smiled with relief as she realized her unexpected guest was about to be retrieved. "He's here!" she shouted again. "You can come around the hedge and then through the front door of my house. It's unlocked."

The thrashing sounds in the bushes next door ceased. Molly imagined she could hear his labored breathing as the man tried to regain a sense of stability in a world that had gone awry. But she knew it was not her imagination when she heard a long, slow, string of less-than-silent curses fill the air. Relief had obviously replaced the father's panic.

Molly raised her eyebrows at the man's colorful language, but got no response from the child in her arms. He didn't look too perturbed. But he did remove his thumb from his mouth long enough to remark, "My daddy," before stuffing it back in place.

"Well, really!" Molly said, more in shock for herself than for the child, who had obviously heard it all before.

She turned toward the patio door, expecting the arrival of just an ordinary man, and then found herself gaping at the male who bolted out of her door and onto her patio.

It had been a long time since she'd been struck dumb by a physical attraction, but it was there just the same, as blatant and shocking as it could possibly be. All she could think to do was take a deep breath to regain her equilibrium and then wave a welcome. That in itself took no effort, and it was much safer than the thoughts that came tumbling through her mind.

She saw the man pause on the threshold, as if taking a much-needed breath, and then swipe a shaky hand across his face. He was tall, muscular, and, oddly enough, quite wet. His hair lay back and seal-slick against his head like a short, dark cap, while droplets of water beaded across his shoulders.

He stared at her backside and then tried not to. But it was an impossible task. Her long, tan legs made short work of the distance to the grill. He tried to remember his manners as he followed behind.

Deep in the Heart

In Deep in the Heart, *it is danger that brings Samantha Carlyle back to her rural Texas hometown, and back into the world of John Thomas Knight, the stunning local sheriff. She left him behind once for the bright lights and big city, but the success she found there—or the threats that came with it—is exactly what brings her into his arms again . . .*

There were no tears left to cry. Unmitigated terror had become commonplace for Samantha Carlyle. She was waiting for the inevitable. Day by day the stalker came closer, and there was nothing she could do to stop him.

She could barely remember her life three months ago when she'd been a highly valued member of a Hollywood casting agency, calmly and competently going about the business of fitting the famous and the not-so-famous into starring and supporting roles.

"And look at you now," Samantha whispered to her own reflection as she stood in the window overlooking the courtyard below. "You have no job. You're running from the devil and your own shadow. You're just hiding . . . and waiting to die."

Until now, she'd never considered what it meant to be "living on borrowed time." She looked again at her reflection and wondered what there was about her that could drive a man to insane threats of vengeance.

Her face was no different from many others—heart-shaped, but a bit too thin, and framed by a mane of thick, black hair. Her nose was still small and turned up at the world, but there was no longer a jut to her chin. It only trembled. Her lips were full but colorless, and the life that had once shone from her eyes seemed dim . . . almost gone. She shuddered and dropped the drapes, rearranging them to shut the sun out and herself in from prying eyes.

When the harassment had gone from hate mail to phone calls with spine-chilling messages left in an unrecognizable voice, she'd nearly lost her mind and, soon after, she did lose her so-called friends.

As if that wasn't enough, she'd moved her residence twice, certain each time she would outwit the culprit. And then came the day that she realized she was being stalked. But by then going back to the police was out of the question. They had convinced themselves that she was concocting the incidents herself. In fact, they had almost convinced her.

Her anger at their accusations had quickly turned to disbelief when they had proved to her, without doubt, that the hate letters she'd been receiving had been typed on her own office typewriter, and that the calls left on her answering machine were traced to an empty apartment that had been rented in the name of Samantha Jean Carlyle. It was enough said. When LAPD reminded her that perpetrating fraud was a crime, she'd taken her letters and her tapes and gone home, having decided to hire a personal bodyguard. Then she'd reconsidered her financial situation and given up on that idea.

That was the day her boss put her on indefinite

leave of absence, after reminding her, of course, that when she got her act together she would be welcomed back.

The victim had become the accused. At first she'd been furious over everyone's lack of sympathy for her situation or concern for her life. Then she'd become too busy trying to stay alive.

It was the constant frustration and the growing fear that no one was going to save her, let alone believe her, that made her remember Johnny Knight.

Touchstone

In Touchstone, *a Dinah McCall classic, fate doesn't bring two lovers together, but instead tries to tear them apart. Rachel Austin has buried her father, and now her mother, and finally they are coming for her family's land. She cannot bear staying in Mirage, where all she'd ever known is lost, but she soon discovers that without her first—and only—love, Houston Bookout, she will never stare down the demons of her past.*

"Rachel!"

He heard fear in his own voice and took a deep breath, making himself calm. But when she didn't answer, the fear kicked itself up another notch.

"Rachel! Where are you?"

He started toward the house, then something—call it instinct—made him turn. She came toward him out of the darkness, a slender shadow moving through the perimeter of light from his headlamps, then centering itself in the beam. She was still wearing the clothes she had on this morning, when he'd seen her last: worn-out Levi's and an old denim shirt. She came toward him without speaking. Fear slid from him, leaving him weak and shaken.

"Damn it, Cherokee, you scared me to death. Why didn't you answer me? Better yet, what the hell are you still doing here in the dark?"

Then he saw her face and knew she was incapable of answering.

"Jesus." He opened his arms.

She walked into them without saying a word and buried her face in the middle of his chest.

He rocked her where they stood, wrapping his fingers in the thickness of her hair and feeling her body tremble against his.

"It's going to be all right," he said softly. "I promise you, girl, it's going to be all right."

She shook her head. "No, Houston. It will never be all right again. It's gone. Everything is gone. First my father. Then my mother. Now they're taking my home."

He ached for her. "I know, love, I know. But I'm still here. I'll never leave you."

But it was as if he'd never spoken.

"The land . . . they always take the land," she muttered, and dropped to her knees. Silhouetted by the headlights of Houston's truck, she thrust her hands in the dirt and started to shake.

Houston knelt beside her. "Rachel . . ."

She didn't blink, staring instead at the way the dust began to trickle through her fingers.

"How can I give this up? It's where I was born. It's where my parents are buried."

He didn't have words to ease her pain.

She rocked back on her heels and stood abruptly. Fury colored her movements and her words.

"Everything is over! Over! And all because of money."

Houston reached for her, but she spun away. A knot formed in Houston's gut. He grabbed for her again, and this time when she tried to shake herself free, he tightened his hold.

"Stop it!" he said sharply, and gripped her by both shoulders. "Look at me, Rachel."

She wouldn't.

He shook harder. "Damn it! I said look at me!"

Finally, reluctantly, she met his gaze. She saw concern and anger; to her despair, she saw fear and knew it was because of her. She went limp.

"Houston."

He groaned and pulled her to him. "Damn it, Cherokee, don't turn away from me, too."

She shuddered. Cherokee. She couldn't deny her heritage any more than she could deny her love for Houston.

"I'm sorry," she whispered.

"It doesn't matter," he said. "Nothing matters but you."

He took her by the hand.

"Wait . . . my car," Rachel muttered.

"Leave it," he said. "You're coming home with me."

"But the sale. I need to be here by seven."

Houston frowned. "I'll have you here by sunup if it'll make you happy. But you're still coming home with me."

They made the drive back to his ranch in total silence.

Rachel felt numb from the inside out until she walked in the front door of Houston's home. The odors of cleaning solutions and pine-scented furniture polish were startling. She inhaled sharply, and as she did, tears blurred her vision. He'd been cleaning for her. Her anger dimmed as shame swept over her. She turned.

"Oh, Houston."

"Come here, girl. Don't fight your last friend."

She shuddered as his arms went around her. Last friend? If he only knew. He was her best and last friend, and in a couple of days he was going to hate her guts. A sob worked its way up her throat, but she wouldn't give in. No time to cry. Not when she wanted to remember.

She tilted her head to look up at him. "Make love to me, Houston. Make me forget."

Chase the Moon

Chase the Moon *will always be remembered as one of Sharon Sala's—here writing as Dinah McCall—most passionate, thrilling stories of love. When Jake Baretta goes looking for his twin brother's killer, he finds instead beautiful Gracie Moon—a woman he could easily fall for, if only she didn't believe he was his dead brother. Sheltered and innocent, Gracie doesn't know about the evil that lurks under the surface of her idealistic Kentucky hometown—but she is in danger of finding out, far too soon.*

Less than an hour later, Jake was startled by a knock on the door, but even more so by the woman behind it.

All Gracie said was, "Oh, Jake," and then walked into his arms.

He froze and tried not to panic. *Damn, Johnny, why didn't you warn me this would happen?*

Her arms were around his waist, her cheek against his chest, and he felt her shoulders trembling. Her long dark braid felt heavy against his hands as he tentatively returned her embrace. The thrust of her breasts, the feel of her slender body against his, were startling. He hadn't prepared himself for this, or for the supposition that John could have had a personal relationship with anyone here—no less with a woman as damned beautiful as this one. Worst of all, she thought he was John.

It took a moment for Jake's shock to pass. He didn't know who she was, but he suspected that this was Elijah Moon's only daughter. From the files he'd read, Gracie Moon was the only unattached female in New Zion. He hoped to God this was Gracie, because if John had been seeing a married woman, then that would pretty much explain why he had been shot.

He said a prayer and took a chance.

"Gracie?"

Gracie sighed. She loved to hear her name on his lips, and then she remembered herself and took a quick step back. There were tears in her eyes as she laid her hands on his shoulders.

"Father said you'd been shot." Her chin trembled, and she bit her lip to keep from crying. "He said you didn't trust us anymore." Tears hovered on the edge of her lashes. "Does that mean you don't trust me, either?"

Jake stifled a groan. My God, how could he answer her? For all he knew, she could be the one who'd pulled the trigger. Just because she was beautiful as sin, and just because there were tears in her eyes, did not make her an innocent woman. But he had to play the game. It was why he'd come.

"I guess what it means is, getting shot in the back put me off balance. Trust isn't something that's happening yet. But I'm glad to see you, too. Does that count?"

Gracie ducked her head, fighting tears, and when she looked up, there was a sad smile on her face.

"Of course it counts," she said softly.

She kept looking at him. At his eyes. At the shape of his mouth. At the cut of his chin. Finally, she shrugged.

"You look the same . . . but in a way you're very different. Harder, even colder." A gentle smile accompanied her apology. "But I suppose surviving being shot in the back would do that to anyone, right?"

"It made me hate," Jake answered.

Gracie touched his arm. "Just don't hate me."

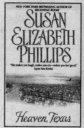

Wacky, sexy, sensational love from
USA Today bestselling author

PATTI BERG

I'm No Angel

0-06-054476-7 • $6.99 US • $9.99 Can

Sexy Palm Beach p.i. Angel Devlin always gets her man—and bad boy
millionaire Tom Donovan is at the top of her Most Wanted list.

And Then He Kissed Me

0-380-82006-4 • $6.99 US • $9.99 Can

Disguising her identity, Juliet Bridger runs from her
problems . . . straight into the arms of a small town vet
with troubles of his own.

And don't miss

STUCK ON YOU
0-380-81683-0 • $5.99 US • $7.99 Can

SOMETHING WILD
0-380-81683-0 • $5.99 US • $7.99 Can

BORN TO BE WILD
0-380-81682-2 • $5.99 US • $7.99 Can

BRIDE FOR A NIGHT
0-380-80736-X • $5.99 US • $7.99 Can

WIFE FOR A DAY
0-380-80735-1 • $5.99 US • $7.99 Can

LOOKING FOR A HERO
0-380-79555-8 • $5.99 US • $7.99 Can

Available wherever books are sold
or please call 1-800-331-3761 to order.

www.AuthorTracker.com

PBE 0404